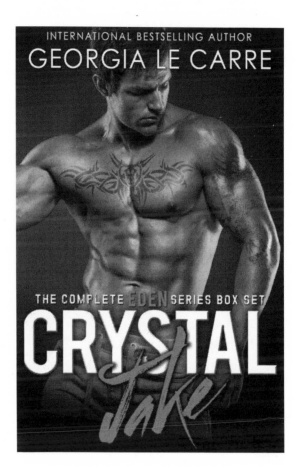

INTERNATIONAL BESTSELLING AUTHOR

GEORGIA LE CARRE

THE COMPLETE EDEN SERIES BOX SET

CRYSTAL

Jake

ALSO BY GEORGIA

The Billionaire Banker Series

Owned
42 Days
Besotted
Seduce Me
Love's Sacrifice

Masquerade

Pretty Wicked
(Novella)

Disfigured Love

.

Click on the link below to receive news of
my latest releases, fabulous giveaways,
and exclusive content.
http://bit.ly/1oe9WdE

Cover Designer: http://www.ctcovercreations.com/
Editor: http://www.loriheaford.com/
Proofreader: http:// http://nicolarheadediting.com/

CRYSTAL JAKE

Published by Georgia Le Carre
Copyright © 2015 by Georgia Le Carre

ISBN: 978-1-910575-11-6

You can discover more information about Georgia Le Carre and future releases here.

https://www.facebook.com/georgia.lecarre
https://twitter.com/georgiaLeCarre
http://www.goodreads.com/GeorgiaLeCarre

For
Samantha Bailey
who wrote Stripped
&
Christian Plowman
who wrote Crossing The Line

This book wouldn't have been the same
without your deep knowledge.

ACKNOWLEDGEMENTS

I sincerely hope I don't leave anyone out, but no doubt I will. And when I do remember I will give myself a hard time and make it a point to mention you in the next book. ☺

Thank you from the bottom of my heart to Nicola Rhead, Caryl Milton, Elizabeth Burns, Sue Bee, Cariad & Nichole from Sizzling Pages, B.J. Gaskill, Rene Giraldi, Chelle Thompson, Sandra Hayes, Terry & Donna Briody-Buccella, Tina Medeiros, Sharon Johnson, Tracy Spurlock, Simona Misevska, Irida Sotiri, Lan LLP, C.J Fallowfield, Drew Hoffman, Nadia Debowska-Stephens, Maria Lazarou & Nancy of Romance Reads.

Book 1

BOOK 1

Contents

Ha, ha, ha, bless your soul.
You really think you're in control.
Well...
—*Crazy*, Gnarls Barkey

PROLOGUE

Crazy

'N<small>OOOOOOO</small>,' I HOWL, but there is gravel or grave soil in my throat, and nothing other than an ugly, dried-up rasp travels out of my mouth. My head shakes back and forth like a mindless wind-up toy. Even my body is denying the horror before my eyes. Without warning my knees buckle under me, and I find myself in a heap at the doorway of his flat. Frantically, I begin to crawl toward him, screaming, babbling.

I can't lose him! Not him! Oh God, not him. Please. Not him.

Two feet away from his body and it occurs to me: this is just a nightmare. Of course it is. It has to be. Any moment now I'll wake up. And the first thing I'll do? Call him and tell him how much I have missed him, how much I love him.

I feel the floor scrape against my bare knees. It isn't a nightmare. It is real.

We haven't spoken for two weeks. I had exams and when I called his mobile, it went straight to voicemail... Shit excuse. I should have called again, I should have emailed. Why hadn't I? I should have known.

I hunker down over his body, my pose ungainly, heavy, that of a suffering beast. My buttocks hit the floor and my legs fold up and cross under me. I press my fingers against my open mouth and stare at him. His lips and fingers are blue and the rest of him is ashen and still. He can't be dead.

It can't be real!

The stillness of a dead body is impossible to describe. And yet when you see it you refuse to believe it. You always think it is a trick. A mistake. A ploy.... But a needle is embedded in his arm, which is blackened with the skin stretched and unreal. It looks as if it belongs elsewhere. That is not my brother's arm. I know my brother's arm as intimately as I know my own.

My breathing is shallow and trembling. I suck a huge burst of air into my lungs and pull the offending needle out. My stomach twists. It should *never* have entered his body in the first place. I throw the syringe away. It hits something and rolls on the wooden floor. It also leaves a tiny hole in my brother's flesh that does not bleed. I swallow hard. My hands are shaking badly.

That means he didn't suffer, a voice whispers in my head. He did not even have time to pull it out before he was gone to wherever it is he went to.

Oh God! He is nineteen. He can't be gone.

CPR. I should give him CPR. There must be something I can still do. I grab his shoulders and try to drag him across my thighs, but his body is so heavy, so cold, and so stiff and foreign that my shocked hands fly away from his shoulders as if they have touched fire. I gaze at him as he lies unmoving. The blood that ran without rest during his short life has stilled within his veins. Everything has cooled and hardened. He is like a piece of wood.

With a sob of intolerable, indescribable anguish I reach for him and with every ounce of my might I drag his cold, dead weight toward me and lift it onto my lap. I touch the soft brown hair that flops across his forehead and it feels different. His scalp has hardened and changed the lie of his hair. I caress his hair, his face, his hands. Holding his head pressed against my stomach I close my eyes and begin to rock him the way a mother would comfort her distressed baby.

But there is no comfort—his head is a hard, unfamiliar weight and the action produces an odd thud made by his stiff hand repeatedly hitting the floor. I stop. In a daze I look down on his face.

3

His mouth is open, the tongue—a strange, dull color—is pushed against his teeth. Without the healthy sheen of saliva it looks gross. I try to close his mouth, but it is locked open. His eyes are not fully shut and through the slits I see the whites. I try to lift a lid to see once more the beautiful blue eyes I have known all my life.

If I could at least see that.

But his eyelids are glued shut. They will not budge. Tremors shoot through my hand as I still the gruesome desire to force his eyelid open. When we were young we used to lick the salt from each other's skin. I am suddenly filled with the strange desire to lick his skin.

I put one hand under his head and the other under his neck and I put his head on the floor. Then I scoot backwards until I am on my hands and knees and my face is hovering inches away from his. My head moves downwards. My tongue comes out. Inches away a voice in my head urgently cries, 'No.'

I stop and listen to peculiar silence around us. It is quieter than falling snow. On the tabletop I notice his fingerprints in the light layer of dust, and then something weird happens. For a second I clearly perceive myself not from inside my body but from outside, crouched over my dead brother, more animal than human. I recoil from the

sight. And then the moment is gone and I lower my head and lick the last salt on the corpse's skin.

It is the beginning of my descent into unfamiliar territory. A place you might call madness.

I'm afraid my stay was excruciatingly long.

Can't read my, can't read my,
No, he can't read my poker face
—*Poker Face*, Lady
Gaga

ONE

Lily

'FIRST STOP, EDEN,' says Patrick, with a quick backward glance, as he pulls the eight-seater minibus out into the lunchtime traffic. 'Just give it your best moves, and no worries if ya don't get picked because we still have Spearmint Rhino and Diamonds after that,' he adds cheerfully.

He has a boyish face, full of charm and guile, but one look at him and you know. Weasel. And he drives like a mad man. The five of us hang onto our battered seats and smile distantly at each other. We are competitors who have been collected from the designated pick-up point outside South Kensington Tube station and are on our way to an audition. Surreptitiously, I watch them.

Traveling with me are a tall redhead, a black girl with a tight body, a life-size human Barbie doll with masses of blonde hair, a beyond believable tiny waist and enormous boobs, and a sleekly beautiful olive-skinned girl. Each one of us has a large shoulder bag. No doubt their bags hold the same things mine does.

A sexy costume, killer shoes, and strong stage make-up.

I gaze out of the window and digest the information that Club Eden is to be our first stop. Shame. I had hoped to practice my routine on a real life stage in one of the other clubs and see all the other girls' routines before we got to Eden, but still, it is interesting to know that Eden has to be paying Patrick the highest commission to have first refusal. No wonder it has overtaken all the other strip clubs and become *the* club to be seen in even though it does not offer full nudity.

In silence we head northwards to the infamous King's Cross area of London. Once it was synonymous with a grimy train station crawling with prostitutes, and rave parties in disused warehouses, but King's Cross has cleaned up its act and fast become a cutting-edge hub for fashion and the arts, attracting even Google to set up its European headquarters there.

Club Eden stands sandwiched between two tall glass office towers.

Patrick drives past the large neon-lit bitten red apple logo and, turning at the

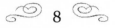

next side street, enters the rear car park. He parks close to the back doors where a guy in a chef's whites is sitting on the steps smoking a cigarette. He watches us through the smoke with uncurious eyes.

'Here we are,' Patrick announces, and switches off the engine.

We climb out, adjust our clothes, and follow him around the side of the building to the front entrance. As soon as we enter the glossy black, double doors and my stiletto heels leave their indent on the carpet, I feel a prickling sensation go up my spine. It is so strong it feels as if a spider is actually walking on my skin. Unable to stop myself I snap my head around.

Jesus!

Deeply tanned, badass black hair, and staring straight at me is the legend himself! Jake Fucking Eden. My heart skips a beat. Fuck me! His photographs have *not* done him justice. Dressed totally in black except for a pair of brown snakeskin boots, he is coming down a broad and rather magnificent stairway with the kind of effortless, lazy power of a tiger.

He is too far away for me to see the expression in his eyes, but the intense, barely leashed tension around him has a thunderstorm effect. It makes the air between us vibrate and crackle like electricity, taking my breath away and

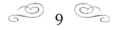

throwing my senses into high alert. My spine goes rigid and all the tiny hairs on the back of my neck rise up like those of a cat that comes face to face with mortal danger.

For a few seconds we stare at each other, instant sexual adversaries.

Then I tear my eyes away from his and train them back on Patrick, who is holding open another door. Taking a deep breath I go through it. It leads into a dimly lit corridor. The air here is cooler. I look at my hands. They are clenched tight with pent-up energy. That has never happened to me before. I have never simply looked at a man and *hungered* to have him inside my body. The sensation is raw.

'Changing rooms are through there,' Patrick says swiveling his eyes toward another door farther up the corridor. 'Meet me upstairs in fifteen minutes and I'll introduce ya to the manager.'

Then he disappears in the direction we came from and the five of us troop into the changing rooms, which I cannot help noting are super clean and resemble those in a posh spa. The other girls immediately start unzipping their bags, but running into Jake Eden has unexpectedly and unfathomably unnerved and unsettled me, and I have to close my eyes and take a quick moment to compose my body, which is

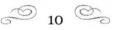 10

still clenched tight with arousal. When I open my eyes, my face is no longer flushed, nor are my eyes glittering bright. I have a task ahead of me. I look cool and composed.

As I open my bag and pull out my specially commissioned, easy to remove red dress my eyes flick over to the others. Already unrecognizably glamorous in a long, sheer robe with sequined edges, the redhead is stepping into sparkly gold shoes. Suddenly she is a six feet tall goddess. She is impressive to say the least. The black girl has taken off her bomber jacket and underneath she is ripped like a racehorse and wearing a black catsuit with fluorescent green and pink geometric patterns. I quickly slip into my dress and take my plastic red platform shoes out. While I secure the straps I notice that the life-size Barbie doll is dressed in a schoolgirl's uniform. She catches my eyes in the mirror and mouths, 'Hiya.'

I mark her as my biggest competitor. It turns out the sleekly beautiful olive-skinned beauty has the longest legs I have ever seen on a human being. To increase the illusion she hooks on glass-effect shoes. As if by unspoken agreement we are all ready at the same time.

Together we go up the grand staircase Jake Eden had come down and through a pair of gold and black doors.

I have been in nightclubs when daylight starts filtering in before, and it always looks dirty and sordid, but not this place. Here it is as if we have stepped back into a decadent time in Paris or Vienna when men wore wigs and high heels. From the hundreds of gilded mirrors to the intricate gold on black brocade upholstery on the armchairs and settees, the rich wallpapers, the heavy velvet curtains, to the massive chandeliers it is just over the top splendor. The rich mix of colors reminds me of a Gustav Klimt painting. Patrick is standing at the lip of the stage talking to a balding man. He beckons us over.

'This is Mark. He's the manager so be nice to him.'

'Hey,' Mark greets with a smile that encompasses all of us. We pipe in with our bright volley of hellos and heys.

Mark doesn't waste time. He zeroes in on the olive-skinned beauty. 'Haven't I seen you before, sweetheart?'

She shakes her head decisively. 'Nope. This is my first time here.'

'Yeah? Weren't you here about six months ago?'

Saying nothing she starts walking away.

Mark looks at Patrick. 'Roamers.'

Patrick shrugs. That's a commission he won't be getting.

I watch her go—one down, three to go. Later I would learn that roamers are hookers who work a few sessions in strip clubs every few months to look for customers they can turn into private clients.

'I'll be at the bar,' says Patrick turning away from us.

'First time for anybody here?' Mark asks.

I raise my hand.

'Right. We run a squeaky clean club here. No drugs. No prostitution. Zero tolerance. Got that?'

'Got it,' I say quickly.

He nods. 'Did you bring your music?'

I nod.

'Great. The set-up is you've got two songs. Keep your clothes on for the first song. Start getting undressed for the second and by the middle of the second track you have to be topless. You have only one objective. By the end of your second track you want every guy in the place to want to empty his wallet all over you.'

I nod slowly.

He turns toward the redhead. 'Want to go first, sweetheart?'

'Sure,' she says with a sweet smile, and gives him her CD. He sticks it into a

 13

small machine that is conveniently just under the stage. 'Ready when you are.'

She takes her time sashaying to the pole.

'Ready,' she calls out once she is in position.

Mark hits play and the club fills with the sound of Pussycat Dolls belting out, 'Don't You Wish Your Girlfriend Was Hot Like Me'. The redhead is OK, but nothing special, and my confidence goes up a notch. As the seconds tick by I realize I am miles better than her. In fact, she does not even get a chance to finish her first number before Mark snaps off the music.

'Thanks, sweetheart, but you need more moves. Get some dance lessons and then come back for another audition with the House Mother,' he dismisses. It is a no, but he has left the door open. He turns toward the black girl.

'Can I have only the ultraviolet lights on, please?' she requests.

Mark shouts over to the barman who slips to the back of the bar. Seconds later when the stage is lit by a purple glow she steps into it and suddenly her dark skin makes her disappear. She becomes a collection of pink and green patterns. Justin Timberlake's 'Sexy Back' comes on and she launches herself with surprising energy onto the pole and begins to execute the most intricate moves. But the real beauty is the way she seems to be a geometric shape moving up and down the pole. The way she gets out of her catsuit is pure class. She is damn good and so impressive to look at my heart sinks a little. If this is the standard I am competing against there is no way I am getting this job. When the music finishes it is a foregone conclusion that she is getting the job.

'Fantastic show. Come back this evening at six,' Mark tells her, and turns toward me. His eyes travel casually down my body, taking in the red dress that I could shimmy out of in two seconds flat. 'You want to keep the fluorescent lights going?'

I shake my head. My heart is suddenly beating so hard I feel my blood buzzing through my body. This is it. It is tits out time.

He hollers to the barman and the lights change back. 'Right. Off you go then.'

The butterflies in my stomach begin to crawl up my throat. I swallow hard and nod.

'Just be yourself and have fun,' he advises with a friendly smile.

I give him my CD and walk to the stage slowly, deliberately swaying my hips, but I am so nervous my knees wobble. I climb the steps carefully. No point falling on my ass before I start the

show. There are large mirrors on stage and I can see myself walking. Five feet five inches on top of nearly seven inches of heels, slim hips, flat stomach, nothing special chest, dark chocolate hair with tints of copper and a wide red mouth fixed into a professional dancer's smile. I guess I don't look too bad. And I can definitely do this. I have practiced this routine for hours. OK, I am not as good as the girl who can magic into geometric shapes, but I can do this. I have a good, foxy routine. Even Ann says so and she has taught hundreds of girls. All I have to do is get to the pole and follow the routine.

I reach the pole.

'Ready?' Mark asks.

'Yeah.'

Mark hits the play button and Marilyn Manson's skin-crawling voice reverberates around me.

Sometimes I feel I got to run away.

Holding onto the pole I circle it with a prowling gait and sinuously rub myself against it. I snake my hands above my head and grabbing the pole jut my ass out and swing it from side to side. I sneak a look at Mark and he is leaning forward. Approval.

Yeah, I can definitely do this.

I grip the pole hard and with all my might I fling myself into the air. It should have been an energetic and impressive one-handed swing around the pole, but instead my sweaty palm starts slipping off the metal. In a blind panic I try to right myself by catching the pole with my other hand but it is too late—I am flying into the air. I end up hitting the stage floor hard with my knees. For a few seconds I sit stunned in the position I have fallen in. My adrenaline is pumping so hard I do not feel any pain. Then my brain kicks into gear. *Fuck. Fuck. Fuck.* With my legs still twisted underneath me I turn toward Mark.

He has slid off the table and is bounding up to the stage.

'Let me try again,' I plead, and putting my palms on the floor I attempt to push myself upright. A sharp pain shoots right up my legs. Wincing, I persist and right myself to a standing position.

Mark is standing in front of me, looking concerned. 'Are you all right?'

Around us Marilyn's raspy voice screams, *Tainted love, tainted love.*

'I really need this job,' I beg, humiliated by my graceless fall and annoyed with myself for being so careless.

He eyes my knees and rubs his chin thoughtfully, and I know just by looking at him that he is going to ask me to take more lessons or something in that vein.

'Please,' I urge. 'That was my first time. I was just nervous. I can do this.'

'Look,' he begins more firmly, but he is interrupted by his mobile ringing. He takes it out of his pocket, glances at the screen and looks surprised. He lifts one finger at me in a gesture that tells me to wait, presses his thumb on the answer button, and puts his phone to his ear.

'Yup,' he says after less than a few seconds of listening to someone speak, and terminates the call.

He turns his attention back to me, but his eyes are now speculative and assessing. 'Good news. You've got the job. You can start whenever the swelling'—he nods toward my knees—'goes down. Arrive at five thirty p.m. with a photo ID, proof of address, and your National Insurance number and report to the House Mother. Her name is Brianna.'

For an instant I stare at him speechlessly. My knees are throbbing like crazy by now. 'I've got the job,' I repeat stupidly.

'Looks like it,' he says with a grin.

'Thanks, Mark. You won't regret this.'

'No problem,' he replies casually, and losing interest in me turns toward the blonde Barbie. 'Want to show us what you've got?'

As I hobble away from the stage, a slight movement in the far shadows

catches my eyes. I turn my head and at the dim edges of the club I see the glint of snakeskin as Jake Eden quietly slips out of the black and gold doors. And I know without a doubt: North London's most illusive gangster, Jake Eden, has just hired me.

TWO

For two days I hobble around my flat, eat junk food, and endlessly replay my disastrous reaction to Jake Eden. Could it have been some sort of freak overreaction caused by nervousness about my impending audition? On the third day I convince myself it must have been, and slapping a bit of concealer on my knees I make my way back to the club.

To my surprise the House Mother is a female version of my bank manager: forties, a sleek helmet of strawberry blonde hair, and a dark blue suit with a classy fitted top underneath it. Then she goes and does what my bank manager never does: she flashes a genuinely warm smile and I know we are going to get on just fine.

'Hi, I'm Brianna.' She extends a hand. 'Patrick told me to expect you.'

Her grasp is warm and soft.

'We're all known by our stage names here. Thank God. I'd go bonkers if I have to remember two names for all my girls. Do you have one?'

'Jewel.'

'Jewel. It's been a long time since I've heard that stage name.'

'Really?'

'Yes, I've been in this business for twenty years, you know. And I danced for the first ten.'

She was so respectable and 'establishment' it was hard to imagine her on a pole. 'You did?'

'I sure did. A part of me still misses the attention and the money, but I'm married with kids now and I wouldn't exchange that for the world. Besides I love being House Mom here.' She smiles charmingly, but her next words are a smooth shift into her business mode. 'About a hundred and twenty girls work at any given time and it is my job to ensure that just the right amount of redheads, blondes and brunettes are on the floor, so that all my girls make good money.' She looks at me curiously. 'You have a very exotic look. Unusual. Your eyes are slanted, but so blue.'

'My grandmother is from China and my grandfather was Nordic,' I offer reluctantly into the expectant pause. I don't ever want to talk about my personal life to anybody here.

'Ah! That will explain the amazing cheekbones too.'

'Thank you,' I accept politely, but my stiff expression closes off that avenue of conversation.

'Right. I expect all my girls to be able to do at least three shifts a week. If for any reason at all you can't make it, you're ill, you've got your period, or you've got a mother of a hangover, just let me know so I can cover my ass. Be honest with me. I expect straight talking from all my girls and I'll do the same with you. Understand?'

I nod quickly.

'It is also my job to act as the buffer between the customers and the dancers so no matter what troubles you find yourself in you can always come to me.'

'OK.'

'Good. Let's get the house rules out of the way. The most important one is: the punters aren't allowed to touch you and you aren't allowed to touch them below the waist. Break that rule and you're out. If the security cameras ever pick up a girl touching a man's groin with any part of her body that girl never dances here again. Understood?'

'Understood.'

'Now, it's pretty standard that while you are dancing for a guy he will have a semi happening in his pants. At that point it is exactly the same with all men. They'll look at their crotch meaningfully and ask you to touch them.'

 22

My belly churns with disgust, but I fight hard to keep my face neutral, and I must have succeeded because she carries on without batting an eyelid.

'They'll plead with you, offer you money, and some of them will even tell you they are friends of the management, and that it'll be OK for you to "help" them. But if you do touch them and they turn out to be undercover officers from the licensing department at the Council or the police, the club will be closed down within the hour.'

'So what does everybody do at that stage?'

'Tell them you'd love to, but it could be seen as soliciting and that *would* be in breach of the club's license. Point coyly to the security cameras.'

'What if they insist?'

'If anybody behaves in a perverted way, is rude or aggressive to you, simply signal one of the security boys and the chancer will be escorted or dragged out, depending on the situation, by the back way where there are no security cameras.'

It is hard to imagine that simply the sight of a pair of breasts will make grown men gladly drop thousands of pounds from their wallets, but I do start to feel better about the job.

Then she explains the financial set-up. For the first three days I will not

have to pay house fees, but after that all dancers have to pay a house fee of ninety-five pounds—sixty-five at the start of the evening and thirty by midnight. Use of the VIP rooms costs thirty pounds an hour, but the men get charged two hundred so my profit is a hundred and seventy for that hour.

Then she tells me the interesting part: money does not change hands between customers and dancers. Instead dancers and punters use plastic chips called Eve's Currency or ECs. The club adds twenty percent to whatever the customer converts into ECs and deducts twenty percent commission from the dancers when they change ECs back into cash at the end of the night. It seems incredible to me that the dancers can make any money at all with all these charges. My thoughts must have showed in my face.

'Most of the men who come in here know the deal. They understand that the girls aren't here for free and they keep the lovely stuff flowing. Don't worry—a girl with your looks *will* make money— lots of it. And when you do always remember to show your appreciation to the finely tuned invisible grapevine circulating intelligence around the club.'

'Invisible grapevine of intelligence?' I thought this was a gentlemen's strip club!

'Let's say a customer pulls up in a Lamborghini. The doorman will radio ahead to reception that someone who needs looking after has just come in. Reception might decide to waive the entrance fee, which will make him feel special and put him in a good frame of mind. While seating the prestige customer the waitress will ask him what kind of mood he is in or if he has any special requests.'

She stops to smile cheekily. 'If he says, "Tonight I'm feeling exotic," she will pass that information on to the DJ who will instantly call you or the other exotic on the floor up to the stage. By the time you sashay over to the big spender to ask if he wants a dance, he will think Eden is the most brilliant place in the world. All he has to do is think of the flavor of girl he wants and lo and behold, by a beautiful coincidence, she is everywhere. He'll never know that it is well-oiled cooperation at work.'

She looks at her watch.

'I'll give you a quick tour, show you to your locker, introduce you to Josh who is head of security, and then take you over to Terry, our resident make-up artist. Since this is your first time you must pay twenty-five pounds for a compulsory complete makeover session with her. She'll teach you how to bring out the most of yourself. If you can learn to recreate that look tomorrow you won't need her anymore, but if you can't you'll have to shell it out again. Are you OK with that?'

I nod.

'After Terry I'll introduce you to our no-buttons dressmaker, Donna. She can make an outfit to cater to any man's fantasy and she's an absolute genius with Velcro. Her dresses are designed to fly off you if you stick your tits out forcefully or squeeze your buttocks hard.'

'God!'

Brianna laughs. 'I think you'll find it good for tips. Punters are usually so amazed and entertained they'll tip you all over again to see a repeat performance. And if you find a "lucky" outfit that you make a lot of money in you can ask her to make you a copy.'

'OK,' I agree, as she pushes the door open and we start the tour. The place is massive. The restaurant and lounge are downstairs and the club is upstairs. At the end of our look around she introduces me to Josh. He must be at least six feet six inches tall. He has small eyes, a shaved head and a neck thicker than my waist. He nods his greeting.

After meeting him I am taken to a small room where I meet Terry. After the introductions Brianna leaves telling me she will send Donna around to look in on us.

'Sit yourself down,' Terry invites merrily. She is in her thirties and full of bright chatter. She tells me I have a very different look and I should play on that. First she does my hair, backcombing it from the top of my head and stiffening it with hairspray before combing the front end back so my hair becomes tall and big. She is very precise and very sure in what she does.

I watch her in the mirror as she quickly and expertly applies a layer of foundation, using a darker tone to emphasize my cheekbones, and give my chin a more pointy look. Then she carefully draws my eyes with blue eyeliner focusing attention to their slant and bringing out their color. Afterwards she glues on fake eyelashes. It is a surprise how foreign and heavy they feel. With a wand she dusts glitter on the ends.

'Nearly there,' she says, and paints my lips rose pink. As a final touch she plants a beauty spot on one cheek.

'And now for the magic touch. We have a Chinese girl here called Jade who carries an intricate fan and makes it part of her routine, but you can become known as...' She brings out a plastic flower from her box and holds it behind my ear. 'The girl with the flower.'

I stare at my transformation. The idea is seductive and even I cannot help but fall for the pure poetry of 'the girl with the flower' line, but... 'Look, Terry, I don't want to insult you or anything, but don't you think it's all a bit much? I look like a transvestite.'

Terry covers her mouth and peals of laughter escape from between her fingers. 'Don't worry. The lights on stage are very bright and afterwards it is very dim in the shadows. You will be the perfect fantasy in both types of lighting,' she says and switches off the bright lights that surround the mirror. And suddenly in the dim there is this fantasy creature. I stare at her curiously almost in disbelief. Is that really me? Some of the glitter has fallen from my sweeping lashes onto my cheeks and they sparkle like magic dust.

'See?' she says gleefully.

'Yeah, I get it now,' I agree with a smile.

She switches the lights back on.

As she is arranging my hair around my shoulders Donna comes in after knocking softly. Her hair is pulled back in a messy bun and she has the look of a harried housewife but her voice is low and melodious.

'Well, dear. What kind of clothes would you like to wear? I could get you a nice long gown with a Mandarin

neckline going. Some of the other girls wear it and it works very well if you have the slit going right up to the crotch.'

I think of my grandmother's beautiful silk cheongsams with their demure side slits and I suddenly miss her so much I lose the ability to speak. I just nod.

'What color?'

'Whatever you think is best.'

'Either blue to match your eyes or deep red to catch attention.'

'Deep red then.'

In full fantasy mode I find my way to the changing rooms. It feels as if I have accidentally stepped backstage during a Miss World contest. Unbelievably beautiful girls of every race speaking a cacophony of languages are in various stages of undress. In all the madness of shaving creams, tampons, sequined G-strings and feather boas I spot the black girl who became geometric patterns in the dark.

I experience an instant sense of solidarity with her. There is something about her I really like. Even at our audition I recognized her as one of those

straight people. No bullshit. What you see is what you get. I go up to her. She is sitting in front of a mirror applying her make-up.

'Hey, remember me?'

She regards me in the mirror with cool eyes. 'Sure I do. How are the knees?'

'Fine. I'm Jewel by the way. What's your name?'

She carefully glues on a strip of false eyelashes and says, 'Melanie.'

'In ancient Greek that means "the black girl".'

She stares at me in the mirror, one eye extravagantly lashed, the other oddly bare. The coolness is gone. She is as impressed as I had wanted her to be. 'Where did you learn that?'

I'm not about to tell her that. 'I was interested in Greek mythology when I was younger.'

'And then you became a stripper.' Her voice is challenging.

'Yeah. Shit happens.'

'Hmmm...'

'Look, I'm about to be kicked out of my flat share. Do you know anywhere I can live? Even temporarily?'

She shakes her head. 'No.'

'OK. I'm sure I'll find something,' I say with a shrug and turn away.

As I am walking away she says, 'My flat mate is moving out in two weeks. If you want you can kip on the couch until

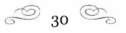

she goes. Just contribute toward bills for the moment.'

I smile. Much better than anything I could have expected. I turn back slowly. 'That would be fantastic. Thank you, Melanie.'

'Two hundred pounds a week plus bills after she goes.'

'Sounds perfect.'

THREE

Jake

The flower behind her ear is a surprise. A large plastic orchid. It is at once bold and innocent. Something a child or an island girl would do. She is wearing a sleeveless red dress with a low cut V-neck and no bra. My eyes flow to the way the material cups her supple breasts. I itch to shape them with my hands, feel their weight, squeeze them, play with them, drag my tongue wildly over the peaks.... Bite them.

Lust trembles in my roaring blood as my cock thickens and lengthens with unsatisfied desire. Damn! I want to fuck her like I have wanted to fuck no other. From the moment our eyes clashed I have been consumed by a kind of madness. I keep thinking of my fingers clenched in her hair, tonguing that smooth flat belly, the fragrant creases between her thighs, and wrapping my lips around her secret flesh. Feeling her buck and come in my mouth.

It is sheer craziness.

Even now, I realize I am stalking her. Watching from the shadows as if I am some carnivore after prey, but I can't seem to stop. The urge to possess her is stronger, miles stronger than my desire for the uncomplicated life of making loads of money and ending my nights between the legs of women I don't own. I used to think life didn't get sweeter than that.

I drain the last of my whiskey, the liquid cool and scratchy in my throat.

With her it is different. I don't want to have sly sex with her. I want to mate with her. I want to wrestle her to the ground and take her with relentless force, so hard that she retaliates with claws ripping into my back. I want to force open her thighs and take her whether she wants it or not.

My mouth dries and the damn lust gnaws like a rat at my guts. The effect this woman has on me is indescribable. I must have her or I will be driven crazy with the itch in my groin, the craving in my blood for the scent and the taste of her skin.

I have never paid for a dance before. But I'm fucking about to.

I raise my hand to signal a waitress. Two notice my hand and eagerly start hurrying toward me. Both are aware of each other, but determined to get to me first. Once it flattered me, people falling

over themselves to please me. But now I have become cynical. I despise them for being so weak and clinging. One of them has nearly reached me. She is smiling broadly, triumphant. Delighted to serve Jake Eden. She knows her tip will be astronomic.

Behind her I see the woman who is quietly but relentlessly driving me crazy. She is standing by the bar, so delicate that she is almost translucent and yet I know she is full of secrets and fire. There is a riot going on all around her, but she looks totally removed, entirely lost to her own thoughts. For a while she looks safe. Locked away in an ivory tower. Waiting for her prince to rescue her.

The waitress is two steps away from me when my blood begins to seethe and boil.

Oh! You hellishly jealous guy, you!

Lily

'Hey, Lily.'

I whirl around warily, startled by the use of my name in this place. A man is leaning against the bar, a small smile playing on his lips. My eyes automatically rove over his face and body. God! These Eden men! They are so fucking gorgeous.

I relax, rest my back against the bar and smile up at him. He has beautiful eyes. Impossible to tell what color in these lights, but probably green or blue. 'Hello, Mr. Eden.'

'Shane,' he corrects softly.

I smile mysteriously. Shane is the younger brother of Jake and the owner of the club. But unlike his brother, who is aloof and elusive, Shane is universally liked by everybody. He is everything you

could want in a man. Movie star looks, charm, manners, and he is supposed to be genuinely nice too. He's not just the kind of man you'd be proud to take home to your parents but will also make all your girlfriends green with envy. The kind of man you could *so* easily say I do to. I have seen him around, but this is the first time he has deigned to talk to me.

'Wanna to go to a party?' he asks, a lazy smile playing on his lips. Wow! He really has perfected his technique.

'Sure. If I'm not working.'

He leans close. 'You're not.'

I grin. 'I do like a resourceful man.'

He laughed. 'I've got a room full of resourceful I'm not using, babe.'

I laugh back. It's easy with him. 'Where's the party at?'

'My brother's.'

The DJ is playing 'Dangerous' by Sam Martin. I tilt my head up and pout, a disobedient, come-get-me pout. I know I am flirting outrageously with him, but I feel safe. 'Which brother?'

'Jake.'

My heart skips a beat. Now that's definitely not the kind of man you want to introduce your parents to. Or you can flirt with safely. 'Great,' I say with a slow smile.

'Pick you up from your place at seven tomorrow?'

'OK.'

'Got anything pretty to wear?'

'What do you think?' I say, batting my false eyelashes with exaggerated coquetry. I swear he makes it too easy.

He reaches into his wallet, takes out a thick wad of crisp notes, and puts it on the bar. 'Buy yourself something stunning.'

I look down at the money, at his strong, long fingers, and then back up at him. He is watching, transfixed. Shit, he really likes me. 'Thanks,' I say softly.

'Right, I'm off to have a shower. A cold shower.'

'I...umm...am looking forward to tomorrow.'

'Goodnight, Lily,' he says, pushing himself off the bar, a smile lighting his eyes, and then he is gone, only his expensive scent remaining.

I watch him leave—the scene is being set—before I pick up the money and stuff it into the red satin bag that comes with my outfit.

The first thing I think of when I open my eyes the next morning is Jake. I hear his

call like an echo in a vast room. A lost, blind sound. I roll over to a cool spot on the sheet and remember the way he looked at me that morning of the audition. The attraction had been immediate, wild, and electric. The promise and the temptation of pleasure and release that only Jake Eden can give shimmer in the morning air.

So: I will see him again tonight.

But I will not let this crazy longing distract me. He uses women the way other people use tissues. And when he discards them he gives them as much thought as people do to tissues they have soiled. I will not be one of his conquests.

When I came home last night I counted the money Shane had put on the bar. Two thousand pounds! If I am going to a party thrown by a gangland lord then I am going in some seriously fabulous gear.

After breakfast I take a taxi into London and end up in Pandora, a secondhand designer store in Knightsbridge. There I find myself standing in front of a mirror wearing a sweetheart neckline, sheer illusion, cocktail-length gown. Its price tag is an eye-watering one thousand eight hundred pounds. Far more than I have ever paid for a dress, but it is gloriously and uniquely beautiful with beads and sparkling blue crystals embellishing the fabric. The assistant, a friendly South American girl, runs to the shoe section and comes back with a pair of blue high heels. I slip them on.

'Wow!' she exclaims dramatically.

'It's very expensive, though,' I worry aloud.

'It is one-third of the price when it was new. It has probably only been worn once.'

I turn my head to look at my side profile. It is a truly breathtaking dress.

'Wait,' she says and going to a glass case takes out a pair of long earrings. She gives them to me and I clip them on. They are so perfect that there is nothing left to do but buy the whole ensemble.

'You'll stun him,' she says sagely as she is counting Shane's money.

At that moment I know. I am not going to this party to be with Shane, but Jake. Even though he is a dangerous criminal and a sexual predator, he is the one for me.

Shane arrives at seven sharp wearing a white dress shirt with ruffles at the front and a black, single-breasted suit. He is a sight for sore eyes. In the daylight I see

that his eyes are the brightest blue this side of heaven. Genuine admiration glimmers in the beautiful depths. He purses his lips and whistles.

I twirl around for him.

'Wow,' he says appreciatively.

I look at the huge bunch of flowers and the obviously expensive box of handmade chocolates he is hugging. 'For me?' I ask.

He holds them out.

'Thank you,' I say and relieve him of them. Truth is I was fourteen the last time a guy brought me anything. Andrew Manning bought me a bar of Aero, my favorite chocolate back then, and put it in his back pocket. I can still remember his red face when he fished the melted, shapeless thing out.

'You look rather dashing yourself,' I murmur, letting my eyes travel over his fine clothes.

'I bet you say that to all the boys,' he jokes in a low, throaty voice.

It could have been silly, but I had to listen to my father bringing the house down with Meatloaf while I was growing up, so it works for me. Suddenly it is as if I have known him for years. I know he's going to be my ally. A friend I can count on. He waits while I put the flowers in a vase and then we leave the apartment together. The weather is unseasonably warm and still, so I don't bother with a jacket. There is a gleaming black Maserati Ghibli parked outside. Shane unlocks it and settles me into the passenger seat before going around to his side. I have never been in such an expensive car before. It is the byword in luxury and it smells heavenly.

'So where is your brother's house?'

'The party is in Essex. About an hour and a half away.'

The conversation is easy and fun.

We leave the highway and hit narrow country roads surrounded by lush forests and finally arrive at electric iron gates. There are paparazzi with long lens cameras hanging around outside. They start immediately snapping their cameras on the off chance that we are famous.

'Why are the paparazzi here?'

'They're expecting a Hollywood A-lister.'

'Who?'

'Leonardo Dicaprio.'

'Really?'

The gates open and we drive through. The road leads up to a fabulous purple-lit mansion with six tall Roman style columns at its entrance.

'Wow!' I cry. '*This* belongs to your brother!'

'Nice, huh?'

'What does one have to do to afford a pile like this?'

'This and that,' he says easily, but evasively.

I turn to look at him. 'Is it a secret?'

He glances briefly at me. 'No, but some things are better left alone.'

Well, that is some warning. I clear my throat. 'Sorry, I didn't mean to pry.'

He grins, the sparkle returning to his eyes. 'It's OK, babe. I don't know what you've heard, but Jake's not the baddest thing in town,' he says, pulling up to the front of the large courtyard, and finding a parking space among all the other highly strung boy's toys. Shane holds open my door and I get out of the low-slung seat as elegantly as my short dress will allow.

I look up at the magnificent house and the first flutter of nerves hits me.

'You look beautiful,' Shane whispers in my ear.

I look gratefully up at him. We walk up to the house and climb the flight of stone steps and two Josh lookalikes in black outfits stand at the tall doors.

Inside, the party is well underway. There are beautiful people everywhere I care to look. We cross the black and white antique marble floor polished to a high sheen and enter a large room full of beautiful furnishings. The music is loud and the room is full of glamour-soaked people.

A statuesque, deeply tanned blonde approaches us with a silver tray of champagne flutes.

'Good evening,' she greets. 'Would you like a drink?'

Shane gets two glasses and putting one in my hand says, 'Come. Let me introduce you to Leo.'

So I meet Leo—as charming and urbane as he was in the Great Gatsby but a bit rounder than I expected—and his escort, a very tall South American beauty. A lot of people seem to know Shane. I say hello to various characters— a TV celebrity, a news anchor woman, and a couple of Shane's cousins, a few decidedly shady. But neither Dominic nor Jake seems to be around. I discreetly glance at my watch. It has just gone ten.

It is only when Shane excuses himself to go to the toilet and I wander over to the open French doors to gaze out at the long, immaculately manicured lawn and surrounding gardens that I hear a man's rich and distinctively husky voice that seems to leap above the music and make my blood throb and rush to my clit.

'Hello, Jewel.'

FOUR

For a couple of seconds I do nothing. Just stand there, a gentle breeze lifting my hair from my neck, savoring the sensation of unfolding drama and the reckless abandonment his voice has brought into my being. I know when I turn around the world will be different.

I prepare myself and face him slowly. Even so the breath catches in my throat. I blink and stare at him.

He towers over me in an emerald suit. Sexual energy glimmers off him like the wavy heat effect in a desert. His eyes—green marbled with violet or black, beautiful at any rate—glow with desire. Every fiber in my body contracts and buzzes as if he is a great dynamo and I am some dumb equipment that is absorbing too much energy. And the worse part: he knows it.

'Or is it Lily?' His sinful lips caress my name like a kiss.

Heat prickles up my arms. 'It's whatever you want it to be.'

He lets his wicked, smoldering gaze drift over my body. 'I want it to be Lily.'

I shrug. 'OK,' I say carelessly.

He takes a drink from a passing tray and hands it to me. Our fingers brush and I shiver. Visibly. His eyebrows lift, but his eyes remain inscrutable. My cheeks flame with sexual tension. I grip the glass tightly. Shit. What the hell is this? Christ in heaven. *Get a fucking grip, Lily.* I can't believe how affected I am by this man. I need time to sort myself out.

I force a smile onto my lips. 'Thank you,' I say politely, and make to move away. His hand shoots out and touches my bare arm. This time my reaction is clear. I jerk my hand away.

'We don't have a no touch policy in this house,' he observes quietly.

'I don't believe we've been introduced. Who are you?'

Green sparks of amusement dance in his eyes. He knows I know exactly who he is. 'Who do you want me to be, Lily?' His voice is lazy like a deadly snake coiled in the sun. One wrong move...

An unfamiliar warmth shivers and fizzles through my veins. 'My lover's brother.'

The amusement vanishes from his eyes—the reptile has been rudely awakened—replaced by a bolt of blazing fury.

 45

My heart stops. I resist the instinctive reaction to back off. For a few moments, or it could have been thousands of years, we stare at each other and then he turns on his heels and strides away, his back ramrod straight.

I grip the champagne glass tightly and watch his tall figure cut through the human crush. He stands out the way a hawk stands out in a crowd of canaries. A woman in a sophisticated ivory velvet evening gown lays a manicured hand on his sleeve. He stops and bends his head to her. She says something. Her laugh is tinkling. I feel a furious tightening in my belly. I am jealous. I am sickeningly jealous of the horny bitch.

'Did you miss me?' Shane asks in my ear.

At the sound of his easy voice, relief floods me. It's like having a stiff drink on a cold day. The warm waves radiate out from the middle of your belly. I turn toward him. 'Desperately.'

'How desperately?' His teeth flash.

'You don't want to know.'

He laughs. 'Come on. I want you to meet my brother.' Before I can protest he puts his hand on my elbow and steers me along toward his brother and the beauty in the ivory dress. She has coffee-colored hair and empty silver eyes.

'Jake, I want you to meet Lily.'

Jake turns stiffly toward me. 'We've already met,' he says dryly.

'Oh! When?'

'Moments ago.' He seems cold and uninterested.

Shane looks at me quizzically.

'You didn't give me a chance to tell you,' I say weakly.

'Aren't you going to introduce me, darling?' the woman says adoringly, as she slides her hand up his black shirt. Her hand dislodges his jacket and I see its pale blue lining. Jealousy shoots like quicksilver into my blood, scorching it. I look up and meet his eyes. They are dark and carefully veiled.

'Andrea Mornington, Lily Hart,' he says curtly, then very deliberately curls his arm around her waist.

'Hello, Lily,' Andrea says, turning her empty eyes toward me, except they are no longer empty but precise and direct, like a key turning in a lock. She perfectly understands what has not been spoken.

I force a smile. 'Please excuse me, I need to find a washroom.' As I turn away, Shane's hand falls on my wrist. 'Are you OK?'

I look into his eyes. Already I can see the weight of responsibility he has taken for my well-being. It warms and saddens me. 'Yes. I'll be back soon.'

I don't have to look at his brother to know he is watching me. I feel it like a dagger in my back or an act of fate.

I don't find the washroom. Instead I drift inconspicuously into an adjoining room. It seems to be a salon of some kind. As with everything else in the house it is beautiful. There is nobody in there. I close the door and lean against it.

The attraction is so inconvenient, so absurd that I had never even considered the possibility. And yet here it is. I want him so bad it is like an ache. I push away from the door, put my glass of champagne on a low table, and walk to a tall window. I stare out of it into the dark and see only my ghostly reflection.

A dozen thoughts come and go. I know I should be going back to Shane, but the part of me that loathes to see them together is the stronger. My thoughts are interrupted by a sound at the door.

I whirl around in surprise.

For God's sake! An emerald suit and a diamond encrusted ring on his pinkie! He should have looked ridiculous, but he does not. He starts walking toward me—sure, confident, leonine. Dazzling.

There is an arrogance and authority to the set of his jaw that is not at all to my liking. His gaze is aggressively bold and virile. His eyes travel down my body.

'Lost?'

'No, I was trying to be alone.'

His eyes dip down and linger suggestively and I am certain deliberately on my breasts. The mental disrobing is meant to unruffle me.

'Positively breathtaking,' he murmurs softly, but with a hint of sardonic amusement.

'Insufferably arrogant, aren't you?'

'It has been said,' he concedes with a wry grin.

'What do you want?' I ask. My voice rings out like a bell in the vast room. I hear the panic in it, the revelation that I do not trust myself.

He stands in front of me, his cheekbones flushed with sexual heat. 'Isn't it perfectly obvious what I want?'

'Not to me.'

'I want you to stay away from my brother.'

I blush. Then I laugh mockingly. 'You're a gangster. Don't act high and mighty with me.'

He smiles slowly, his eyes crinkling with amusement. 'Say that word again.'

I blink. 'What word?'

'Gangster.'

'Why?'

'Because you make it sound so sexy I want to go out and become one.'

'Am I supposed to believe that you're not one?'

He shrugged disinterestedly, but his eyes take on a new glitter. 'I can be if you want me to be.'

Suddenly I feel so flustered I can't even look at him. I drop my eyes.

'Is that what you really want...Lily? A gangster?'

'It's the last thing...'

He moves, and fast. 'So what the fuck are you doing playing nice with his brother,' he snarls and gripping my forearms pushes me roughly against the wall by the window.

I do what I did when I was nine years old and I opened the front door of my nan's house and there were two unsmiling skinheads outside. One of them was holding a hammer. I didn't pause or consider. I simply reacted.

'Let loose the two Alsatians, Nan,' I screamed.

For a second the heavily tattooed heads looked at each other, and then they bolted away so fast there was not enough time to say skin. My nan didn't have a dog.

Again I let my instinct guide me.

I grab Jake's surprised face and, pulling it down, kiss him hard on the mouth, except, unlike the skinheads situation, the problem does not run away.

His mouth opens to mine. The kiss sears my lips, shocking. I stagger and

50

grab a handful of dark hair. Supporting hands come around my waist like bands of warm steel forcing me into his unyielding body, and I melt into it, fuse with it. My insides turn to fucking mush and my toes curl in my shoes. Thick juices leak into the gusset of my panties. For those few seconds I even stop breathing!

Then, without warning, he tears his mouth away from mine, and coiling strong hands around my forearms pushes me back against the cold wall. He stares at me with these wild, animal eyes, the pupils so huge it is as if he has been running or has come out of a dark room. Mesmerized, I gaze up at him. I have never seen anything like it. Anything so feral and beautiful. He takes a deep breath.

'What the fuck?' he bites out harshly.

'Sorry,' I say as coolly as I can manage. 'When a man shoves a woman up against a wall he usually wants to ravish her.'

He is breathing hard. Through short gasps of air he grates, 'Stay the fuck away from my brother.'

His voice is cold and menacing and a great white shark is swimming in his eyes, but I know that if I reach out and touch the front of his five thousand pound suit trousers I will find him tight and hard inside them.

'So I'm good enough for you but not good enough for your brother.'

He laughs bitterly. 'No, you're good enough for any man's bed. The problem is Shane would want to marry you, and we both know you're not the marrying kind.'

'What makes you think I wouldn't marry Shane?'

He reacts swifter than a Tasmanian devil. His hand shoots out and pulls me so hard and fast I gasp with shock as I slam into his body. His cock juts into my belly. 'Don't play with me, Jewel.'

I look up at him defiantly. Heat glitters in his pale eyes and fierce sexual heat has tightened his jaw. 'If Shane wants me he'll have me.'

His eyes flash with anger, but he drawls, 'Oh, baby. You have no clue, have you?'

'Are you threatening me?'

'Take it as a warning.'

'What are you going to do, hmmm?' I challenge.

'For a start, this.' And he bends his head and crushes his mouth against mine. The kiss is possessive and demanding. It is nothing like the other. This one is pure punishment. With this one he is branding me. Putting his seal of ownership on me. I twist my head and try to push away, my knees preparing to connect hard with his crotch, when suddenly the kiss changes and I am helpless to resist. It is a kiss like nothing I have ever experienced. There is no discordant note. Everything about it is hot and wet and wild.

My mouth opens and his tongue thrusts in, boldly, the way his cock would enter my pussy. I suck on it and electric energy snaps through me, scraping the back of my neck, as if I have received a shock from an old electric appliance. His hands lift me off the floor and put me back down with my legs farther apart. I feel him pull my dress up and over my bum. I hear the small scrap of lace and satin tear and then I feel his finger slide into my heat. I moan helplessly into his mouth.

'What the hell is going on here?' a voice demands.

His broad shoulders block my view of Shane, but I freeze with horror. My torn panties are lying on the floor, and Jake's hard fingers are still inside my naked pussy.

Very casually, Jake lifts his head from mine, extracts his fingers out of me, and smoothing my dress over my hips, turns around to face his brother. He keeps his hand firmly around my waist.

'What do you think is going on, Shane?' he asks coolly.

Shane stares at me, hurt etched in his beautiful eyes.

I try to twist out of Jake's grip, but it is iron hard. 'I'm sorry,' I whisper.

He smiles. A bitter twist of his lips and I know what he is thinking. *He'll just use you and discard you.* No longer able to meet my eyes, he draws himself up with great dignity. And at that moment I see what a fine man he is. And how much he must have liked me before this. And I find myself wishing that the sparks between Jake and me had flown between him and me instead.

He nods distantly and looks out of the window. 'You will see her home safe.'

'Of course,' he replies.

'Goodnight then,' he bids and walking out of the door shuts it behind him.

Jake takes his hand away from around my waist, but his eyes never leave mine. Feeling strangely bereft I wrap my hands around my waist. 'You knew he was going to be here, didn't you?'

Green swirls in his eyes. 'I asked him to come.'

I nod slowly. So easily I had fallen into his trap. 'That was a very cruel thing you did.'

His voice is strangely soft, almost regretful. 'I did warn you.'

'To your brother.'

'He'll survive. He knows I have his best interest at heart,' he dismisses callously, but I see the glimmer of a

fierce loyalty to his brother, his family. His pack.

'Why do you think I'd be so bad for your brother?'

'I think I just proved my point a few minutes ago.'

'You don't know me.'

'I beg to differ. I know exactly what you are.'

'I'd like to go home now.'

'You're staying the night. I'll get my driver to run you home tomorrow.'

My mouth drops open. 'You think I'm going to sleep with you after what you just did? I wouldn't sleep with you if you were the last man on earth,' I declare with great unoriginality.

A slow masculine smile splits his face. If he was good looking before he is devastating now. I stare at him. Jesus! I am crazy about him.

He reaches out a hand and touches my face with the backs of his fingers. I flinch away. He drops his hand to the side of his body. 'Don't flatter yourself. I have a date for tonight.'

Of course, Andrea Mornington of the velvet gown. Fucking bastard. At that moment I think I *hate* him.

'My housekeeper Maria will set you up in one of the guest bedrooms.' He turns away from me and strides to the door. At the door he hesitates. 'Enjoy the party, won't you?' Then he is gone.

I touch my mouth with wonder. Fuck!
I was a nightmare looking for a dream.

FIVE

I toss and turn on the silk sheets of the king-size bed, constantly moving my body to find a cool spot. The air is balmy and still, but it is the thought of him with her that makes me sick with jealousy. I keep thinking of him pushing into her, filling her up with long, smooth strokes.

Suddenly I hear the sound of feet in the corridor outside my room. The noise stops outside my door. I lay dead still. Only my heart crashing into my ribs. My eyes riveted on the door handle. He wouldn't dare. He wouldn't fucking dare come to me after he has been with her. There is another heart-wrenching moment of silence and then the sound of his footsteps passes on. I sit up, feeling hot and flushed.

He didn't come in!

I had been maddened by the thought of his audacity but now I am devastated by acute disappointment. It rushes into my system like a physical ache. Fuck you, I think. Fuck you, Jake Eden. I stand up and run to the big oak door. I have my hand on the handle when I stop myself. *What the fuck are you doing?* I clench my hands into fists and press them against my mouth.

What the hell is happening to me? I feel as frustrated and unsated as if I have been left unfinished by a lover. What is it about this man that makes me desperate to feel him inside me? I press my ear to the door and hear him going down the stairs.

I remove my fist from my teeth and turn the lock on the door. The metal click is loud and final. I feel glad that I have done it. I have taken back control. I step away from the door. My hands are shaking with emotion. I am suddenly startled by a light coming on outside the window. It is him. He has tripped the security lights. I move fast. I run to the window and stand in the shadows, behind the curtains.

I watch him walk across the terrace toward the lip of the swimming pool, full of the restless energy and the deadly grace of a puma on the prowl. Bathed in white light, he kicks off his shoes, tugs his T-shirt over his head, peels off his jeans, and with his thumbs pulls his underwear to the floor. I should stop watching him. I should go back to bed, but I can't. I am transfixed by the muscular buttocks lit by the neon blue of the underwater lighting.

 58

Backlit, he steps out of his underwear, and stands for a moment at the pool's edge. I see the rough dusting of hair on his calves, then, gloriously and fabulously naked, he turns slightly toward my window so that his long thick dick is exposed to me. He looks up then and I feel his gaze seeking me out.

Meeting his eyes like that is like being kicked in the guts. Wrenching. There is nothing I can do except stand in my hiding place. Guilty. Shameless. We stare at each other. Then he turns away and glides cleanly into the water. For a few moments more I watch him cut powerfully through the blue water.

Then I stumble away from the window.

At that moment I realize two things. One: the utter primitiveness of the man, and two: the fact that I am not in charge. I never was. Fantasies spill through my head. His hands, his tongue, his cock. Riding me until I scream. I squeeze my thighs hard.

I sleep badly and wake up at five thirty. It is already light outside, but blessedly cool.

I get out of bed and after a quick shower pad over to the clothes and shoes that Maria brought for me last night. Matching peach underwear, a blue tracksuit and white sneakers, all still with their tags on. Shockingly they all fit me perfectly. He must have random women staying over unexpectedly all the time, I reflect sourly.

Outside my door the house is totally silent.

I walk down the grand staircase and let myself out. Mist clings to the ground. It all looks very Sherlock Holmes and I smile to myself as I cross the lawn and head off toward the woods.

A thundering sound breaks the peaceful stillness of the morning. I reel around, startled. Out of the mist a man on a shining black stallion appears. He is riding without a saddle. His horse is like him—a terrifying presence, raven-eyed. A big brute. Hard and unyielding. I am struck by how animal and man are so blended, so in tune.

He stops beside me. The stallion snorts restlessly. Its eyes are wild. I drag my gaze back to the man, in awe at the sight of him on that big black stallion. In the soft morning light his face is hard and watchful.

'Come for a ride with me,' he commands, from a long way up. He sits dead still, his expression intense, his eyes picking up every detail of my person. Despite the stillness there is no mistaking the intent in that big body. At that moment it seems as if nothing can stand in his way.

I open my mouth but nothing comes out. I shake my head. I have never been on a horse, let alone a gleaming black monster like this one.

'You don't talk much,' he notes and offers his hand. He knows inside I am clamoring for him.

Dazed by his appearance and the way he makes me feel I put my hand in the cradle of his. His hand is huge. It feels like hot damp earth. It closes over mine tightly. He hauls me up so suddenly, I yelp. I find myself dangerously unbalanced at the back of him. The horse neighs at my panic. He places his calm, steadying hand on its strong neck and holds it there until it stills. He squares my weight on the horse.

'Put your arms around me,' he says.

I do it gladly. The heat and scent of him envelop me. I hear the staccato of my heart, loud, strong, fast. I have to resist the desire to lay my head on his taut back.

'OK?' he asks, turning his head to look at me.

'OK,' I croak.

He clicks his tongue and eases the horse into a canter through the fields. There are no sounds but those we make.

 61

The horse's snorting breath, the twigs crackling underneath. He does not speak and neither do I. There is something magical about our ride.

He slows the horse to a walk as we enter the woods. Here the air is colder and darker and full of the scent of summer, wildflowers and clover. Squirrels and small animals scamper in the underbush and trees. When we get out of the woods we are suddenly on a beach.

'Wow,' I whisper.

'Hold on tight,' he says, and puts the horse to a gallop along the shoreline. For a few seconds I am shocked and a little bit afraid and then I laugh. The wind tears at my hair, tossing it about wildly. Beneath me I can feel the stallion flexing gracefully as he flies over the ground with amazing speed.

The hard man against my front, the horse underneath me, and the fantastic sensation of total freedom: it is old magic. Magic that can only be conjured up when all the trappings of civilization have been stripped away. The horse stops. Jake throws a leg over and deftly jumps to the ground. With his hands around my waist, he lifts me down. He pats the horse's sleek neck and it runs away from us.

I look up at him. 'The horse...'

'He'll be all right.'

I notice then that he is barefoot. And unlike all the other times I have seen him, he is wearing an old, ripped T-shirt and faded brown corduroy trousers. I take my borrowed shoes off and hold them in my hand.

'Come on,' he says and we walk together, our hands almost touching but not quite. We never speak. There is not a soul in sight. Salt water laps at our bare feet. Above our heads a lone seagull circles the sky. I cannot explain the sense of peace or the inevitability of the moment. It feels as if there is no other life for me but this. I am not a dancer in a gentlemen's club and he is not a gangster.

I want to ask him why—why is he sharing his paradise with me?—but I find the words choke in my throat. Maybe because I know that this is temporary and words will only taint it. Once, I turn sideways to look at him and find him watching me. His hair is windswept, the hard cheekbones flushed, and his eyes bright in the morning sun.

'What?' I mouth.

He shakes his head and whistles. The horse flies toward us, mane flying. A beautiful sight. It stops in front of him and he carefully cups its face and in hush tones speaks to it in a language I cannot understand. Maybe Gaelic.

 63

'What are you saying to him?' I ask.

'I am introducing you to him. We gypsies have always talked to our animals.'

'What are you telling him about me?'

'That's our secret.'

He takes my hand and brings it to the horse. I feel its hot damp breath on my palm. I touch its cheek and see a flare of panic in its eyes. It paws the ground. He cups its face and soothes it.

'What's his name?'

'Thor.'

'He loves you,' I whisper.

'I love him,' he says simply and kisses the horse between the eyes.

With a clean hop he mounts the horse and, sitting squarely on it, reaches for my hand. With me securely seated behind him we return to the house. The journey back seems much faster and too soon we are outside the front entrance of the house. He dismounts and helps me down.

I look into his face and already he has changed, become distant. He regards me carefully. 'I have other matters to attend to and will not join you for breakfast. After breakfast Ian will take you back to London.'

Other matters to attend to. And suddenly I remember the woman he spent the night with. A flash of jealousy rips through me. Fuck her. Fuck them both.

'Thanks,' I call out casually as I walk away from him.

I am dying to, but I don't watch him gallop away.

Inside the house, I find Maria hovering in the living room. She seems to be fluffing some cushions, but she must have been at the window watching us arrive.

'Good morning,' she says brightly.

'Morning.'

'Well then, young lass, what would you like for breakfast? Waffles, cereal, full English, continental, or something different?'

'Continental sounds good.'

'Excellent. Breakfast will be served in the dining room in ten minutes.'

After she leaves I wander over to the window. How strange it all is. Me in this house. Me on a horse with Jake Eden. Ten minutes later I go into the dining room. It is exactly like the rest of the house. Rich and splendid and unlived in.

I eat my warm, perfectly flaky croissant with lashings of butter and jam and drink my cup of freshly brewed coffee alone. But as I am finishing my food Jake appears at the door.

His hair is still wet from his shower and he is dressed in a charcoal shirt, black trousers, a white silk tie and

maroon shoes. I remember again the way he looked coming in from the mist, at one with his beast. Uncivilized and utterly beautiful. He is holding a box in his hand.

I stare at him, surprised. I did not expect to see him again this morning. I brush croissant crumbs from my fingers and wipe them on the napkin on my lap.

'I got you something.' He seems awkward, totally at odds with his usual macho bravado.

I stand, the chair scraping on the carpet. 'You got me a present,' I say stupidly.

He comes toward me and holds it out. I take it cautiously. It is a square box, five inches by five. It is wrapped in dark gray paper with a broad red ribbon. It screams expensive.

I undo the ribbon and tear the paper open. Inside a transparent plastic box is a spray of white orchids. The stem is immersed in a small plastic tube of water and attached to a comb-clip.

'For your hair,' he says softly. 'Wear it tomorrow night... For me.'

White flowers. I remember the poem: *Somewhere there's beauty. Somewhere there's freedom.* I nod slowly, my eyes locked on his. Hypnotized by what I see in them. 'So you're coming to the club tomorrow?'

'Yes. Wait for me?'

 66

I register a surge of uncontrollable joy inside my body. It makes my ears burn. I smile—happy, wistful.

'And one more thing—Miss Mornington didn't stay the night.'

SIX

It is a slow night at the club and I worry about how awkward it will be to see Shane there, but as it turns out he does not come in. At two Melanie and I take a cab back to the apartment.

'I'm hungry,' I say walking to the fridge. 'Do you want something?'

'Get the ice cream out,' she says flinging herself on the sofa.

'Chocolate or vanilla?'

'Both.'

I bring two bowls of ice cream out into the living room and Melanie is taking crumpled, damp notes out of her bra.

'Whoa,' I say, kicking off my shoes and curling up on the couch opposite her. 'I thought we all have to use ECs.'

'Yeah, we do,' she admits. 'But some guys want me to have cash. They know I'd lose twenty percent during cash out and they'd rather I had the whole thing.'

'Does Brianna know?'

'Sure.'

'So how much money do you make in a night then?' I ask curiously.

'About a thousand on a bad night and three to five on a good night.'

My eyes widen. 'Three to five?'

'Why? How much do you make?' She looks at me with narrowed assessing eyes.

'After paying the house fee and other costs about three hundred quid. Once I made seven hundred.'

'No fucking way,' she erupts, clearly as shocked as I was that she was taking in up to five thousand in one night.

'Why is that so shocking?'

She shakes her head. 'Damn, girl, if I looked like you I'd be making five thousand a shift. That's what those blonde bimbos take home *every* fucking night.'

'Really?'

'Yes, really, and you know what else? If you don't start earning at least four figures soon Brianna is going to ask you in for a little chat, and if your income doesn't improve real quick after that you'll be politely asked to leave.'

'Shit,' I curse softly. I can't afford that to happen.

'What did you think? You're taking up the place of a girl that could be earning thousands for the club. We are the sweets in the sweetshop.'

I stare at her stupidly.

'Look, it's not hard. You just have to apply yourself. Do you know what Jolene takes home?'

'Jolene?' I frown and shake my head. Jolene is the least good-looking girl at the club. She even has buck teeth. When I met her in the changing rooms it surprised me that Brianna had taken her on.

'That girl takes six to seven thousand. Sometimes I've heard she even makes ten when her regulars come.'

My jaw drops open. 'Ten thousand *pounds*?'

'Yup.'

'A night?'

'Yeah. You should see when she cashes out at the end of her shift. It's like someone hitting jackpot at the fruit machine in a Vegas casino.'

'What does she do to get them to give her all that money then?'

'To start with she doesn't act all high and mighty like you do.'

I open my mouth to deny it, but Melanie holds out a warning hand. 'I've seen you. You will be sitting down with a guy and your body language will be screaming, I don't want to be here. I mean which man is going to pay a girl who clearly tells him she finds him unattractive.'

'But they are unattractive..'

'True, but,' she licks her spoon, 'why did you become a dancer?'

'To make money.'

'You're not going to make any with your attitude. You know what Jolene does? She goes and sits next to them and whispers in their ears, "I'm here to be anything you want me to be. I can be the dirtiest, most forbidden whore of your fantasies. Tell me what you want me to be? Talk dirty with me." And guess what? They never get to touch her, she talks dirty, they empty their wallets, and they come back for more. Now that is a clever dancer. She'll even invite other girls into the VIP room to dance for her customer and pay them for it.'

The whole idea puts me off. I feel decidedly glum. 'I don't get why they just don't all go to a knocking shop and buy a prostitute.'

'Aha!' she cries triumphantly. 'That is why plain Jolene is taking home ten thousand and super gorgeous you is bringing in three hundred. Because you don't understand the job. The "no touching" rule means there is no longer any pressure for the man to sexually perform. It's all about his fantasies. For a few hundred quid he can be that guy of his dreams with beautiful girls hanging on his every word, laughing at his most inane jokes.'

She leans back and takes off her boots. There are more sweaty notes stuck to her calves. As she peels them off and straightens them out on the table I see that some of them have phone numbers scribbled on them.

'And here is something else you should understand. Dancing can be incredibly empowering and a great turn-on. Why do you think all the girls wear tampons even when it's not their period?'

My eyes widen.

She just nods sagely. 'When your garter starts to bulge with twenties and fifties you know you're not just hot, you're bloody good at what you do. I always make them sit with their legs spread wide so I can see them get a hard-on. This gives me total control of the situation. I will then roll my body inches away from their faces so they feel the heat coming off me.'

She puts her feet up on the coffee table and wriggles her toes.

'And I'll purposely let my hair trail their cheeks or let out a long sigh close to their ears. Usually they will start breathing heavily, which means I've done a good job, but sometimes they will become so fixated, so paralyzed they actually forget to take a breath and have to take a sudden sharp intake, and that is when I know. They are ready for the VIP room.'

Melanie looks at me as though seducing strange men is the simplest thing in the world to accomplish.

'And if you know a guy is really satisfied with your service you can even ask for a tip.'

Wow! It had not even occurred to me to do such a thing. 'Won't they feel robbed after they've paid all that money for the dance?'

'Don't ask, don't get.' She grins. 'These men know the game. They know what I do and where they are and that means if they spend my time it has to be in exchange for money. Exactly as they would pay their lawyer, by the hour. I'm not there for fun. I'm there to make money.'

'As a matter of fact,' she adds, 'the more wealthy and powerful the man the more cheeky and forthright you can be with them. They'll think you're hilarious and that's another tip there for you. It's a hustle only if they feel they've been harassed. I take pride in never letting them feel they've blown away good money.'

I think of her dangling from the top of the pole and doing splits mid-air to David Guetta's electronic music and a voice screaming, 'Let me see your fucking hands,' as she starts tumbling

down the pole. And when the male voice asks again, 'A party without me?' the lights come on and the club fills with lines from the song, 'I Might Be Anyone'. But she is not anyone. She is as beautiful as Lupita Ny in that iconic Lancôme advert. After her performances the club always erupts into applause.

'I know you are very good at what you do,' I tell her sincerely.

'Damn right. I'm not just showing them a pair of tits. I'm giving them a performance that will blow their heads off. And if a customer treats me with contempt—some of them come in there just to do that, a stripper and a black stripper at that, I must be despicable—I'll use his money the next day to buy me something that will make me feel good, and that will be my revenge.'

Melanie yawns hugely.

'Thanks for the advice,' I say gratefully. She is absolutely right. I'd better get off my high horse or forget dancing altogether. And since leaving Eden is not an option I'm going to have to do things very differently from now on.

SEVEN

The club has a carnival air to it. Men throwing money into the air as if it is confetti, champagne flowing like it is free, gorgeous girls dressed for showtime, and then the cabaret starts, and ladyboys from Thailand flutter onto the stage. They are bold, highly talented, and gregarious.

I stand backstage and hear the DJ announce my name. As I walk up to the door I remember Ann, my instructor, saying, When you are on stage wave a wand and become a tigress. Make eye contact with the punters, hold their gazes for a long time. Make them think you want them. Make them squirm in their seats. Make them feel your power, so that when you have finished your routine and are walking toward them they know it's time to reach for their wallets.

At the doorway of the stage I hold onto the doorframe and strike a pose while I survey the darkened audience of men. The lights are hot and bright in my eyes, but I see him immediately. He stands out like a sore thumb, the only man who does not look like he is looking for a good time. His pose is relaxed, his knees spread apart, one hand on a thigh, another loosely curved around a glass of amber liquid, but he stares directly at me with intense, unsmiling, furious eyes.

What the fuck is he angry about?

I freeze and almost lose my self-confidence. But then a blast of candy white smoke from the stage bathes me. A blue strobe light cuts me in half. Then the music comes on and my heart starts to pound with sexual energy, the kind that Melanie uses in her performances, and I think, fuck you, Jake Eden. I haven't done anything wrong.

Totally ignoring him I strut onto the stage. There are whistles and catcalls from a stag party that are seated right at the edge of the stage. There are about twelve of them and I am glad for them. They straighten my spine. I will give them the best performance of my life. I'll take their money. My time has to be paid for.

I concentrate on the music. I let it fill every cell in my body as I dance around the pole and rub myself sinuously on it. Flicking my hair back, I grip the pole hard and perfectly execute the flying around the pole move that landed me on my knees at the audition. The men from the stag party seem impressed judging from the whistles.

I search for the bridegroom. Early thirties, red hair, pleasant face and has an L sign pinned to his shirt. I will dance for him. It's hard to explain, but it's so much easier to dance for someone you don't fancy. You look into their eyes and you pretend. So I do. And the more I stare at him the more rowdy and boisterous his mates become. I am clearly a success.

It is almost time to lose my bikini bra. I climb the pole. Slowly, seductively. They hoot their encouragement. I focus totally on the bridegroom—his eyes are on stalks. Gripping the pole with my thighs I lean right back so I am looking at the crowd while I am upside down. Hanging in that position I let my breath out in a hard puff. The bra pops open and flies off. The boys go crazy.

Far in the shadows another man is watching, calling. Helplessly my eyes flash across the crowded room, the crush of bodies, and clash with his. All the sounds and smells and chaos recede. He is as still as a statue. For a moment I am suspended on the pole and caught in his world. In this world I am in trouble. I have done something very wrong. Somehow I have betrayed Jake Eden.

Then gravity asserts itself and I pull my body upwards, and slide down the

pole. I bend to pick up my bra from the stage floor and the bridegroom is standing at the edge of the stage holding a fifty. We look at each other. There is *hunger* in his eyes, the kind of hunger that Melanie talked about. And I feel sorry for his bride. Then I pull my stocking out and he slips my very first cash tip into it.

I look again at him—we are less than ships that pass in the night, and yet we are more.

'Thanks,' I say, blowing him a kiss as I exit the stage. I go backstage and get back into the deep red cheongsam with the slit that goes up to my crotch. I touch the orchid Jake gave me and it is exactly where I pinned it. With a deep breath I walk out onto the floor. I know exactly what I will say to Jake.

A waitress sidles up to me. 'Table twenty-three has just left a black Amex behind the bar and thinks you're hot,' she whispers.

I look at her little name tag, and say, 'Thanks, Toni. I'll be sure to remember you later.'

'No problem,' she says with a wink and moves on.

For a second I think about not going to table twenty-three and then I think: No, I'm working. I need this job. Toni has taken the trouble to send a customer my way and she'll be expecting her cut. I'll make it real quick.

I walk up to table twenty-three. He is wearing a smile that could light up a Christmas tree.

'Hey.'

'You were great on stage,' he says.

'Thank you. Would you like a dance?' I ask.

'Sure, I'll buy a private dance off you,' he says, another bulb on the Christmas tree lighting up.

Shit, what bad timing! My first big spender and I'm in a horrible hurry. From across the club I can feel Jake's animosity searing my back. I realize now I shouldn't have come. I should have passed table twenty-three onto another dancer.

Jake

What the fuck! I cannot believe my fucking eyes. Not only did I have to sit through a roomful of horny men staring at her nearly naked body—now the fat bastard is standing up and following her. She's going to go into one of those VIP rooms and give him a *private* dance. Frustration claws at my heart. I grit my teeth. I have never wanted to be shackled to anyone, no matter how enticing the chains. But damn her. I cannot even bear the thought of any other man in a room with her, looking at her.

I want her to belong to me. And only me.

From the corner of my eyes I see Brianna walking toward me. She is smiling. I don't smile back. The thoughts

in my head seethe so bitter and dark that I lose control. I stand up and begin to stride toward Lily and her punter. I see Brianna's experienced eye sizing up the situation. She stops smiling and picks up her speed—not so she would make a scene, though.

I grab Lily's hand. Her first reaction is interesting. It is one of pure repulsion. Then her gaze collides with mine and the expression is replaced by a mixture of joy, lust, and anger.

The man turns to look at me. 'Excuse me,' he says pompously, as if it is *I* who has trod on his property. I've collected money from men like him before. Without their fancy lawyers they are sniveling, pathetic messes. They'd give up their mothers to avoid a scratch.

Fortunately for him, Brianna reaches us at that same instant. She is so smooth I have to admire her anew.

'Mr. Walsh,' she coos. 'Jewel has a personal emergency that she has to take care of, but I have found two beauties to dance for you instead. Obviously, your champagne is on the house.'

Mr. Walsh accepts with ill grace. He has no idea how close he was to being floored. Brianna leads him away quickly.

Hiding the black lust in my heart I look down at the brazen little hussy coldly. 'I believe this dance is mine.'

'Yes, my lord,' she says sarcastically.

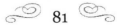

I am still furious, but her scent drifts over me like a sweet cloud and lust writhes hot in my blood as my cock hardens too fast and painfully.

Lily

The walls and ceiling of the VIP room are mirrored. It is empty except for a small, round, low table, a large upholstered red and gilt chair, and another much smaller black one that the dancers use as a prop. He kicks the door shut, his heel slamming into the wood, and stands there, tall, proud. Pure alpha. Great! I am alone in the VIP room with one pissed off gangster.

In a silky, dangerous voice, 'Did you enjoy that?'

Nervously, 'What?'

'Taunting me.'

'I wasn't.'

'You looked right into my eyes. You knew I was waiting for you.'

I lick my lips. 'This is my job.'

He walks over to the red chair and lowers himself into it. He takes two blue chips out of his jacket and puts them on the table. Blue chips are a hundred pounds each. Then he looks up at me.

In a voice like the crack of a whiplash, 'Now strip.'

I feel my cheeks start to burn. Doing a dance for someone that you fancy like crazy is totally different. The adrenaline rush is undeniable. It surges inside me. I finally understand why the other girls wear tampons all the time.

Without taking my eyes off him I unzip my dress and let it slip down my body and pool around my ankles. His eyes rush down my body greedily, hungrily. From the speakers Snoop Dogg is singing, *'Tell me, baby, are you wet? I just want to get you wet.'*

Just perfect.

Jake

She flicks her head flirtatiously like an animal in heat and deliberately presents her buttocks to me. I see her sex clothed in satin and puffed out between her spread thighs. I know exactly what she is doing. She is showing me the sweet wet heat at the center of her. The urge to reach out and touch. Fuck!

She moves her hips from side to side, slowly, teasing, provoking. Then she pushes back until she is inches away from my face. I can smell the heady scent of her arousal. It has hidden itself within the noisy smells of cheap perfume, sweat, sex, and seedy thoughts. It flowers in my face.

Like a wolf scenting the air, I inhale in quick bursts. She pulls back and my nose moves forward, following the intoxicating trail of her scent. Her hands

skim lightly over her ribs and linger over the tops of her breasts, the skin satiny. She cups her breasts. I stare at her utterly riveted. She hooks one leg over the chair's back and in one deft, smooth movement, sits down on the edge of the seat.

Keeping her body arched and her legs straight, she opens her thighs so her long, long legs make a fabulous V. The position is obscene and bewitching. She is good enough to eat.

I stare at the wet patch hungrily.

She holds the pose.

I raise my eyes up to hers. 'How much to push the material aside?'

Something flashes into her eyes. She lids them quickly.

'One thousand.' Her voice is flat and cold.

At that moment no one else in the world exists. Only her, me, and something raw and too hot to touch. I reach into my pocket and pull out a handful of chips. There might have been two, maybe three thousand there. I hold them over the table and let them fall. Some hit the surface and roll away to clatter onto the floor.

Very slowly she reaches into the material and pulls it to one side. My eyes drop. God only knows how many pussies I have seen in my lifetime, but this time it takes my breath away. I stare riveted

at the pink glistening whorls of wet flesh. In that position the hole gapes, as if begging to be filled, taken, fucked. Enticingly thick nectar drips out of it.

I raise my eyes to hers. Very deliberately she moves her gaze to my crotch, to my hard-on. I get it. She is angry. Even in this humiliating position she is helpless to fight the sensual call of her own body.

She smiles. 'Want anything else?'

'What else is for sale?' My voice sounds cool and distant, but my heart is hammering in my chest. Afraid of her answer. Afraid she will become more than just a cock tease. Terrified she'll become another fallen flower littering the ground I walk upon.

I see it clearly then. A flash of something far stronger than the liquid dripping out of her. Hatred. The violence of it shocks me. She doesn't close her legs. She doesn't pull the material over the gaping wound between her legs.

'You've already bought everything that is for sale,' she says quietly.

My heart leaps in my chest. Alive with some sort of great wild joy. 'Cover yourself,' I say curtly to hide the joy.

She pulls the material over her sex and puts her legs back down.

I take a black chip out of my jacket pocket. I didn't know what I was going to use it for tonight—if I was going to use it

at all—but I am immensely relieved and glad it is going to be used and for this purpose. I put it on the table and watch her eyes widen with astonishment.

'This is for you to get dressed and go home right now.'

EIGHT

Lily

The door shuts softly behind him. I walk over to the table and pick up the black chip. It weighs the same as all the others, but wow! I never thought I would ever see one of these. Ten thousand sweet pounds! I sweep all the chips from the table into my satin bag and gather those that have fallen on the floor.

Then I get back into my dress and go looking for Melanie to tell her I am leaving early. I change back into my normal clothes and head to the cashier's box where I cash everything except the black chip, and ask for the money to be put directly into my bank account. Shockingly, there is nearly three thousand pounds.

I pop over to reception and ask Toni to call me a taxi. Less than five minutes later she tells me the cab is outside. Steve, the doorman, walks me out. It is a thing they do, see us into our cabs. As we walk out we see the taxi driving off.

'Hey,' Steve shouts, and then goes silent when he sees Jake walking toward us.

'Good evening, Mr. Eden,' he greets politely.

Jake nods but does not look at him. 'I thought I might as well give you a lift to mine.'

I gasp at the audacity.

Steve starts backing off. 'I'll be off, then,' he says, and makes himself scarce pretty quick.

'How dare you give him the impression that I'm going back to yours?' I storm.

'Aren't you?'

'No.'

'You can come in my mouth.'

I gasp. My insides lurch, like being in a very efficient lift. 'For God's sake!'

He shrugs. 'Better, surely, than having to hear all those men telling you they want to come in yours.'

I look down at the ground and see his expensive boots polished to a mirror shine. I regret it even before I say it. 'I won't bother, thanks.'

'Why not, Lily?'

'The truth?'

'Of course.' He gazes at me with those smoldering eyes.

And fire flows into my blood. Jesus! I've never had it this bad for any man. 'I don't do one-night stands.'

'Whatever gave you the impression that it would be a one-night stand?' His eyes are curious, quizzical, fascinated.

My heart swells. He sure knows which buttons to press. He takes a step closer. I should make him try harder. 'I want to go on a date.'

He smiles, a look of genuine happiness on his face. 'On a date? With me?'

I nod. 'Could be fun.'

'I knew I'd like you.'

I grin, feeling protected and precious.

'Come on,' he says, and leads me to a white Porsche 918 Spyder.

I don't know where the night is taking me—some distant warning that it could be dangerous clamors in my skull—but the call seems distant and inconsequential, and I turn away from it. I tell myself it is just a snapshot in time. Here, there, and then gone forever. Why shouldn't I have this night? Without thought. Without consequence. Embrace, kiss, no rules, no guilt, just get and give pleasure. Only tonight. It will never be more, anyway. Not with men like him. For men like him, women come and go. So I will just do this one time.

I slide into the cool interior, and he shuts the door behind me.

'Nice car.'

'Yeah, I like it.'

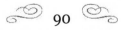

He doesn't have to drive far. The car stops in front of a deserted bar. All the windows are shuttered. A young man runs out of a darkened doorway and Jake chucks the car keys to him, and, putting his palm on the small of my back, leads me toward the darkened doorway.

I look up at him. 'The place looks closed.'

'It's closed to some and open to others.'

The door is opened from inside. There are doormen just inside who nod respectfully to Jake and two receptionists who fuss obsequiously over him. We go through a side door and come upon a room that looks like the interior of a pub. It smells of beer and feet. The stools have been overturned on the tables ready for the floor to be cleaned in the morning.

'What's this place?' I ask.

'A gambling den.'

'What?'

'Yup. When the bar closes, the real activities begin in the back rooms.'

'An illegal gambling operation?'

'Something like that. Have a seat,' he invites, and I sit on one of the tall padded stools next to the bar.

He goes behind the bar. 'Do you want champagne?'

I shake my head. 'I'm a bit sick of the smell of champagne.'

'What would you rather?' he asks softly.

'Whiskey.'

He nods, grabs two glasses, puts them on the bar and reaches for a bottle in one smooth move. It tells me he has worked a bar before. He tips the whiskey bottle the way bartenders at swanky nightclubs do, from up high and continuously. The bottom of the bottle finds its way to the bar surface with a thump. We lift our glasses—there is no toasting—and drink. He downs his and picks up the bottle and refills his glass. A pulse throbs at his throat and he looks restless and edgy.

'So this is your idea of a date?'

He takes a large swallow. 'At this time of the night? Yeah.'

I really have to stop staring at him. Even if he is heart-stoppingly beautiful. 'If it wasn't this time of the night?'

He looks at me with those amazing, bottomless green eyes and pours the rest of the whiskey down his throat. 'I'd have tried to impress you by taking you to a fancy restaurant.'

He pours another glass.

I look at the glass and back up to his eyes and try to remember him as he was on the beach, the warmth of his smile, and I can't, because the man in front of me seems so far removed from that man.

 92

About him is an air of danger and expectancy. My skin sizzles with it. I know just lurking underneath our apparently meaningless conversation are deep sexual undercurrents.

'Should you be drinking so much? You still have to drive me home,' I say to cover my awareness.

'I'm not driving you, Lily. If I drive you somewhere I'm going to end up fucking you.' He smiles, but it doesn't reach his predatory eyes. At that moment he looks sexy as hell.

I hurriedly look down at my drink. My thighs are clenching like fists.

He rests his elbows on the bar and leans forward. 'So, tell me about yourself.'

I look up and lick my lips. His eyes drop to my mouth. 'Not much to tell, really. A life wasted.' I pick up my glass and empty it. The alcohol goes straight to my head.

He frowns, picks up the bottle and refills both our glasses. 'Where are you from, Lily?'

'I'm a runaway kid who didn't make it good, OK?'

He didn't seem even the slightest bit affected by all the alcohol he was consuming. 'You've made it just fine.'

'Not many people would agree with you.'

'Doesn't matter what anybody else thinks. You did fine.'

I finish my drink and put the glass down with a thud. 'I'm a stripper, Jake?'

He chugs his down, refills our glasses and pushes mine toward me. 'That's OK. Gangsters and strippers go together like toast and marmalade. We keep the same hours, the tax man doesn't hear much from us...'

I grin. 'Are you trying to get me drunk?'

'What do you think?'

'Yes.'

He shakes his head.

'So what's with all the whiskey?'

'You don't have to keep up with me. I'm trying to dull the urge.'

I keep my breath steady. 'What urge?'

'At the risk of sounding like a compulsive, obsessive possessive fool, the urge to fuck you, of course.'

I feel the heat rush up my cheeks. 'You're the kind of guy every mother warns her daughter about.'

'Did yours?'

Suddenly I am on shifting sand. 'She didn't get the chance.'

'Don't you ever want to go back?'

'No.'

'Have you brothers, sisters?'

Here is the test. Here is where Lily passes with flying colors. I lock eyes with him. 'I was their only child. Can we quit the questions now?'

He looks at me with an unreadable expression, his lashes wickedly long and dark. 'I'm not actually one for talking. I thought you wanted to.'

I slide off the stool. 'Let's go back to your place.'

My chest rises and falls at the excitement that flares in his eyes. He comes around the bar, grabs my hand and we leave the way we came. As if by magic the car is already waiting outside. We slide into it and roar through the empty streets.

NINE

We stop outside a town house in Bloomsbury. He turns off the engine and looks at me and I feel a sharp thrill of pleasure run through my body. I open the passenger door and step out. The night air is deliciously cool. He comes around to my side and, taking my hand in his, pulls me up a short flight of stone steps.

He must have found a key and put it into the door—there might even have been some sort of alarm set-up he had to turn off—but I am in such a haze of lust that the only thing I recognize is when he grabs my body in an iron embrace and bruises my lips with his. The sensation of being overpowered and taken is so great my body starts to tremble violently.

He pulls away from me. 'Are you all right?' His eyes glitter with the look of a man possessed, a man who can barely control himself.

Warmth glows in my guts. I open my mouth and no words come. Perhaps I am possessed of the same lust. I nod wordlessly.

For a second he stares at me oddly, his shadowed face lit by street lamps from outside the windows, then he swoops down again on my mouth and I am vaguely aware that hard hands are sliding inside my top and unclasping my bra. I moan helplessly. It feels as if I have been starving for a lifetime. Cool air touches my skin and warm hands cup my breasts. My nipples harden against his palms. My mouth clings desperately to his. Between my legs I ache desperately for him. Suddenly he takes his mouth away.

'More,' I beg hoarsely. Like an addict.

He gets on his knees and his hot hands roughly drag my skirt upwards. Hooking his fingers into the sides of the skimpy triangle of cloth stretched between my hip bones he pulls it down my legs. Then he parts my thighs and with his fingers opens me up and stares hungrily at my naked, slick flesh.

'Beautiful,' he breathes. His voice is thick with lust. 'So damn beautiful.'

He dips his head and, dragging his tongue over the slit, laps up the juices dripping from it. And that simple greed is far more erotic than sex. He has claimed my body in a way that no other man has. He has drunk my juices as if they are nectar. He looks up into my glazed eyes. There is no need for words. He bends his head and devours me with the hunger of the damned. I buck wildly against his gorging mouth.

There is no time to tell him that I want him inside me.

The rough, sweet drag of his tongue through my soaked folds sends me over the edge quickly. I come violently, screaming, my fingers grabbing his head, grinding his mouth against me. It is not pretty and it is not feminine. It is animalistic. It is basic. It is Jake fucking me with his tongue and me losing control to a man for the first time in my life.

And for the first time in my life I don't just come: I fall away. I feel my body start falling backwards and would have fallen too if strong hands had not caught me. *It's safe, Lily. It is totally safe to let go.* And so I come in his mouth the way he planned it all along and go to a place where there is no me and no him, no one lives there. Only bliss. When I return to my body he is standing up and holding me tightly. I feel too raw to look him in the eye. I try to move away, but he grabs me tight.

'It's my turn,' he growls urgently, his lips glistening from eating pussy.

And suddenly I am galvanized. I don't feel as if it is an obligation, as if I *have* to return the favor. I don't even feel mildly

resentful that the delicious lull after my orgasm is going to be interrupted. And I certainly don't feel what I always felt, as if he should have a wash first. In fact, I want him, every inch of him, unwashed and raw. Let him taste like old wine, bitter and enticing. Dark like the taste of danger.

I don't even want to do what I always do, tell him he can't come inside my mouth. I *want* him to spill his seed down my throat. For the first time ever I don't fake wanting to give a man a blow job. I want to pleasure him. I get down on my knees and open my mouth so it looks wet and open and hungry.

I hear a quick indrawn breath as I reach for his belt, fumble with it, open it, slide down the zip, and see his muscular cock thrusting against his briefs. I put my hand into his underwear and find the skin hot and silky. I bring the thick throbbing length out and gasp.

His cock is inked. Fabulously so.

Fascinated, I pull his hips into a patch of yellow light and look at the artwork. The skin around the massive head has been tattooed to resemble an apple. A black and yellow snake holds that apple in its mouth while its body coils around and around the entire fleshy rod until its tail disappears into the nest of pubic hair above.

'It's fucking beautiful,' I tell him.

 99

With a shiver of anticipation I grab him by the base and stretching my mouth open greedily take the man, the snake, and the red apple between my lips. I watch him close his eyes and throw his head back in pure ecstasy. He swells further in my mouth, making me gag, so I slide him out and swirl my tongue around the snake's head.

The taste of him coats my tongue and I feel my own juices leaking out of me. I start sucking him slowly and feel a strange sense of power and pride. On my knees pleasuring him feels good. I start bobbing my head faster and faster.

Until he can stand it no more.

He grabs my hair and fucks my mouth. When he looks down our eyes catch. Something ancient passes between us. He holds my head tight to his groin, emits a harsh cry, and erupts in my mouth. Hot liquid gushes down my throat. He jerks and more salty semen discharges into me.

He holds my head in place and watches me suck him clean. Then he pulls me upright and slides his hand between my legs. I am so ready and wet, I moan. His gaze is watchful and unsated. We are both unsatisfied. Hungry. Starving hungry.

He takes my hand and we hurry upstairs. He opens a door and I see a white room with a massive red

chandelier and a very large black bed with white bedding. It is glamorous and strangely soulless.

When he peels off his shirt I see two things I did not expect. A tattoo of a cross over his heart—unlike the tattoo on his penis, this one is roughly inked as if it is homemade—and a chain made of beautifully cut red crystal beads around his neck. It is a woman's accessory, but strangely it does not look odd or feminine on a man who is so seriously ripped and tanned. If anything he seems more mysterious and masculine for it.

I touch the smooth, glittering facets.

'Why are you wearing this?' I ask, my voice a whisper of wonder.

'Because I like it,' he says simply.

In his eyes I am suddenly startled to see something that makes him different and more special than any other man who has undressed me or pressed his body into mine. This man has done bad things, but he alone has decided that I am his and only his. That I will always be his. He will willingly give up his life for me.

He rips my top off in one vicious tug and flings it into one corner of the room. My skirt sticks to my thighs. The air thuds in my lungs.

The sex is furious. Relentless. Glittering. We fuck hard and fast and dirty, sweat running down his curving muscles and dripping on my bare skin.

TEN

That night I dream of Luke. He is standing on a bridge in a foreign country, perhaps China or Japan, and his back is turned to me.

'Come to me,' I call to him.

Although he turns and looks at me he doesn't move, so I put my foot on the bridge to go to him, but instantly his face changes to one of terror. He starts to shake his head. In my dream I ignore his warning and put my other foot on the bridge and to my shock he starts to disintegrate the way a statue would. Bits fall off him. His hands drop off. I take another step and his hips crumple and he crashes to the ground on the stump of his waist. The closer I get to him the more he disintegrates, but even though I am horrified by his destruction I am unable to stop moving toward him.

Tears start pouring down my face, but still my feet move forward. His head falls on his chest. His face turns to dust and starts flying off. And still I cannot stop walking toward him. Finally I reach him and he is a handful of dust.

I take the handful of dust and eat it.

I wake up naked and flushed and stuck to Jake's skin. I can still smell the heady scent of our raw, primal pillow-biting fuck. I suddenly remember that time when I ran on pure rage. Rage against the world that had taken Luke away. For a few seconds I do nothing. Simply lie listening to the thud of my heart and feel the sweat pouring out of my skin.

The window is open and a soft breeze is blowing in.

Slowly I turn my face and look at Jake. Sleeping the sleep of the innocent. I touch the sheet and it slides off his massive shoulder, baring the crudely inked cross on his chest. Very gently I turn around and, going close to his face, smell his fragrant throat.

Desire radiates off me like the heat of a sultry summer night. My breasts begin to ache. I never thought I would ever feel this sweet ache for any man, let alone Jake Eden, the criminal. I let my nipples gently slide over his chest. They are so hard even that hurts. I watch the sensuous, relaxed curve of his mouth. He is delicious. I bend my head toward the sleeping man and viciously bite his lower lip.

His reaction is shockingly precise and immediate. Like a trained special ops force under attack his hands fly up, fit around my neck and tighten like bands of steel. My mouth opens in a startled gasp and his lip falls out from between my teeth. We stare at each other, breathing hard. There is no condemnation, only desire glowing in his eyes. His thumb caresses my throat in a silky, sexual fashion. Excitement hums between us.

No rules. No guilt. Here. There. Then gone.

We move toward each other at the same instant. His two fingers thrust deep into my throbbing sex. I look at his hand disappearing into my pussy and widen my thighs shamelessly.

'I'm gonna make this even better for you,' he says as his thumb begins to swirl around my clit and I moan with the pleasure that flowers. I curl my fingers and dig them into the mattress, as if I am getting ready to fight my ground. In fact, I am holding on. It feels as if I am about to fall from a great height.

His thumb presses down on my clit and my sex clenches with need. Suddenly, he starts jamming into me. So incredibly fast my entire body vibrates like a jackhammer. I climax without warning, my body convulsing.

He lifts me by the waist and holds me over his erect cock and pushes me down hard, stretching my swollen pussy over his blunt thickness.

'Ride me,' he commands.

Impaled on his thick, full cock I place my hands on the taut muscles of his stomach, the skin under my palms burning, and slam myself on him. He grabs my ass and spreads the cheeks so I am even more open when he plunges upward into me.

It is the thrust of pure possession. He is claiming me as his and erasing away the memory of every other man who has been inside me. I allow him to fuck me harder and harder, flattening my thighs and pushing my sex into him until it is too much to bear. Our struggle is raw and wild and age old. *This soaking wet cunt belongs to me*, his body tells me, *and I'll fuck it any way I want.*

I twist and struggle, but he is so much stronger there is simply no contest. His pubic bone keeps on hitting my clit and I feel myself begin to break open. My drop down on him is no longer slow but frenzied. My breasts bounce wildly.

The climax comes while I am wide open and taking every inch of that massive cock of his. As he unleashes his hot cum deep inside me I clench wildly around his flesh. We are both panting. I rest my forehead against his chest.

Slowly, he lifts my body so I am looking into his eyes.

We gaze at each other.

'Lily, why are you so scared?' His voice is soft, curious.

'I'm not scared.'

'No?'

'No.' I lightly graze my fingernail on the red crystals. He catches my fingers. They look so tiny inside his big hand.

'I'm just reckless,' I tell him.

'Hmm... That's what I would be if I was not what I am.'

'What are you?'

'Lucky. I'm very lucky, Lily,' he says drowsily.

His eyelids flutter down and I watch him fall asleep while he is still inside me. I lift away from his body gently, but with a sucking sound that does not wake him. I lie beside him—not so our skins touch, but so I can still feel the heat that comes in waves from his body. I cannot comprehend the connection I have with this man. I cannot understand the way we fuck, like wild animals. I have never been like that with anyone. And I simply cannot comprehend the deep way I feel about him.

I stare at the window until it lightens.

Then I get up very carefully, my body sore and my sex swollen and puffy between my legs, and I go into the bathroom. When I use the toilet it burns

like crazy. He must have torn me last night. I close my eyes and lean my forehead against the cool tiles. He did not use protection. And I did not ask him to. I have never done that with anyone. Not even when I was a teenager. I have always been so careful. So cautious.

I splash water on my face and go back into the bedroom. It reeks of sex. Very quietly I collect my clothes off the floor. My top is ripped beyond repair and my skirt is torn and the hook missing, but still usable. I borrow his shirt. Of course, it is too big, but I roll the sleeves and it will have to do.

For some minutes I stand over him and watch him sleep. He is deliciously manly and the desire to wake him and have sex is so strong I have to force myself to turn away. I tiptoe down the stairs and let myself out of the front door.

Outside the air is cool. There is no one about. I look at my mobile phone. It is five thirty a.m. I start walking down streets blindly. This is the good part of London and there are no tramps. In fact I meet no one for a good ten minutes. Then a man on a bicycle passes me by. He does not spare me a glance. I look at the time. Nearly six.

Finally I see a red telephone box. I go and lift the receiver to check that it is working. It is. I go back outside and find a little corner shop where I buy a bar of chocolate and get some change. I go back to the telephone box and check the time again—six fifteen a.m. She should be awake by now. I go into the box, drop some coins into the slot and dial.

A woman answers, and I release the breath I am holding. Her voice is dear and familiar. I feel tears rushing into my eyes. I blink them away.

'Hello,' she says again.

'Hey, Mom,' I say. My voice sounds small and broken. I shouldn't have denied her existence. No matter what, I shouldn't have done it.

ELEVEN

Jake

I park my car and sit inside it for a while. My pulse is too erratic. I feel too jumbled and unsettled. I need to calm myself. I get out of the car, lock it and cross the road. It's an old square building in a shitty area. She shouldn't be living here. I make a mental note to move her into better digs in the next couple of weeks. I go up to the door and ring her bell. She answers almost immediately.

'Yeah?'

'It's me.'

There is a pause and then the buzzer sounds. I push the door open and enter. The walls are white, the floor is smooth concrete. It's basic but clean enough. Her flat is on the first floor. I take the steps two at a time. She opens the door before I can ring the bell. Her face is scrubbed clean of make-up and her mouth looks swollen and red. She is wearing an old flannel dressing gown. There is a faint bruise on her throat. I feel a stab of unease. I did that.

'Melanie is asleep,' she explains in a hushed voice.

I reach out to touch the bluish mark on her throat and she flinches away.

'Come in,' she says, and starts walking toward the sitting room to cover her involuntary movement away from me.

I follow her silently. The room has two sofas, a glass-topped coffee table. A biscuit tin is on it. She sits at the edge of a sofa. I don't sit. I am too wired. I stand over her.

'Are you all right?'

She nods.

'Why didn't you answer my calls?'

She doesn't look at me. Just shrugs.

I get down on my haunches and look directly into her eyes. 'What's the matter?'

I see her eyes go to my lip. It is still red and swollen.

'I don't think we should see each other anymore,' she whispers hoarsely.

Every cell in my body rejects that statement, but my face remains calm, my voice cool. 'Why not?'

'Because I behave like an animal when I am with you.'

I take her hands in mine. She tries to pull away, but I don't allow her to. 'We will behave like animals until we no longer need to,' I tell her calmly. It is also my most persuasive voice.

She stares at me with those strangely beautiful eyes of hers. And God! I just want to rip her dowdy clothes off and fuck her right there on that cheap couch. That's the real truth. I don't want to talk. I don't want to reassure her that it's all going to be OK. I just want to fuck her senseless. Because when she is around I lose all control. I become a beast.

'Love shouldn't be like this. It should be beautiful.'

I don't let myself react. I don't let her see that she has unconsciously called what we have love. But it is a heady head rush.

'Let's take it step by step then. Let's get to know each other. Let's go out to dinner tonight,' I murmur.

'I can't tonight. I'm working.' Her voice is dull and matter-of-fact.

I feel the hot ball of jealousy slam into my gut. I try to control myself, but I can't. I stand up and stride away from her. My hands clench. 'You're not going to work tonight.'

'I have to. Brianna has me down for today and tomorrow. We can go out the day after.'

She has absolutely no idea. 'You're not working in Eden again, Lily.'

Her head snaps up. She rises to her feet. 'What? I need that job.'

'I can't let you take your clothes off for other men. Even the thought kills me.'

'That's not fair. I have debts to pay.'

I walk up to her. 'What debts?'

She looks up at me. 'I don't want you to pay my debts for me.'

'What debts, Lily?'

'That's my business.'

'Everything about you is my business.'

'I'm not ready to talk about it. Just leave it, please. It's personal.'

I frown at this new complication. What the fuck is she involved in? I don't show her my horror or the horrible thoughts that are running through my head. 'I don't want my woman chased by debt collectors,' I counter reasonably.

'Please, Jake. Leave it. All this is too soon. Just give me some space, please.'

'Space? Is that what you want from me?'

I see a flash of something fierce in her eyes. No, she doesn't want space. She wants to tear my clothes off too. I grab her by the forearms and take her mouth. Sweet. Soft. The taste of her sends me wild. It is as if last night never happened. It is as if I have still not had her yet. The yearning for her rages insides me.

I force open her mouth and she wraps her smooth tongue around mine and sucks hard as if she is feeding on me. She presses her stomach into my fully erect dick, wanting it. I feel myself beginning to lose myself to her.

There is a sound nearby and with a gasp she pulls violently away from me. I feel as if some part of me has been torn away. Her housemate puts a hand up. 'Don't mind me, I'm just on my way to the kitchen.'

I spare her half a glance before my attention returns to Lily.

She is holding a shaking hand against her mouth. 'You'd better go,' she says. She looks white and alone and so troubled that all I want to do is hold her in my arms, but I know it will be the wrong thing to do.

'I'll pick you up at seven tonight.'

She nods and I walk out of her flat and call Brianna.

TWELVE

Lily

I get out of the shower and choose my underwear carefully: expensive, lace and net. The heat wave has not let up and it is so hot and humid I put my hair up and wear a white dress that leaves my back bare. I slip on strappy heels and for some reason, perhaps because I have never seen my lips look so plump and swollen, I paint my lips crimson. They dominate my face and make me think of the female monkeys whose butts turn bright red when they are in heat and ready to mate.

The doorbell rings at five minutes to seven.

I open the door and see emerald fire kindle in his eyes.

'Jesus,' he exclaims softly, and strokes my cheek with his knuckle. He is wearing a dark red shirt, two buttons undone, the red crystal chain visible when he moves, and black trousers with knife edge creases in them. His shoes are mahogany colored.

He looks like a gangster and leads me to a ridiculously souped-up Range Rover with massive wheels and a row of headlights on the top. I raise my eyebrows and he smiles, guileless as a child. 'People expect gypsies to have such things. Get in. It's fun.'

I seriously doubt him but as it happens it *is* fun and a laugh to be so high up.

He takes me to the fancy, oak-paneled, Michelin-starred restaurant Hibiscus. Wine bottles gleam from their silver buckets. Inside it doesn't smell of food, but the perfume of Mayfair fat cats. The staff are discreet and faultless in their superlative attention. There are complimentary cocktails, small delicacies and copious amounts of sour bread. The menu is intriguing.

'What will you have?' I ask Jake.

'The roasted suckling pig spread with warm Irish sea urchins.'

'I've never had sea urchins before. Are they good?'

'They are an acquired taste. They have a dirty, sexy flavor,' he murmurs, his eyes dropping to my mouth.

There it is again, the sweet ache for him. I avoid his gaze. 'I'm having the yellow fin tuna with roasted artichokes and Herefordshire pine tree foam.'

He makes a face. 'Ugh... I can't eat foam. It reminds me of cat sick.'

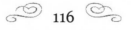 116

But it is not the foam, but the raw sea urchins on sweet potato that are sick making. I almost have to spit out the mineral-like concoction Jake slips into my mouth. He laughs at the expression on my face.

When Jake laughs he becomes a different person. He is no longer a hard-assed, cold-eyed criminal. Fancy that— he becomes stunning. I stare at him, surprised at how carefree, handsome, and young he suddenly seems. A voice full of disquiet whispers up my bare arms, tingling and raising the hairs, *'You will fall for him... You will... You will.'*

I shift in my chair, my appetite lost. Unease like a drop of castor oil slides down my throat.

'What's the matter?' he asks.

'Nothing.'

It turns out that neither of us has much of an appetite after all. We skip dessert. No coffee. The little chocolate petits fours lie uneaten. Jake pays and we are back in the car. The night air is cool. It ruffles his hair. The music is loud, the beat insistent. I shift restlessly on the fragrant leather seat, my guts warm and tight.

When we get inside the sandstone foyer and into his elegant living room, Jake lights candles. I drape myself on a pristine white rug on the floor.

'Want a drink?'

'Nope.'

He walks over to the polished bar filled with downlights and pours himself a good measure of whiskey. He chucks it down his throat and goes to sit on a low white couch. It has claw feet. For a while he lies back and stares at me. I look up at him, unmoving. His eyes are shiny with the flames from the candles. His skin is dark and seems very beautiful, almost as if he is carved from wood. I think of the spicy scent of his cock. Of taking him in my mouth. My thighs part.

'Come here,' he orders softly.

I get onto my hands and knees and *crawl* toward him. Toward his erection, *craving* it. I rest my chin on the white couch between his spread legs. He releases my hair with gentle fingers and runs his hands through it. His hands move down my naked back and pull the small zipper down. My dress withers away.

'We gypsies believe in faeries and faerie glamour. Humans are easy prey. Once they cast their glamour on a human he becomes bewitched. He never sees what is right in front of him. He wanders the world dazed in a tangle of lust. Like a junkie.' He traces my jaw with his thumb. 'You look like one. Your eyes. Are you faerie, Lily?'

I shake my head slowly, a weight in my heart.

118

'It's been a long night,' he mutters, as he bends his head to claim my mouth. Our lips touch. His mouth demands total surrender. I accept the velvet hardness with a contented sigh. He's right, it has been a long night. Too long. As if I am a slippery, limbless fish he puts his hands on the sides of my body and pulls my body up onto his lap. With his lips still attached to mine with allure, heat, and promise, my body is arranged on the couch and divested of its last scrap of covering.

He raises his head, his mouth crimson with my lipstick. 'We didn't use any protection last night,' he observes.

'I took care of it this morning,' I whisper, looking deep into his eyes. They are as an ocean in a storm.

'I haven't come inside a woman since I was seventeen,' he admits.

'Jake?'

One elegant dark eyebrow quirks upward.

'No man has ever come inside me,' I tell him.

His skin flushes with the triumphant red of a conqueror, and his eyes roam my body with the deep satisfaction of ownership. His gloriously strong hands cup my breasts possessively. He revels in the extraordinary fact that my body belongs to him. My nipples pebble and my spines arches. I gaze up at him with fascinated eyes.

He is breathing hard, his jaw is clenched, his cock is so hard it is straining against his pants. The memory of his smooth, naked muscles against my skin comes back as does the smell of his arousal—strong, smoky. Between my legs it feels wet and hot. I reach for his zipper. My hands are sure, fast. He is out in an instant. I watch him rise up over me and peel off his shirt, trousers, and underwear. His skin glows in the candlelight.

He bends to retrieve his trousers, his hands searching for the pocket. I know what he is looking for. I hear the crinkle of the condom foil and cover his hand. He looks at me.

'Are you sure?'

I nod.

The trousers slip from his fingers. His large hand rests a moment on my stomach. I watch his manhood. Beautifully decorated with ink it stands proud and thick. His knees come between my legs. Slowly he tries to nudge the apple head into me, but I must be so sore and swollen from the night before because it feels as if I am being split asunder. I swallow my scream of pain, but my eyes widen and my mouth gapes open in a shocked O.

He freezes.

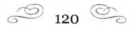

My flesh feels raw and ripped, but I grab his shoulder. 'No. Don't stop,' I urge.

He retreats gently, but it scorches all the way out.

'Sweet Lily. I couldn't hurt you even if you asked,' he breathes. The burning eases. It is relief but at a price.

He moves lower and puts that hot, wet mouth on my swollen, bruised sex. I sigh with pleasure. He licks gently, with great dedication. It soothes me. I feel bright and shiny again. My fingers dig into the lustrous black hair and pull his mouth harder onto me.

I come quick and hard and gasping, my spread thighs shaking uncontrollably. The pleasure is so intense it is agonizing.

I try to rise. He puts one finger on my breastbone. 'Stay. You look good when you are open and ready to be taken.'

'Take me in the ass.'

And in this way, inch by inch, slowly, carefully, painfully he goes where no other man has gone. No matter what happens after this, this is my gift to him.

Afterwards, I lie on his chest and listen to his heartbeat pulsing—slow, definite. A sheltering sound. He deserves more than I can give. Something tears at my heart. He deserves much more.

Can he feel the beat of my treacherous heart? I shouldn't have begun this. Too

late. I just never dreamed someone like him would ever want me. I feel suddenly so lonely it hurts. Aching tears swell my eyelids. I stamp them down. He explores my hair, curling it around his fingers. I open my eyelids and the tears run out and smear between our skin. His hand stills. He takes my chin between his thumb and his fingers and lifts my face up.

'Why?'

I realize I want to make him feel good. I want to pretend a little while longer. 'I'm just happy.'

He stares at me for a moment longer. He is about to speak again so I smile. So easy to execute. So disarming. Such a lie.

I trace the cross over his heart. 'When did you do this?'

'I was fifteen. I built it over time. It is made of seventy-seven scratches.'

I lift my head higher and look at him curiously. 'What does it stand for?'

'Matthew 18:21. Then Peter came to Jesus and asked, "Lord, how many times shall I forgive my brother when he sins against me? Up to seven times?" Jesus answered, "I tell you, not seven times, but seventy-seven times." My seventy-seven times are up, Lily. No more forgiveness for me. Only hell awaits.'

He doesn't know but I already know his story. I think of him as a fifteen-year-old boy. Lanky with long muscles.

 122

Arrogant on the outside, but fragile and broken inside. Scarring his own skin, filling it with ink, counting his sins, and I suddenly feel so sad I want to weep.

Life is so strange. So unfair. What has a starving child in Africa done to deserve its fate? Or a gypsy child who has to take over a criminal enterprise at the age of fifteen? I think of my brother bringing me an abandoned bird's nest with the broken shells still inside. Doing handstands on Brighton Pier. Sweet, clueless Luke. Making lumpy pancakes on a Sunday morning. A knot forms in my throat. I swallow it. My throat aches. I will not cry in front of him.

'Why didn't you stop at seventy-seven?'

'Because I couldn't.'

'Why?'

'The more money I made, the more entitled I felt.'

The child is gone now. The man is impenetrable. He fucks. He comes. He doesn't feel. He leaves. And yet he is different with me. As I am different with him. I nod. Yes, money. It makes the world go around. All of us little puppets in its thrall.

'I found you a job,' he says softly.

I feel tired. 'Yeah? Where?'

'You'll work in my organization.'

'As a drug mule?'

His face is serious. 'I have legitimate business ventures.'

'What will I be doing?'

He shrugs. 'Alicia, my PA, will tell you all about it.'

'You mean you created a job for me.'

'Lily, Lily,' he whispers.

THIRTEEN

'Friends, we have a new member amongst us tonight. Let's welcome Lily,' announces William, the group leader of RSSSG (Relatives Surviving Suicide Support Group).

The introduction is for me, being that I am the only new one in the group and everyone has turned to stare at me, but I am unable to acknowledge it, since my mind and body have suddenly become blank. I stare ahead, unable to look at the faces searching me, unable even to speak.

My grief, a deep tattoo covering my heart, starts bleeding anew. Maybe this is a mistake—too early (that's a laugh)—or maybe I'm simply not ready yet.

Just act normal.

Whatever that means in a place like this. I take a deep breath and forcing myself out of my paralysis nod a general greeting. A girl stands up and goes to get a chair from a stack in the corner of the room. The clanging noise is loud in the empty, uncarpeted space and I have to stop myself from jumping. Other participants are moving their chairs, widening the circle to accept me. The girl slides my chair into the newly created space.

'Take a seat, Lily.' William's voice is firm, but in a reassuring, hypnotic kind of way. It struck me that way even on the phone. I walk to the vacant seat and gingerly perch myself on the edge of it. The woman sitting next to me turns my way and smiles warmly.

'Relax, we're all friends here,' she says and presses her hand on mine.

'Hi,' I say, resisting the impulse to pull my hand away.

I first heard about this center when a friend suggested it four years ago. She said it kept her sane when her father took his own life. But I never wanted to come. Until a few days ago. I'm only going to observe, I told myself again and again. But now that I am here, I no longer know why I am even here at all.

'So who wants to begin the session?'

It's that time when someone gets up and bares their naked soul!

William looks directly at me. Oh no. I'm only here to observe. I'm not ready to reveal anything yet and certainly not to a room full of strangers. I realize then that it has taken a long time for me to stop putting flowers on the grave of my memories. I don't want to talk about him now. Maybe not ever. I bow my head and hope he will take the blatant hint and give me a pass.

'How about you, Lily? Would you like to share with us?'

Heads turn my way. I look at him reproachfully.

'Tell us a little about why you're here?' he coaxes.

'I'd rather not. Not just yet, anyway.'

He smiles gently. 'That's all right, you don't have to participate yet, only when you feel ready.'

A weight suddenly escapes my body and I ease back in my chair. This man has a way that soothes and calms me. Someone else starts speaking. His voice drones on, becomes a buzz that I don't listen to. I lose sense of time.

The next thing I know, I'm being awoken by a soft but insistent touch. My body involuntarily recoils. William is hovering above me. My violent reaction causes him to back off with his hands raised.

'I'm sorry. I'm so sorry,' I apologize and his face breaks into a kind smile.

'Would you like to talk for a few moments, Lily?'

'Everyone has gone,' I note.

'Yes, the session ended. You fell asleep quite early into it but you seemed so worn out and since you were reluctant to participate just yet, I let you rest.'

Inside I feel awful—I mean, who the hell comes to therapy and falls asleep on the very first session? 'Thank you,' I say shamefully.

'Hey, that's what we are all here for, Lily. Shoulder to cry on. Nobody here is going to judge you. It's obvious you are very troubled and if there's anything I can...'

'No,' I deny, instantly going into defensive mode, closing the door to any hint of pity. I get to my feet. 'Really, I'm OK,' I add, avoiding eye contact.

'It won't do you any good, locking it all away.'

'Yeah, well maybe it won't, but it was a mistake coming here,' I respond sharply, and try to move past his large frame, but he moves directly in front of me.

'It's never a mistake to seek help, Lily. You need to find a way to deal with your pain or rage or perhaps your guilt. Bottling it up will only make things much worse, and believe me, you are hearing this from someone who has been there.'

Even though I try to resist the wisdom of his words, his gray eyes have a depth and knowledge that command my reluctant attention.

'People come here because they've lost control of their lives and they want to heal—they're tired of the grief, the tears, the immobilization. Promise me, even if you never come back, that you will focus on something positive. Take back the control you lost, Lily.'

Strangely, as I search his eyes, I feel calm. I've told him nothing of my problems yet there is some thread of connection between us. He has suffered himself, it's clear he's no fake.

'I will.'

He steps aside and nods with approval. I start moving toward the exit.

'You take care now.' His words punctuate the empty silence.

I leave the strangely echoing, sad building and insert myself into the bustle of the real world, but something's different about the way I feel now. I'm actually glad that I took this route, because I know.

I will never come back. The pain cannot be talked away, it has to be exorcised away. The destructive emotions buried deep inside me tear free, like a hand protruding from a grave.

I begin to sprint, blood rushing to the powerful muscles in my thighs, my movements long and sure. My pounding step accelerates until it jars on the pavement. The wind whistles by my ears. Sweat beads on my skin and makes my clothes cling to my back. My muscles start stinging, my chest heaving as if it will burst. But I don't stop running.

Maybe I will never stop running.

FOURTEEN

My new job is in Jake's import and export firm. I have been stuck in the administration department. The job is terribly legitimate and terribly, terribly boring, but I do get to keep my clothes on and the money is far better than I could have hoped for. Everybody is really nice to me and Ann, my co-worker, picks me up in the morning and drops me off after work. So no complaints.

That day I work till late and when I get out of the car the night air is warm and thick with an imminent storm brewing.

'See you tomorrow,' I call and wave as Ann drives away.

I fish my keys out of my bag and start walking up the path to my front door. I swear I never felt even the slightest premonition. When the man's hands clamp down on me I am totally taken by surprise. My heart stops cold, but my brain works perfectly. The impressions are fleeting but clear. Caucasian. Skin gleaming sickly in the white glare of the

fluorescent lighting from the adjacent building. Breath smelling of cigarette smoke. Wrists full of dark hair. Pale eyes: blank and empty like a reptile's. Black shirt. Dark blue jeans. Five feet nine. A hundred and ninety pounds.

I know him.

From the club. He wanted me to touch him. I said no and walked away, but not before I had seen the flash of hatred.

My nerves scream for me to run, but he has the element of surprise. He jerks me toward him and drags me into the undergrowth. I try to lift my arms up to fight him off and he pushes me roughly to the ground. I stagger and crash backwards into the bushes. Branches scratch the sides of my face and neck.

He falls on me, his fingers digging into my shoulders. I lie underneath his weight, winded. Unable to move.

'Refuse me, will you? You skanky, stone cold, cheap whore,' he hisses, his jaw quivering with fury. Immobile I stare into his eyes. Whatever else he is, he is vicious. My heart thumps wildly with fear. Terrified, I know I cannot run.

He grins hatefully. 'Still think you're too good for me, slut?'

'No,' I say, shaking my head, and he punches me in the face.

The blow stuns me. Colored stars dance across my vision, blinding me and

making me wobble, before my brain actually registers the explosion of fierce pain. Blood erupts from my nose, splatters his hand, and pours down the sides of my face. Sick fear spreads in my stomach. I want to vomit or piss myself.

He digs his knee into my chest and taking his mobile out of his pocket, starts taking pictures of me bleeding and pinned under him! Terror is like an enveloping coat of freezing cold leaves. This guy means to kill me. But it is a good thing he does that because it allows me to recover slightly. My brain starts rolling into action again. He is too big for me to push off and his position means I cannot even knee him or do any damage to him with my hands.

My only option is to pretend to become unconscious and find a way to open my purse, which is still hooked to my elbow. I let my head loll to the side. If I can just get inside my purse. He takes his knee off my chest and starts unzipping his pants. I do nothing. I keep my breathing even while my fingers are slowly moving into the flap of my bag. Suddenly he drops over me and like a rabid animal bites hard into my neck. So hard I am no longer able to pretend to be unconscious.

I scream. My hand searches frantically inside my bag. He slaps me hard. I feel a knife at my throat. I close

 133

my mouth. I have located my mace. Very stealthily I bring it out and in a flash I spray it into his face. He falls backwards, his hands clawing at his face. I seize the moment, pick myself up, and run screaming toward the building. A man— I have seen him before, he must live in the building too—runs to me. He wants to call the police but I say no. I tell him I am too frightened to call the police. I definitely do not want him to call the police.

'You've been attacked. You must tell the police.'

I look at him. 'It's someone I know. An ex. I don't want to call the police, OK?'

He shakes his head in a disgusted way. Together we go back and get my handbag. I thank him, find my keys and go into my apartment.

Melanie is on the phone ordering a Chinese takeout.

'Fuck! What happened to you?'

'One of the customers from the club. Remember that creep I told you about?'

'That pervert Simon?'

I nod. 'He took pictures of me with his mobile camera.'

'What a nasty piece of work?'

I go to the mirror. My nose is bleeding copiously and one side of my face is starting to swell badly.

I hold my head tilted upwards while Melanie applies ice packs that she uses on her feet on my face. 'It'll be a bit smelly but you'll survive,' she tells me. Then she picks up her phone. 'I've got to tell Brianna. Ban him and warn the other girls. You need to make a police report.'

'No police. But yes, warn Brianna.'

She comes to sit beside me, her forehead creased with concern. 'Why no police, Jewel?'

'I've got history. Minor things, but I can't go to the police.'

'OK. No problems. No police.'

'Thanks, Mel.'

Literally a minute after Melanie ends her call, my mobile goes.

'Jake,' I say, with a frown.

'Wow! Brianna was fast,' Melanie comments.

'Are you all right?' Jake barks urgently into my ear.

'Yeah, minor bruises.'

'Are you sure it was him?'

'Yeah, I got a good look at him.'

'Right. I'll be there soon. I got something to take care of first. And, Lily...'

'Yeah?'

'Don't go anywhere until I get there, OK?'

'OK.'

FIFTEEN

Jake

I ring on the little cunt's bell and wait, nausea clawing at my guts. He put his filthy hands on *my* woman.

His disembodied voice comes through the intercom. 'Yeah?'

'You hurt one of my employees this evening. I'd like to come up and talk to you about it. Discuss some compensation.' Jesus, I sound calm.

'What? You've got the wrong guy, mate. I've been in all day.' He does offended and indignant very well.

'Or if you prefer I can go to the police and let them sort it out. You decide.' I do rational and threatening very well.

For a moment there is silence and I think the coward is going to take his chances with the police, but then the buzzer sounds. *First mistake, Motherfucker.* I push open the door and run up two flights of stairs to his door. I lean the baseball bat against the wall next to his door, ring his bell, and affect a relaxed pose. He looks at me through the spy hole, then takes his time about opening the door. But he does.

'I'm telling you, you've got the wrong guy,' he says strongly.

I shove him hard and he flies backwards and lands sprawled in his corridor. His eyes widen with terror as he sees me casually retrieve the baseball bat from its place. I come in and kick the door closed. Shame. He has cream carpets.

He starts moving backwards. 'It wasn't me. You're making a big mistake,' he whimpers like a fucking pussy.

I throw him a ball gag. He doesn't catch it. It bounces off his body and falls on the floor. 'Put it on.'

'I'm not going to put it on. I'm innocent. I want the police here. Now.' His voice trembles with fear.

I lift the baseball bat and strike him in the gut. He doubles over in agony, staggers back two steps and drops to his knees clutching his stomach. Then he starts blubbering like a fucking two-year-old brat!

'Not so big and strong now, eh?'

'You got the wrong guy,' he sobs.

'Yeah? Put the gag on or I'll crush your skull with one blow. A beating or a quick death. Choose.'

He is struggling to breathe through the pain. He takes wet-sounding breaths. The ones people take when they are

dying. It sounds like a rattle. But he is not dying. Not by a long shot. Oh no. Death would be too easy. I watch him put the gag on with shaking hands. Cowards never fail to fascinate me. Fucking idiot! Why would you put something on that is meant to silence you?

A savage growl tears from my throat. The rage in the sound surprises me. I thought I was through with all that years ago. I haven't swung a baseball bat in ten years and yet here I am. For her.

Using my foot I push him to the floor.

Then I lift the bat high over my head and bring it crashing down on his kneecap. The shocking pain makes his eyes bulge and roll upwards. I think he might pass out, but fortunately he doesn't. Cold sweat pours out of his skin as his hands rush to hold the smashed bone. I pick up the bat and shatter the other kneecap. He spasms with shock.

After that I rain his body with blows. Each one precise and destined not to kill but to maim permanently. Finally I am done. I stand over him. He is lying on his side: alive, but only just. His breathing is shallow and his eyes are half-closed. I use the tip of my shoe to tip his inert body on his back. A groan escapes his bleeding mouth. Two of his teeth are lying on the carpet.

'This is just a little warning. Open your fucking mouth and heavy comes next,' I say mildly.

I take a handkerchief from my pocket and wipe his blood off the bat. How strange! So many years since I did something like this and I still carry a pristine white handkerchief on my person and a baseball bat in the boot of my car.

Calmly, I walk out of his flat. There is a phone box around the corner. I get into it and call nine-nine-nine. I change my accent to a Cockney one and tell them a man is dying in his flat.

'Looks like he's been beaten bad. Get an ambulance, man.'

I ring off and look at my hands. Dead steady. I feel ice cold. I get into my car and drive to Lily's apartment.

Melanie opens the door.

I go through and come to a dead stop. My hands start shaking. Tears sting my eyes. Shit. I haven't cried since I was fifteen years old, when I saw my father fall down dead at my feet.

Hell! This hurts so bad I want to bellow.

She stops too and we stare at each other. Both shocked. Her by my reaction, me by her appearance. Minor bruises! Fucking hell. Her face is so swollen and blue-black I can hardly recognize her. Then I start advancing on her. My gait is

that of an angry bear. I want to be normal but I can't be. The raw fury simmering inside me is making me shake.

I reach her and she touches the blood splatters on my clothes. Then she looks up into my eyes—hers are huge pools of fear. I see her eyes change, widen. I am alien to her. In her nice candy-floss world what I did to her attacker is wrong. 'What have you done?'

'Gangster rules,' I say harshly.

'Is he dead?'

'No, but he's wishing he was.' Tears are slipping down my face. I just can't help it. My mate has been badly injured.

'What is it?' she whispers.

'You need to go to a hospital.'

She shakes her head. 'I'm fine. It looks worse than it is.'

I have never experienced this fierce need to protect before. Ever. The way I feel shocks me to the core. This is not me. I'm tough. I'm in and I'm out. I don't trust anyone. In this business you can't. A king is never killed by his enemy but by his courtiers. They are the only ones who can get close enough to poison the wine, stick the blade in. I'm not saying, 'Et tu, Brutus,' to anyone. The easy way—never let anyone get close.

Except her.

She opens her arms. Her lower face is too swollen for her to smile but I see it in

 140

her eyes, a smile of comfort as it is I who have been attacked and am in pain. The tears fall faster as I catch her to my body and hold her tight. She's still here. She's still mine. I squeeze my eyes shut. And then I lift her into my arms.

'I can walk,' she whispers.

But I don't put her down. I turn around with her in my arms and Melanie wordlessly opens the front door. I walk out with my baby in my arms.

I could have lost her. But I didn't. Never again will I be so careless with her.

I put her on my bed and she looks up at me drowsily. The stress has worn her out. She looks so small and defenseless in my bed. Her fingers are curled into a light fist. I circle the wrist, shocked at the fragility of the bones in her hand. Gently I rub my thumb along the pulse leaping on the pale underside of it. Her vulnerability terrifies me. Scares me. Makes me feel weak.

'Sleepy?'

'Hmmm...' she hums.

I sense her slipping away, drifting into dreamscapes where I will not be. I pull

her closer toward me. When she is awake there is always a part of her that remains aloof and watching. She is like a forest. Deep and dark. You can lie or howl in it. She murmurs something that I don't catch, and snuggles in, accidentally scrapes her face against my forearm, and winces.

My breath catches. I can't bear to watch her in pain.

She is wearing cotton pajamas. An erotic seduction it is not. It is so demure it makes her seem a child. I guess this must be what fathers feel when they watch their daughters sleep—absurdly protective. The collar of her top shifts and my heart fucking stops. I stare in horror at her neck.

Fucking bastard bit her.

Bit her so fucking hard he broke her skin. That piece of shit marked my woman! I ease myself out of the bed carefully and pad into the living room. The rage is nauseating and gut-churning. It is so all encompassing I can't even think straight. I want to go back to his fucking poky little flat and finish the job, but he won't be there. He'll be behind glass in Intensive Care by now. I go to the bar and pour myself a large measure of Jack Daniel's. I drain it in one swallow and slam the glass on the bar surface, so hard the noise reverberates like a gunshot. I press my palms to my temples.

'Stop. Just stop,' I tell myself.

But the desire to go out and bash his sick head in is so strong I have to physically fight myself. I stride out to the balcony. It could rain anytime. I throw my head back and take large gulps of air. I feel like a volcano about to erupt. I would have loved to go out running. A couple of miles and some of this pent-up energy would've been gone, but I can't leave her alone.

'He's not worth going to prison for. I have already broken his legs and hands in at least a few places and smashed his kneecaps. Not to mention the shitbag's ribs and jaw.'

I reach into my pocket and retrieve his mobile phone. Before I click into his photo file I take a deep breath. Then I press the button. The shock of seeing her pinned on the ground, her eyes full of fear and horror is harder to take than I had anticipated. I stare at it hard. And yet she didn't want to call the police!

My fists clench hard as I force myself to calm down. 'Let it be. Leave it be.'

Eventually my pulse returns to normal, the boiling rage goes. In its place comes guilt. I shouldn't have left her alone and unprotected. I should have protected her better. That was my job.

I take the battery out of the phone and toss them both into my safe. I very much doubt it, he is a little coward, but I might still need it. Chance favors the prepared mind.

I go back to the bedroom and stand over her. Her hair is fanned out on the pillow, her lip is split, her face is swollen and bruised. How strange that the split, the swelling and the bruise have only made her more precious and intriguing. She moves, dislodging the sheet down to her waist and exposing a small strip of skin between her pajama top and bottom. It is milky white and flawless and it gives me great pleasure to claim ownership of it.

I watch the easy rhythm of her breath going in and out. It is strangely seductive and I watch her for a long, long time. Part of me is shocked by the strength of the emotion I feel. Part of me is in awe of it. I never thought I would ever feel this way for a woman. The signs are all there.

I watch her slip into a restless dream. She turns and tosses. I reach out and slot my finger inside her loosely curled fist. She makes an odd sound and tightens her grip. And then, while still deep in her dream, she says the oddest thing. Something I never in my wildest dreams thought I would hear from her lips.

SIXTEEN

Lily

I wake up with my head throbbing and my body aching. I stretch and wince and then realize that I am in Jake's bed. He is sitting at the foot of the bed watching me.

'Good morning,' he says softly.

I groan a reply.

'How do you feel?'

'Worse than yesterday.'

He stands up and comes to my side. 'Need some help getting out of bed?'

'I don't think so,' I reply, but he bends down and gently lifts away my upper body, and puts pillows under my back.

'Thank you.'

'You're welcome,' he says so close to my ear, I am filled with the fresh scent of him.

'Have you been awake long?'

'About an hour. I've got to go soon, but I wanted to get some food into you before I leave. Alicia will be around later with some magazines and if there is a book you want she can get it from the bookstore. Just call her.'

'Am I going to be staying here tonight?'

His jaw tightens. I recognize it. He is about to impose his will on me again. 'I've moved all your stuff here. You'll be staying here from now on.'

'What?'

'It's not open to discussion, Lily. You're staying here.'

I lift my hands in disbelief. 'It's impossible.'

'Impossible is a dare.'

'Jake, you can't do things like this. You can't just move my stuff in here and tell me I'm going to be living here from now on. You have to ask me and I have to agree.'

'Asking would imply a choice.'

I give a gasp of laughter. 'Yes, that's right. At least give a girl the illusion of choice.'

He folds his arms across his wide chest. 'Would you like to move in here?'

'I'll stay here for a few days and then we'll talk about it.'

'See why asking is stupid?'

'I'm not a child, Jake. You can't decide for me.'

He walks up to me. 'Don't you get it? I won't be able to sleep if I don't know you are safe.'

I look into his face and I know he is telling the truth. 'It could have happened to anyone,' I say quietly.

'It didn't happen to anyone. It happened to you.'

'I don't think he will be in any fit state to come back after last night, will he?'

'I protect what's mine, Lily.' No remorse. His face is icy calm.

I sigh. My head is throbbing and I simply don't have the energy to fight with him. 'OK, OK, let's talk about it when I'm better.'

'Want some breakfast?'

'Yeah, I do. I want some ice cream.'

'For breakfast?'

'I was always allowed to eat ice cream when I was feeling poorly,' I say without thinking and realize what I have said.

In the morning light his eyes are suddenly sparkling emeralds. Impenetrable. But what comes out of his mouth is mild and friendly. 'What flavor?'

'I like pistachio and vanilla, but I'll have whatever is in your freezer.'

He only has cookies and cream so I have a bowl of that. He watches me eat and then he has to leave. 'I'll be back at lunchtime,' he says, and kisses me lightly on the cheek that is not swollen and throbbing.

When I hear the door shut I slowly get out of bed and limp into the spare bedroom where I know my things will have been put temporarily. I see my guitar propped up against a cupboard. I

fetch it and sitting on the bed I strum it. I'm a mess inside. I've got all kinds of crazy emotions. Maybe I am still in shock about what happened to me yesterday, but I feel totally numb. No emotions at all. All I can remember is Jake, blood splattered with helpless tears pouring down his face. I think of the last time I cried and cried and could not stop. My fingers start moving on the strings. My mouth opens and words come out.

Strumming my pain with his fingers.

Always the same song. Always the same sadness.

Killing me softly with his song. Killing me softly.

I forget my surroundings and go back into that place where everything is right in the world. My parents have gone to the movies. I can hear my brother downstairs eating jam sandwiches and making a mess of the kitchen. It is raining outside and I am lying on my bed, my palms folded under my head, looking at the lightning flashes in the sky.

I finish the song and there is a noise at the door. I turn around too quickly, pain jars in my ribs. Jake is standing there staring at me. He seems pale under his tan.

'Why are you home?' My voice sounds accusing. I did not mean it to be so.

 148

'I don't know why I came back,' he says. He walks up to me and kneels in front of me. 'I didn't know you could play the guitar so well.'

I shrug. It hurts to. 'Now you know.'

He slides his finger down my unhurt cheek following the path of my tear. 'Who were you crying for, Lil?'

I freeze. 'No one. I wasn't crying for anyone.'

'Do you come with instructions, Lily Hart?' he asks gently, but his eyes are searching and concerned. Who knows how much longer he will be so patient with me?

Three days later I sit on the toilet seat and watch him immerse himself beneath the bubbles. When he pops up again he is wearing a hat of foam. He wipes the suds from his eyelids. So endearing it makes my heart beat faster. When he opens his eyes I am startled anew by how beautiful they are. I try not to stare at the taut muscles of his shoulders.

'My mother wants to meet you.'

My eyes widen.

'You'll like her.'

'It's a bit early.'

A shadow passes his eyes. 'It's not too early, Lil. We are a very close family.'

'I'm not ready, Jake. Anyway, look at the state of me. I can't meet your mother like this.'

'OK, I'll take you when all your bruises have faded.'

I breathe a sigh of relief. 'Thanks, Jake.'

SEVENTEEN

Mara Eden

My firstborn comes to visit me, and the instant he walks through my door I know: there is a new woman in his life. It is there for all to see. The sparkle in his eyes, the faint flush on his cheekbones. And I am ecstatically happy. I am forty-nine and I want to see my first grandchild.

I never tell anyone, but my Jake is my private sorrow. From the time he was fifteen he has known nothing but responsibility and brutality. At fifteen he was held down and made to watch his father cut from ear to ear and given the choice by the men his gambler father had borrowed money from: work for us and pay off your father's debts or watch your entire family die in the same way.

When he came home that day, the Jake I knew was already dead. There were no tears. No mourning. He set to work immediately and relentlessly. He would work all night, sleep for three hours and go back to work. It took him two years to pay off his father's debts. I know he had to do a lot of bad things, but he did it for us, for me, Dominic, Shane, and for our little'un, Layla.

In time he made a lot of money, he bought me this beautiful house, the car I have, pays for my holidays, and he gives me a monthly allowance that I never seem to be able to spend all of. He himself lives in a mansion with a swimming pool, wears fancy clothes, owns fancy cars and has too many fancy women, but until yesterday I have never seen him happy.

'Is she one of us?' I ask.

'No. But she's beautiful, though,' he replies. And there is such pride in his voice that I marvel at it.

'Bring her to see me, then,' I say.

After I tuck a basket of homemade jam and a Tupperware of his favorite Madeleine cakes into the well of his passenger seat, I wave him off, close my door and run to my altar. I go to give thanks to the Black Madonna. She is the patron saint of my family. For generations we have venerated her and she has given us visions. My grandmother, my mother, even me. She told me when my husband was going to be murdered: I was standing in prayer when I had a vision. I saw him raise his hand and apologize to me.

'I'm sorry, Mara, but I have to leave.'

The next day he was dead.

With a smile I light a red candle and stand in front of the Madonna's statue. But as I begin to pray I have such an awful feeling in the pit of my stomach that my knees buckle and I fall to the floor. While I am sprawled on the floor the vision comes. I see a bullet rushing toward my Jake. And I see blood. It seeps quickly into his clothes. I lie on the floor stunned and biting the fist that I have jerked to my mouth.

You see, from the day Jake's innocence was snatched away from him I have never known peace. Not even in sleep. The terror lies coiled like a snake in the deep, dark pit of my belly ready to rear its head at a moment's notice. Its day has come. It stares at me with baleful eyes.

With a cry I race to my phone and call Queenie. She is my grandmother's friend. A woman with a great gift. The spirits talk to her through the cards. I call her and I am weeping.

'Come now,' she says.

She lives in a caravan on a field. I get into my car and drive the twenty miles to her. I park my car at the edge of the field and walk quickly to her home. She opens the door in her dressing gown and invites me in. Her face is round, the eyebrows plucked clean and penciled with brown eyeliner. Underneath them are a pair of large black eyes with a rim of white between the pupil and the lower lid that gives her face the look of a victimized saint. Her mouth is small, the lips shriveled. On Brighton Pier she is known as Madame Q, a charlatan, and loony bin.

I climb the steps and enter her abode. It is spotlessly clean and the sun is shining in through the net curtains, but it is full of mysterious shadows. It reminds me of my grandmother's caravan—same net curtain, same love of crystals, little painted porcelain figurines, and potted plants on the windowsill.

'I'll make some tea. Or would you like something stronger?' she asks.

'Tea,' I say quickly.

She nods and puts a kettle on to boil.

'Sit down, Mara. You'll wear my carpet out,' she says, pouring tea leaves into a teapot.

I stop pacing the tiny area and sit on a dainty sofa with embroidered, tasseled cushions. My leg shakes. It always does when I am nervous or frightened. It shook when my mother was ill, and it shook uncontrollably when Jake used to go out in the night to take care of 'something'.

She pours boiling water into the teapot and, placing it on a tray that she has already set with dainty cups and saucers, a milk jug and a sugar bowl, carries it to me. She puts the tray down on the small table in front of me, sits back and looks at me with her large, soulful eyes.

'We'll let it sit for a moment, shall we?'

I nod gratefully. 'I'm afraid for my son.'

'Let's see what the cards say.'

'Yes. Please.'

She reaches under the table and takes out an old wooden box. It is carved with intricate patterns. She puts it on the floor next to her legs and takes the cards out. They have strange markings on the back that are almost obliterated with use, and yellowed dirty edges. She shuffles them lovingly in her gnarled hands—the arthritic knuckles are the hue of church candles. She hands the pack to me.

I take it with frightened hands. Many times in my life the cards have revealed true things about my life—some small, some vitally important, some painful.

'Think of him,' she instructs.

I shuffle the cards and think of Jake. Deliberately, I think of him looking happy. I think of him strong and vital. I don't infect the cards with my own fear and worry.

'Give them back to me when you are ready.' Her voice is level and diagnostic, and as pitiless as an immigration officer or prison warden.

I shuffle the deck one more time and give the cards back to her.

She takes them and spreads them into a semicircle on the table. 'The Black Madonna protects you. Let your cry come unto her,' she says softly.

I make the sign of the cross over my chest.

'Pick only one.'

I ignore the creeping sense of foreboding and choose a card. *The lovers*.

She glances at it with a carefully blank expression. 'Pick another.'

I take the card that is second from the last on the left-hand side and hand it to her silently. My heart is thudding against my ribs. My hands are clasping and unclasping incessantly on my lap. *A diabhal*. The devil.

She looks at the card and raises her eyes appraisingly toward me.

'One last card.'

I close my eyes and let my trembling hand hover over the semicircle. With a prayer in my heart I fish one out. I hand the card to her without looking at it, but I already know. Something is wrong. Very wrong.

She frowns at the cards. It's a hot day but I feel the chill spread over my skin, making my hair stand on end. She lays

the three cards down on the table. Slowly she strokes the card in the middle with her forefinger. Her nail is thick and yellow.

'*An túr,*' she says. The tower. She doesn't look up at me. Finally, she raises her martyr's eyes, her expression portentous, and speaks.

'Beware the woman who is wounded, beautiful and ruthless. She has soot and death in her mouth.'

My mouth opens with horror at her terrible words.

Her black eyes flash, her voice is a shade fainter. 'You can still pray to the Madonna for a miracle. The abyss may not come to pass.' She gathers the cards with a snap. 'Perhaps.'

There is a sign on the door that can't be
missed.
It reads:
Enter but at your own risk.
—Whodini

EIGHTEEN

Lily

That morning Jake gets up early. There is something he must do at the office.

'Unimportant, but necessary,' he says when I ask him what.

It is too early for me to eat, but I sit and watch him wolf down three slices of toast thickly spread with butter and homemade marmalade that his mother bottles for him. I walk him to the front door, snake my arms around his neck and stand on tiptoe to kiss him and he lifts me up.

'I'll crumple your suit,' I whisper in his ear.

'Wrap your legs around me, woman,' he growls.

I laugh and wrap my legs around his hips.

'Have I told you today how beautiful you are?'

I tilt my head and pretend to think. 'Let me see. Yes. Yes, you have.'

He looks into my eyes seriously. 'You're beautiful, Lily. Truly beautiful.'

'Is everything OK?' I ask him.

He smiles softly. 'Yes, everything is just the way it should be.'

We kiss gently and then he leaves me.

I stand for a moment looking at the door. A small cold leaf of worry clings to my back. *Is he doing something dangerous today?* I go back to bed and lie down for a while, thinking. Why has he not told me where he is going?

By nine thirty a.m. I have showered, dressed and am closing the front door behind me. I walk to the bus stand down the road, and I sit on one of the red plastic seats and wait for the bus. It comes at nine fifty-two a.m.

I climb aboard, pay the bus driver, and take a seat upstairs. The bus takes me all the way to Leicester Square. I get off and walk up to Piccadilly Circus. It is full of tourists and I sit on the stone steps under the statue and look at them, with their maps and their cameras and their great enthusiasm.

Afterwards, I walk down Regent Street ambling in and out of shops. I try on a hat. When I look in the mirror I find my eyes huge and frightened. I turn away quickly. I flick through the hangers without real interest and my behavior earns me the attention of a security guard, who starts following me around. I leave that shop quickly.

I enter a shoe shop and after trying on about ten pairs I buy a pair. I am outside

the shop when I realize I don't even know what color the shoes are. By now it is one forty-five p.m. I go into a small café and order a salmon and cucumber sandwich, but I am unable to finish it. I pay my bill and set off toward the Embankment Bridge.

As I walk across the bridge I start to feel the first frisson of nervousness. It settles like lead in the pit of my stomach. I have blocked it out all this time, but the moment is here. It is time. I train my eyes not on the Tate Modern, but on St Paul's Cathedral in the background. Eventually I come upon the giant black insect creature made of metal. Creepy and perfectly War of the Worlds.

I go through the front door of the Tate Modern and up the stairs. Down the corridor there is an exhibition by Marlene Dumas that I would like to see but I don't go in there. Instead I pass into one of the smaller rooms where a man is sitting on a bench contemplating a collage called 'Pandora' by a new artist, Miranda Johnson.

The colors are bright and bold, but there is no difference between this painting and Picasso's 'Weeping Woman'. Both are violent and raw with suffering. To enter the painting is to enter pain. I let my eyes wander over it. There is an eye in the collage, a full pair of bright pink lips, and a flower. There are also words like bitch, suck, liar, arsehole, abuse, and on the very top, cursive writing that says, *You are invited...*

I walk toward the painting, my soul aching.

The man on the bench speaks. 'She shouldn't have opened the box.'

I don't look at him. I simply sit next to him, but not close enough to touch. There are six inches between us. I feel frozen inside. I think of my brother lying on the floor with the needle sticking out of his arm. And I am suddenly caught by his pain, the pain of the painting, my pain. I can do this. Of course I can do this.

I look at the painting and all I can see is the word 'Bitch'.

'You called for a meeting,' the man says without looking at me.

'Yes.'

He turns his head briefly to look at me. I turn my head quickly to meet his gaze. I want to look into his eyes. I want to stand again on firm ground. His eyes are dark and expressionless. Exactly the way I remember them. I stare at him. He is first to look away.

'Well?'

'There is something big happening on the sixteenth,' I say.

'What?'

'I don't know yet. But something is coming in through Dover.'

'Good work, but we won't act on this one. It will compromise you. We'll let this one go. You have something far more important to do.'

I swallow hard.

He turns to stare at me. 'Are you falling for him?' His voice is hard and cold.

I think of Jake's skin pressed against mine, his tongue tracing an erotic path to my ear, his lips whispering, 'I love you, Lily. I never believed anybody could be as beautiful as you.'

'No. Of course not. This is just a job,' I say, my insides twisted in a hard knot.

He looks at me with narrowed eyes. 'Good. Because you are a servant of the Crown and our best hope to bring Crystal Jake and his criminal enterprise down.'

'Yes, sir.' I stand to leave.

'Keep your wits about you, Hart,' he cautions.

I don't turn back and I don't allow myself to think of Jake. I walk away with the sound of my feet echoing on the hard floors and Luke's beautiful, helpless face in my mind.

To be continued...

Book 2

BOOK 2

O Mother, I have made a bird of prey my
lover,
When I give him bits of bread he doesn't
eat,
So I feed him with the flesh of my heart.
                              —Shiv Kumar
                Batalvi

ONE

Lily 'Hart' Strom

If I should die before you, cremate my body and commit my ashes to the ocean.
—A note from Luke Strom to his sister

A month after my brother's remains were brought home in an earthenware urn, my father and I—my mother was still too distraught—took the container out to sea.

I remember that day well.

The sky was cloudy, the light tinged with pink. Windless. At the pier the driver of the chartered boat held out his hand, weathered to leather, to help us in. My father and I sat side by side on plastic cushions. I jammed my hands into the pockets of my wind jacket and my father lovingly cradled the urn. Neither of us spoke. The motor began and we sliced cleanly through the water, the cold salty morning air buffeting us, flattening our clothes against our bodies, and tearing at our hair.

When we were three nautical miles out, the driver cut the engine, and the boat began to gently drift. For a few seconds the air held only the sounds of water lapping against the sides of the boat and the whispered creak of wood as my father and I moved toward the rail. The sea was a gray blank, quiet, waiting. Like a cemetery.

I stood beside him while he opened the mouth of the urn and undid the knot of the plastic bag inside. We each took a handful of the pale gray ash. One last touch.

'Oh, Luke,' I whispered brokenly, unable to reconcile that handful of *dust* with the living breathing being I had loved so dearly. When we were young we had been like Siamese twins, sharing one heart. Inseparable.

Without warning, it began to drizzle. I raised my eyes at the sky in surprise. Was it a sign? A final goodbye? Luke had always loved the rain. When he was young he used to cartwheel in it. Laughing, happy Luke. But the arms of my memories were cold. He was too young and sweet to die.

I began to cry.

Thousands of water droplets struck me and mingled with my silent tears as I stood perfectly still, fist stretched over the railing. I was aware of my father opening his hand, and the cloud of ashes

pouring from it. As if that was not enough of a magic trick, he took the plastic bag out of the urn, and upended its contents into the sea. I watched Luke blossom in the water, temporarily disarmed by the gentle beauty of his new form. Finally I understood why they call incinerated bones white flowers in India.

My father turned to me.

I swallowed hard. I had no magic tricks up my sleeve. I had nothing.

Gently he nudged my arm. 'Let him go, Lily,' he urged, his voice lowered and solemn.

I looked up at him blankly. His blond eyelashes were wet with rain or tears or both, and in the milky light his eyes seemed paler than I had ever seen them. I noticed the deepening lines that fanned out from the corners of his eyes. Poor Dad. Somehow life had defeated him, too. I felt the first flash of helpless anger then.

With his left hand he wiped the damp strands of hair away from my cold cheeks. 'It will be OK,' he promised. He had no idea how hollow he sounded. His eyes flicked down meaningfully to my hand.

I nodded in agreement. Of course, it was what Luke wanted. And yet I could not open my fist. The drizzle became a freezing steady rain that plastered my hair to my head, and ran down my neck into my clothes, making me shiver. I could hear my father's voice in the background, like a distant buzz, pleading with me, but still I would not let my brother go. I could not. My hand was red and frozen tight.

Finally, my father pried his fingers into my tightly clenched fist and forced my hand open. Numb with horror, I watched the rain turn the ash into gray mud on my palm and wash Luke away forever.

On our way back the clouds opened to reveal a sky as brilliantly blue as my brother's eyes had been. So blue you could have wept.

I did.

TWO

I fell apart after that. No one could understand how painful it was for me. No one. They had *absolutely* no idea about the sharp teeth of guilt tearing at my insides, or the inescapable sorrow that wound itself around my heart like a thickly muscled anaconda tightening its hold every time I exhaled.

I had not been there for him.

My dreams became footsteps that kept taking me back to his killing ground. In my dreams I stood at his window, pale, limp, my hair waving like seaweed in water, and watched him push the needle into his arm. I was the witness. I was there to see the stair I had missed in the darkness.

I woke up in a trembling fury. Rage at everyone. No one was immune from it. Especially me. I sprang to the floor and like a caged animal paced my bedroom restlessly for hours at a time.

That last sniff of him—his perfume after the cells of his body had stopped replicating and replacing themselves—the bouquet of raw meat became a friend. Calling. Calling. Dangerously seductive. My existence had become

171

hellish. I wanted to escape. That day on the boat I had seen Luke become the ocean, the rain, the wind and the blue sky. I wanted all of that and Luke within me, too.

The otherworld... I nearly went.

After one failed attempt, while my mother looked at me with shocked, reproachful eyes, my despairing father who is a doctor quietly persuaded me to consider a temporary treatment of antidepressants.

'No one outside this family need ever know,' he said, the terrible guilt of not being able to save Luke skulking in his eyes.

I took the wretched things he gave me. They did the job. They banished my intolerable grief, but I lived in limbo, speaking only when spoken to, eating when food was put before me. And I think I might have been content to exist in that walking dream, on that cloud of dull edges forever, if not for the visit to the toxicologist.

It gave me a fresh pain. It woke me up.

Mr. Fyfield was small, assiduous, clean-cut, well groomed. He opened my brother's file as if that was the most important thing he had to do that day and in a funeral director's voice proceeded to explain some of the details contained within. I listened to his voice drift around the room idly until one sentence sent blood rushing up into my brain, so fast I felt it slam into my head.

Whoa! I opened my mouth and made an odd choking noise.

Both my parents turned to stare at me in surprise.

'But Luke died of an overdose,' I blurted out. My voice was unnatural, guttural.

Mr. Fyfield spared me an oddly sterile glance before returning his eyes to my parents. 'He overdosed because the heroin he consumed was spiked with acetyl fentanyl. Fentanyl is an opiate analgesic with no recognized medical use. It is typically prescribed to cancer patients as a last resort. It is five to fifteen times stronger than heroin and ten to one hundred times stronger than morphine.'

The jargon was difficult to comprehend in my state, but one fact was inescapable. I stared at Mr. Fyfield, wide-eyed and trembling. 'Knowing it could kill him...they sold it to him,' I whispered.

He looked at me as if I was either stupid or insanely naïve. 'I'm afraid so.'

I began to hyperventilate. My parents gathered around me protectively. I gasped that I needed a glass of water, which Mr. Fyfield's secretary immediately fetched. I drank it down and didn't say a word after that, but finally I was ready to start living again.

Over the next few days I decided that I would join the war on drugs. I made a promise to Luke's memory. I would do all I could to stop what had happened to him from happening to others. Anyone I saved would live because of Luke's memory.

I came off the pills. I did research. A lot of it. There were many agencies that I could have targeted, but I found myself gravitating toward undercover work. The idea of using deception to fight deception was perversely pleasing. But, more important, I thought it would be cool to no longer be Lily Strom, the basket case, but an alter ego. Someone new. I could decide who I wanted to be and build her from ground up.

There were two lines of work available as Test Purchase Officers (TPOs) and Undercover Officers (UCOs). Generally TPOs undertook a lower level of undercover work, usually presenting themselves as prostitutes or drug addicts to lure in the small-time dealers. Their assignments were unglamorous, quick in and out jobs that typically lasted only hours.

UCOs were a totally different kettle of fish. They lived in a different world, one shrouded in secrecy, taking on different names, different addresses and totally different ways of life, sometimes for years at a time. The most elite and secretive of these units was called SO10 or SCD10. So secret most police officers didn't even know it existed.

Although it was easier to be accepted as a TPO I knew I didn't want to be a TPO. My heart was set on being a UCO. They brought in the big fish. The kingpins. The ones I wanted to target.

'You'll have to finish your education if you want to be accepted in an agency like that,' my father said.

So I diverted all my rage and energy into work, graduated with honors, and applied to be a police officer. They accepted me and sent me to the Police Academy in Hendon. It was a flat, depressing place that looked exactly like one of those eyesore housing estates from the seventies; only it had a large swimming pool and a running track.

The training was undemanding: for twenty effortless weeks they taught us to unthinkingly and unquestioningly obey the chain of command at all times. But I was strangely glad of the strict parameters of authority that we had to conform to.

I came out of it a police officer.

THREE

One year later I stood in front of my commanding officer. 'I want to be in SO10,' I said.

He raised his eyes heavenward. 'They are a bunch of wannabe gangsters.'

That and all further arguments swayed me none at all. SO10 in my opinion was the pinnacle, the elite.

The very next day I made my way to New Scotland Yard carrying a docket of twenty-five pages of forms that I had painstakingly filled in and signed. I had made particular mention of the fact that I could speak Chinese, Norwegian, and my BA was in the Russian language.

On an upper floor, down a narrow, faceless corridor, I found a stable-style door with the magic words SO10 printed on a tiny sticker the size of a matchbox. Male voices and raucous laughter could be heard from within.

I took a deep breath—I had worked so hard and so long to get to this moment— and knocked on the top half of the door. There was no let-up to the mirth and voices within so I was startled when the top half of the door suddenly swung open.

Facing me was a bully of a man: close cropped red-brown hair, a navy blue North Face sweatshirt, gold sovereign rings on every finger, and an insufferably arrogant what-the-fuck-do-you-want expression on his face. It changed when he clocked me, though. In a totally leisurely and insulting way his gaze mentally undressed me. Eventually, his eyes traveled back to meet mine.

'The ladies' toilets are not on this floor, petal,' he advised, a patronizing smirk curling his lip.

'I...ah... I've brought my application form,' I stammered. I had never imagined such a blatantly sexist brush-off.

Reddish eyebrows flew upwards with exaggerated surprise. 'Yeah?'

I clutched my application form tightly and nodded.

'Give it to me, then,' he said. There could be only one way to describe his expression: highly amused.

He opened it and let his eyes run down it, sniggering and laughing intermittently. When he looked up his face was serious. 'Right then. You can go now.'

'Um... Someone will call me?'

'No doubt,' he said, in a tone that implied the opposite, and rudely closed the door in my face.

For a second I was too stunned to move and simply stood there. I heard him move into the room and say, 'You will *not* believe the skirt that just dropped this off.'

He must have then showed them my photo because the room broke out in low whistles and totally inappropriate comments. One guy said, 'Call a doctor, I think I've just caught yellow fever.' The group erupted in laughter. My face flamed.

Then a voice, more raspy and authoritative than all the others, said, 'Give that to me.' Later I would learn that his name was Mills—Detective Sergeant Mills.

Silence descended while he studied my form. I held my breath.

'Well, well,' Mills' voice pronounced mysteriously. 'Looks like we found the mouse to catch our lion.'

I turned away and ran down the stairs, my heart pounding like crazy. I knew then: I was going to be a UCO. But at that time I never thought about the logistics of the crazy idea of sending a mouse to catch a lion. I was just ecstatic: I *was* going to become an SO10 undercover officer.

Two days later I got a withheld number phone call from a woman administrator who said, 'You have been selected to join the SO10 team. Are you available to come in tomorrow?'

I gulped. Was I available? Bloody hell. 'Yes,' I replied smartly.

And just like that I was back at the stable door. This time, though, I had dressed conservatively in black tailored trousers, a white shirt that was buttoned close to the throat and a gray, loosely fitting jacket. My hair was pulled back in a tight ponytail and I wore no make-up. After the last visit I knew what I was in for. And I was not wrong.

The brute who had laughed at my application form came toward me. 'Get us some tea, will ya? Black, no sugar,' he said, as he passed me by.

I didn't miss a beat. 'Where's the kitchen?'

He pointed his thumb over his shoulder to indicate somewhere at the back.

I nodded. 'Anybody else want tea?'

There were two other guys there. Both had the same macho attitude.

'I'll have mine with milk and no sugar,' said one leaning back in his chair and stretching.

'Black. One sugar,' said the other without looking up from a book he was reading.

I nodded. No one was wearing name tags so I had no idea who anybody was and no one seemed inclined to introduce me.

I went into the kitchen, a small area with a microwave, toaster, a small fridge and a kettle. I found tea, sugar and milk, and from the back of a cupboard a tea-stained tray.

Just as I finished serving the men, another man walked in.

'Jolly good, tea. I'll have a cup, love. Two sugars and plenty of milk.'

I walked to the kitchen fuming, but my expression remained as cool as a cucumber.

I fixed the tea and put it in front of the man.

He waved vaguely toward some filing cabinets. 'How about putting some order into that fucking mess over there?'

'Right,' I said and walked toward it. He was right. It was a fucking mess. I decided to take all the files out and start from scratch.

'Come on,' a big, shaven-headed white man said as he walked past me. I recognized his voice. The man with the authority. I quickly jumped up and followed him into a small office.

'Close the door,' he said, as he lowered himself into his chair.

I obeyed. You could tell he had a hair-trigger temper just by looking at the tension in his shoulders. In fact, he reminded me of a standard issue brutish gangster.

'Sit.'

I sat.

'How's it going?'

'Great,' I said.

Something flicked very quickly across his eyes. 'Nice one. Off you go, then.'

Sorely disappointed, I stood up, thanked him and walked out of his office. I closed the door and another tough-looking guy walked in through the stable door.

'I'm gasping for some tea and toast,' he said, looking me right in the eye.

That morning I made twenty rounds of tea between bouts of 'administrative' work while they sat around regaling each other with tales of their bravery and the times when they had narrowly and heroically escaped death through relying purely on their wits. It became quickly obvious to me that the fastest way to gain their respect was to administer some sort of violence.

And the next day the routine was the same: round upon round of tea and toast and having to listen to their misogynistic and snide comments. But my grandmother had taught me, when you live in a lake you don't antagonize the crocodiles.

I was determined to stick it out and live in that infested lake. They were not going to break me. I was there for a reason and all those thinly veiled attempts to provoke me were not going to get a rise out of me. Although the atmosphere was macho, intimidating, and openly contemptuous of the rest of the police force, these men thought of themselves as the elite: I had not been brought there to make endless cups of tea. I knew I had something important they wanted. I was the mouse they needed to catch a lion. Let them have their fun until then.

On day five, Robin, one of the marginally nicer guys, stopped by my table where I was knee-deep in their antiquated filing system that still used paper receipts.

'Want to go out with us tomorrow?' he asked.

Going out with inarguably the most ignorant bunch of men I had ever had the misfortune to meet was not the most appealing offer I could think of, and there was also the distinct possibility

that this was a means to humiliate me in public, but... 'Sure,' I said softly. 'Where are you guys going?'

'To a crack house.'

I smiled for the first time since I had come to SO10. 'Yeah, I do. I definitely do.'

'Great. Briefing is at eleven. You'll be going as a crack whore. So don't wash your hair and bring slutty clothes and skanky shoes with you.'

I nodded happily.

Finally!

FOUR

'Just relax. If it all goes pear-shaped a vanload of big guys in riot gear will rush in,' Robin said, while Federica, another undercover agent, expertly applied stage paint to make me look like a junkie.

I nodded, unable to stop staring at him. A very experienced ex TPO, he had incredibly transformed himself into a convincingly sad addict with a pasty face, bags under his eyes, greasy ropes for hair, fake ear and nose piercings, grimy nails, and stained clothes and shoes.

In a little hand-held mirror I watched Federica blacken my front teeth and paint a disgusting sore on one side of my mouth. When she was finished I stood still in a faux leather miniskirt, a purple Lycra tube top and cheap stilettos with heels that I had deliberately scuffed, while Jason fitted my 'technical' (body-worn recording equipment): an Apple iPod that had been equipped with a tiny camera and monitoring device that would allow the monitoring team to see and hear what was being said.

'Here,' Robin said, and gave me a battered packet of cigarettes. I unzipped my bag and put the packet into it.

'Rinse your mouth out with this,' Federica said holding out a bottle of red wine. I took it and swallowed a mouthful. Pure vinegar. Robin took it off me and glugged it down as if it was water.

'Ready?' he asked.

'Ready,' I said, shrugging into a filthy, fur-trimmed hooded parka. We got into a battered brown Renault and Jason drove us to the crack house. I sat in the back seat and mentally prepared myself for the unknown. I was going behind the locked doors of a real crack den to see the lost souls inside it.

It was two in the afternoon and the street was dead quiet. It was quite a nice area, actually. I wondered what the neighbors must think of having a crack den right in their midst.

Robin swiveled his head to look at me. 'Remember, the back door is welded shut, so don't ever make for it in an emergency.'

'I'll remember,' I said nervously.

He thumped a few times on the door and a black, well-built, twenty-something man with suspicious, darting eyes opened it. In his hand was a large hammer. This was not Robin's first time and the man—his name was Samson—

touched fists with him and opened the door wider. I flashed Samson a quick smile, which was not returned, and totally ill at ease followed Robin and Federica into a darkened hallway.

'When is he coming, bruv?' Robin asked.

'Soon, man,' Samson said with a Jamaican accent. 'Soon.'

Behind me I heard three heavy bolts slide shut.

For better or worse we were locked in with a man called Samson who was armed with a large hammer. Samson told Robin that the dealer had not arrived and that everybody was still waiting for him. He led the way to the living room, an *awful* room. There was neither furniture nor curtains. The windows were shrouded with moth-eaten blankets.

Crammed into that dim, smoky space were dozens of junkies leaning against the walls and sitting close together talking quietly. But from the flare when someone lit a cigarette or a crack pipe I saw the vacant desperation on all their faces. Humans of every race and age had been reduced to creatures that were beyond pitiful.

Their degradation and devastation was unbelievable. They were living corpses. Their stench couldn't be described. You had to experience it to believe the rotten reek of the accumulated weeping of the human body; blood, sweat, oil, urine; and dirt, layers upon layers of fetid filth.

It was *intolerable*.

There was also a great restlessness about them that made them appear to be a heaving mass united by a single all-consuming purpose. To score. They were all here for smack or crack.

Suddenly, fear gripped me that just as I could smell them, they could smell me. I felt wild-eyed with paranoia. Federica fitted her hand over mine and squeezed. I knew what it meant. *Calm down.*

I pressed her hand. *I hear you.*

Federica led me to a corner and we sat on the bare, dirty floor. I was glad to do so—my knees were shaking. I could not comprehend the utter wreck of the humanity around me. For a second I thought of Luke, the spoon on his coffee table, the rubber rope fallen on the floor, and the old tree of my sorrow shed a few leaves, but I pushed the thoughts away.

Not now, Lily Strom. Not now.

After a few minutes I came to realize that there was no talk of family or hobbies or work. Nothing. Just drugs. The only topic of conversation was about gear—they spoke about it endlessly. It was the only thing they lived for. And *everybody*'s main preoccupation was to know when the dealer would be arriving.

Every once in a while someone would ask, 'When's he coming?' and the answer was always, 'Soon, man, soon.' I felt incredibly sorry for them, for their wasted lives. I thought of their parents and their sisters and maybe even their children.

Every few minutes more junkies knocked on the door. The place became more and more packed.

A gaunt man and his friend turned to me.

'Where you from, girl?' he asked.

It was only junkie small talk. Who were we? How did we hear about the house? The kind of thing that Robin had already briefed me I might be asked, but I was terrified I would slip up, or my accent would sound too forced and fake. So I started to pretend to be suffering from withdrawal systems, twitching, jerking, pulling faces and looking generally unwell, or I bit my nails furiously.

Federica fielded their questions expertly.

'Soon' turned out to be hours. I was exhausted from pretending to be in withdrawal. The longer I remained in that room the more anxious and worried I became. Finally, Samson announced that the dealer was five minutes away. The room became charged with an electric excitement; the mass began to prepare for its feast of delight.

Then a whisper spread like wildfire. 'He's here. He's here.' And everybody scrambled up from their sitting positions. Ready.

We heard the three bolts slide back, and the door opened.

The dealer, a strutting East Ender, in a Nike tracksuit, came with two minions. They immediately started dishing out the drugs to the addicts who had the presence of mind to line up as if they were in a supermarket queue. But some of them were so desperate by then that they lit up or stood against the walls shooting the drug into their veins instantly. Standing in the queue I gazed at one boy, high as a kite, bent from the waist swaying like a plant in the wind. Robin, Federica and I produced our crumpled tenners and got our little rocks of crack.

When it was my turn the minion looked directly into my eyes and my throat constricted. An Eastern European *boy*. He couldn't have been more than nineteen. I held out my two tenners.

'One of each, please.'

I noticed the notes were trembling, but he snatched them from me, and gave me a tiny white rock (crack) wrapped in white plastic and a small brown rock (heroin) in blue plastic. I closed my fingers around them and... Suddenly all hell broke loose.

The riot boys were coming in. The door imploded with an enormous crash at the same time as the windows were being smashed to smithereens. To the sound of splintering glass they were pouring in screaming, 'Police, police,' ordering everyone to, 'Show your hand.'

It was like being caught in a tornado. I had never seen anything like it before. Helmeted, flameproof balaclavas and massive in their heavy-duty uniform, some were wearing glass suits (special material that protected them when they climbed windows full of glass splinters). They mowed into the gaunt addicts, screaming, 'Get on the fucking floor. Now.' And beating them with batons. The poor junkies! *The war on drugs was total crap! A political sleight of hand.*

Both the drug dealer and I had frozen in terror. He looked at me—his eyes were wide with fear. In that second I realized that he was no tough kingpin, but a frightened little boy who was as much a victim as the desperados he served. The small-time drug dealers were just as vulnerable and in need of *real* help as the addicts were. He, me, Luke we were all victims. At that moment: did he know? Who I was?

Then he was running to flush the drugs. He didn't know Federica had already blocked the toilet. He ran straight into a beefy figure in black. One second after he was pushed face first into a wall. I was toppled. A large officer pressed my face into the ground and I felt the grit and the dirt from the filthy floor scrape into my skin. The two rocks in my hand fell out.

The cuffs were on me in seconds. 'You're nicked. Possession of Class A drugs,' the officer gleefully proclaimed.

'Just do exactly as you are told,' Federica muttered under her breath next to me.

I went limp.

Then, just as suddenly as it had begun, it was all under control. They had completely trashed the place and everybody was in cuffs. Incredibly, it had all lasted only seconds.

I could see Robin play-acting, calling the cops 'cunts', and Federica was yelling abuse in Italian, but I could also see that they were high on the adrenalin of a successful bust-up. Of knowing they had closed down another despicable crack house. I knew I should have felt the same, but I was too much in shock. I could not forget the look in the drug dealer's eyes. None of those arrested would be given the help that they desperately needed, and were too ill to obtain themselves. They would simply be holed up somewhere for some time and then released, and the whole cycle would repeat again. This was a war where there would be no winners, only 'good' crime figures, praise from superiors, and more funding for the drug squad.

Out through the smashed door I staggered in the bright light of the afternoon. I could have wept from the relief of the light. I took deep gulps of fresh air and turned my face upwards as if in prayer. For a few seconds my soul blossomed and then I was roughly uprooted as if I was no more than a dandelion that does not belong and pushed into a waiting drug squad car. I looked out of the window and saw that neighbors had gathered to watch. One of them met my eyes. There was no pity or compassion, only condemnation and disgust in her face. I was just another junkie fouling up her neighborhood.

I turned to the arresting officer. 'I'm a cop. I'm a UCO.' It ran hollow. So hollow it echoed in my brain.

And so hollow the cop said sarcastically, 'No doubt.'

I said nothing else until Robin came to get me at the local police station where we had been taken.

'We got them,' he said, still buzzing.

'And you were great,' Federica added. She looked elated.

I was too shocked and shaken to reply. I felt my lip start trembling and tears welling up behind my eyes, but somehow, I clenched my teeth, swallowed my emotions and put on a brave face. I realized that both of them had known that it was not going to be a simple test purchase exercise. It was a full-blown bust-up, but they had not informed me because it had been a test of sorts.

I was not going to fail by falling apart.

I wanted their report to note that I was strong.

That I was the mouse to catch a lion.

FIVE

The next morning I stood in DS Dickie Mills' spartan office. He used to be a UCO—for many years. Now he was top brass running the Met's covert ops program together with five other undercover officers. He drove a 7 Series BMW and was unashamedly and brazenly tough as nails.

He was wearing a gray Armani polo neck, cream trousers with knife edge creases, and Prada loafers. When he rested his palms on the edge of his desk his gold Rolex peeked through.

'There's an undercover course in two days' time. I want you on it.'

'Yes, sir.'

'Get the details from Robin.'

'Yes, sir,' I responded confidently.

'That will be all.'

'Thank you, sir.'

'Come and see me after... If you pass.'

The undercover course, held at Hendon Training Centre, turned out to be a two-

week long, bloody hard training session packed with interrogations, role-plays, cameos, pretend UC operations in real time, psychometric tests, psychological evaluations, and a final interview with cold-eyed UC officers.

There were twelve of us on the course. If I had thought my Police Academy training was a means of sucking the recruits' individuality out and brainwashing them to unquestioningly obey the chain of authority at all times, then the undercover course was breaking down and hardwiring recruits on steroids.

For two weeks we were kept tired, stressed and disorientated with an incredibly intensive schedule and lack of sleep. Once I went to bed at 5.30 a.m. and had to be back in the classroom at 8.00 a.m. Our tutors frequently subjected us to abuse and degrading names. One even called me a cunt. Three students were simply arbitrarily dismissed and we never saw them again. Two broke down in tears and left.

We were expected, in fact compelled, to drink until the early morning hours with the staff and sometimes with the role-play carried on throughout the night to see if we could keep our created personas when we were drunk. Even the weekends brought no respite—we were given tasks that necessitated us traveling all over London and finishing at midnight.

My first time in the interrogation chair left me a shaking mess. I was supposed to take on the persona of a runaway turned stripper who dabbled in drugs and was looking for a job in a lap dancing joint. Tensely, I took the chair and perched on the end of it nervously. They began.

First they lulled you into a sense of false confidence by asking simple questions. With me it was the kind of drugs I had taken.

Easy. I felt myself relax.

Then they asked me for the street prices of those drugs.

I sailed through those.

Then they asked about the last hostel I had stayed in.

I was prepared. I told them.

'What street is it on?'

I swallowed. I knew that. I had memorized it. But my mind was a blank.

'Is it the one near Aldi supermarket?' one of them asked, his eyes gleaming, sensing weakness.

I floundered. I had absolutely no idea. 'I'm not sure. I didn't go out much,' I evaded. Black thoughts swirled in my head. After all this, I was not going to pass, after all. I felt so bad the tears pricked at the backs of my eyes, but crying, I knew, would only make them jeer and hound me mercilessly. I had seen them heap abuse on others for crying. I bit my lip hard and looked them in the eye.

'So who was running the hostel that year, then?'

Oh shit. 'I... I've forgotten,' I stammered.

'This is fucking bullshit,' he roared.

'Load of old bollocks,' the other interrogator agreed, fixing me with a mean stare.

I was falling apart inside, but I kept my face calm. 'Look, I didn't want to say this before, but when I was in that hostel I was a total wreck. I took so many drugs I didn't know whether I was coming or going,' I said in a contrite tone of someone confessing.

I batted more questions. By the time I rejoined the others I was shaking with nerves and exhilaration. The fuckers had not broken me down.

By the end of the course, I was mentally exhausted, and had lost nearly half a stone in weight. There were five of us left standing. There were no awards or medals or ceremony to tell us we had passed. We just gathered in a restaurant for a meal and that was that.

Two of us went off to join foreign forces, another two were taken as part of the part-time index, which meant that they would be available for part-time UC work alongside their day job in whatever police department they belonged to. And I alone was taken on as part of the full UC unit.

I had passed!

SIX

DS Mills swiveled his large black chair and contemplated the bleak gray sky outside his window, as I stared in wonder at the chiseled, savagely handsome face of Jake Eden—a.k.a. Crystal Jake, the kingpin drug dealer. I could hardly believe it. The assignment was for me to infiltrate one of the Eden family clubs and find out how their secretive and vast drug empire was run.

Ever since I joined the police force all I had ever dreamed of had been just such an opportunity. Going after the big guys. Making a difference. To think that such a plum assignment had fallen so easily into my hands was shocking. I wanted to punch the air.

I put the photograph carefully back into the thin file it had come out of and picked up the photos of his brothers: Shane and Dominic Eden. Both extremely good-looking, but without that dangerous panther-ish quality of their brother.

'We've been wanting to insert an agent into his organization for some time, but it needed to be the right person.'

I looked up at DS Mills. He was watching me expressionlessly. 'What makes me right?'

'The man at the helm of this evil gang is so mysterious and secretive that he is almost mythical. He trusts no one. Using a male officer in these circumstances would likely yield no result and could be dangerous for the operative. Gypsies have their own ways of dealing with snitches.'

'And I'm the spider who will lure him into our web?'

'Something like that,' he admitted impatiently, obviously disgruntled by the analogy I had used. 'We're hoping that by inserting you into one of his clubs you will eventually meet him or one of his brothers and over time you will attempt to disarm one of them with your abundance of charm. These tinker families are close-knit. There are no secrets between them. One is as good as the other to bring Crystal Jake to his knees.'

I frowned. There was a touch of bitterness and envy in DS Mills' voice. I wondered if this was a personal vendetta.

'This is a level one assignment. High risk and long term. It requires someone intelligent with social insight, able to react quickly and adapt accordingly to situations. You will be living under your

assumed identity for months and socializing with people that you must never forget are the enemy that you have been employed to finger. These are cunning, ruthless criminals who will kill to protect what is theirs.' Mills kept his small, sharp eyes trained on me: seeking out my fears or telltale signs of weakness. If I was going to back out, this was my opportunity to walk away.

But I kept my expression as impassive and calm as the surface of a lake. He could *never* know what a seething mess lurked deep beneath. 'This is what I trained for, sir.' I noticed my voice was shaking.

Mills' eyes searched me relentlessly for what seemed like minutes, but was obviously only moments. He frowned suddenly. A look of uneasiness crossed his features. Had he seen under the surface of the lake? But if he had, he had decided to ignore it. People were expendable to DS Mills. What was important was a job well done. And more commendations for him. 'Good,' he said curtly. 'But be warned—do not underestimate Eden, he is a formidable man, a persuasive man with the ladies. And do not *ever* trust him no matter how close you get. Your life may depend on it...'

The sharpness of DS Mills' tone was resoundingly clear. Suddenly, an unfamiliar feeling stirred the tiny hairs on my arms, and I didn't know whether to feel terrified or excited about meeting Jake Eden. But I was certain that when I did my heart would be like a rock—strong, unflinching.

'Robin will sort your cover alter ego with you.' A semblance of a smile escaped. The interview was nearly over.

'Sir, can I just ask, why me?'

His eyes shifted downwards. He hesitated, but he knew it was a valid question.

He smiled. It was rather unpleasant. 'I guess it comes down to your looks.'

'My looks, sir?' My face was flaming. So it had nothing to do with my language skills or the accomplishments in my CV then.

Mills showed me a concealed skill, an adeptness in diplomacy that had once propelled him to become one of Britain's best UC officers. 'A hardboiled, experienced officer would be no good. You have the right amount of innocence and mystery. I believe you could be Crystal Jake's Achilles heel.'

My eyebrows rose in shock. This was not what I had signed up for. 'You want me to sleep with him?'

'On the contrary. That would be improper and illegal. Such an activity could only be as an abject failure of the deployment and a gross abuse of your

role and position as an officer of the Met. If he sleeps with you, you are finished. He will discard you like an old shirt. I want you to flirt with him. Tease him. Court him. In the old-fashioned way.'

I nodded, but I was confused. It seemed an impossible task. First that such a man would be interested in me and second that I would be able to keep him on such a tenuous string. It was more likely that sexual relationships between covert deployed officers and those they were employed to infiltrate and target were not officially sanctioned or authorized, but I could read between the lines. What he was really telling me was that Crystal Jake would lose interest in me as soon as he had had me! And that was why I was not to sleep with him.

'If you cannot get to Crystal, then suck up to one of the brothers. You sure you're up to this task, Strom? It's not going to be a quick or an easy one and you're going to have to keep your wits about you.'

'Never been more sure of anything, sir,' I replied firmly.

'By the way...' His eyes flicked to my nails, bitten to the quick. 'You'll need a new set of nails.'

'Yes, sir.'

When I came out of Mills' office I saw that the other officers were gathered

around Mark's desk. Mark was the man who had taken my form that first day.

'A piss,' he was saying, as he put his feet up on his desk.

Ah well, more testosterone-fueled posturing, telling stories of jobs gone by and bragging about who had brought in the biggest cache of guns or drugs: the usual dick swinging contest. I noticed that Robin was not around.

'Who wants some tea and biscuits?' I called out.

'Sure. Get us a round,' someone shouted. The rest of them laughed. The mood was jolly, as it usually was around there.

I smiled brightly. I went into the kitchen and made them all tea, just the way they liked it. I brought it out and handed them their mugs.

'One sugar, two sugars, milk, black.'

Then I went to my table and noticed that since I had been gone the filing system had gone to pot again. I was gathering all the files that had not yet been properly categorized into a pile in the middle of my desk when I heard the first howl of fury. I looked up calmly. Mark was looking at me with a murderous expression. He had spewed the coffee all over his desk and some had spilled onto his precious Ralph Lauren trousers. Two others looked like they had had a sip of their tea, too. The others were warily putting their mugs down.

I dumped all the files back into the cupboard and smiled at them. Surprised. For a group of people that were always taking the piss out of others they had turned out to be pretty thin-skinned.

I had used salt instead of sugar.

SEVEN

Robin grinned at me. 'If you want to bag a tiger you need the right equipment. You need a whole new set of clothes, bank account, the works. We need to create a package your targets cannot resist.'

'Ready when you are,' I replied, with a fierce thrill of excitement.

'First, we'll have to install you in a rented flat.'

And that was how I came to be sharing a flat in South London with another UC officer, but she was never there as she had her own 'other' life. Then for four months Robin and I painstakingly constructed my alibi and cover story.

'We usually use our real Christian names,' he said. 'If someone from your old school recognizes you from across the street the hope is that they will simply call out your Christian name.'

I nodded, but I had pushed all my friends away after Luke died.

'Do you have a name you'd like to assume?'

'Hart,' I said immediately. 'Lily Hart.'

'Right, time to apply for a passport dating from three years back and a driving license.'

'Why would a runaway have a passport?'

'Because she toyed with the idea of dancing in Amsterdam?'

They arrived in less than a week. Both fake passport and DVLA issued driving license had been created in collusion with the appropriate governmental departments and were good for travel and if I was stopped by the police. Using those, I opened bank accounts and applied for credit cards.

Robin took me to lap dancing clubs so I could watch the girls, the way they behaved, and how they interacted with their customers. I saw them rub their naked flesh against men and I thought I had cringed inwardly, but Robin must have sensed my discomfort.

'The most important thing I learned, first and foremost,' he said quietly, 'was that whatever I was doing, I had to always remember that I was a police officer.'

I turned to him. His face was unusually serious.

'Don't allow yourself to get psychologically mixed up. Always keep what you are doing and who you are separate. At the end of the operation you will ditch all the physical trappings of your undercover alter ego, the hair, the clothes, the people you have befriended, and return to your own normal world.'

'Is that really possible?' I asked, surprised.

He looked me in the eye. 'You have to. If you don't maintain the line between the job and who you really are you will become a wreck. For example, if you find yourself in a position where you have to take a drug then you have to come out of that personality as soon as possible and tell your handler, in your case DS Mills. And if necessary you will have to go for counseling.'

'Will I have to take drugs?' I asked worriedly.

'No, we will put it into your cover story that you've had a very bad experience, nearly died, et cetera, and no longer touch the stuff.'

'When and how do I start asking for information?'

'Work your way in very slowly,' Robin said. 'This is a long-term assignment and so requires a huge element of deception. We don't want the target to get suspicious. He is very intelligent, wary, and uncommonly aloof. Don't appear too eager for information. In fact, don't ask for any information. Let some chances to ask for information go by. Don't even appear curious. Lull him into a place of complete trust before you sink the hooks in.'

He then warned me that constant fear of discovery and letting the side down, which was part and parcel of undercover work, could manifest itself as sexual arousal. 'Watch for it and be prepared for it.'

That night he also introduced me to Anna.

Over the next two months she gave me pole-dancing lessons and taught me some really cool moves that looked good and professional, but didn't take an athlete to perform.

A week before I was due to start my assignment I had my nails done and glamorous red highlights put into my hair. I looked into the mirror. There. My alter ego was ready to be unleashed.

On the day before I was due to meet Patrick, who would take me on my audition at Eden, I went to see my parents. We had dinner together at a restaurant. The hole that was Luke was bigger than ever. My father told me he was very proud of me.

'When will you come to see us?' my mother said, crying quietly.

'I don't know, but I will call.' The reality was I wanted my new life to begin. I wanted to stop being Lily Strom and begin my new existence as Lily Hart.

I had become quite close to Robin and on that morning before I left to start my assignment he hugged me. His parting words were, 'Never let your guard down. Remember, one false move can give you away.'

But what stayed in my mind and haunted me was what he had once told me when we were dining at a Chinese restaurant. He told me the loneliest place in the world was the place inhabited by the undercover police officer when they are deep inside the mind of a fictional person.

Take me down to the paradise city
Where the grass is green
And the girls are pretty
Take me home
(Oh won't you please take me home?)
—Guns N'
Roses, *Paradise City*

EIGHT

Lily Hart

Have you ever been compelled to take a step that you know is a mistake but you simply can't stop?

The return home from the Tate Modern is a blur. I walk through the streets of London blindly, telling myself over and over again that I did it for Luke. I try to remember him, but his image eludes me. All I see is Jake, shirtless on a horse, Jake looking at me. Jake standing blood-splattered in Melanie's apartment. Jake with tears in his eyes. Jake holding me. Jake kissing me. Jake smiling. Jake laughing. Jake. Jake. Jake.

I stop walking and hold my head. It feels as if it is about to burst.

'Are you all right?' someone asks.

I look up. A man is looking at me. He seems concerned. 'Yes,' I say automatically. Nothing could be further from the truth.

'OK,' he says, and moves on.

Robin's words flash into my mind.

At the end of the operation you will ditch all the physical trappings of your undercover alter ego, the hair, the clothes, the people you have befriended, and return to your own normal world.

A small, hesitant voice in my head asks, what about the people you fall in love with? I drum it out with the militant message they have brainwashed me with. *First and foremost you are a police officer.*

I *have* done the right thing.

I walk until my legs start to ache, then I stop and hail the first taxi I see. Inside it, I sit with my face turned toward the window, seeing nothing. The taxi drops me outside the house. I watch it drive away and stand at the bottom of the short flight of steps for an age. My legs are like lead. Eventually, my heart weeping, I climb the steps.

I open the front door and I know straight away: he is home. I walk down the corridor and open the living room door.

Seeing him is like jumping into an icy river. The guilt. God, the guilt. I know: I'm in too deep. I have broken the most important rule—I didn't keep what I am doing and who I am separate. I have allowed myself to get psychologically mixed up.

He is sitting on the white leather sofa, but he must have been pacing the floor until he heard me at the front door, because there is that look of restlessness about him. A glass of Scotch sits on the table. He looks pale under his tan and his green eyes burn feverishly bright in his face.

I smile as I shatter inside. The heaviest tears never reach the eyes.

He doesn't smile back. He seems very still. His eyes hold onto me so hard it almost hurts.

'Hi,' I say.

'Where have you been?' I see that his hands are clenched hard and he seems to be controlling himself.

'I was shopping.'

His chest heaves and his eyes flick to the bag in my hand. 'Why did you not answer your phone?'

'I had it on silent.'

He nods gently, but seems somehow inconsolable. I feel the vibrations of his despondency in my blood as if it were my own.

'I'm sorry, I didn't think you would worry,' I murmur.

He takes a deep breath. Again I see him making a Herculean effort to control himself. 'You were attacked less than a week ago, Lily.'

'I'm really sorry,' I say again.

'You look tired,' he observes.

'I am.' I try to smile at him.

'Come here.'

 214

I go to him and climb into his lap. His hands come around me, the palms hot. I nuzzle him like a cat, my hand stroking his thick hair, straightening it. It is ruffled. He has been running his hands through it. He takes my shoes off and lets them drop with a thud on the floor. I sigh with pleasure when his big hands start massaging my foot.

'I didn't know where you were. If you had simply run away. I know so little about you.' His voice is a deep, honeyed rumble. It has a song in it. I could listen to it all my life. But I won't. I was fooling myself before.

'I didn't run away. I'm here.'

The hardness between his legs pushes into my hip. I look up into his eyes. There is only one word for what is in them: *hunger*. I have never seen such extreme desire, such ravenous craving. The air trembles with it. A voice inside my head cries, 'What have you done? What have you done?' I ignore it. My body loses its tiredness and responds to that yearning. My lips part, my nipples swell and pebble tightly, my sex opens like a night flower.

'Would it be really horrible if we had sex right now?' he murmurs.

'Yes, that would be utterly, utterly horrible.'

He carries me to the bedroom and kicks the door open. The large

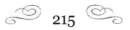

chandelier is not lit. Instead only the narrow bronze lamps over the paintings on the walls are on, creating their own individual pools of yellow light, making the paint look thick and oily. I glance at the bed and my mouth opens with astonishment. I turn back to look at his face. 'What the—?'

'Indulge me,' he says languidly and throws me on the bed covered thickly with money.

'Oh,' I gasp.

'Get naked,' he orders.

Giggling, I pull my top over my head and, lifting the upper half of my body slightly, unclasp my bra and pull it off. I raise my hips off the bed and shimmy out of my skirt. There are only my panties left.

'Help me,' I say.

He reaches down and, sliding his hands along my bare thighs, pulls them down my legs and flings them over his shoulder.

Hungrily he looks down at me lying naked on a bed of money. I gaze up at him, and slowly biting my lower lip, grab two handfuls of money, and throw them up into the air. They fall over and around me.

'Hello,' I say, covered in his dirty money.

He nods slowly, formally. As if he approves of my actions. We continue to

stare at each other. I could have stayed there looking up at him forever. I actually feel faint with longing. He is so beautiful, I want to reach out and touch his skin to see if he is real.

'Do it again.'

I lift handfuls of money and pour them onto my body. One note lands on my mouth. I blow it away. Here I am, an undercover cop, bathed in money, about to fuck a criminal, and not wanting to be anywhere else in the world.

He gets down on his haunches and cupping my buttocks in his large hands, lifts my hips bodily and, bringing my open sex toward his face, deeply sniffs in my female scent. I have been walking all day and I imagine the smell to be scandalously strong and musky. But I am not embarrassed. I know he likes dirty sex. This is the man who thinks warm raw sea urchin tastes good.

He lets his tongue swirl between the pink folds. The velvet brush is succulent, bringing with it whispers of sensations. Deep within I begin to tremble indescribably. My body instinctively arches, and my hips grind into his mouth, feeling his teeth, and begging for more and more. He slips his fingers into me. I grab his head and force it against me. With his fingers impaled inside me, his tongue works my clit.

'Get up on your elbows and let me look at you.'

I obey his demand and look into his eyes. They look stunning. He gazes into my glazed ones. Suddenly, I can't hold his gaze. I am the dirt that has betrayed him. I close my eyes.

'Open your eyes and look at what I am doing to you.'

I open my eyes and, unable to meet his eyes, watch his mouth fasten down on my sex and suck it like a hungry babe at its mother's breast. My body feels no guilt. It pushes me on until I break apart with a stifled cry inside his mouth, his fingers deep inside, his eyes trained on me, my head thrown so far back it touches the wings of my shoulder blades.

I lift my head slowly.

He is watching me, his lips shining with my juices. 'I like watching you lose control.'

I flop back down on the bed, roll over, and getting on my hands and knees, money sticking to my damp skin, offer my throbbing, eager sex up to him.

'Lay your face on the bed,' he growls. The sound wells up from deep inside him.

I hear the sound of his trousers hitting the floor as I lie on my cheek. The scent of money rises into my nostrils: soiled ink, slightly disagreeable. He grabs my hips, and, with a snarl of hungry desire, plunges into me. His cock feels more swollen than usual, voluptuous. I marvel at the sensation even as my muscles ripple around him to accommodate the intrusion. Coated in hot, slick juices he pushes in harder. I tilt my hips so he slides in deeper.

'Who does this hole between your legs belong to, Lily?'

'You,' I gasp, as another thrust makes more notes detach from my body and rain down on the bed.

Another thrust. 'Say it again.'

'You,' I pant.

'And who do you belong to?'

'You. I belong to you.'

And with that he explodes inside me, wild, hot cum shooting into me.

I hear him breathing hard. With me still speared to his body, he leans forward, his body barely brushing my back. He kisses me on the base of my neck where there is a little nerve that makes me shiver, and whispers in my ear, his breath hot and moist, 'You can keep all the money you can hold in your hands.'

Baffled, my spine prickling, I turn my head back to look at him. Is he...?

But his face is innocent.

He moves back and pulls out of me. My body immediately misses him. I watch his eyes latch onto the blood-engorged, reddened flesh between my legs, his milky seed seeping out.

I can read his mind. If I stay in that position one moment longer he will slide his fingers into me. I crawl forward and sit cross-legged on the money. There is a note stuck to my calf. I peel it off, thinking of Melanie, thinking of her saying, 'I take their money and spend it and that is my revenge.'

Dust motes are swirling magical specks in the last rays of the evening's sun pouring in through the windows.

I let my gaze travel over the notes. They are mostly tens and twenties. There must be at least fifty thousand pounds I am sitting on. I could ask where the money has come from, but I remember Robin saying, *Let some chances to ask for information go by. Don't even appear curious. Lull him into a place of complete trust before you sink the hooks in.* So he wants to play the games low-level gangsters employ to show off to their women? When again our eyes clash my face is calm, my thoughts hidden.

'Do I have a time limit?' I ask.

'Nope.'

'OK.' I start gathering the money, carefully, in bricks. Afterwards, without looking at him, but knowing he is watching me, I slide the bricks together. Six bricks. I double them so their height will be slightly higher than my palm and

fingers spread to their fullest. I push them together and notice a note lying on the floor. I look up at Jake, standing with his arms crossed over his chest.

I arch an eyebrow. 'Do you mind?'

Wordlessly he bends, picks it up, and holds it out to me. I take it and, putting it on top of my pile of bricks, lift them all by pressing them together on either side of the tower with my spread palms. The whole thing comes up in between my palms.

I look up at him, fifty thousand pounds richer.

He grabs my hand—the bricks fall down on the bed in a heap—and pulls my naked body to his. 'Do you know what I am thinking?' he mutters.

My heart somersaults. I take his lower lip between my teeth and pull it experimentally as far away from his face as I can while my hands start undoing the top button of his shirt. He drags his lips in a trail of fire along my throat and my chin and catches my mouth with his. His tongue delves in, seeking mine, like a grounded child whose friend has come to knock on the door to ask if he can come out to play.

'Someone should bottle you,' he says softly, much, much later.

NINE

Jake

The sound of a bird chirping wakes me up. Shit. That's no fucking bird in my bedroom. Immediately I tense. It can only be bad news. I feel Lily moving in the pitch dark. Her bedside lamp comes on. She blinks and squints blearily against the glare of the light. I lay a hand on her shoulder.

'Go back to sleep,' I say softly, and quickly go out of the room holding my phone. The light clock flashes 3.50 a.m.!

'What is it, Dom?' My voice is not sleepy. It is a bark, at once urgent, worried and irritated. I run down the stairs.

'They've only gone and torched Eden, haven't they?' He sounds like he has been drinking.

My stomach lurches. My first thought: 'Where's Shane?'

'He's all right,' my brother says instantly.

I feel almost sick with relief.

Without drawing breath Dom carries on ranting, 'It was the Pilkingtons that did it. I fucking know it was that big bastard. No one else would dare.'

I get into the living room and start walking toward the window. 'Calm down, Dom.'

'Calm down? Calm down?' he bellows. 'I'm gonna kill him. I'll fucking kill the ugly vermin. These motherfuckers need to know who they're messin' with. I say I get some of our boys to Red Ice and turn it into a nice bonfire tomorrow night.'

This is not good. Dom is in one of his volcanic rages. I can picture him, his lean, wiry body crashing about whatever room he is in, his neck popping with purple veins, his mind an unthinking red mist. I need to calm him down. The situation is bad enough without another bonfire. Outside it is beautifully still.

'Take it easy, Dom.'

'Are you kidding me? That lowlife scum is trying to muscle in on our patch and you're asking me to take it easy? He'll be dead meat before I call this feud between the Edens and the Pilkingtons over,' he screams into my ear.

'Shut up. Your head is fucked,' I snarl furiously.

That gets through to him. He goes silent.

I take a deep breath. 'Let me think. We need to remain calm and focused,' I say seriously.

'And then what?' he spits, still boiling, but disaster has been averted for now.

My temples begin to throb. This silly generational feud. Will I never be free of it? Still, I'm in no mood to argue.

'And then *I* decide. I'm the head of this family and don't you forget it.'

Dom subsides like a soufflé that has seen daylight too early. 'OK, I hear you. I'm sorry. What do you want me to do, Jake?'

'Take your boys and go down there and see what the gossip is and report back to me in the morning.'

'All right, I'm gonna do what you ask, but this needs to be sorted quickly. I'm not gonna let that cocky cunt walk all over us—'

I terminate the call and fling my mobile across to the couch. Shit, fucking shit. The last thing I need is for Dominic to go crashing into this delicate truce between the Pilkingtons and the Edens. Nobody can even remember anymore why our two families are feuding, but we are. We stay out of each other's way. Why on earth would the Pilkingtons decide to reignite the feud now? There is no sense to it. Neither of us wants an all-out war. I call Shane.

He answers on the first ring. 'Dom called you?' He sounds stressed.

'Yeah. Where are you now?'

'At the club.'

'Is the fire out?'

'Yeah, looks like it.'

'How bad is it?'

'They firebombed the front and the back. There was hardly anything to burn in the front and the sprinklers contained the fire but the kitchen looks bad.'

'Do you need me to come there?'

'Nah. I got it under control. The police are here now.'

'Right. I'll see you in the morning.'

I flick on a light switch, go to the bar, and reach for a bottle of Scotch. I pick it up to down it and see Lily is standing at the door. I take a swallow, my fingers gripping the cold glass.

'You want a drink, Lil?'

Before she can answer I pour a second shot into another tumbler. I walk up to her, pass her the drink and raise my glass against hers. I swallow in one but she doesn't even pretend to drink.

'What's going on, Jake?'

'Someone set fire to Eden.'

'What?' Her eyes widen with shock. 'Why?'

I shrug. 'Could be just kids.'

'Do you have to go there now?'

'No, Shane is there.'

'Do you need me to do anything?'

225

I shake my head and kiss her on the top of her head. 'Go back to bed. I've got some calls to make. I'll be in shortly.'

'OK.' She turns around and starts walking toward the bedroom.

'Oh, Lil, would you like to go on a trip tomorrow?'

She turns around slowly. 'By myself?'

'Of course not. With me, obviously.'

She beams at me. 'Of course I would.'

I feel that dizzy rush to my head. It is unbelievable how crazy I am about her. She is waiting for me to explain. Tell her where or why. But I don't and she walks away from me. Smiling, but confused.

Lily

I don't close the door to the living room and go back to bed. Instead I stand at the top of the stairs and listen, but there are no more sounds to be heard other than Jake going into the dining room and shutting the door behind him. I go back to the bedroom and lie on the bed.

So the Pilkingtons have firebombed Eden. I frown. The information in the file Mills gave me clearly stated that both crime families maintain distant but cordial relations, and have their areas clearly drawn up. If it was the Pilkingtons, there is no doubt that this is a declaration of war. But why? There is no benefit to either family to engage in all-out turf war.

Hours later, when a small sliver of light seeps under the curtain, Jake comes back to bed. I pretend to be asleep. He stands over me watching me sleep. I keep my breathing even and deep. Eventually, he goes over to his side of the bed. I can hear him peeling off his clothes before the mattress gives way to his weight.

I make a small sound, as if I have just woken up, and turning around mumble incoherently. He is sitting with his back to me, but his head is turned down to look at me. I blink up at him. In the blue light of dawn his back is an intriguing play of shadows and gleaming muscles, but his eyes are densely black.

All I want to do is grab his silky hair and drag his mouth onto mine. This is exactly the moment of vulnerability that I have been waiting for. It must be exploited. I reach out a hand, and a frisson of electricity goes through me when our skins touch.

'It's not just random kids, is it?'

'Probably not,' he admits very softly.

'You know who it is, don't you?'

His voice is guarded. 'Maybe.'

'Why did they do it?'

He sighs. 'I don't know yet, but I intend to find out.'

'Why are we going away tomorrow?'

'Because I need to think.'

'Where are we going?'

'Ibiza.'

I could have pushed more, but suddenly I am filled with an odd and surprising sensation. Not to take or break. But the acute regret that I am unable to savor him, as I would a fine wine. If only I was his real girlfriend. If only he could really trust me. If only I could help him instead of finding a way to trap him.

The thoughts are burdensome. Willfully breaking what I have believed in for so long. But mostly because they betray the promises I have made to Luke. And I am faithful if nothing else. My loyalty must be to Luke at all times.

He lies down beside me. For a while there is only the sound of our breathing.

'I'm here for you,' I whisper. And the odd thing is I mean it.

He turns his head to look at me. Our gazes meet and hold. The look in his eyes is so intoxicating I can't look away.

'Thank you,' he says, and his voice is strangely breathless.

TEN

Lily

Jake's house in Ibiza is a triumph of cubist modernist architecture. Set into the clifftop it is held up by an impressive framework of poured concrete, steel columns and beams. A concealed garage opens remotely.

'Wow,' I exclaim.

'That's what I said when I saw the artist impression of the design.'

At the entrance, a suspended steel framed cube hovers in mid-air while the frameless pivot door welcomes us into a stunningly minimalist entrance hall. It opens out to a space into which natural light pours through floating roofs. Sliding doors and the extensive use of glass make the threshold between the open plan interior and exterior convincingly invisible.

Jake slides open the glass doors and we are standing outside facing a swimming pool. Beyond it is the blue-green sea. It is so beautiful my breath catches. Now I know why he wanted to

come here to think. This place is so modern and yet so wild and natural. It's taken me some time but I am slowly starting to understand him a little better. He is a sensuous man who needs wildness, nature. They are almost a part of him. That is why he rides horses bareback.

For a while we are both silent, drinking in the salty sea breeze. Then he looks down at me, tousled, but somehow refreshed already.

'Come, I'll show you the rest of the house.'

Natural light floods even the deepest parts of the house and there is always that sense of space that comes from vast expanses of glass. There are two receptions, three bedrooms all facing the sea, a kitchen, a dining room, and a cellar. We don't go down into it.

He opens the freezer and takes out a bag. 'I'm going for a swim in the sea,' he says. 'Wanna come?'

'How will you get to the sea? We are so high up.'

'I'll show you,' he says, and takes me to the bottom of the garden where there are steep steps that go down to a small private beach inaccessible by any other means.

'What's in the bag?' I ask, as I carefully follow his lead.

'Breadcrumbs for the fish.'

'We're going to feed the fish?'

'Yup.'

He leads the way and at the end of our descent we are standing on a strip of yellow sand that is totally enclosed by rocky cliffs and sea.

He pulls me toward his body and puts a finger under my chin. 'I'm going for a long swim. Can you amuse yourself until I come back?'

'Why can't I come?'

He frowns, instantly worried. 'It will be too far out for you.'

'OK, I'll swim for a bit, and then I'll lie on the beach and wait for you.'

He bends his head and lightly brushes his lips against mine. 'Don't go anywhere.'

I shake my head. 'And leave this paradise?'

He puts the bag into my hand.

'What do I do with the crumbs?'

'Go into the water until you are waist deep and throw a handful.'

'OK.'

He smiles and starts shedding his clothes. He is so fast it is as if he can't wait to get into the water. He takes everything off, and, naked, strides into the waves as I stare at him, bronzed, strong and so perfectly beautiful. When he gets to hip level he raises his hand in a wave and plunges in.

I step in myself. It is so clear it practically compels you to dive into it. When I get waist deep I start throwing handfuls of frozen breadcrumbs. It is a shock to me to see the sudden burst of activity. In seconds all the crumbs are gone. Fascinated I throw another handful and this time I submerge my head to look at them. They are small and silver with black patterns, and utterly beautiful. When all the crumbs are gone I swim for a bit and then I go to lie in the sand. I can see Jake is still swimming out.

I close my eyes and let the sun dry my skin. But after a while I find I am unable to relax. I sit up and I can no longer see him. In a panic I rush to the water's edge. I can just about make him out. My eyes become riveted to his powerful arms as he goes farther and farther out to sea. When he is just a dot on the horizon my throat constricts with fear. What if a really strong current sweeps him away?

Jake

With every stroke my mind becomes clearer and clearer until it sparkles like crystal. All kinds of scenarios play in my mind. I am sitting at the back of a white transit van, wiping blood from a baseball bat. I am sitting in the dark in someone's apartment and when he comes in and puts on the light he nearly has a heart attack to see me there. And me smiling at him as if he is a long lost friend. That's the thing you learn as a debt collector. People are fuckers—they will cry poverty, until they are threatened with physical violence. Yeah, he paid.

Images of Billy Joe Pilkington come into my mind. His cold, empty eyes. Billy's a legend on his turf. His reputation is one of fearlessness and ruthlessness. His name usually only comes up as a whisper when there is talk

of violence and mayhem on the streets, in certain parts of London.

They call him the bat, the bat that came straight out of hell. Nobody has ever dared to cross him. Nobody has dared defy him and lived to tell their story. Nobody except for me. But that was a long time ago when I had nothing to lose.

I know I am *never* going back to that life. It is clear what I need to do. No turf war. Not while I am alive. Carefully, I weigh all the options open to me, all the situations that could arise. Each one of them calls for a true truce. We've had an uneasy truce for too long.

In the distance I can see a yacht. People are sunning themselves on the deck. A woman is standing in a bikini, a hand shading her eyes against the afternoon sun.

She starts waving to me. I stop and turn to look at the beach. I could have gone farther, but I can see Lily standing at the water's edge. I cannot see her face, but I can tell by the tense and fixed way she is standing that she is worried about me. I turn around and start to swim back toward her. As soon as I am standing on the sand she runs to me. She does not say anything, just hugs me tightly.

'I'm so sorry. I'll never put my phone on silent mode again,' she almost sobs.

I lift her out of the water and lay her on the sand. The sea has rejuvenated me but has made her tense and frightened. Her eyes are wide and bright. I place my wet palms on the insides of her thighs—they are warm and gritty with sand—and part them. The sun shines down on us, warming my back. Droplets of sea fall on her face; it is already a lovely shade of gold. Her nipples taste salty when I bite them. She pulls at my hips and screams for more. I force more of me into her. Our coupling is frantic, urgent and wild. There are no sea breezes, but watched by the sea, the sun and the rocks it is the perfect fuck.

Afterwards, we dress and go up the steps hand in hand. I have never felt closer to another human being. Then Dominic calls and I know that once again I will be wiping blood from my body.

Lily

Evening descends and from every corner night fragrances rise. Every living thing, the grass, the trees, the flowers, the people all bring into the leisure of night their own scent.

And that crowd of odors surrounds us as we sit in the open-air restaurant that Jake has brought me to. I raise my glass of wine and take a sip. It is perfectly chilled. I lick the beads of condensation off the glass. They have their own taste. I look up and he is staring at me. I blush.

'Tell me about your childhood,' I say to cover my sudden gaucheness.

'Until my father...died, I was happy. We never had much money because he was an incurable gambler. I remember that my mother kept debts with everyone, even with the butcher who provided her with the cheapest cuts of meat, but even so we were truly a happy family.'

I look at him with surprise. How accepting he is that his father was a gambler. There is no condemnation, no anger, no feeling that he has been deprived. Only a strange and impressive loyalty to family.

'What about you? What was your childhood like?' he asks.

I had it all down pat—an alcoholic father, a downtrodden mother, everything, the whole shebang, at the tips of my fingers—but I found I couldn't say the words. I didn't want to lie to him! I blinked in surprise. What the hell? I was going to fuck up my first assignment. Make him suspicious.

'I'll tell you about my family another time,' I say, and wanting to distract him I reach out and touch his fingers. Immediately, they move to clasp mine.

I look at our entwined fingers and an old, tired ache of once when I was insane breaks into me and eats at my bones. Its return makes me angry. How pathetic. Sentimental fool. There is no one here I can call my own. This man will never be mine. He will never share my pain. I am here to do a job. I am here to crush him, not to long for him as one does a beloved. I am here to save other people's sons and brothers from dying unnecessarily because of men like him. I look up at him.

'Are you all right?' he asks.

This time I won't allow myself to dissolve in my own grief. This time I will recognize myself. It is simple. It is beautiful. I am not lost. I am strong. I can do this. I smile. Harden my heart and speak.

'I'm fine. You want to know about my family? Let me tell you about them. My father was an alcoholic. I'm not sure if he is still alive. And my mother was a downtrodden, weak woman. She let him beat her and me. When I was fifteen I ran away.'

'I'm sorry,' he says softly, and begins to stroke the inside of my wrist. The movement is gentle and tender, and suddenly I feel like bursting into tears.

'I'm so sorry I asked,' he says.

I look at him. There is an expression of such caring tenderness in his face. Oh, the irony. He thinks I am upset to remember my past. That makes me feel worse. I shake my head. 'It's OK. You said you wanted to come here to think. Have you managed to?'

His eyes darken. 'Yeah, but I'm afraid my plans have been rather turned on their heads.'

'What do you mean?'

'My brother, Dominic, you haven't met him yet, have you?'

I shake my head.

'He's a bit of a hothead. He got drunk and went to one of the Pilkingtons' clubs and challenged Billy Joe Pilkington to a bare knuckle fight.'

'God! But how does a drunken dare affect your plans?'

'Billy Joe Pilkington is an animal. If he fights my brother he will do serious damage to him. I cannot allow that. I am the head of this family and they are my responsibility. I will fight on behalf of the Eden family. Maybe that will be the end of this silly feud.'

I stare at him aghast. 'That's just barbaric. Nobody fights to settle a dispute anymore. This is the twenty-first century.'

He looks faintly offended, but his voice is calm. 'Bare knuckle fighting is a noble and proud pastime. For us travelers, family is the most important aspect of life. My mother, my brothers and my wife and children when I have them are the most important things in my life. I will do everything in my power to protect them.'

When he says 'my wife' I freeze, my gut constricting with horror. It shocks me to hear him talk about another woman as his wife. The pain is sharper than I can ignore or explain away as a crush or a passing infatuation. How foolish I have been. Of course he will marry some other woman and speak of her possessively. By then I will have ditched all the trappings of this assignment and disappeared into my real life. And then it hits me. Maybe by then he will be behind bars. Because of me.

Because of me this fine man will be behind bars.

And I feel pain in my gut. My body doesn't want me to betray him. 'You are a police officer first and foremost,' Robin's voice says in my head.

I grip the stem of the wine glass and swallow a mouthful. It goes the wrong way and I start coughing and choking. He comes around and drops to his haunches next to me and asks with great concern if I am all right. I look at him in shock. No other man would do that. They would worry about what other people would think of them. He doesn't care. He honestly couldn't give a shit what anyone else thinks of him. And I clench my hands with rage.

By design this man was made for me, yet I cannot have him.

ELEVEN

I come out of the bathroom and stand in the doorway. He is lying on the bed totally relaxed. The illuminated wall behind the headboard creates an intimate ambience and makes him appear as if he is on a stage. I walk up to him and he opens his eyes slowly and gazes at me, as if he has been dreaming and has woken up to find himself still in the dream. What he has been dreaming of is impossible to say: the expression in his eyes is unfathomable.

His warm hand slides between my thighs. A secret smile plays on his lips. 'Mmmn...' he says. The sound is low, a hum, an invitation.

The hand moves higher.

I take a quick, sharp breath. I am not wearing panties. His fingers touch the wet whorls of flesh, and tendrils of excitement snake across my body. He drags his fingers through the soft, sensitive layers. My head tilts back involuntarily, my eyes half close.

The expression in his eyes changes: gold-green lust shimmers in them.

He pinches the protruding fleshy nub. Quite hard. My eyes widen. He pulls me by my clit toward him. I follow helplessly. He pulls his knees up so his body makes a seat. Awkwardly, with the most sensitive part of me trapped in his firm grasp, I climb onto his body and sit on his crotch, facing him. His penis is so hard it is like sitting on a piece of wood. His eyes are level with my open sex.

'Wider,' he encourages softly.

I comply.

He releases my clit and blood rushes to the numbed flesh making it tingle. For a few seconds he studies the blood-engorged bud while I tremble gently with anticipation. 'For fuck's sake, start,' I want to scream.

He grasps the outer lips of my sex and pulls them apart so the secret, pink inner tissue is exposed, and stares at the glistening flesh. I squirm impatiently. My whole body is hot with desire and excitement. To my disappointment he lets the lips spring closed. His eyes rise up to meet mine.

'Play with yourself.' His voice is thick with need.

I hesitate. I have never done it with someone watching me.

His expression is enigmatic. 'I feel voyeuristic.'

Crystal Jake wants to watch. I take a deep breath. Yeah, sure, you can watch, Jake Eden.

I bring my right hand between my legs and move two fingers in a slow circle around my tingling clit. His eyes drop from my face down to the show between my legs. He watches my actions avidly, greedily. I never thought it would be, but it is an incredible turn-on. I feel dirty, and slutty, and shameless, and absolutely fucking vibrant.

My fingers travel in the familiar practiced movement. I know exactly how I like it. Exactly what makes me come. But there is a different layer this time. He is watching me. It is almost like when he was watching me dance. I feel powerful. Desired. Wanted. I close my eyes, my hips lifting, my muscles tightening. Small moans of pleasure escape from my lips as I welcome that gathering knot, the bunching muscles, the promise of an impending orgasm. I am so close to my climax... Almost there.

'Yes, yes,' I breathe.

Then his hot hand closes over mine.

I open my eyes and stare at him, needy and frustrated. Knowing. He is not going to let me come.

'No,' he says softly, and inserting two fingers into me, orders, 'Take your top off.'

With his fingers impaled deep inside me I hurriedly pull my top off, my movements clumsy. I am not wearing a bra and his eyes latch onto my naked breasts.

'Come closer,' he says, in the kind of deep, seductive voice that I have always imagined the big bad wolf using on Red Riding Hood.

Oh, Mr. Wolf, how long I have waited for you.

I lay my palms on either side of him and lean forward until my back is arched like a bow and my breasts are almost brushing his lips. He captures one swollen nipple in his mouth and swirls his tongue around it.

''Yes,' I encourage.

He starts sucking the tip gently and with such a soft mouth that I groan. Shockwaves of pure pleasure course through me.

'Offer me the other,' he commands.

With unseemly haste I fit the other tip into his warm, wet mouth. So gentle. The way I imagine a toothless baby would take a nourishing nipple. I let out a long breath of satisfaction and start grinding my sex against the heel of his palm. He lets me until the tremors begin shaking my whole body, and it is clear that I'm going to climax. Then he pulls his hand away and catches my nipple between his teeth. I look at him. I am almost screaming with frustration and the sadistic fucker is enjoying this.

'Let me come, damn you,' I groan.

He lets go of my nipple and smiles slowly. 'Persuade me.'

'There is this,' I say, and lifting my hips away from his crotch, I unzip his trousers. His erection is straining against the waistband of his boxers.

'That's the most persuasive argument I've heard all day,' he says.

'Wait till you hear the rest of my argument.' I slide my hand around his shaft and it swells even more.

'Can't wait,' he mutters.

'Get your knees down,' I order suddenly.

His eyes flash at my strict tone, but his voice is even: 'Done.' He flattens his legs.

I lift myself off him and on my knees walk along his body up to his face and then carefully turn around so I am facing his feet. I lower my sex until it is suspended a few tantalizing inches away from his mouth.

'Smell me,' I command. I hold still while he lifts his head and sniffs me. I know what is coming next. And it does. His tongue flicks out. I allow one lick. It makes me shiver with pleasure. The desire to let him carry on is immense, but I control myself.

'Who told you to lick me?' I ask sternly, and lift my hips away from his mouth. 'You've ruined it. You'll just have to wait until tomorrow now.'

He moves so fast I register the sound of his muffled laughter before I realize I am immovably trapped between two hard hands around my hips.

'You wait till tomorrow if you want to. I'm having you tonight,' he growls and suddenly I am sprawled awkwardly on his body with my legs spread, my pussy opened on his mouth, and his tongue thrust into me.

'Hey, I'm supposed to be in charge,' I protest as I try to push myself up on my hands.

'Cock teasers don't get to be in charge.'

His hand comes down around my waist to force me down while the other slips underneath my body. His fingers work my clit in exactly the way he learned from me earlier. In that exposed, helpless position, him devouring my pussy, and his fingers doing exactly what I love to my nub, my orgasm comes so fast and so hard, my nails claw into his thighs.

When it is all over, I find myself lying with my cheek on his belly and panting hard while he is still sucking my swollen folds softly. It's very, very delicious and unspeakably decadent, but I lift my cheek, turn my head, and find myself looking at a very beautifully decorated, very erect throbbing penis. Clear liquid is running down it.

On my belly I shimmy toward it and extending my tongue follow the body of the snake all the way to its open mouth.

'Oh yeah,' he encourages hoarsely.

With my lips held in a tight pout, slowly, inch by hot inch I swallow that deliciously bulbous apple, and then as much of that thick and twisting snake as I can. I bob my head faster and faster, not even stopping when I feel one long finger slide into me. It occurs to me then—the kind of view he must have of my open pussy with its gaping, glistening hole begging to be penetrated. I squirm encouragingly and he fits another finger in and starts pumping into me while I suck him as furiously and as fast as I can.

Suddenly, he grabs me by the waist and pulls me off his shaft. My mouth comes off with a wet, slurping sound. Before I can say Jake Eden I am put on my hands and knees. Threading his fingers into my hair, he pulls my head back, as he rams into me.

'Ahh...' I scream, my head jerking back.

'That's what I was missing. Watching my cock disappear into you,' he says, pushing himself in so hard I shudder.

He fucks me harder and harder, forcing his cock deeper and deeper, and I start to feel the verge of another climax.

'Yesssss...' I push into him, my muscles clenching and tightening as we climb the heights together.

He wakes me up in the night.

'Want to go for a midnight swim?'

It is too dark to see his expression, only the bulk of his naked shoulder, the way it rises out of bed, strong and full of power. 'Yes,' I whisper.

We pad down to the swimming pool. He dives in. I dip a toe in. The water is cold. But it is OK. Under the stars we swim together like two carefree eels, sparks flying whenever we touch. Later his body is warm as it moves on top of me.

TWELVE

I wake up alone and touch the indent on the pillow where his head has been. Then I roll over to his side and bury my nose in the scent of his shampoo.

'Oh, Jake,' I whisper.

I get out of the bed and walk to the living room. The house is very quiet. For a while I think he has gone out and then I know where he is. The sliding doors are open. I walk around the swimming pool and stand at the edge of the cliff and far away in the ocean, much farther than he went yesterday, I see him, swimming furiously. He only came back yesterday because of me.

Once again, I am beset by gnawing fear and worry.

I go into the kitchen and open the freezer door. Other than a couple of trays of ice it is filled with bags of breadcrumbs. I take a bag and go down the steps. I go into the water and feed the fish. I watch them as they frantically snatch at the crumbs and it is a beautiful thing, but I feel restless and distracted. Suddenly, impulsively, I decide to swim out to him. I know I won't be able to swim that far, but perhaps I can meet him halfway on his return.

I strike out toward him. I must have been swimming for a good ten minutes, and yet he seems even farther away. I realize that I am already very tired. I stop and start treading water. I look back at the shore. It looks dauntingly far. It was a stupid idea.

I holler out to Jake, but my voice doesn't carry. I have a little moment of panic. Suddenly, as if he has somehow felt my distress, he stops, turns, sees me, and immediately begins swimming powerfully toward me. I tread water and watch. He is a fine swimmer, sleek and fast. He dives under and pops up in front of me, water sluicing down his hair and face, as ageless and as at home in the sea as a seal.

His eyes are thunderous. 'What the fuck are you doing so far from the beach?' he demands furiously.

I feel stung by his anger. He has never spoken like that to me before. I stare at him in astonishment.

'Don't you know how fucking dangerous it is?' he snarls.

'Fuck off,' I spit at him, and begin to swim toward the beach. He grabs me from behind. His body is hard and slippery.

It is a relief to stop kicking and simply relax into his body.

He nuzzles my neck, his breath warm. 'Can you make it back on your own?'

'No,' I admit reluctantly.

He catches me under my arms, and slowly we make it back to shore.

We lay at the water's edge, naked. I look up at the wonderfully blue sky and feel the heat of the sun penetrating my skin. 'It was a stupid thing to do, I'm sorry.'

He turns his head and our eyes meet. In the sunlight they are bright and intense, dizzying: the color of spring grass. His eyelashes are all long and dark and stuck together with seawater, like a child that has been crying. 'I'm sorry I shouted at you, Lil. But you scared me.' He blinks. 'If anything had happened to you, I would have been too far out to do anything to help you.'

I raise my hand and lay it on his flat stomach. He takes his hand and traces my mouth and desire starts to stain his eyes. He moves forward and leans his forehead on my shoulder and takes a deep shuddering breath. 'Oh, Lily. What am I going to do with you?'

I wriggle myself so I am underneath his body, sweat seeping into my skin. 'I have an idea,' I say, focusing on his brutally masculine chest.

He looks down on me. A hint of that which is centuries old, plain ol' human lust, shines in his face. Fire explodes in my skull. I am so addicted to this man.

'I really like the way you think.' His amused whisper slides into my head like a little mind trick.

Some may call it love. I don't.

'Hungry?' I ask.

'Starving.'

We toss a coin to decide who is to make breakfast. He loses and to ease the pain I promise to make dinner. I stand against the counter and watch him put a pan on the stove.

'Who taught you to cook?'

He smiles, cheeky. 'Let's get something straight, Lil. I don't cook. I'm frying a couple of eggs because I lost a coin toss.'

I can't help smiling back. Like this he is pure magic. The twinkling of his eyes warms my heart the way standing next to a three bar heater in a freezing room in winter warms the body. It actually makes me want to kiss that sexy mouth.

'You don't smile very often, do you?' I say.

'No?'

'No.' I look at him from beneath my lashes. 'What would make you smile right now?'

An inscrutable expression crosses his eyes then is gone as quickly as it came. Then he smiles suddenly, dashing and irresistible. The pull of it is undeniable. I feel my knees weaken.

'How's that?' he asks.

'Not bad, considering how out of practice you are,' I tease.

He steps closer and taking my shoulders in his hand, lowers his mouth to mine. The power of the unexpected kiss is shocking. It whips through me, setting fire to my senses. I hear the roaring in my ears as my mouth opens. He draws me closer and my whole body presses into his hard, clear need, and gives without questioning. My body knows what I refuse to acknowledge: I need him. I open my eyes quickly.

'I'll make the toast,' I squeak, and walk unsteadily away to put some slices of bread into the toaster.

We have breakfast on the terrace and I eat with relish. I wipe my plate clean with a piece of toast and grin at him. 'That was delicious, thank you.'

He leans back in his chair and smiles, beautiful eyes flashing. 'So, my little wildcat, how would you like to take a tour of the island?'

I let my gaze travel over him, cool. 'You know all my buttons.'

'Good. Because I'm trying to impress you here.'

'You're doing great so far.'

He rises and holds out his hand.

Putting a sway into my hips, I walk with him through the house into the garage. He hits the button that opens the outside garage door and pulls a plastic cover off an absolutely stunning red and black Ducati Multistrada.

'Wow! This is some bike,' I exclaim walking around it, my sway forgotten. It is so spanking new there is not a scratch on it. I look at him, impressed.

He is beaming like a child. 'Great, isn't she?'

'Awesome.'

'Come on,' he says, throwing his leg over the machine.

'What? You're going to go like that!' He is wearing the same faded jeans, old sneakers and nothing else.

'Why not?'

'No helmet?'

'Ah, Lily. Do you need the government to be your nanny and tell you what to wear all the fucking time?'

'What if we meet with an accident?'

He sighs. 'There's a helmet in the cupboard.'

He kicks the bike over and it roars dangerously into life the way a really

good bike should. The smell of exhaust fumes fills the garage. He turns to look at me as I fit the helmet on my head.

He winks at me and I gingerly swing my leg over the seat of the bike and place my feet on the passenger pegs.

'Hold me tight,' he says.

I scoot forward until my body is leaning against his and wrap my arms around his hard midsection.

'Ready?'

'Ready.'

He takes off and as he leaves the driveway and gets on the road he accelerates and I hold tighter. He rides with precision and skill as if the bike is an extension of him. When he dips I follow. We cruise along the open road, the wind in our faces, my body glued to his. We travel downhill through the labyrinth of cobbled lanes and make for the roads lined with pines, almond trees and juniper bushes that hug the coastline. Ibiza is full of goats, picturesque coves, tall rocky cliffs, lovely beaches and old-fashioned boatsheds made of wood. Contrary to what I believe about the island being the playground of celebrities and fashion models, so much of it is green and undeveloped. We pass a lonely, whitewashed, hilltop church and at the end of it an olive grove starts. I tap Jake's shoulder and shout over the roar of the bike for him to stop. He slows down and pulls up at the edge of the road then cuts the engine.

'What?' he says, turning to me, his hair wind-blown, his cheeks flushed.

The whole time the tips of my breasts encased only in the thin bikini top have been rubbing against his naked back and I am feeling unbelievably horny.

'I want you,' I say, and taking my helmet off I get off the bike and walk into the grove.

By the time he comes for me I am lying naked on the hot orange soil, my legs spread. When his hard cock enters me, his eyes raping me, raking over my exposed body like rough hands, I hiss with relief.

THIRTEEN

Jake

From the open door I watch her wash vegetables in the sink. She turns off the tap and reaches for a knife. Her hair falls forward and she flicks it away carelessly. The gesture arrests me. Compels me to stay and watch. It is as if I am watching a movie. She is someone else. I am someone else. The picture of domestic bliss is so foreign. So alluring. It warms my heart.

What is it about her that makes her so magnetic? Even the simplest thing she does becomes a movement of grace and beauty. I have to stop myself from going into the kitchen, lifting her onto the counter and fucking her until she claws at me.

She leaves the tap running and turns to check on a pan of boiling water. As she puts the lid back on it she looks in my direction, sees me, and for an instant loses her concentration. The lid slips from her hand and falls to the ground, catching a ladle resting by the side of the pan on its way. The ladle pings up and falls into the pan of boiling water and splashes boiling water onto her hand.

I hear the ladle clatter to the floor as I rush to her and try to pull her toward the cold water tap, but she shakes her head vehemently.

'Flour,' she gasps. 'Find me some flour.'

I stare at her, confounded; convinced I have heard her wrong. 'What?'

'Where's the flour?' she barks urgently.

Flour! As if I would know where that is. I start opening cupboards and clumsily rifle through them. Dropping packets on the counter and floor. Cursing. I find an unopened packet in the third cupboard I open. I turn around quickly,

'Open it,' she instructs, white with pain.

I open it and pass it to her. She takes a handful of flour and holding it against her burn, closes her eyes. It must have given her some relief because she looks up at me and smiles tremulously.

'I know it looks weird but it's an old Chinese trick my grandmother taught me. She actually keeps a packet of corn flour in the fridge so it is cold and ready for use whenever she burns herself.'

I stare at her in shock. This is the first time she has offered a tiny little snippet

of herself, without being prompted, and something real!

'It's brilliant,' she adds. 'It actually helps heal the burn faster and stops the skin from marking.'

I keep my voice casual. 'Your grandmother is Chinese?'

She smiles. A tender expression comes into her eyes. 'Yes.'

'And you love her very much, don't you?'

'Yes, yes I do.'

'And she is still alive?'

Suddenly the expression in her eyes changes, becomes guarded and fearful. And all I want to do is hold her close to me and tell her it doesn't matter. It does not matter a damn. She has ruined nothing by telling me that.

Lily

I stare at him in horror. Oh! My! God! I have totally slipped out of character. My alter ego doesn't even remember her grandparents. I can't believe I have fucked up so bad. What if he wants to know more about her? Or, worse, wants to meet her? I can't tell him she is dead. I think of her, her head tipped back, roaring with laughter. My grandmother is very superstitious—Chinese believe all mention of death and dying is bad luck, and she would be so hurt if she knew I was telling anyone she was dead. I'll have to tell Mills and the agency will have to come up with a fake grandmother. But that will be embarrassing, too. Admitting that I slipped up this early in the assignment.

I drop my eyes to my hand.

'How long do you have to do that for?' he asks.

I put my head up and see him looking at the flour I am holding against my burn.

'Ten minutes.' The flour has helped, but it is still painful.

He switches the fire off. 'Come on,' he says, and with his hand on the small of my back leads me toward the living room. 'We'll order in tonight.'

To my great relief he loses interest in my grandmother and does not ask anything else about her.

It will be our last night on the island. Some part of me doesn't want to leave. I have been happy here. Happier than I have ever been in my life. We have watched the sunset over the water and had our takeaway pizza, and now Jake has gone in to have a shower.

I stand on the terrace for a little while longer soaking in the magic of the island. A lizard scampers up a tree. I know a faint tinge of envy. It lives in this paradise. I watch it until it disappears into some bushes. With a sigh I go indoors and pull out a book from my bag. Curling up on the sofa I start to read. Three pages later Jake is standing in the doorway.

'Hey,' he says.

I gaze at him. He is wearing a pair of faded jeans. They hug his strong thighs. Something about him always makes my mouth dry. 'Hey, yourself,' I reply.

'What are you reading?'

'The Billionaire Banker.'

'Any good?'

'Not bad.'

He comes forward, the muscles of his chest gleaming in the down-lights. Desire floods through me, so hot and fast that my clit aches.

I pat the sofa next to me.

He raises his eyebrows.

'I want to try something.'

His eyebrows rise. 'What?'

I turn my book to the appropriate page and hand it over to him. 'I want to try that.'

He takes the book from me and reads. I watch him, the way the light caresses his cheekbones, the shadows his long eyelashes make, the straight mouth. A beautiful man, a truly beautiful man. When he looks up his eyes are dark and amused. 'I've got whiskey.'

'I know where I can get some ice,' I say with a grin.

By the time I come back with a bucket of ice, he has stripped naked. His big thighs are bunched and ready and his decorated, satiny soft cock is erect and magnificent in the soft glow of the lights. He is so hot and so perfect my thighs quiver. In one hand he is holding a bottle of Jack Daniel's.

I lean weakly against a pillar. 'Already so hard?'

He doesn't answer. Instead he opens me with his practiced fingers and does to me what the billionaire banker did to his woman.

FOURTEEN

The first thing I do at work when I return from our little holiday is go on the Internet and find out about bare knuckle fighting, a sport where the opponents ram their unprotected fists into each other to decide who is the hardest of them. What I discover scares the shit out of me.

The activity is considered to be the ultimate tear-up, no fucking around, no holds barred and with plenty of blood. It could be pouring from a fighter's ears or even from his groin, bitten by his opponent.

I also learn that the impact of one man's bare fist on another is equivalent to the force of a four pound lump hammer traveling at twenty miles an hour. The effect could be devastating, even after a bout lasting just a few minutes. There are no official rounds to this blood sport; instead it just goes on until one of them cannot take it anymore, or has sustained so many injuries that he can no longer stand.

It reminds me of the Chinese proverb my grandmother used to tell us grandchildren: *When two tigers fight, one limps away horribly wounded, the other is dead.*

That evening, profoundly disturbed and unable to wait, I run to the front door as soon as I hear Jake enter and confront him. 'Is it true that in bare knuckle fighting you could be bitten so hard in the groin that you start bleeding?' I demand.

He closes the door with a deliberate click. 'It won't be like that, Lil. Both Pilkington and I are too proud to bite like wild animals.'

I clasp my hands together nervously. 'But you could end up with a broken eye socket or a smashed fist?' The thought makes me tremble.

'Unlikely. The fight will be marshaled by a referee.'

'But the possibility exists that you could get hurt?' I insist.

'Yes, I could,' he admits.

I take a deep breath. 'And what happens when you do?'

'There will be a paramedic on standby.'

'It says on the Internet that you could be brain damaged. What could a paramedic do then?' I cry.

'I could die tomorrow crossing the street.'

'I don't want you to fight,' I blurt out unhappily.

He takes my trembling hands in his, but looks at me with an unyielding face. 'It is tragic, but we both have to go through this fight simply to sustain our identities. I *have* to fight him, Lil. It is all arranged. The date has been set. Saturday coming. And there is no backing out.'

I gasp. 'And when were you going to tell me that?'

'Saturday.'

Angrily I pull my hands out of his grasp. 'Before or after the fight?'

He runs his fingers through his hair. 'Before. I was trying to avoid a scene like this.'

'Where will it be held?' I ask coldly.

'In a barn somewhere.'

'I hope you've reserved a good seat for me,' I throw at him sarcastically.

'You're not going.'

My eyes widen. 'Why can't I go?'

He folds his arms over his chest. 'Do you really want to watch two men inflict savage injuries on each other?'

I narrow my eyes. 'I thought you said the injuries are not going to be savage?'

He frowns. 'Just stop it, Lil. You're not coming, OK?'

'It's a spectator sport so won't there be others there, including women?'

'Yes.' His voice is cautious.

'And you said it is a noble tradition.'

'Yes.'

'Well, I want to be with you while you engage in this noble tradition.'

'Well, I don't want you there.'

'Why not?'

'Because I will be distracted and unable to concentrate if you are. I want to know that you are in a safe place. *At home.*'

Some part of me is relieved to know that I am not going to see the fight. It makes me sick to even watch a boxing fight between total strangers. I don't know that I can take watching Jake bloodied in such a barbaric way. 'Will you at least let me come and wait in the car for you?'

He sighs. 'All right, you can wait in the car with Shane.'

I look at him. 'Will many people be going?'

'Entrance is by word of mouth and the location will only be revealed a few hours earlier by the organizers, so nobody really knows how many will turn up until the day.'

'Will people be betting?'

He shrugs. 'They usually do.'

Saturday flies into my life. Nobody talks and I sit in the back of the car, sullen

268

and fearful, as Shane drives us to a barn in the middle of nowhere. Dominic has gone on ahead and will meet us at the location of the fight.

A swarthy boy is directing cars down a beaten track to a field. I am shocked to see what looks like hundreds of cars parked there. Shane passes them and comes to a stop outside a barn. There is a van selling hot dogs and burgers. As I watch, people are going into the barn.

Dominic has been waiting for us to arrive. He comes striding toward us. He is tall and broad like his brothers, but it is immediately apparent that he is not the thinker of the family.

'It's a fucking zoo in there,' he says bending down at Jake's window.

'Is Pilkington here yet?' Jake asks.

'Just arrived. He's got a lot of supporters. His women are going crazy, but don't worry, it won't take you long to put him to sleep.'

Jake gets out of the car. I scramble out, too. Dominic acknowledges me with a nod. I don't nod back. I know it is him that has caused this fight.

Jake turns toward me and smiles. 'Kiss me good luck?'

I fling myself at him and, holding the sides of his face between my palms, I kiss him desperately. His mouth is warm. His hands come around my waist. And his tongue traces my teeth gently.

But there is no passion. There is only the sense of cold fingers crawling all over me. I break away. He smiles again at me.

Shane comes around to stand beside me as I watch Jake stride away with Dom.

Close to the barn, he stops, and turns around to look at us. I wave at him, but he simply stares at me as if this could be the last time he will see me. The thought makes my throat constrict with fear. What if something happens to him? Brain damage. Or...death. People have died during these fights.

The thought galvanizes me, and I take a step to run toward him, but Shane's arm shoots out and grasps my forearm. I stop and do not move. He holds me still while Jake carries on staring at me.

Finally, Jake nods and, turning away, walks into the barn. He never turns again. He enters the door and I hear the crowds roar their welcome. I feel a shiver go through me. Shane removes his hand. I hug myself. I don't want to think of what is going on in that barn.

I turn my head to look at Shane. He is staring at the entrance, his face tense and anxious.

'It's going to be OK, right?'

'Yeah, it's going to be OK,' he says very softly, not looking at me.

This is the first time I have been alone with him since that night at the party when he found Jake with his fingers inside me. 'I'm sorry,' I say.

His head whips around. 'About what?'

'About that night. I didn't mean to hurt you or cause trouble between you and Jake.'

He stares at me incredulously. 'You don't understand at all, do you?'

'Understand what?'

'My brother would never have done that if you were right for me.'

I stare at him curiously. This unshakeable loyalty they all have toward each other even at their own expense.

'My brother is the father I never had. Did you know that his burning ambition was to be a vet? He wanted to be the best vet in the world. He was convinced he could talk to animals. Maybe he could. Even fierce dogs used to wag their tails at him.'

His eyes harden.

'He gave it all up for us. We are what we are today because of him, because he took the tough decisions and did whatever was necessary for us to stay alive and thrive. I owe my life to him. So yes, I liked you, but contrary to what you think, I had no problems stepping aside. And I am proud that I did something for him. I introduced him to you.'

I flush bright red with guilt. 'I'm not special,' I mumble.

'You're so clever and yet so blind,' he says, shaking his head. 'When you see him, what do you see?'

I shake my head. My thoughts about Jake are so jumbled, so conflicted and so confused that even I have not tried to analyze them yet.

'You see a flashy criminal, don't you? He dresses that way because those are the trappings of those he deals with and it is a disguise he wears so they do not see that he is not one of them.'

I think of Jake on the horse and the way he was when we were alone on the island. He was most comfortable when he was unshaven, barefoot and shirtless.

'Do you really think my brother treats *anyone else* the way he treats you? I've never seen a woman get as close as you have to him. In fact, to my knowledge no one has. Don't fuck it up by mistaking the strong emotions he has for you with weakness.'

FIFTEEN

Jake

The atmosphere in the barn is buzzing. All around me side bets and cash seem to be changing hands. Dominic has rounded up some of our boys to shout their welcome for me, but they are few compared to the people who have come to see The Bat.

At six feet two, an inch shorter than me, but weighing well over nineteen stones, and with a chest that is reported to be fifty-five inches, he is not just a veteran of at least thirty bare-knuckle fights, but a champion, too. I made light of it to Lily, but Billy Joe Pilkington has never lost a fight. His opponents are known to be either out cold or crawling pathetically away from him at the end of the fight.

And now he believes no one can beat him.

Taking a deep breath I walk toward the makeshift ring. It's been so long since I have been in one. The ring is a claustrophobically small six by six feet square made of three bales of hay stacked up to mid-thigh level. Billy Joe stands in one corner, shirtless, his chest puffed out and covered in tattoos, the largest being a bat with its mouth open in a red scream, and the letters No Fear written in olde English font.

His eyes, black with cold intent, are fixed on me, as he pulls a mouthful of Guinness from a can. He swallows and slowly and deliberately clenches his fist. White frothy liquid shoots out of the can and pours over his large hand. He flings the crushed bit of metal aside and, with a savage roar, repeatedly bangs his chest with his fist in an astonishing show of bad ass.

Staring at me he punches his fist—one of the knuckles has been smashed to smithereens during a fight—into his open palm. He's getting off on the adoration of the crowd and trying to intimidate me.

I step over the cordon of hay and I am in the ring with Pilkington.

I feel the eyes of every single person in that packed barn. All hoping to spot a telltale weakness, a slight twitch, a nervous smile, a dropping of the eyelids. Any small sign to decide which corner to put their money in. But I keep my attention totally focused on Pilkington. He is much bigger than I remember, stronger, and more muscular. There is a new scar on his face. It looks like a bite mark.

In that moment I realize we are two different species. He's fighting to die and I'm fighting to live. This is totally against everything I am supposed to be doing with my life. Nevertheless, this fight is real and it is happening. For a second my mind shifts to Lily waiting outside. I push the thought away. Shane is watching over her. She is safe. I need to get this done. I train my thoughts back to my adversary.

'What you waiting for, Eden?' Pilkington taunts.

His voice inspires an instant eruption from the crowd. They jeer and bay for blood. Anyone's will do, it's all part of the bare-knuckle sport!

Pilkington takes a step forward into my space and I take one into his. I meet him glare for glare. We are so close our noses are practically touching. This is as primeval as it gets. Two rivals locking horns in a battle for supremacy.

His raging black eyes blink, and suddenly he head-butts me and swings a thunderous right my way. I register the breeze that slithers up my cheek as his iron knuckles swish by and hear the sickening crack of his fist connecting with my temple, before my brain rattles in my head and my ears start ringing. My legs give way under me and I go crashing to the ground. But I am so hyped up and racing with adrenalin I don't feel the pain. All around me his supporters are going crazy.

'Do him. Fucking do him,' they howl.

This is a bad start. I know that he already has one on me.

Every punch takes a little out of me. It isn't like it is on TV. It's exhausting. Unfortunately for Billy Pilkington, though, we're not yet half an hour into the battle when I'll be weaker. His blow disorientates me only momentarily. I look up and see him, feet apart, hands raised, as if he is a conquering gladiator who has already delivered the final blow. Boy is he wrong. I'm not done. Not by a long shot.

'Come on, Jake,' Dominic screams somewhere from my left.

I shake my head to clear it and get to my feet. This time Pilkington doesn't have surprise on his side. I explode forward with a powerful uppercut. He leans backward to evade it, and I kick him. He staggers, but stays upright.

I throw a punch into the side of his jaw. He ducks, and I land a solid blow to his liver. The pain causes air to whoosh out of his lungs. He retaliates with a blow to my left kidney. I gasp with the flash of pain and land on my knees. Fuck that hurt. I'm gonna be pissing blood for the next few days.

I scramble up, but he sideswipes my legs from underneath me. I topple backwards. He staggers toward me, and with a furious screech, throws himself on top of me. The weight of him landing on me is unreal. My body jerks. His large hand spiders across my face and digs into my eyes. I slam my elbow into his ribs, and hear the crack of bone. His eyes widen. He rolls off me.

We are both on our feet.

I unleash a powerful uppercut down the middle that catches him on the chin. Whack. He grimaces and falls with a dull thud, almost as if he's unconscious before he even hits the floor. For one moment I think it's done, but the next thing I see, he is sitting up, blood spilling from his mouth, and what the fuck? Smiling at me. Well, that's a fucking first, no one's ever got up without help from my best shot. That shot should have dropped a horse.

I realize single punches are not going to crack this tough nut as I watch him get back on his feet and turn to face me. With a grunt he takes a lurching step forward. The odd move disarms me. He swings out and connects heavily with my ribs. A searing flash of pain ripples through my torso.

Winded, I double over, and stagger back unsteadily. The punch has the effect of knocking in the backs of my knees. My head is swimming, but blindly I hit out for his body.

I know I'm in a fucking war when a left body shot opens me up to a pair of knuckles that feel like they're encased in steel. My head snaps around from the unbelievable force. My mouth fills with blood. I swallow a mouthful and, protecting my head, fire back, unleashing multiple combinations that rain down on him.

His head looks like it might come off his shoulders. Fuck knows how he's staying on his feet. One thing I got to say for him, he is as strong as a damn bull. He keeps coming forward throwing bombs. One lands hard on my jaw. I see a vapor mist of my blood spray the onlookers. It makes them yell louder. The more blood the better, just so long as it isn't theirs.

I suck up the pain and catch him again, this time with a devastating blow to the solar plexus that bends him in two. I watch him drop to his knees, face etched in pain, blood pouring from his mouth and a gaping eye cut. He's a fucking mess, but the fucker won't stay down.

I gulp some air as he staggers toward me, and I remember the hard way what I've learned with fighters—no matter how exhausted your opponent is, the last thing to go is the power of his punch—

when a crunching punch lands on my ribs followed by an exploding right to my jaw. It sends more blood spraying all over two guys closest to me. The impact of the rib shot sends me winded to the floor. I choke and cough violently.

'Fucking give it up, Eden,' Pilkington bellows, swaying over me, his face snarled and bloodied.

But quitting is not in my genes. I can take his best dogs. I get to my feet—it is only adrenalin that is keeping me going now—and start dancing the famous Eden shuffle. It's been so long, but it comes back to me as clear as if it was yesterday. It mesmerizes and dazes Pilkington. My jabs come from every angle making his life a little worse with every shot. They're too fast for him to see them coming out of that swollen eye of his and he's too fatigued to block any.

The sustained assault on his face and body leaves him gasping for breath. I watch him finally wilt and collapse after three more hard blows. The crowd becomes frenzied: they know as do I. He won't throw another punch. He's done. He's not the only one—the earlier strength in my legs deserts me and I slither to the ground beside him, blood and sweat dripping from my body.

We've neither won.

The referee will have to decide on points.

But before he can make his decision, a decision that could start another feud, the barn is split by the sound of a man's voice screaming, 'Police, police.'

The lookout has spotted them a mile away, which gives us a few minutes to get out of here. The two hundred odd people in this warehouse panic and start running for the exit in a mass exodus.

Dom and another man are beside me. 'We got to go,' Dom says.

'Wait.'

I turn my head and Pilkington's heavies are trying to help him up. I grab his upper arm. Pain shoots through my ribs. His mouth spills a long cable of saliva, his face is split and bruised, his hair and clothing are slathered in blood, grease and mud. He looks like a wild man. We both look like wild men, blindsided by lightning.

'It's over between us,' I squeeze forcefully, and he just looks at me. His eyes are no longer electric, replaced by the aftermath mellowness of a punishing battle.

'I respect you, Jake Eden,' he says, and a spray of blood hits my face. 'You have fucking balls. You met me head on. Your family and mine are tight now. You won't have any trouble from the Pilkingtons.'

I stick out my bleeding hand. He takes it. Like a man.

'You're one tough fuck, Billy Joe Pilkington, and I wouldn't want to do that again.' He breaks into painful laughter that makes him wince. A mutual rush of respect flows through me.

In typically modest fashion he says, 'You're the greatest fighter of all time... Next to me.'

I grin.

I hear the sirens now. His men slide their hands under his armpits and help him away.

In a daze, I hear a woman's voice calling me frantically. Ah, Lily.

And then I see her face. God! She looks like a fucking angel.

SIXTEEN

Lily

'**O**h, my God, Jake! You're covered in blood,' I scream, falling to the ground next to him. I cannot believe the state he is in.

'Have you seen the other guy?' he jokes, blood dribbling out of his mouth.

I stare at him in horror.

'Come on,' Dom shouts urgently. 'We better get the fuck out of here. In a few minutes the pigs will be swarming all over this place.'

'Shane's waiting in the front with the engine running,' I say automatically, remembering what Shane had told me. The sirens sound a whole lot closer. 'Come on,' I say, my voice high and shrill. 'We have to hurry.'

Pilkington's men rush forward to grab an arm each. By a weird chance my gaze collides with one of his helpers and the man's eyes register recognition before he moves his eyes swiftly away. But I have never seen him in my life. Then they are making for the exit and I turn my attention back to Jake, with all my thoughts back to the worry of getting Jake into Shane's car before the police arrive.

Dom and another guy support Jake. It is shocking that in his state he can still walk. I run ahead to open the back door of the car. Jake is put in, Dom and the guy run off, and Shane takes off. The sirens are deafening now, but the coppers are about to find that they're too late again. It is shocking how quickly all the cars have sped away.

I turn to look at Jake.

'Oh my, Jake. Look at you,' I whisper.

'Most of this blood is not mine,' he lies.

'We're going to see a doctor, right?'

'Nope. A doctor is coming to see us.'

I lean back and close my eyes. I feel shocked and shaken.

'Hey,' he says.

I turn my head.

'The feud is over.'

I nod sadly. The price seems too high to me. 'Are you in agony?'

'No, I'm still buzzing.'

'Buzzing?'

'Yup. Buzzing. It's up there with sex.'

I raise my eyebrows.

'Maybe not,' he grins, then winces with pain.

I look at him worriedly and he touches my face gently. And for some crazy reason tears start slipping from my eyes.

'Don't, Lily. Don't. *Everything* is just the way it should be.'

'It's just the shock,' I sniff. Even I don't know why I am crying. It seems so silly, but I feel unbelievably choked up and shaken.

We hurtle through country lanes, with Jake wincing now and again.

The doctor comes and to my horror tells us that Jake has fractured ribs. He prescribes a course of anti-inflammatory meds and painkillers. I set up an ice bath and Jake gingerly lowers himself into it. The buzz of adrenalin has worn off and the damaged ribs make even talking an incredibly painful thing. He lies in the ice bath for about an hour. I can see huge purple bruises and bumps coming up on his legs, his midsection and his face.

'How do you feel?' I ask, coming to sit on the toilet seat.

'Like hell. Even breathing makes me feel miserable. And I've got a splitting headache.'

When he gets out of his ice bath, he is shivering and I gently help him to bed

and cover him with a blanket. Then I wrap his hands with gauze bandages—the skin over the knuckles is all broken and raw.

'Why don't you have a little nap?' I say.

He sighs. 'I'd like to have sex.'

I look at him in astonishment. 'How?'

'I could if you did all the work.'

I shake my head in wonder. He can't even breathe without pain and he wants to have sex. Incredible!

'Will you?' he cajoles.

'No. Look at the state of you. Your face looks like a damn balloon. And you can't even breathe properly. I'm not going to have sex with you. What if I cause you even more injuries?'

'We haven't had sex in three days,' he says sulkily.

'And whose fault is that? Who had to conserve energy to prepare for his big fight?'

'How about a blow job?'

'You're mad.'

'I thought you liked a swollen cock.'

I grin. 'I'm not doing it.'

'Right then, just open your legs and let me see your pussy.'

I blush.

'Right, at least just talk dirty to me.'

'Stop it, Jake. I'm not doing anything like that. You're supposed to be resting.'

'Go on. I just want to see my cock in your pretty mouth.'

I lift the duvet and fucking hell he is as hard as a piece of wood. I lay the duvet back on his body.

'Spoilsport,' he grumbles.

I grin.

'By the way, we have to go see my mother in a few days' time. She wants to meet you.'

'Wake up, Lily. Wake up.' Jake's voice startles me awake. Disorientated, there is still a great rage left over from my dream. I turn to look at him in the light from his bedside table. He is too stiff and in pain to move too much and is lying on his back looking at me with worried eyes.

He reaches out and pulls me gently backwards onto the pillow. 'You were shouting.'

My skin is damp with sweat. I inhale deeply. 'Can't you sleep?'

'It hurts to sleep.' His voice is dry.

I rise up on one elbow. 'Is the pain really bad?'

'I'll live. Are *you* all right, Lil?'

I take a deep, calming breath. 'It was nothing. Just a nightmare.'

'What was it about?'

 286

The hole that cannot be filled yawns. I can't tell him about Luke. There is only one way I know to distract him. I give a tiny laugh. 'Do you still want to have sex?'

For a second he seems confused, and then I see that familiar gleam of sexual arousal flickering in the depths of his eyes. 'What do you think?'

I lift the duvet off our bodies and then I place both my palms on either side of him, very, very gently lowering myself onto his erect cock, sighing with pleasure as that big cock invades, stretches and fills me.

'God! I've missed your tight pussy,' he groans.

Carefully, so my body never touches anything but his cock, I clench and tighten my muscles around him and drag myself up and down that deliciously thick shaft. The nightmare falls away in pieces like leaves in autumn and makes me forget the tide of emotion that was aching to come out.

I whimper with pure pleasure and feel him get harder and bigger deep inside me. I know he will soon be at the point of no return. I feel his fingers move and locate my moist, swollen clit straining and protruding from its hood.

As his seed rushes upwards through his shaft he firmly grasps the tight bud between his fingers and squeezes it hard.

The sudden furious sensation is so different from my gentle manipulations that it triggers my climax. I try not to buck too violently as the blissful spasms of my orgasm shake me from head to foot, but with his own climax upon him he instinctively forces more of his shaft into me, causing my buttocks to land on his thighs.

His groan is one of explosive ecstasy tempered by pain. For some time I hold him trapped within my body until our bodies are finally quiet. I remember once reading that the heart is like a tendril—it cannot flourish alone. It will always lean toward the nearest and loveliest thing it can twine itself with and cling to it. When I try to gently lift my body away he makes a sound of protest.

'What is it?' I whisper, thinking I have hurt him.

'I am so...' He hesitates. 'Proud of you.'

SEVENTEEN

A week after the fight, when only yellow bruises and unhealed ribs remain, we go to Jake's mother's house for lunch. She lives in a cottage with a charming English garden. English gardens are always best in spring but hers still looks good. There are hanging baskets of purple petunias by her front door. The door opens before we can knock and a surprisingly small woman, perhaps five feet three inches, with extraordinarily bright green eyes, smiles at us.

She kisses her son warmly on both his cheeks and formally extends her hand toward me. I am relieved by this show of formality. Her hands are small but strong—a gardener's hands. Jake introduces us.

'Nice to meet you, Lily,' she says. Her voice is soft but her accent is more pronounced than her son's.

'It's a pleasure to meet you, Mara,' I reply.

She withdraws her hand rather quickly and clasps it along with the other close to her chest.

'You better come in,' she says, and leads us into her living room. It is exactly as I expected it to be. As clean as two new pins with net curtains, family photos galore, and dainty china figurines on the windowsill.

'Take a seat,' she invites, and hovering uncertainly at the door asks if we would like something to drink.

'No, you sit down and I'll fix us all a drink. What will you have, Mother?'

I take the sofa and she perches on the end of a velour-covered Queen Anne chair. 'I'll have a sherry,' she says. I notice that her hands are tightly clenched in her lap.

'Lily?' Jake looks at me with a raised eyebrow.

'I'll have whatever you're having then.'

Jake walks to the carved armoire and opens it. One shelf holds an impressive selection of alcohol.

'So how did the two of you meet?' Mara probes.

I return my gaze to her. She is smiling politely, but her eyes are sharp. 'Shane introduced us,' I reply.

She frowns. 'Shane?'

'Yes, I was working as a dancer at Eden.'

'Dancer?'

Ah! Malice disguised as moral outrage. She just about stopped herself from crossing herself.

'She was,' Jake interrupts smoothly. 'She doesn't dance anymore.'

His mother turns to him. There is a puzzled, curious expression on her face. 'Oh!'

'Now she works for me.'

'Really?' she says softly, taking her glass of sherry from her son.

I have the urge to down the entire contents of my glass, but I don't. Instead I hold the glass in my hand and endure fifteen minutes of interrogation disguised as polite chat.

Finally, his mother stands. 'Please excuse me. I think lunch might be ready.' She disappears into the kitchen and I feel the tenseness in my shoulders go.

'I think she likes you,' Jake whispers.

'I think she doesn't,' I whisper back.

'I think she'll come around,' he consoles, and kisses me on the nose.

For some weird reason, his words touch me. I look into his eyes and he looks back and we are both so lost in each other's gaze that we don't hear his mother come back into the room.

She clears her throat and both of us turn to look at her. Her face is white and she seems shocked by something.

Even Jake notices. 'What's the matter, Mum?' he asks, standing up and going to her. He puts his arm around her narrow shoulders, making her appear smaller and quite fragile.

She shakes her head and smiles weakly. 'Someone walking over my grave.'

I stand, too, but I am conscious that she doesn't want me near her. The truth is that she can barely bring herself to look at me.

'Come on, lunch is ready,' she says briskly.

'Would you like some help?' I ask, knowing what the answer will be.

'Absolutely not. Everything is done.'

So Jake and I take our seats at a dark wood dining table. The room faces her beautiful back garden full of flowers and fruit trees. His mother then disappears from the room and returns with a trolley.

'Be careful, the plates are hot,' she warns, setting our plates of a lamb chop, peas, carrots and potatoes in front of us. She places a basket of bread rolls and a gravy boat in the middle of the table and sits herself.

'May it do you good,' she says.

'May we all be together at the same time next year,' Jake says.

An expression of alarm crosses her face.

'Bon appétit,' I say.

Jake picks up his knife and fork.

His mother turns toward me. There is something in her eyes. For a second I think it is envy, the normal envy a mother feels for her son's chosen mate, and then I realize it is not envy. It is fear. She finds me terrifying. I am still staring

at her in shock when her eyes slide away. She busies herself with tearing at a piece of bread, which she then lays down on the plate.

I turn to look at Jake. He has missed it all. He is cutting into a piece of meat. He catches my eyes as he carries it to his lips.

'What?' he asks

'Nothing.'

I look down at my plate. She wants to rub me out. Like a pencil mark that has been made in error. She cannot know who or what I really am, but some instinct is driving her. Telling her I am not to be trusted. Not to be taken into her family.

The meal is a disaster. Both his mother and I hardly eat. As soon as Jake puts his knife and fork down, his mother turns to him. 'I need more ice. Will you get a bag from the freezer, Jake?'

'Sure.' Jake gets up and makes for the kitchen.

'Can you get it from the big freezer in the shed?' she says.

'Would you also like me to walk back very slowly?' he asks with a grin.

'That would be nice,' his mother replies, but there is no mischief in her voice. Only worry and trepidation.

As soon as the door closes she says, 'I've always preferred sketches to paintings. Paintings are closed, finished

293

things that hide layers of lies. Sketches are the bones of what will be. They are more honest. They haven't learned to lie. What do you prefer?'

'If we are truly talking about sketches and paintings, then I prefer paintings. I know the finished product is a series of accidents, but I appreciate that the grand design of life allows accidents to become beautiful.'

She frowns. 'I want to have grandchildren. I want them to think of me as the old woman who wears shawls and silly hats and reads tea leaves. Are you the woman to give me that?'

I swallow. 'Look, Jake and I have just met. It's too early. It's not on the cards.'

'What do you want from my son, then?'

I shift uncomfortably. 'Did you ask this of all women he brought home?'

'He has never brought a woman home before.'

My mouth drops open.

'You haven't answered my question.'

'I don't want anything from your son. We're just in a relationship.'

'Liar,' she says very softly.

'What did you just call me?'

'You heard. You are a dangerously manipulative woman, Miss Hart. And I am here to tell you that I will never allow you to break this family, or my son for that matter.'

EIGHTEEN

As we fly into Las Vegas airport, I look out of my cabin window, and the sparkling city appears almost magically from the miles of desert surrounding it. The heat outside the airport hits me like a wall. We walk quickly toward a gleaming purple SUV, which is waiting outside for us. It is wonderfully cool inside.

'Purple?' I ask with a laugh.

'It's the Hard Rock touch,' Jake says.

We are in Las Vegas for the weekend, because I have never been, and when I told Jake that, he said, 'Well, you haven't lived until you've been on the Strip.'

The journey to the Strip is only about fifteen minutes. I gaze at the infamous street with wide eyes. It is an over the top, glamorous fantasy playground, almost like a giant Hollywood movie set with its miniatures of the Sphinx, pyramids, the Statue of Liberty and the Eiffel Tower. I even take a photo of the M & M store to show my mother.

I wonder what she will make of it. She once told me a shocking thing about the gorgeous black torch performer Lena Horne, who was allowed to stay at The

Flamingo as long as she was not seen at the casino, restaurants or public areas. When she checked out, her bed sheets and towels were burned.

Over the massive, gold guitar door handles are the words: *When this house is rocking, don't bother knocking. Come on in.* And it really is rocking in there for Jake. There is no check-in for Jake and me. He is greeted by name by a smiling host and we are quickly and efficiently whisked past the awesome, fifty-five feet digital screen stretched behind the reception desk, straight to the elevator bank and up to the Provocateur penthouse suite.

The Provocateur suite is like no other hotel room I've been to.

We are greeted by walls covered in black vinyl embossed to look like crocodile skin in the foyer. In that deliberately darkened hallway there is a birdcage, large enough and strong enough to hold a grown man and a whipping cross! With handcuffs!

On our left, silhouettes of naked women start swaying provocatively in the shower as motion sensors pick up our movements. There can be no doubt that the design is fetish orientated and I turn to look at Jake.

Beyond the foyer are claret walls and sophisticated shiny black furniture and more dominatrix accessories. We are shown the heated plunge pool in the balcony and taken to the bedroom with three beds pushed together, presumably perfect for orgies. The other master bedroom has an enormous four-poster bed and a mirrored, trellised ceiling. The man shows us how to work the 3D projector system behind the bed to make it throw patterns and themes onto the walls.

At the flick of a button the shades come down, the lights dim and two women wantonly writhing are projected onto the bed. It is so over the top and creepy-crazy I start giggling. My laughter doesn't deter our host. We are taken to a secret vault full of toys, equipment and costumes for sex play.

When he is gone I go to stand by the ceiling-to-floor windows. The view is fabulous. Down below, the swimming pool is heaving with beautiful bodies on purple floats. I turn around to look at Jake.

'Like it?' he asks.

'Are you trying to tell me something Fifty Shades-ish?'

He laughs. 'No fucking way. I don't need to beat a woman to get my kicks. I just thought you'd enjoy this more than the Venetian. It's all Liberace style opulence, chocolate-covered strawberries and beluga caviar served by butlers with white gloves over there.'

'And you don't have to pay for any of this?'

He grins, at once boyish and delicious. 'Nope.'

'How come they treat you so good?'

He shrugs. 'My claim to fame is that I once lost a whole million at their baccarat table and they're hoping I'll repeat that lack of judgment,' he says dryly.

My eyes widen. 'One million? Dollars?'

'Yup. I used to be what they call a whale.'

'What's a whale?'

'At the lower end a high roller is someone who bets between a thousand to five thousand dollars a hand. A serious high roller would play upwards of five grand to about twenty, twenty-five thousand. A big high roller would spend between twenty-five and fifty thousand.' He stops and smiles. 'And then you have the whales. Whales start at seventy-five thousand dollars a hand.'

'And you were one of them?'

'I was. But now I only come two, maybe three times a year.'

'God!' It's hard for me to even think of anyone blowing that kind of money on the roll of a die.

'But I still get the eight o'clock reservation, the cabana, tickets for the best concerts in town, and... I get to be imaginative with my requests. So far the management has always said yes to everything I've asked for.'

'Wow! What kind of things are available?'

'Lunch on a yacht, a helicopter ride somewhere, a game of golf with Tiger Woods...'

'What have you asked for this time?'

He smiles slow and full of meaning. 'Lingerie. I have asked for the most expensive, most beautiful lingerie they can find.'

I can't help it, I flush hard. I can feel my cheeks flaming. 'You didn't.'

'I did. Go and have a look.'

For a few seconds I don't move. We just stare at each other. Then I turn around and go to the bedroom. At the door I stop and look around. He is watching me, his eyes unfathomable.

By the bedside I see the white box with a black design on it. I open it and it is full of whispers of baby blue lace: a half-cup bra, a thong, suspenders with white bows, and nude stockings. There is a card with a message to open the cupboard. I open the cupboard and gasp. A real cheongsam. Not the cheap thing that looks more like a Hong Kong waitress's uniform and with a dirty slit that runs all the way up to the crotch like I wore at the club, but the softest, most beautiful, pure white Chinese silk brocade. I run my fingers over the pretty little blue flowers. My grandmother would love this. I turn around and Jake is standing in the doorway.

'It is so very, very beautiful,' I whisper. I am so touched my voice shakes.

'Good. You can wear them all tonight.'

'Thank you.'

His eyes darken. 'Thank me later.'

'You look beautiful,' he tells me that night.

'So do you,' I say.

And he does. He looks good enough to eat. He is wearing a perfectly fitted black suit that totally showcases his great physique, an oyster gray silk shirt that is almost translucent, and polished black shoes. I have never seen him so subdued in his color scheme.

We go for an early dinner at Shanghai Lily. The food is exquisite. The last time I ate lobster that good I was in Singapore with my grandparents. There is even gold leaf on the food to gladden the hearts of the Asian high rollers since gold is considered a good luck charm.

We end up at the Shadow for drinks. I gaze in amazement at the giant backlit

screens with the enlarged shadow of a woman dancing behind each one. It looks different from anything I have seen.

I drink a green cocktail and watch the bartenders, who are actually performers who throw bottles up into the air and catch those their colleagues have thrown. The atmosphere is young, fun and totally hip, and I turn my head, smiling, and catch Jake looking at me. The smile dies on my lips. His eyes are smoldering.

'What is it?' I ask.

His hand slides into the slit in my dress and up my thighs, parting them. 'I've always wanted to finger fuck you under a table in a public place.' One finger rubs suggestively against the string of my thong. He drops his voice to a whisper. 'Maybe because you won't be able to scream when you come, because everyone is watching.'

The green cocktail sings longingly in my veins as wetness seeps between my legs. My clit swells, begging for his touch. I put my drink down, suddenly daring and uninhibited. 'Knock yourself out,' I choke.

With a sensual growl he inserts one long finger into me.

I gasp.

His teeth flash in the dimness. 'Look at you. Always so wet and hot,' he says

moving his finger in and out of me. 'Open your legs wider,' he invites, sliding the thumb of his other hand into my mouth. I catch it between my teeth and suck it. His thumb strokes in circles around my clit while his fingers curl inside me.

'We could get thrown out for this,' he whispers.

I release his thumb, my eyes glancing around furtively. It's dark and no one is looking. 'They wouldn't throw a whale out,' I choke.

'No, I guess not.'

'It will be a stern warning, though,' I mutter, wriggling and rubbing myself against his hand, loving the feel of his fingers inside me, his thumb working my clit.

'Damn, I love how filthy and greedy you are. How you'd let me do *anything* with you.'

He plunges his fingers deeper in and my muscles start clenching around them. 'I can't wait to get back to our room and see my big cock disappear between your sweet lips until I am balls deep in your mouth. And then I'd like to slide that saliva soaked cock, every fucking inch of it, into your poor little pussy. I am going to stretch her and fuck her until cum shoots out of her. And then I'm gonna suck her as she drips.'

'Oh Fuck! I'm coming,' I warn in a strangled gasp.

'Turn and look at me.'

I turn and look at him, my eyes wide, my face struggling to remain normal. Then the climax rips through me and I clench my teeth and shudder against his hand in an effort not to scream.

Afterwards, he puts his fingers into my mouth and makes me suck them.

NINETEEN

It is eleven o'clock on Saturday night, the lights are flashy, the rock ephemera is hip, and the gamblers are rocking, when we make our way through the casino toward the high limit gaming area called the Peacock Lounge, where once Jimi Hendrix's peacock vest was hung.

The high limit gaming area is a circular elevated platform off the main floor. It has its own cage and bar. It has obviously been arranged beforehand, so a roulette table has been wheeled in especially for Jake.

I look at Jake. 'Albert Einstein once said, "No one can win at roulette unless he steals money from the table while no one is looking."'

'If you look at roulette through the language of physics, then it is the universe in miniature, a whirling, glittering mix of forces all playing out their elegant tiny dances.'

'Very poetic.'

The croupier is an Asian girl. She smiles and nods. A man in a suit brings a tray of really cool psychedelic-colored chips and leaves them on the table in front of Jake.

Jake looks at them and smiles his thanks. He pushes five chips toward me. The chips have purple orange, yellow and green in them. Each one says five grand on it.

'I can't gamble this much money. I'll be devastated if I lose,' I say pushing the money back toward him.

He laughs and pushes it back to me. 'Keep it for now. Give it back to me later if you don't use it.'

He places a chip on Red and a chip on Even. The croupier starts rolling the wheel. The ivory ball spins on the outer ring. It leaves the outer track. No more bets.

'Thirty-three black,' she calls.

She places a marker on the 33 Black square and sweeps away his money. I swallow. Wow! That was ten thousand dollars gone in just seconds. When I look at him, his face is impassive.

This time he puts two chips on Red and two on Odd. The ball stops on 23 Red. I take a deep breath. He has won twenty thousand. People have begun to gather behind us to watch.

Jake repeats the same sequence and wins again.

A large suited man walks toward our table and stands unobtrusively at the side of it. His eyes are alert and watchful. Now more people come to watch. This time Jake puts five chips on Black and five on Even. A man puts his two chips next to Jake's.

The wheel turns—8 Black.

He has won a hundred thousand. I place my hand on his. I know how casinos work. The smart player never stays. The longer you stay, the more unlikely you will walk away with anything. 'Shouldn't you stop now? You've won so much.'

He looks at me, a strange expression on his face. 'Remember what I told you, Lil? I'm lucky. I'm always lucky.'

He puts the entire winnings, a hundred thousand dollars, on 34 Red. The crowd behind us gasps. It's straight up betting. Pays thirty-five to one but the chances of winning are so small.

I touch his sleeve, my eyes confused. I can't understand what he is up to. Why abandon his earlier winning and more careful strategy? 'Why?'

'Lucky at games and unlucky in love. If I win then I am unlucky in love and if I lose it means I am lucky in love. What do you say, Lily? Is a hundred thousand dollars worth it?'

The woman spins the wheel. I stare at the wheel in bewilderment. Then I put my chips behind his.

'No more bets,' the woman says.

I look at his face and he is staring at me, totally unperturbed. He has no interest in the outcome of his bet. There is a disappointed hush. Hazily, I hear the words, 'Fourteen Red.' All the chips are swept away.

'They don't call it The Strip for nothing,' he murmurs. He is strangely calm.

He slips his hand into his pocket and comes up with a small velvet box. I stare at it in shock. He opens the box.

A huge, glittering diamond solitaire stares back at me. I am shaken out of my daze by a commotion at my side. I lift my head and see the award-winning Blue Man Group! Their shiny blue painted heads bob and they widen their eyes and start to turn placards around that read:

Will
You
Marry
Me,
Lily
Hart?

My mouth drops open. The people around us 'Oh,' and 'Ah.' What the hell is going on? The whole thing is so unreal I almost can't believe my eyes. I glance at Jake and he is grinning at me. The men start pantomiming beating hearts in their own inimitable way. They produce a bottle of Cristal champagne and pop that open. Two flutes appear from somewhere and get filled. One is handed to me. Utterly bemused I take it and turn toward Jake. My mind is a total blank.

'Will you?' Jake asks softly.

'Was this your high roller request?' I whisper.

'Part of it. It's not finished yet.'

My brain can't get into gear. The cocktails have made it sluggish. It has all happened so fast. I don't know what I would have done in different circumstances, but with no time for thought or reflection, this moment seems like the most beautiful thing anyone has ever done for me. It is the most romantic and certainly the most dramatic. And all these people are waiting for me to say yes.

Caught in the moment my voice is a whisper. 'Yes. Yes, I will.'

With a triumphant smile he slips the ring onto my finger. It is a perfect fit and the crowd starts clapping and congratulating us.

'Come,' he says, and we go out to the pool area. It has been turned into a magical wonderland full of flowers, balloons and lights. There is an altar and a priest is waiting for us.

'What the hell?' People are clapping, laughing, and cheering us on.

'Feel like becoming my wife tonight?'

'Tonight?' I squeak. 'It's nearly midnight.'

'Why not? This is Las Vegas—the land of dreams and twenty-four hour marriage ceremonies.'

I suddenly remember Mills and what he would say. Shit. What the fuck am I doing? This is not part of the plan. A feeling of uneasiness slithers down my spine, cold and restless. I want to say, 'We should wait. This is all too fast,' but I am unable to. He has gone to so much trouble and everyone is looking at me with a mixture of envy and awe. I look up at him.

A warm gust of wind ripples through his hair, as if it is teasing fingers. He looks down at me, reckless and intense. I stare at him, mesmerized. He is as gorgeous as a technicolor dream. I am the luckiest girl here.

I open my mouth and words tumble out. 'Yes, I'll marry you.'

With a smile the priest announces, 'You may kiss your bride.'

As if in a dream I watch Jake drift closer, his eyes flashing, triumphant. Daring me? Daring me to what? Then I feel his mouth come down on me and drown out every thought in my head. My legs go weak. I'm married. I'm married

to Jake Eden. Without my parents or grandmother. A sharp guilt pierces me.

What the hell have I done?

But everybody is shouting. There is glitter and noise. A photographer and videographer appear. Hotel staff are congratulating us. And there is a pink cake to cut. A small piece is put into my mouth. It feels soft, but I don't taste it. It must have been sweet.

Then Jake is pulling me by the hand. He pulls me into the elevator. I look up at him, still dazed, unable to believe: I'm married. We just got married. In the confines of the lift I can't look into his eyes. I look down at my ring. Wow! I'm married. I'm *really* married. A tendril of happiness touches my heart.

We start kissing in the lift. He pulls me out and we stumble through the doors, our lips glued. Suddenly he breaks away and, putting his hand under my knees, lifts me up.

'What are you doing?'

'Carrying you over the threshold.'

I laugh. Who would ever have thought I could be so carefree and happy again? He carries me past that dim foyer and puts me down in the living room with its scarlet walls.

'Show me what's underneath the dress, Mrs. Eden.'

I am suddenly shy. I bite my lip. He propels me to the middle of the room

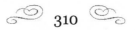

and drops himself onto the black couch. He leans back, his legs wide open, relaxed, wanting a show.

I undo the clasp on the high neck and pull down the zip. The dress shimmers all the way down to the floor, leaving me standing in my underwear, suspenders, stockings and high heels. I step away from my dress and slowly sway up to him. Once in front of him I stand with my legs apart. He lets his gaze travel slowly over my body.

'Turn around and show me your bum,' he says.

Intoxicated by the hunger in his eyes, I turn around and jut my bottom out provocatively. I look back and see his eyes rush to my crotch where the pale blue string of my thong is caught between my sex lips. Without removing his eyes from me, he takes his jacket off and pulls his shirt out of his trousers.

I turn back around and, with my hands behind my back, fiddle with my bra strap, while I slide my tongue over my bottom lip. I know that always drives him crazy.

'Go on,' he mutters, unbuttoning his shirt.

I take the bra off.

'Jesus, you're so fucking sexy.' The pupils of his eyes are dilated and huge.

'What do you want off next?' I sound all breathy and bimbo-ish.

'That bit of string stuck to your pussy.'
I laugh giddily.

His expression doesn't change. He stares as if bewitched. I used to wonder what it would be like to be with someone who made me feel so desired, so wanted, so special. Now I know. I don't know what the future holds. But it can never take this moment away from me.

I take it off and holding it in my hand, scandalize myself by bringing it to my nose and smelling the string.

He catches his breath and standing up steps out of his trousers and boxers. He runs his hand along the curve of my buttocks. My skin burns faintly at his touch.

'So slender,' he murmurs, the sound warm and intimate. Then he bends down and swipes his velvety tongue slowly and tantalizingly along the crack. 'And as sweet as sin,' he whispers. He moves upwards, flicks his tongue on the rim of my ear, catches the lobe between his teeth, and suddenly nips me. My stomach curls and I moan.

He catches my waist and spins me around, his gaze adoring. I slide my wrists around his neck and press my body invitingly against his hardness. I am desperate to feel my breasts crushed against the dark hair on his chest and his hot, wet mouth on them. I want his hands to spread my open thighs and gorge himself on the swollen whorls of flesh there.

But he doesn't.

Instead, he pulls me toward the ceiling-to-floor windows. My palms connect with the cold surface and I see the panoramic view of the city glittering with neon lights surrounded by miles of dark desert. I feel him tilt my hips up toward him, and enter me in a fierce thrust. And I see my shining reflection open its mouth in a startled gasp.

'You like it rough?'

'Yes.'

He thrusts again, harder. 'Like this?'

'Yes,' I gasp.

I feel him pull apart my buttocks and the next thrust is so hard and so deep that my body jerks like a puppet. My eyes swivel upwards, dimly noticing the stars like jewels in the soft blackness of the night sky. A thought hits me: All that I need is to be his. Like this. Forever.

'Nobody has taken you so hard before, have they?'

'No.'

'Nobody ever will again, will they?'

'No,' I moan.

'Because this is all mine. I own all of this now, don't I?'

'Yes, yes, yes.'

His finger drums relentlessly at the side of my clit. The sensation causes a rush of aching warmth to start flooding

my body. He keeps up the thrusts and the drumming until I explode and splinter into a thousand pieces. I am slumped against the glass when I feel him climax. He comes with a fierce bark of humorless laughter.

I rest against the glass panting, slowly returning.

'Do you know,' he whispers close to my ear, his voice sensation soaked, lazy. 'I dreamed about you.'

'Really,' I murmur. I am pleasantly satiated. I want to keep him inside me forever.

'Don't you want to know what I dreamed?'

'What did you dream?' My voice is lazy, playful.

'We went out, we had dinner, we had sex... And then you betrayed me.'

I freeze, the blood congealing in my veins. He saw me coming!

In the glass I see his face gleaming dimly, as insubstantial as a ghost. It is a moment so simple, but so heightened because of that very simplicity. Life rarely offers such moments of profound clarity. It is as if I have trained for years for this moment. I see its preciousness glittering like a cornered rat's eyes. Kill or be killed. Hesitating is to make the second choice.

I whisk around, eyes wide, clumsy and unsteady in my heels.

 314

His face is tight as a carved marble bust. The glass behind my back is shockingly cold and the silence between us is leaden. Suddenly I feel the way Eve must have felt, so naked, so exposed, and so *fucking* guilty.

He stands a foot away from me, touching distance, and simply looks at me. As if he is looking at a piece of modern art and trying to figure out what the artist intended to say with his senseless splashes of color. I try to imagine what he must be seeing.

After you cut all the bullshit about making the world a safer place and my gnawing shame that I was not there for Luke when he needed me, what is left? A sad, lonely, despicable bitch, who tried to use her body to get some information and failed miserably.

I open my mouth and, honestly, I don't know what I was planning to say, but he lays a silencing finger across my lips.

'Don't lie, baby,' he advises softly.

I shake my head. I can feel the tears gathering at the backs of my eyes. I blink hard and fast. He takes his hand away.

'Did you tell them about the sixteenth?'

Dismay curves my spine. I close my eyes and nod.

I hear him sigh softly.

I open my eyes and he is looking at me with an expression so sad that I want to press my body against his and hold him, but I can't. I couldn't bear it if he pushed me away. God! It had seemed so real only a moment ago and yet it was all only a mirage. I feel my body trembling.

'When did you find out?' My voice is just a string.

'Maybe I always knew. I just didn't want to believe it.'

'How?' A part of me wants to know where I went wrong.

One corner of his lips twists. 'Everything about you was off. You were too clean to be a runaway. And a runaway who has never let a man come inside her before? And there is one more thing that you might want to reconsider before you go back to being an undercover asset. You talk in your sleep.'

'I do?' I say hoarsely.

'That time when you were attacked you said, "Get Crystal Jake." I knew then for sure. No one calls me that anymore.'

'So you admit dealing in drugs?'

He frowns. 'How have I just admitted to dealing in drugs?'

'Crystal Jake because you were selling crystal meth.'

'Is that what they told you?' He grasped his crystal chain and tugged hard at it. It broke, sending sparkling crystals flying across the room, hitting the floor. With his other hand he took my hand, opened my palm, put in what was left in his fist and closed my hand. 'That is why I was called Crystal Jake. I have *never* sold hard drugs.'

My gaze moves from my closed fist up to his eyes. I don't know whether to believe him, but he has never lied to me, and it is true that the whole time I have been with him I have not seen any evidence of drug usage or dealing either at Eden or on a personal level.

I stare at him as I have never seen him before. As the man I am in love with. All this while I have been pretending—to him and to myself—that I'm not. But I love him. I love this gangster who seems more honest and sincere than a priest. Other than the bed covered in used money I have no evidence that he is a gangster anyway.

He walks away from me and begins to dress. I stand at the glass, naked and frozen, all kinds of thoughts churning through my mind. He comes back fully dressed and looks at me. There is contempt in his eyes.

'Why did you marry me if you knew?'

'So that no one will be able to force you to testify against me. If you do, it will be because you want to.'

My mouth drops open. For some reason his answer is painful on a shocking level. 'How could you marry me for that reason?'

'How could you show me your naked body and keep your heart covered? Tell them the next time they want another swipe at me it might be an idea not to send such a rookie.' He looks at me with hard, derisive eyes. 'Enjoy your wedding night, Mrs. Eden.'

Oh
The damage is done
So I guess I be leavin'
—Cry me a River,
Justin Timberlake

TWENTY

For a long time I stand staring at the closed door. A part of me is horrified, but a part of me that I have hidden for so long is strangely elated that the lie is finally out in the open. I don't have to pretend anymore. Nude, I walk to the fully stocked bar. I open a bottle of whiskey and drink it straight from the bottle. It glugs down my throat, burning all the way down. I cough and pat my chest. The sound is loud in the empty suite.

Tears press against my eyelids. I feel alone, helpless, and so incredibly lost. I have failed miserably. And I have only myself to blame. I pick up the cheongsam from the floor, and carefully hang it in the closet. It is my wedding dress. I let my fingers skim the silky material one last time. The chambermaid will find it. It will be a nice treat for her. Then I go into the bathroom and, avoiding my reflection, dress in my own clothes.

Then I sit on the bed and wait for him. I am convinced he will come back through the door. He could not have just walked out on me. But an hour later I know he is not coming back. Reality hits. The truth is like switching on a light. All this time I had thought my eyes were accustomed to the dark. I had made out shapes from the shadows and guessed their names.

But it was a lie.

He knew I was an undercover cop the whole time and he was only pretending. Everything we had was a lie. Maybe the lust was real, but what is lust but dust without love? All that time he knew. I think of all the people and the planning that must have gone into hiring The Blue Man Group, the lavish wedding. He had lost all that money on purpose. To keep the invisible balance ledger between him and the casino straight.

The breath comes out of me in a rush. Now I understand why he asked for this particular suite. The Provocateur suite.

The message was there for me to see. Only I was too proud of my own ability to deceive and too blinded by my own feelings. I feel tears prickling at the backs of my eyes. No, I won't give in now. I know what happens when I give in to grief. It takes over. I become a total wreck. No more introspection. I can't stay here anymore.

My instructions are very clear in the event that my cover is ever blown.

I pick up the phone, make flight reservations. Then I pack my bag quickly and with little fuss. There is not much to pack, anyway. I open my purse and take out the black plastic chip. Worthless here, but worth ten thousand dollars at Eden.

I remember that sweltering night as if it happened yesterday. How exciting it had all been then. How naïve I was to give in to temptation and not think it would scar me for life. I put the chip on the pillow on his side of the bed. I don't know why I bother after the cavalier way he lost all that money in the casino earlier, but I know I can't keep it. *At the end of the operation you will ditch all the physical trappings of your undercover alter ego, the hair, the clothes, the people you have befriended, and return to your own normal world.*

Then I go out to the lounge to sit and wait. I know I am a wreck waiting to happen, but at this moment I feel strangely detached and calm. It is simple, I tell myself. My cover is blown. I am not the first undercover cop it has happened to. It has happened many times. I will simply report back and they will assign me somewhere else. Somewhere I can go to lick my wounds. Where there won't be a Jake Eden I will fall in love with and suffer over.

I look at the time. I call reception and order a cab. In thirty minutes the cab will arrive and take me to the airport. I will be fine. Of course I will be fine.

A small voice says, 'Don't run away. Stay. Fight for your man.'

But he is not my man. He is nobody's man. He was pretending the whole time. I have been silly. I allowed myself to fall in love. It is not so despicable. Other cops have done it. Over the course of years of being undercover some have married their targets and even had children with them. I am not so despicable.

I stand. I can't stay in this room any longer. I will wait in reception downstairs. I pick up my luggage, take one last look at the opulence around me, and walk resolutely to the door.

I open it and stop dead in my tracks. My luggage falls from my disbelieving hands.

Jake Eden is sitting sprawled out in the corridor. His back is resting against the opposite wall and beside him is an empty bottle of Scotch. He has another in his right hand, which is already half empty. He looks up, trying to hold his lids open.

'Leaving so soon?' he slurs.

Last part out sooner than you think... ☺

CRYSTAL Lake

Book 3

BOOK 3

ONE

Jake

"Whoever fights monsters should see to it that in the process he does not become a monster. And if you gaze long enough into an abyss, the abyss will gaze back into you."

—Friedrich Nietzsche

Not many people end up sitting sprawled and dead drunk in the corridor outside their suite in a Vegas hotel. Waiting for the door to open and desperately wanting it not to. I guess I am what Edna O'Brien meant when she described the Irish character as 'maimed, stark and misshapen, but ferociously tenacious.'

In my maudlin state I contemplate a mysterious madness. If it is true that your soul alone keeps the map of your destiny, then the geography of my destiny to this expensive corridor must have been known to the highest and most hidden part of me even while I was a destitute boy. A boy who ran barefoot on grassy, sunlit meadows, visited horse fairs, and watched with hungry eyes but never touched the other traveler girls.

I have memories of digging up armfuls of carrots and potatoes, eating soda bread crusts, and dressing in rags and cast-offs even though I was the oldest. One Christmas my mother paid ten pounds for a pair of stained maroon velvet curtains in a charity shop. She cut them up and sewed all her three boys identical trousers and my sister a dress. My sister was something beautiful even then, and, of course, the dress looked gorgeous on her. I had to knock a boy down after church for staring so lustfully at her. 'Unfortunately' for me, one day after Christmas I caught my new curtain trousers on a nail and tore them so badly they were unusable even as a pair of shorts. Within a week both my brothers had 'accidentally' and irreparably ruined theirs, too.

As children we didn't know we were dirt poor because my father was a compulsive gambler. Cards, dogs, horses, sports, fights, dice. Anything that he deemed required some form of skill he found irresistible. Once he started he didn't know how to stop. Sometimes he took me with him and I used to sit big-eyed and watch him. He was my hero. What the fuck—maybe he still is.

Patrick Eden was special. While the rest of the world was telling me that the Irish were thick—'they'd bring a fork if it rained soup'—my father had a totally different philosophy.

'There are only two kinds of people in the world, my boy,' he said often and with cheerful certainty, a proud finger raised in the air, 'the Irish and those who wish they were.'

Obviously with such a philosophy he was absolutely convinced that he was a winner. The other gamblers were banking on luck, and he alone had found an infallible technique to beat the odds. And when he was winning it did seem that way. I can't forget what he was like when the pile of money in front of him was growing. Cocky? Oh! You never saw anything like my dad when he was winning. A larger than life character he was. Even now the memory brings a warm glow to my heart.

So I bought the lie. I was young and I wanted to believe. Even when the inevitable 'losing streak' struck, his confidence remained invincible. His bets became bigger, sometimes doubling. Forget doubling—every penny ended up on the table. He borrowed money from anyone who was fool enough to lend it.

This was the time desperation ruled: nothing was sacred. Everything could go into the pot. His wife. His sons. His daughter. Anything. Because he was that cocksure that a losing streak always preceded a big win. On the other side Lady Luck was waiting with open arms. He was the big winner. All he had to do was believe in himself. So he readied for the losing streak to end by betting heavily on long shots.

And then he lost.

The shock might have stopped another man in his tracks, but not my father. At that point there was no yarn too outrageous, no lie that was beneath him. He *had to* recoup his losses. That was when he began to embezzle from the bosses. That period didn't last long.

They are bosses because they are one step ahead of everyone else.

One day he was patting me on the back, looking me in the eye and boasting about a non-existent big win on the dogs, and the next day I was being held back by two of Saul's heavies while another slit my father's throat from ear to ear. I was so shocked I went limp. I just stood and watched the blood gushing out of his severed arteries. It squirted out so far I was covered in it.

That moment can be likened to when a great tree is felled. The air becomes barren. A shocked silence ensues. The forest knows another one of its guardians has been murdered. The savagery of the waste stuns it.

My soul, dependent upon his nurture, wizened and shrank even as my mind sharpened. I watched the radiance and the light die out of his bright eyes. How they went from wide-eyed shock to nothingness. I saw with hurtful clarity all the words unsaid, the potential lost, and the promises missed. Nothing would ever be the same again. His last whisper, a gargling, unintelligible sound, was that of someone on his way to a dark, cold space.

'What do you want to do, tinker boy? Are you going to work the debt off or is your sister going to do it on her back?'

The question had only one right answer.

TWO

Jake

The next phase of my life has only one word to describe it. Saul. Before that afternoon when he made me watch his men slaughter my father like a farm animal, I had only seen him twice and spoken briefly only once. I had made a mental note: mean, dead eyes disguised by superficial charm. I was a big lad even then and I knew he always wanted me to work for him. It was only my father that had stood in the way.

What can I tell you about Saul Schitt?

Pay your fucking debts.

He hated unpaid debts. And I hated him.

I hated working for Crocodile Saul. I hated the ugly, unconscionable, inhumane things I was forced to do. And I hated the coldness that was slowly seeping into my heart. I cannot describe how it destroyed my soul to be his enforcer dog. For four fucking years I paid off my father's supposed debt on an interest rate that was calculated daily. Do you get the picture of my hatred?

I was nineteen when the debt was finally deemed paid. I went to his house.

'The debt's paid and I want out,' I said.

'You've been good to me. I want to do something for you in return,' he rasped.

When Saul wanted to do something for you, you didn't refuse. Warily, I accepted his invitation to go to Vegas with him. I had never been anywhere outside England. To me Vegas was not a destination, it was a glittering, glamorous fantasy playground that rose from the heat of the desert like a mirage. I loved it. I loved the burning heat, I loved the American accent and I fucking loved the Strip.

He checked us into the Venetian. It was amazing, I had never seen anything like it, with lofty, beautifully painted ceilings. It was my Sistine Chapel. And, shit, you should have seen the way they treated Mr. Schitt. Like he was royalty. The king of Schittland. He got the works. *Nothing* was too much trouble. They even had his favorite, a fucking key lime pie, waiting in the penthouse suite's fridge. King Schitt opened a line of credit for me. Fifty thousand dollars.

'My gift,' he said with the smiling generosity of a godfather.

In that rarefied air of unmatched opulence I became royalty too. I was so young, so naïve, it all went to my head. That Irish saying knocked on my door—what would a cat's son do but kill a mouse? I sat at the baccarat table. My father with his throat cut and blood gushing out invited, 'Have a seat, my son. There are only two kinds of people, my boy, the Irish and those who wish they were.' In a daze I sat. It turned out I was my father's son, after all.

God! How fast I lost that fifty thousand.

As if by magic Saul was by my side, smiling his benign crocodile grin. 'No problems. Extend his credit to two hundred thousand.'

I looked at my father's murderer, and you know what? At that moment, I just wanted the credit. With unutterable desperation I wanted the dirty money of that disgusting man so I could continue gambling. Like my father.

Then the strangest thing happened. I heard my mother's voice say clearly in my head, 'Even what he thinks he has shall be taken away from him.'

Luke 8: 16–18, The lesson of the lamp.

And it was like someone had flicked a switch in my head. I stood up and walked away from that table. I could feel Saul's eyes on my back, one of his men calling me back, but I was in a rage. With my father, with myself and with Saul. He had taken me and molded me into a man with vices. A man he could control.

I walked for more than an hour, without knowing where I was going, just walking in a straight line, passing dangerous, low rent areas, hardly seeing anyone, and looking for buildings in the distance.

At some point I burst open the double doors of a bar that advertised cold beers and cocktails. It was dark and seedy inside. So grimy you didn't want to touch anything. The locals turned to look at me. Whoa! Unfriendly. This was not the Strip. Tourists unwelcome.

But I was already in and I wanted a drink. And no one was stopping me. As Saul would say, What's wrong with my fucking money? One drink and I'm out of here, I thought. I walked up to the bar and ordered me a whiskey.

The bartender, a surly guy with spiky hair, hesitated and then looked at the breadth of my shoulders and that foul light in my eyes and thought better of it. He went in search of a bottle while I looked around the bar. The exits were close enough. I let my eyes wander restlessly into the darkness. I had found out something ugly about myself.

From the shadows a woman of mixed descent got up from a chair. Ordinary

 334

looking. Black hair, brown eyes, skin like chocolate, and the kind of plump lips you know are going to be so soft when your teeth nip into them. I felt nothing. Not even curiosity about what she could be like in bed. The whiskey hit the bar surface. The measures are larger in America, but I swallowed it in one gulp, threw a note on the table, and turned to go. It was the wrong place, wrong time. The exit was ten steps away.

I must have taken five when she started singing, that ordinary brown girl. And fuck me, I froze in my tracks. I could not move.

She had the voice of a siren, you know, those mythical creatures from the Greek fables who lured sailors to their death. As if in slow motion I turned back and looked again at her.

She was looking right at me. She was singing to me. There was nothing I could do. I was like a rat mesmerized by a cobra. From the roots of my hair to the tips of my nails I tingled with her magic. I thought—I was only nineteen, don't forget—that I was going to spontaneously combust. The chemistry was that strong. How could someone with her talent be singing in a joint like this? She should have been up there with Beyoncé and Madonna.

Afterwards, she came over to me. She almost had a smile on her face.

'Buy me drink?' she said.

The prosaic request shocked me. I had to beat down a hysterical desire to laugh. That's it? That's what you want from a man you have stunned to a slow faint?

'What do you want?' I asked.

'Champagne,' she said daringly, but her underbelly was soft.

Did a place like this even carry champagne? 'Sure,' I said.

It came then. Her first real smile. 'I knew you were good for it.'

Her name was Indigo and I felt for her. Singing in that dive, for men who wouldn't know talent if it hit them with a wet fish. I got her their best bottle, piss water as it turned out, and watched her get drunk on it. I was dizzy for her and I had a packet of condoms burning a hole in my pocket.

She lived within walking distance, so we went back to her place. The building was dark. Her apartment was at the far side. Somewhere in the gloom I could hear people talking in low voices. I gripped the Beretta in my waistband, but it didn't cross my mind to turn around and walk away. I was that wired on lust.

Her skin was smooth. She was generous. I was generous. Things got hot. Real hot. We fucked to the sound of spilling dustbins in the alley under her window. I don't know how many times. Maybe nine, maybe ten. I couldn't get enough of her. Inside her body I forgot about Saul. And his poison.

During the night it started to rain. Droplets drummed on the window.

'I haven't felt rain since I got to Vegas,' she said.

She got out of bed and went to look at the rain. You could see the drops shine silver where the streetlight illuminated them. She placed her palms and then her forehead on the cool glass. At that moment she seemed lost and sad, as if life had cheated her. Then she opened the window and allowed the rain to come into the room. She laughed as the drops hit her naked skin. She came back to me wetter and wilder. I was wrong. Life could never cheat this woman.

In the morning I lit two cigarettes and passed one to her. She was actually younger and far more beautiful without all that gunk on her face.

'I love your accent,' she said.

'Yeah?'

'Yeah. Where you from?'

'England.'

'Where Princess Diana came from?'

'Exactly.'

'So what were you doing in that bar?'

I shrugged. 'I just wandered into it by accident.'

She giggled. 'I figured you for a guy who gets on all the best guest lists and stays in one of those fancy casino hotels

with white leather sofas and purple and blue lighting.'

'What makes you think that?' I was curious. She glanced at the leather trousers she had peeled off me last night. 'You've got ambition. It's in your eyes. Even in the dark, I saw it. You'll be as rich as Croesus, one day. You just wait and see.'

I felt a rush of sympathy for her. She'd never be rich or famous the way she was going. 'Listen, you have a truly beautiful voice, way better than Beyoncé. You should record a music demo and send it to some record companies.'

'Now no one after lighting a lamp covers it over with a container, or puts it under a bed; but he puts it on a lampstand, that those who come in may see the light.'

And I froze in astonishment. No fucking way. It could not be a coincidence. If I had turned left when I exited the casino. If I had gone into the bar before this one. If I had left as soon as I saw the state of the bar. If she had not at that moment stood up to sing. I would not be lying here listening to *Luke 8: 16–18, The lesson of the lamp.*

'What are you talking about?' I croaked.

'The gates to the entertainment industry will only open for those who are willing to sell their souls in exchange for

wealth and social admiration. I'm a spiritual person. I will never allow myself to be an industry puppet flashing the one-eye symbol, or making horns and pyramids and the six-six-six symbols with my hands and fingers at every photo opportunity and in every video I make. Better for my lamp to shine its light honestly in that dive you found me in last night than have it covered by the sick and the depraved.'

I looked at her and I did not see a one-night stand, a woman I had no intention of ever seeing again. She was glowing with inner beauty. I saw only the truth of the quote—All god's angels come to us disguised.

When I got back to the hotel Saul was waiting for me. His gift had morphed into a loan. I now owed him fifty thousand dollars plus interest. What did I expect? Saul Schitt hangs a black cloth over every lamp he sees.

I went back to England and for six months I laid my plans down, carefully, meticulously. I took advantage of the fact that though Saul trusted no one, other than maybe his mother, he had made the mistake of underestimating me. He thought I was a sapling clinging to his mighty branches. He paid for his error dearly. I avenged my father's death in the gangster's way.

An eye for an eye. A life for a life.

For four years I had sat quietly in the background and absorbed the workings of Saul's little empire. No one knew it better than I. So I was confident I could take it. The sycophants never saw me coming. I behaved in the only way the power structure understood. Extreme violence. I exerted my will, established myself as top dog, and quickly took control.

But I desired a different organization.

One of the first things I did was sit down with BJ Pilkington and his father. Our families were in a generational feud, and they were not happy to be drawing up territories with me, but even they understood that I meant business. Ruthlessly I trimmed and cleaned up the organization. There would be no more dealing in class A drugs, no more human trafficking, no more prostitution, and no more loan sharking.

I reduced the rate but kept the protection racket going since abandoning it would have created a dangerous power vacuum. Besides, we would need it for the gambling dens and the clubs. I kept the contraband going too, because I'm a gypsy after all, and I have an aversion to paying taxes. Plus I'm really, really good at it.

I found myself a genius of an accountant and I started buying up properties in the most sought after areas of London through perfectly legal shell companies. And whenever possible I invested in Internet start-ups. Only two out of every twenty ventures were successful, but they were cheap to get into, they were great for washing dirty money, and when they were successful the rewards were astronomical. My best venture I sold for forty million.

Two years after that fateful trip I went back to Vegas to look for Indigo. I was the rich man she had predicted. I felt nothing for her but pure gratitude. I wanted to set her up so she could sing her songs without being a puppet of the industry. This time I didn't walk. I was driven in a limo to that bar. The sign still proclaimed cold beers, but a different barman served me.

I described her.

'Sorry, man. We've never had a singer here as far as I know. And I've been here near a year now,' he said.

Ah, Indigo. I only want to give you what you deserve: FAME, FAME, FAME.

I tried looking for her through various detective agencies, but she had left nothing but a stage name. And that was too cold a trail to follow even for the best money. In the end I had to give up. She was not meant to be found.

I thought I'd never see an angel again in my life. Until the day I came down a set of steps in my brother's club and saw

Lily Hart. Here was another woman to change my life.

If she is not an angel then she is the devil in disguise.

-Just gonna stand there and watch me
cry,
But that's alright
Because I love the way you lie
I just love the way you lie—

THREE

Lily

For a few seconds I simply stare at him in shock. It's a sight I never thought I'd see. The great Jake Eden wasted and lolling on the floor of a hotel corridor. He attempts to straighten himself by pushing his palms to the floor and fails. There is something boyish and endearing in his futile attempt. Resting on his elbows he looks up at me and wriggles an eyebrow.

'There's a whole closet of sex toys we haven't tried yet,' he says and grins seductively.

I shake my head in a disbelieving daze. 'I've booked a cab. I have to go,' I whisper.

He blinks up at me. 'I thought you wanted to see me in handcuffs.'

'I don't,' I reply tightly.

'Could have fooled me.' His voice is rolling and mellow.

I take two steps forward and crouch in front of him. His breath reeks of alcohol and his eyes are glazed. 'Well, you're wrong,' I say softly.

'No? Well, I'd like to cuff you to my bed.' His hand comes up and strokes my face clumsily. 'I don't care if you're a cop, Lily. I just want you to stay.'

The graceless, unrehearsed gesture throws me. Oh God! How much I want to stay. But I have to leave. He is intoxicated and does not know what he is saying. I still remember the cold look in his eyes before he closed the door in the early hours of the morning and went away leaving me naked and frighteningly alone.

Confused and conflicted, I stand up. To put some distance between us I take a step back and cross my hands over my waist.

His right hand comes out to curve around my ankle. He slides his hand up my leg. 'Such soft skin. Like a baby,' he croons.

I have to make my exit, but I can't leave him in the corridor in this state. I have to get him into the room before I go.

'Can you stand?' I ask him.

'I was born standing.'

He is amusing in this state, but my cab will arrive in about thirty minutes. I reach down, take his hand and try to heave him up, but he is a dead weight. I sink down next to him.

'Come on, Jake, help me. We have to get you inside the room.'

345

He laughs carelessly. 'Take your panties off.'

'Stop it, Jake.'

'Just take them off and stand over me with your legs spread so I can look up your skirt into that delicious velvet darkness.'

'I'm not doing that.'

'Then I'm not going into the room,' he says, his jaw set into a stubborn line.

'I can't believe how drunk you are.'

He looks at me, his eyes not properly focused. 'Drunk is when you are over the edge. I'm not there yet. I know exactly where I am and what I am doing. Besides it is not pertinent to our discussion.'

'Well, I'm not taking my panties off and standing over you so you can look up my skirt.'

'Why not?'

'Because anyone could come along!'

He chuckles. 'That's the best bit. The fear of discovery always makes you come faster.' He slides his hands between my legs and rubs the silken crotch of my panties. His eyes glitter as his hand finds that despite my prudish objection I am already aroused by the thought. And it hasn't escaped him that I haven't swatted his hand away either. He strokes the damp material and smiles triumphantly.

'Come on, be a devil. Just one little lick. I'm dying to get my tongue inside you.' His eyes are half closed and heavy with drink and desire. I can feel myself getting more and more turned on, the material he is digging into becoming soaked.

'One little lick,' I say sternly.

'Scout's honor.'

'And then you come with me into the suite?'

'Cross my heart and hope to die,' he promises solemnly.

I stand and quickly take my panties off while he watches. Wordlessly, he holds his hand out and I put them into it. While he clumsily pockets them I furtively look right and left. The corridor is empty so I take a step forward and stand over him with my legs spread.

He looks up and smiles broadly. 'I could die now and be happy.' He raises his eyes up to mine. 'Now squat on my face.'

I lean my palms on the wall in front of me and lower my hips until my sex is close enough to touch his mouth. Turns out it is not one little lick he wants after all. He captures my clit between his teeth so I am trapped into that horribly gauche position.

'One little lick you said,' I remind desperately.

His hands slide up my thighs and grip my bare buttocks firmly.

'I lied,' he says airily and starts sucking my clit.

'I've got a taxi coming,' I cry urgently, but the sensations that are coming from between my legs make me moan and grind myself against his teeth. I can always get another taxi. And then another voice, much stronger, says, *What happens when he sobers up? What happens when Mills and the boys at the department find out?* The thought is like a bucket of cold water in my face.

With all my strength I wrench myself away from him and stepping out of his reach stare at him panting, aroused, and terrified. 'Right, you've had your fun, now let's get you in,' I say shakily.

He holds his hand out meekly, and I take it and pull him up. He comes so easily I realize he never needed my help.

'You OK?' I ask.

'Never felt better.'

I help him to the bed. He falls on it and purposely brings me with him. With him on top of me he gazes into my eyes.

'So you are planning to leave, huh?'

'I thought you wanted me to anyway,' I whisper.

'Yeah, sure. You're one strange gal, Lily.'

'Why did you walk out then?'

He gives a bark of laughter. 'I wanted to see what you would do. I didn't realize it would take you so long to make your move.' He rolls off me and lying on his back brings out a packet of cigarettes from his shirt pocket.

I frown. 'You don't smoke?'

'I do...in times of extreme provocation.' He lights it and inhales deeply. He blows out the smoke and turns to me. 'I smoked a pack a day until I was nineteen.'

So much I don't know about him. 'What did you do when you left here?'

He makes an amused noise. 'I sat outside the room and called down and got someone to bring me a bottle and some cigarettes. They're very good here. They wanted to bring me a glass as well, but I told them not to bother.'

There is ash gathering at the end of his cigarette, and I move to find a saucer or something to use as an ashtray, but he immediately tightens his hold on my wrist. 'Where do you think you're going, young lady? I haven't had my way with you yet.'

I put my mouth close to his ear. 'Isn't your dick a bit too limp for that?'

He laughs, a lovely deep rumble, then puts his mouth to my ear and whispers, 'I'm rock hard and hungry for you, babe.'

Suddenly my body feels tight and jittery. 'Really?'

'It's a done deal. All nine inches.'

I can't help, but smile.

'Try it and see.'

I lean back and look into his eyes. They are hazy, almost smoky with sensuality and seductive promise. I run my hand over the material of his crotch. Indeed the man is rock hard. My body instantly responds. My mouth is dry. I lick my lips. 'Let me go get an ashtray first.'

I find a glass on the coffee table and bring it back. Jake has taken his shirt off and is sitting slumped against the pillows. He is holding between his thumb and forefinger the black chip worth ten thousand pounds from Eden and is staring at it reflectively. His hair has fallen over his forehead and he looks up at me slowly. At that moment he doesn't look drunk. Just devastated. Utterly devastated.

I stand frozen in the doorway.

It is impossible to tell what he is thinking. He takes a drag of his cigarette and blows it out slowly. He puts the chip on the side table and turns toward me. 'Come in,' he invites softly. 'Because I'm dying to fuck you with my tongue.'

'That's so dirty,' I say as I discard my skirt on the way to the four-poster. I climb onto the mattress, take the cigarette out of his mouth, kill it at the bottom of the glass, and position myself

with my sex right slap bang on his mouth.

My back arches as he begins to devour me. I come quickly and intensely. When I look down into his eyes, they are almost black with desire. Leaning back I slowly rub my hand over his crotch. I pull my body away from his face and I start to take his trousers off.

'I need to take a piss. Don't go anywhere,' he says.

I listen to the strong splash of his urine hitting the toilet bowl and I remember my nan saying, 'You can tell a man's health by the strength of his morning piss.' Well, it's confirmed. He's one healthy man. I hear the tap running and then he comes back. There is still a little sway in his walk, but he seems more sober now.

He stands at the edge of the bed looking at me. 'Every time I see that sexy little mouth of yours I just want to fuck it. I want to fuck it until it is all red and swollen and then I want to fuck it some more.'

And that is exactly what he does after he picks up the phone and cancels my taxi. He puts the phone down and fucks my mouth long and deep and then he finishes off in my pussy. There is no tenderness given and none asked. This is just lust. Pure lust. Both of us craving each other's bodies and taking it hard and fast because we can't have what we really want. At least that is true for me. What I want is shimmering in the distance. Way beyond my reach.

Afterward he lies beside me. I can see that the alcohol is shutting him down. He is valiantly fighting it, but the edge of a deep sleep is less than a blink away.

'You're going to have one hell of a hangover when you wake up.'

'I'll live,' he mutters.

'Go to sleep, Jake,' I encourage.

'Will you be here when I wake up?'

I pause. 'Yeah.'

'Don't leave me, Lily, or Jewel, or whatever your real name is.'

'My real name is Lily Strom,' I whisper.

His eyes widen. 'No, your name is Lily Eden,' he murmurs.

I smile sadly, and he runs his fingertips along the curve of my hip. My body quivers at the delicate touch. My nipples come alive, hardening, darkening, tingling, calling. I stop thinking about anything else but him and the strong sensation that he is touching my very soul. The emotion is unbearably intense, maybe too intense. A tear leaks out of each corner of my eyes.

No matter how many obstacles, our bodies can always find each other. My brain says no, but my body tells me this man has to be part of my future. I have to find a way for us to be together. And staying here while I am confused and vulnerable is not the way. I need time to sort out what I am going to do about Mills, my job and my terrible guilt about the love I have for this man.

He stops stroking my hip and drags his thumb down the path of my tears. I swallow hard and blink. He puts his thumb into his mouth.

'Salty,' he pronounces.

I flash a wobbly smile.

'Did you know that otters hold hands before they go to sleep so they don't float away?'

I slip my hand into his and he tightens his hold on it.

He smiles and his eyelids droop. He forces them open. It's a lost battle. Not long to go now.

'The first time I saw you I thought you were an angel come to save me,' he mumbles.

I say nothing, I just watch as he slips into a deep drunken stupor. I lie next to him for another few minutes watching him, listening to his even breathing. When his body is totally relaxed and dead to the world I slowly pull my hand out of his grip, but even though his entire body is limp as if passed from this world, his hand is clinging onto me like a claw. Gently, one by one I pry his fingers away. Very gently I kiss his forehead.

Quietly I get out of bed and into my skirt. I retrieve my panties from the pocket of his pants and go into the living room. On hotel stationery I write a note.

I'm not running away.
I just need a bit of time
to think and sort my head
out.

xx Lily

Then I softly close the door. I have a plane to catch. I am in such a daze that it is only when I am high in the sky that I realize I am still wearing both my engagement and wedding rings. I twist them around my finger in horror. I can't believe I have left him. My body feels hollow where my heart should be.

FOUR

Lily

I clear customs in Heathrow and head straight for the payphones. I find one that is coin operated and lay my coins in a row along the metal ledge. I lift the receiver, pick up a pound, push it into the slot, and dial Robin's number. His answering service clicks on and for a split second it occurs to me that I have done the wrong thing. In that split second I even consider terminating the call without saying anything, but then I hear myself speak.

'Hey, Robin. No panic. Everything is just fine. Just touching base. Saying hello. Call you another day. Byeeee.'

I click the disconnect button quickly and close my eyes, full of regret, wishing I hadn't called him. That was another mistake. My voice had been normal, cheery even, but while I was talking an announcement had been made. He will know I am calling from an airport and, being the bright button that he is, alarm bells will be going off as to why if all is well I would be calling him from an airport simply to say hello. With every decision I take I seem to be digging myself deeper and deeper into a hole.

On the spur of the moment I decide not to go back to the company flat, and instead take a taxi to my grandmother's house. Staring unhappily out of the window I fret about whether to call my mother. I know I should, but ever since Luke died, she has become so fragile I have learned to either bear my burdens silently or take them over to Nan.

The driver drops me off outside her ground floor flat, and I go up to her blue door and ring the bell. Her little face appears at the window. I wave and she breaks into a massive grin. At that moment she is no longer a sprightly seventy-two-year-old woman, but a mere child.

In seconds her beaming face is at her open door.

She greets me in the traditional Chinese way, by asking me if I have eaten.

'Yes,' I reply automatically, but she bundles me energetically through the door past the Feng Shui cat with its waving arm, and into her small, rather dim kitchen. It has old-fashioned, dark wood furniture and the air smells of incense that has been lit in the red prayer altar of the Kitchen God, Zao Jun.

In front of his statue she has left an offering: a blue bowl of oranges.

'Sit, sit,' Nan says, and starts filling her electric steamer with water.

'I'm actually not hungry,' I protest.

'You're never hungry,' she grumbles. She switches on the appliance and turns around, her hands on her hips. 'Look at you, as thin as one of those throw-away chopsticks.' She narrows her eyes. 'And have you been lying in the sun again?'

'It's called a tan, Nan.'

'Tan, my foot. These unattractive Western traditions that you have picked up. You should have seen your great-grandmother. She was as white as a lotus blossom.'

'Talking of traditions, didn't she also have bound feet?'

She stares at me disapprovingly. 'What's that got to do with taking care of your skin?'

'Nan,' I say tiredly, 'I haven't come here to talk about the state of my skin.'

She shakes her head and moves toward her freezer. She rummages around and brings out white buns made of Hong Kong flour with chicken and pork filling. She shows me the packet. 'See? Your favorite brand.'

'Thanks,' I say weakly. The last thing I feel like is food.

While she busies herself placing the buns into the steamer I look around me.

Nothing in Nan's kitchen ever seems to change. From the time Luke and I were kids everything looks and smells the same. We used to love coming here. There was always some kind of celebration—moon cake festival, lanterns, Chinese New Year festivities when we used to eat sticky sweet cakes, get money in red packets, and burn fire crackers to speed the Kitchen God on his journey back to heaven.

Nan wipes her hands and comes to sit beside me.

'Nan,' I begin. 'You know I became an undercover police officer, right?'

'Of course. You told me this yourself. I'm not senile yet, you know?'

'Well, anyway, I was sent on this assignment and...er...'

Her sharp dark eyes gaze at me curiously.

'I think I've developed, well, feelings for my target.'

There is no discernible expression in her face. 'Tell me about him. What kind of man is he?'

'He is loyal to his family, kind to animals, and... He is fair.'

'Why do the police want him?'

'He's supposed to be a drug dealer.'

I see fear whip into her eyes and she clasps her hands tightly together.

'But I don't think he is one, though.'

Her hands unclasp with relief.

 358

I bite my lip. 'But I am also afraid that my judgment may be colored by the way I feel about him.'

She leans forward. 'Can it be the police have got it wrong?'

'Unlikely,' I admit reluctantly.

She frowns and studies me. 'So why have you come to see me then?'

For a moment I stare into her familiar eyes. And then I realize that I have come to see her because I trust her. I trust her not to bullshit me about anything. And because I know she is non-judgmental, except about things like getting a tan and modern Western ways. But more importantly because I know that something is wrong. If I put it all out on the table for her to peer at she might pick up what I have missed.

'I've come because I'm feeling confused and guilty. And I know you can't make it better, but maybe just talking about it all to you will clear it up for me.'

'What are you feeling guilty about?'

'I believe I am betraying Luke in the worst possible way by falling in love with a suspected drug dealer. Even if the police are wrong, and that is a very unlikely scenario, it is still all a horrible, horrible mess. I feel as if I have become so steeped in filth and mire that a part of me will never get out of it.'

Nan leans forward. 'When you were born I wanted your mother to name you Lotus, but she refused. She said that name was too old-fashioned. In an attempt at compromise she named you Lily, but she didn't understand. She thought because my name, Lan, means orchid, I wanted you to be named after a flower too. I didn't. I wanted to call you Lotus because I looked into your big blue eyes and I felt the sheer strength and purity of your personality. My granddaughter is going to grow up to be strong and pure. Like the Lotus she can remain in filth and mire all her life but she will rise out of it clean and pure. Not a tiny drop of mud or slime can stick to her.'

Tears fill my eyes. I blink them away quickly. 'I don't feel very pure, Nan. In fact I feel as if my feelings for Jake and my guilt about betraying Luke are clouding my instincts and intellect, and making me miss something. Something very important.'

She covers my hand with one of hers. 'When you were a baby, not even two years old, I would sit you on that cabinet.' She points to the high, lacquered cabinet where she stores her odds and ends. 'And I would tell you not to move. And you wouldn't. You wouldn't move at all. You'd sit there with your legs dangling down.'

I look at the cabinet. It does seem a high perch to put a small child on.

'It was amazing how you were aware of the danger, but unafraid. I could even leave the room. I did a few times too. But I could never do that with Luke. I could never trust him. I always knew he didn't know what was good for him. You have to trust your instincts. If you think he is a good man, then I trust you. If your instincts are telling you something is not right then I would trust them implicitly.'

I nod gratefully. I know Nan is right. The only times I have gone wrong in my life are when I have not followed my instincts.

'There is something else, too, that is really bothering me. I am so in love with him I can't imagine my life without him, but I don't know whether he really cares about me, or if it's just sex for him.'

Nan's eyes flash. 'A man can find sex anywhere.'

'Yes, but not the kind of sex we have. We can't keep our hands off each other.'

'Intimacy is the flesh clearing the path for hearts and souls,' she says primly.

'What happens if the lust goes and there is no love?'

'Wait here,' Nan commands, and goes into the hallway. I hear her enter her bedroom and open her armoire. She comes back with a small box. Seashells have been crudely stuck all around it.

She puts it on the table in front of me, sits down and looks at me.

'Go on, open it,' she invites.

I do and it is full of an assortment of small, worthless objects, a yellow button, a bit of shiny foil, a bright orange earring, a screw... I raise my eyes back to her. 'What are all these things?'

'Don't you remember them at all?'

I frown. Vaguely. Something...almost dream-like breaks into my memory. I pick up the orange earring. It is smooth and old. I look up at her. 'I remember this. I know it's mine, but I don't remember where it came from or how it slots into my past.'

She smiles.

'Yes, these are all yours. From the time you were about three years old until you were five you lived with Granddad and me in a rented house close to an abandoned factory. Many crows lived there. At first they would swoop down and eat the food that you accidentally dropped. But then you began to feed them, nuts, breadcrumbs, dry dog food. And they began to bring you presents. All these were brought to you by the crows. They were showing you their love.'

'I don't remember,' I say with a frown.

'It was a long time ago.'

And suddenly I have a memory, of a flock of crows on the ground beside me.

They are all busy feeding. I smile at Nan full of wonder. 'I remember them now. Why did you show me this today?'

'Bright shiny things are given to us by people who love us.' She looks at my rings. 'Like those.'

'You noticed?'

'I'm old. I'm not blind,' she says, and goes to take the buns out of the steamer.

I sigh. 'Yeah, we got married. I'm afraid it's all a huge mess.'

'Never mind. Let's eat now. What is this thing the British are always saying? It will all come out in the wash.'

'Nan, why did Luke and I come to live with you?'

Nan doesn't turn to look at me. 'Your mother was ill at that time.'

'She didn't want us, did she?'

She whirls around suddenly, her face as fierce as I have ever seen it. 'She wanted both of you, but she was ill, Lily. She was ill, the same way Luke was.'

There is so much I don't know about my own family, but I am learning. Finally, the pieces are falling into place. I understand now why Luke and I always felt like outsiders. Our mother rejected us even when we were babies. No wonder I am so afraid of love. And perhaps it was why Luke turned to drugs. There is something missing inside us.

When Nan puts the buns in front of me I realize that I am actually starving. I hardly ate on the plane and I haven't eaten a proper meal since my dinner at Shanghai Lily.

That night I stay over in Nan's house. Uncle Seng, an old friend, comes for dinner and we eat noodle soup with fishballs and Kitato playing in the background. Uncle Seng is funny and Nan laughs a lot. It gives me time to lean back in my chair, sip my white tea, and feel the loss of Jake by my side. Uncle Seng leaves early and I go into the kitchen to wash up. I tell Nan to relax, but she comes and helps to dry the dishes.

'You must be tired. You better go to bed,' she says, hanging up the towel.

'Yes, I suppose I am. Goodnight, Nan. Thank you for today,' I say and bend to kiss her.

'You won't tell your mother I put you on the cabinet, will you?' she asks.

I laugh. 'Why did you do it, anyway?'

'Because you used to look so cute and solemn up there.'

'Oh, Nan, how I love you,' I whisper, and hug her small delicate frame tightly.

Her rib bones seem so small and birdlike.

'Sleep well, little Lotus.'

I climb into my old bed and fall asleep almost immediately. I dream of the crows. They come bearing gifts. Their unrelieved blackness is neither startling nor offensive. I open my arms and receive them gladly. They are my special friends from another time.

FIVE

Lily

I left my keys to Jake's house in his suitcase before I left the Hard Rock Hotel, which means I won't be able to let myself into his house if he is not in. Fortunately, standing across the road from the house I see that his car is parked close by but in a different place from when we left for Vegas. So I know not only that he is back, but also that he is in. I do not know what kind of reception I am going to get, but I know he won't turn me away.

His body won't let him.

Maybe that is why I have not called first. Calling would mean our bodies don't get to talk. I cross the road. At the bottom of the steps I stop, courage suddenly deserting me. It is startling just how nervous I am. My organs feel like they are floating inside a hollow space. I take a deep breath. I think I am afraid of what he will be like without the alcohol.

Come on, Lily, just a few steps more. You've come this far. It's not like you

 366

ran out on him or anything like that. You left a note. You just needed a bit of time to think.

I look up at the sky. It is a hazy white.

I want to take those last few steps and ring the bell. I want to see him again, but I am terrified I will see a stranger with cold, mean eyes. I debate the matter. What's the worst that can happen? He slams the door in my face. A small voice speaks, *I'm not prepared for that. I can't go back to what I was when I lost Luke.* This is a bad idea. Maybe I should leave and then call first. Prepare him. My body starts turning to walk away when in my peripheral vision the curtain twitches. Oh God in heaven! He has seen me.

It galvanizes me. I don't want him thinking I'm a coward. I run lightly up the stairs and ring the bell.

The door opens almost instantly and my voice dies in my throat. My eyes widen with shock and I feel my soul shrivel. This I had not prepared for.

'Well, well, look what the cat dragged in,' Andrea Mornington drawls as her eyes travel down my body derisively, while she stands in Jake's fucking shirt! The buttons have not even been done up. She has just thrown it over her naked body and is clutching the edges together. Underneath the shirt her legs are long and bare and her toenails are painted a pretty peach.

Fuck him.
He went back to her!
Just like that.

The sensation of shock is so immense that I feel physically ill. I want to vomit. I am jealous, horribly jealous of her standing in my man's shirt. At that moment I don't think of what I have done to him or how I have betrayed him. I just feel betrayed. Utterly and completely. I really believed we had something rare and special. A kind of deep connection that I have not had with another human being.

Her eyes note my suffering with great satisfaction. There is not an ounce of pity in them. I see her clearly then. She has never in her life sung the song of pain, or had the branches torn from her tree. She is one of those lucky women. Bestowed with everything.

I open my mouth and no words come out!

'It's always a good idea to call first,' she advises insolently.

It is not rage I feel but pain. Such pain that I don't want to punch her, or scratch her eyes out. I just want to run away somewhere no one will see me and howl in pain.

Some part of me refuses to believe what I am seeing. What if she is tricking me? What if he is not in? I force the words out.

'Is he in?'

'Obviously,' she says, with an amused smirk.

I won't scratch your smug, spoilt face, but I'll leave you with this: 'Tell him... Tell him his wife was here.'

Without waiting to see her reaction I whirl away from her, and lurch toward the steps. But my legs are so unsteady that I miss the first step and, with arms flailing and an involuntary cry starting at the back of my throat, I begin flying face first toward the hard, concrete pavement below.

Oh shit! Now she will witness my utter humiliation, too.

My descent is stopped suddenly by an iron hand. Wet and strong, it curls itself around my forearm and jerks me backwards. The force is so great I slam into a hard wall of solid muscles running with water droplets. The clean smell of soap and shampoo envelops me.

In a daze I feel myself being pulled through the entrance past an open-mouthed Andrea. I turn my shocked face to the owner of the hand. His hair is plastered to his head and rivulets of water are still running down his face and neck. My stunned brain makes a mental note: he was in the shower. His only covering is a small, white towel slung around his delectable hips. He must have just pulled the first thing that came to his hand, and run down the stairs when he heard the doorbell.

Did he know it was me ringing?

He propels me into the living room, and keeping a firm hold of my hand turns to glare at Andrea. She has followed us in and is standing at the door watching. An odd, unfathomable expression crosses his face. He shakes his head slightly to himself, part irritation, part exasperation.

'Get back into your own clothes and leave, Andrea,' he says tightly.

'What about lunch?' she asks sulkily.

'What about lunch?' It is obvious that he is finding it difficult to keep his temper in check.

'You promised to take me.'

'And I will, *another time*... If you get out of here right now.'

Huffily, but with impressive flamboyance, she flings his shirt to the floor and in her underwear stalks to a sofa where her clothes are. The bitch! She had wanted me to think she was naked underneath Jake's shirt. That I had interrupted them at an intimate moment. Jake turns his gaze back to me. I have so many questions eating at me, but I am too frozen to say anything. My mouth is still hanging open.

I clamp it shut—I can wait until she is gone before I go ape shit.

She shoots daggers at me before bestowing a fake, happy smile on Jake. 'See you later, then,' she calls and flounces out of the room.

We hear the door close and Jake says in a weary voice, 'Don't make me come there and put you out, Andrea.'

There is a muffled sound of outrage and then the door slams hard.

'How did you know she hadn't gone?'

'When things don't go Andrea's way she tends to slam doors.'

My mind is a seething mess of emotions. How dare he? How dare he act so cool?

'What was she doing here?'

'When she came I was training. I went to take a shower. She was supposed to wait...in her own clothes.'

I still don't like it. She obviously feels she has some sort of hold on him. And what is that thing about taking her out to lunch? But I can't act all jealous. Now is not the time. We have other far more important things to talk about.

I gaze at him, and suddenly I am aware that he is standing in an inadequately small towel. And he is staring at my mouth. Heat is coming off him in waves. My gaze leaves his smoldering eyes and skitters down to his throat.

'I'm glad you came,' he murmurs.

'Why?' The sound is strangled. His nearness is doing things to me. We have been apart for so little time and yet, it feels as if it has been ages since I have had him inside me.

'Because it's saved me the trouble of going down to Vauxhall to fetch your ass back here.'

My eyes rush up to his. 'You know where I live?'

'There are two things wrong with you, princess. You're too naïve for your own good, and you're always wearing too many fucking clothes.' His voice is low and husky and he watches me like a hungry beast.

I flush and feel wetness pool between my legs. The air around us is thick with all kinds of emotion.

'Um, yeah, we really need to talk, Jake.'

'Everything in good time, but first...' In an admirably smooth movement he unbuttons, unzips and pulls my jeans down my legs. 'I've got to have you.' Sitting on his haunches, his mouth is so close to my sex I feel his breath as warm puffs of air through my panties. I take a shaky breath. Mother of God, this man is something else. I rest my palms on the thick knots of strong muscles on his shoulders as he slides my panties down to the floor. I step out of them.

'We really should talk first,' I whisper without any conviction.

'Aren't you even a little bit keen to have my cock inside you?'

'Not really,' I gasp.

'You're dripping, babe.'

'You're an asshole, Jake.'

He grins, his eyes flashing.

My breasts feel heavy, my nipples hard and hungry. *Should I be doing this?* my mind tries to reason fleetingly, but it is gone when he sticks a thick finger inside me. 'Oh,' I cry.

'Oh, indeed,' he says and standing up, walks me backwards until I am pushed up against a wall. He whips that ridiculously inadequate towel off his bronzed body and throws it to the ground. I have only a flash of him in all his erect glory before my right thigh is grabbed and hoisted up. I wrap it around his hard waist. This is where I belong. I am back where I belong. He drags his fingers along my crack, already slick with juices.

'I can't wait to feel your sweet pussy around my cock,' he says softly, as his thumb massages my clit knowing that the light caresses will drive me insane.

'Fucking give it to her then,' I snarl.

He laughs softly and forces his shaft up into me.

'Oh God!' I whimper, staring up at him. Jesus, how I've missed having this

 373

thick pillar of meat buried deep inside me. The fullness of him is perfect. Absolutely perfect.

His eyes blaze into mine.

Utterly drunk on the look in his eyes, I groan. Possibly because I have come to accept that I love him and will do everything in my power to keep him, it is more satisfying than at any other time.

He rams into me relentlessly, until my supporting leg begins to twitch with tension. I fear my leg is about to give way under me.

'I can't take it anymore,' I gasp, my sex clenching like crazy.

'Yes, you can,' he says. 'Remember I *own* your pussy. She starts when I start and she stops when I stop.' He swats my ass hard, the sound is loud and meaty, and pounds me even harder. Pain blurs into pleasure. My leg buckles and I wind both legs around his thighs and my hands around his neck and hang there, trembling. His hands come around to grip my bare buttocks and hold me in place.

'Jaaaake... I'm coming,' I warn.

'No,' he snarls. 'You come when I tell you to fucking come.'

'I can't wait,' I moan desperately.

'Yes, you can,' he bites out and pushes his tongue into my mouth. I suck on it greedily. I can feel the rush beginning to take hold of my muscles, and I strain to hold it back. My pulse pounds in my ears and between my legs so hard that my body starts vibrating with the intense effort of holding back the oncoming climax.

'Let me come,' I cry harshly.

'Come,' he commands, and I plunge, trembling, twisting, jerking, into a void that is more vast and fantastic than the night sky while my hands grip him hard and close to my body through the splendor of his own orgasm.

SIX

Lily

Breathing heavily and with his eyes closed, he leans his forehead against mine. I feel his wet hair tickling my skin and his cock still spurting his seed inside me. Suddenly, he opens his lids and I am staring into the star-burst of his eyes. This close, they are beautiful gems that have the ability to see right into my soul. I feel naked. All my secrets laid bare. *Do you know about Luke, Jake? Do you know why I was willing to betray you?*

He raises his head, gently pulls out of me, and unhooks my legs from his thighs and sets me back on my own two feet. Very shakily I lean against the wall and look up at him.

'Are you purposely being succulent?' he teases.

I shake my head. I can't say anything. My throat has closed over. He leans forward and bites my mouth. I reach down and rub his glistening cock. He starts kissing me, no, not kissing, devouring me. It is rough and it is possessive. I rewrap my hands around his neck and the empty ache between my legs starts again. I want him back inside me. And I know exactly how to do it. I pull away from his mouth and drop to my knees.

With him I am a dirty girl. Nothing is taboo. All is allowed.

He rests his palms on the wall at shoulder level and throws his head back as I hold his semi-hard shaft by the base and swirl the tip of my tongue around the crown. Languorously, I lap up the shaft as if I am licking ice cream melting down a cone on a summer's day. Then I suck it voraciously, as if it is a massive, muscular tongue. I swallow it halfway... Then I take it so deep into my throat, a growl smolders in his throat. The sound is so damn hot, it's sinful. It shivers onto my skin, scattering goose bumps wherever it touches. God knows how long I suck him because my lips have become numb, but I do get him rock hard.

I slide him out of my mouth and look up at him, my lips parted.

He looks down at me with naked hunger. Mother of God! His eyes are almost lime! I want him. No, I need him. I stare back, my eyes speaking a language of their own. Cock. Dick. Hard. Delicious. Ready. You. Get inside me.

'Fuck my mouth,' I whisper, but it comes out harsh and throaty. I fit him back, hard and thick, between my lips. A hand slides into my hair. Clenches. Tugs. But this is not me submitting. This is me at full power. This is me entirely in control. Me deciding. Me being greedy. Because I already know exactly what he is going to do.

He is Mr. Generous. I *never* come away with nothing.

He begins to thrust. Softly first then harder and harder—enough to see me gag and choke. Then he comes out of me, and grabbing me by the waist, picks me up as if I weigh no more than a feather. He puts me face down over the armrest of the sofa. Shivering with anticipation, my ass in the air, I twist back to watch.

He opens my legs wide and looks at my bare ass and my sex, open and smeared with sex juices. Glossy, swollen, needy. For a second his eyes rise up to mine. What is in his eyes is pure, unadulterated possession. I get it immediately. My sex belongs to him. And only him. Woe betide any man who comes between him and me.

With a wild cry, he grabs my hips and plunges into me. He is branding me. With an answering cry, I push back into him. It is crude, it is primitive. It is what we both are. His skin slaps against mine as he fucks me so hard I feel the leather of the sofa chafe against my thighs.

With the solid heat of his body pressed against me I feel strangely safe. As if the outside world with all its problems and demands does not exist.

'With you the burn never dissipates, even slightly,' I whisper.

'I'm glad,' he mutters. 'Because I wish I could tie you to my bed with your legs wide open so I could come and bury my tongue or my cock inside you any time I please.'

Considering how hard and intensely passionate we have been, it surprises me when I feel my cheeks burn.

He strokes me with the back of his finger. 'What a strange little thing you are. Big-eyed innocence and—'

The word innocence pulls me out of my languor. And suddenly the air between us changes. I start to wriggle under him. He rises and pulls out of me. My sprawled position feels awkward and embarrassing. His seed is leaking out of me. I try to right myself, but he puts a restraining hand on the small of my back.

'Don't hide from me, Lil. Just relax,' he says. There is husky control in his voice, and I cease all movement. He picks up the towel he discarded earlier and kneeling at the apex of my spread thighs tenderly wipes my swollen sex.

After the rough fucking his touch is so gentle I am surprised.

'I love your pussy. It is so beautiful,' he murmurs and plants a kiss right on my core, making my stomach clench.

Then he opens my flesh wide and whispers something into my sex. Hazily, I hear my name, but I cannot make the rest of the sentence out.

He cannot not have feelings for me. It is impossible. He must care some. Nan is right. He cares. He must. I can't even imagine the alternative. He pushes his tongue into me and gently licks me. As if he were a cat or dog cleaning its baby.

'More,' I whisper feverishly. 'Fill me up, Jake. I am so empty without you.'

He pushes a thick finger into me. 'You're not empty, Lil. I'm here.'

He plays with me, never-ending circles, until I feel my back arching. 'I think I'm coming. Can I come?'

'Yes.'

The sensation is so intense, so wild, I try to pull away, but he tightens his hold and makes me submit. I climax with my slick clit inside his hot mouth.

He stands, closes my legs into some semblance of respectability and pulls me up. Our eyes meet. God! This man is so beautiful.

'You look like you could do with a drink,' he says, tying the towel around his hips.

I find my jeans and pull them on. He walks to the bar, pours us a glass of whiskey each. He passes me a glass and our fingers touch. A spark goes through me. I withdraw my hand, spilling whiskey. His eyes are dark, but I can tell by the set of his mouth that the sex is over. It is time to talk.

I pour the whiskey into my throat. It burns all the way down.

He raises his eyebrows, but says nothing. I notice that he doesn't drink, but puts his glass down on the counter. He swivels his head.

'You wanted to talk?'

'Yeah.'

Suddenly I am nervous. What if it is only sex with him? What if Nan is wrong? I swallow hard. I open my mouth and his phone rings. He frowns. I have noticed that his phone almost never rings. The last time it rang it had been Dom telling him about the fire.

'Can you wait one moment?'

I nod.

He moves toward it. Looks at the screen and immediately presses the answer button.

'Yeah,' he says and his voice is worried.

I can hear a woman's voice. It sounds panicked and hysterical.

'Calm down. Calm down,' he says.

The voice becomes slightly subdued.

'Yes, it's true,' he admits.

And the voice screams so loud he stares at the phone in disbelief. Then he looks at me and silently mouths, 'It's my mother.'

I nod solemnly. A family problem of some kind, obviously.

'Look, Ma. I'll come around tonight. Just please calm down. I'll explain everything when I get there, OK?'

Even from where I am I can hear her ranting, not in the least comforted. At one point Jake has to hold the phone away from his ear.

'What the hell are you on about? I'm perfectly fine.' He runs his hand through his hair distractedly.

'All right, I'll be there in less than an hour,' he concedes.

I hear another explosion of sound.

'OK, OK, I'll leave now. I'll be there in fifteen minutes.'

I hear quiet sobbing.

'Ma, stop it. Ma?'

I hear another hysterical outpouring.

He sighs with frustration. 'I'll come right now, OK? Just wait for me.'

He terminates the call and looks at me. 'She's a *bit* distraught.'

'What happened?'

'Apparently, Andrea called and told her I married you.' He raises an eyebrow. 'Any idea how Andrea knew?'

'Oops, sorry,' I say, biting my bottom lip.

He grins at me. 'It's not like I wasn't going to tell her anyway, but it does mean I have to go see her now. Will you wait for me here? We'll talk when I come back.'

I nod.

'Come upstairs and keep me company while I dress.'

'Yeah?'

'Yeah.'

And I thought it was going to be difficult and awkward. It is not. I smile. God! I'm so in love with this man. 'OK.'

I watch him pull on a pair of black jeans in silence, just drinking in the sight of him. He pulls a black T-shirt over his taut muscles.

'Why does your mother hate me?'

He looks at me seriously and doesn't try to gloss over the issue. 'I don't know. But I know she doesn't know you the way I do and when she does she'll absolutely love you...' For a moment it seems as if the sentence is not complete, then he smiles and goes to the door. I follow him.

At the door he turns and kisses me.

'You smell of sex and me,' he whispers in my ear.

I rear back. 'I'll have a shower before you get back.'

'Don't you dare. I love it.' A smile tilts his mouth and warmth kindles in my belly. He goes down the steps, turns back and starts walking backwards mouthing, 'Be back soon. Don't go anywhere.'

He blows a kiss and I shyly return it. Maybe, it's going to be all right.

I watch him get into his car and drive off. Then I close the door and lean against it. The house is large and deathly quiet around me. I shut my eyes and hold to the fierce joy that burns in my chest. I think of the way his gaze had followed my tongue as it licked my lower lip. I remember the heat and I recall the tenderness between us, almost surreal. And I cover my mouth to hide the smile of pure happiness.

And what do the gods do?

They make my phone ring. I look at it and for a few rings I do nothing. Just stare at the number. I knew I shouldn't have called Robin. Then I press Answer and put it to my ear.

A woman says cheerily, 'Hey, Lily. It's Amber.'

'Hey, Amber,' I say automatically. Amber is the way that Robin makes contact with me.

'How are you?'

'Fine.' I clear my throat. 'I'm fine.'

'We should meet. Go out for coffee or something.'

'OK. Where do you want to go?'

 384

'How about Starbucks? You like the green tea thingamajig there, don't you?'

'Yes, I love it. Let's meet there. When?'

'How about now?'

'Now?'

'Yes, I have so much to tell you.'

'Right. I'll be there in the next twenty minutes.'

'Oh, good. Can't wait to see you again.'

'Same here,' I reply.

'Bye,' she says in a high, bright voice.

'Bye,' I say in a low, sad voice.

You take your aim. You fire. And shoot me down. Fuck you, Fate.

My legs feel like lead. I go into Jake's office. I have only been here once. I know the drawers are all locked and the desk is always stunningly bare. I take a piece of paper from the printer.

I take the quill from the ink stand. Just like him to have a fucking quill instead of a ballpoint pen. I feel the tears pricking at my eyes. No, I will not cry. There is a way out. I know it. I am unlucky but he is lucky and he will get what he wants. And he wants me. I know that. Well, I think I know that. Maybe he doesn't love me. But he wants me. I can tell. With every action he shows me. And Jake always gets what he wants.

I write my note. It is short and to the point.

Jake,
I have to go out for a bit. I'll see
you when I get back, OK? x

Should I add another kiss? One seems so informal. A jeering voice says, *WTF!* So I add three more kisses.

And then I leave my sanctuary.

SEVEN

Lily

The Starbucks in Baker Street is quiet. Robin is sitting on a sofa in a corner at the back. He stands and waves to me. I walk toward him. He is wearing jeans and an expensive leather jacket over a Ralph Lauren T-shirt. His face is familiar—his eyes travel my face and body quickly, assessing, assimilating. I can see that he hasn't ordered anything yet.

'Look at you,' he says loudly, so that anyone watching would just think we are friends meeting after a long time.

He kisses me on the cheeks enthusiastically while I stand awkwardly in the loose circle of his arm. 'How've you been?'

'Fine.'

'What will you have?'

'A latte.'

'Anything to eat?'

I shake my head.

'You sure? The company is picking up the bill,' he tempts with a grin.

'Not hungry, Rob,' I reply.

'Right,' he says in a more serious tone, and goes off to the serving counter. I look around me. There are only two other customers in this back section—a woman scrolling through the messages on her handheld and a man who is immersed in a newspaper. I turn away and stare at my handbag. There is no queue and Robin is back quickly. He places my latte in front of me. He is drinking a cappuccino.

'Thanks,' I say, reaching for two sugar sachets. I tear them and upend them into my coffee.

He sits and does the same.

Then he looks around him casually again, sees what I saw and lets his eyes come back to me, his face creased into lines of concern. 'Lily, what the hell is going on? Why did you initiate contact from an airport?' he asks in a low, urgent tone.

I take a deep breath. ''Cause I fucking need your help, Robin,' I choke.

'Jesus,' he says. 'Oh fuck!'

I close my eyes.

'Is that a fucking engagement ring on your finger?' he asks.

It is hard to tell at a glance since the stone on the engagement ring is so big that there is another plain band there. 'Yeah, and a wedding ring,' I say.

His mouth opens. 'You better start from the beginning,' he says cautiously.

I have a speech prepared. 'I...er...um... I... Well...uh...ah...um... Fuck, Robin, I went and slept with him and now it's all a mess.'

He exhales audibly. 'Look, it doesn't matter. You're not the first agent who has slept with their target. Just, well, just keep your feelings separate.'

The way a prostitute does, I think, and suddenly I realize I can't talk to him. I can't tell him anything. Not a thing. Calling him was definitely a mistake. He doesn't know that I am bonded with Jake. He doesn't know that I would die for Jake.

Robin's back straightens suddenly and his expression changes into one of alarm. 'Fuck it, Lily, he's here,' he says. He forces his expression back into one of normality and leans back into the leather couch.

I freeze.

'Anyway, did you know that Andy's wife has just had a baby?' he says.

I want to reply. I want to be normal but I can't.

'Nine pounds, the nipper was,' he adds, smiling.

I open and close my mouth like a demented fish.

And then the seat next to me depresses and I feel my life spiraling out of control. Slowly, I turn my head and feel a stab of pain in my gut. Jake is *nothing* like the man I know. I stare at him in perfect astonishment. His eyes are like green ice. Impenetrable. He does not spare me a glance. He has locked eyes with Robin. Hostility and animosity come off him in waves that you can feel and almost touch.

'Introduce me, then, Lily,' he says silkily, his eyes blazing.

I sit frozen. Unable to utter a single word.

Robin is one cool customer. 'I'm an old classmate of Lily's. We just bumped into each other. I should be going, really. The wife is waiting at the supermarket,' he smiles. His smile is just right. His manner is just right, but Jake doesn't buy it.

'What are you? Her handler?'

Robin's look of incredulity is not faked.

'What?' he says. 'Look, mate, I don't know what you're talking about, but I'm not getting involved. We're just old friends. I was getting a coffee and I saw Lily. That's it. I'm off.' He starts to stand.

'Yes, run away, but if I see you around her again, I swear I'll break every fucking bone in your body.' Jake smiles. The smile is pure menace. Why did I think I knew him? I know only the tip of the iceberg. I remember Shane saying, 'Do you think he treats everyone the way he treats you?' I stare at him, amazed.

Robin is on his feet, his hands raised, palms showing. 'Look, mate, I don't want no trouble.'

'Fuck off, then.'

Robin's eyes bounce to me. I nod quickly, and he leaves.

Jake turns to look at me. 'You want to play undercover detective? Be my guest, I can play the fool for you, but if I ever fucking see you meet him or any other man behind my back again you'll have to watch me fucking kill the cunt,' he snarls.

'Robin is my go-between.'

'I don't care what the fuck he is. You want to meet him? Tell me first.'

It's so fucked up it's unreal. He doesn't care if I want to spy on him, he just doesn't want me to do it behind his back. It would be laughable if it was not so weird. The only thing I can think of doing is using what has always worked. I touch his groin. Mistake. Big mistake. He grabs my hand, so hard I gasp.

'Don't, Lil. Don't degrade what we have.'

He lets go of my hand suddenly. I rub it. 'How did you know I was here?'

'How do you think?'

My eyes widen. 'What? You're having me followed?'

'Yes.' He says it like it is the most natural thing in the world to spy on your girlfriend or wife.

'Why?' I breathe. Too shocked to be angry.

'Because you got beat up by a pervert. Because I care. Take your fucking pick, Lil.'

I shake my head as if to clear it. 'And what about Andrea?'

His turn to frown. 'What about her?'

'Didn't I hear you arrange to meet her for lunch?' I ask, sarcasm dripping from my voice.

'Andrea is an old family friend. She takes care of my house when I am away. She picks the mail up from the floor and makes sure that no pipes have burst et cetera. I pay her for that. She's nothing to me.'

'Well, it doesn't seem like that from where I'm sitting.'

He frowns. 'What does it seem like to you?'

'It seems that she is in love with you.'

'Andrea is not in love with me. She's got her hook in the water for a rich man. And she knows the score with me.'

'Her behavior today was not that of someone who knows the score,' I remind.

He shrugs carelessly. 'All right, I'll hire someone else.'

'Good,' I say as nonchalantly as I can, but inside all my cells are coming alive with joy: Not only do I never need to see her snooty, insolent face again, but I won't have to worry about their relationship anymore either.

I look at his beautiful face. Even in a public place all I want to do is rub my body against his. I turn away and look at my untouched latte and Robin's cappuccino. 'Are you not afraid I will uncover something that will send you to prison?'

'No,' he says shortly.

'Why?'

'Because, Lily, my dearest, for the past ten years I have extricated myself and my organization from almost all that is illegal. I've nothing to fear.'

'What about that bed of money then?' I challenge.

'Protection money.'

I frown. 'You don't need to collect protection money.'

'It's true, I don't need it. It is one of the last bastions of an organization that I want to give up, but it would mean abandoning Eden and Dom's clubs to other far more dangerous and mercenary rackets.'

'I see.' But I don't.

'I'm not a drug dealer, Lil.'

'What came in on the sixteenth, then?'

He sighs. 'Contraband. It didn't just come in on the sixteenth. It comes in all the time. I don't believe eighty-two percent of the price of anything should be tax. I feel like a modern day Robin Hood when I sell a packet of cigarettes or a bottle of whiskey for the right price.'

'But when we met you told me you were a gangster.'

He shook his head. 'You wanted to believe I was one. I just didn't disabuse you of the idea.'

'Luke told me you wanted to become a vet.'

'Yeah. A long time ago when I thought I could talk to animals and they talked back to me.'

I cover his hand with mine and tell him the story about the crows. The anger dissipates as I speak. His eyes become warm and full of some strong emotion. 'My grandmother still has all those shiny objects in a box,' I finish.

I see the glimmer of tears in his eyes.

'What is it?' I ask.

He shakes his head and for a long time he simply looks at me with an expression I have never seen before. I dare not name it. If it is what I think it is then it will reveal itself in time. I won't try to second guess it. It would be too frightening to do that in my delicate emotional state.

'Sometimes I don't know what to make of you, Lil. I'd love to meet your grandmother some day.'

'That's what she said,' I say with a smile.

He smiles back. 'Come on, let's get you home.'

'Sorry, I forgot to ask. Did you manage to solve your mother's problem?'

'Nope.'

'Oh?'

'Ask me why.'

I bite my lip. 'Why?'

'Because while praying she had a vision. She saw me with blood pouring out of my chest and you standing over me. You were the cause.'

I stare at him in shock. The idea is a terrifying, unimaginable vista. His words are like a monstrous tsunami wave rolling forward to envelop and swallow me whole. Foam and lies crash around me. In sheer panic I gasp a single breath of air. It rushes violently into my lungs. There is ice, too. In my heart.

'I don't want to hurt you, ever,' I whisper.

His eyes suddenly soften. 'I know,' he says quietly.

'I'm going to go into work tomorrow. I need to tell them that my cover is blown and that I really need to be taken off this case. In fact, I need to tell them that there is no case. Jake Eden is no kingpin drug dealer.'

'Ah, my little lost lamb. Strayed into a
den of wolves, did ya?'

EIGHT

Lily

The next morning Jake kisses me tenderly on the forehead.

'Are you absolutely sure you don't want this done through a lawyer? All I have to do is pick up a phone and you'll never need to see any of them ever again.'

'I'm not afraid, Jake. I want to do this.'

'All right, but no matter what happens, never forget I'm here to support you,' he murmurs. His eyes are intense and full of some strong emotion.

'I think I kinda already know what's going to happen. I'm gonna get the book thrown at me,' I say softly.

'Call me when the meeting is over, OK?'

'OK.'

I dress carefully in a long black skirt, a striped white and gray shirt and a mannish gray jacket. I pull my hair back in a severe bun and stand in front of the mirror. And the mirror says, 'Slut in disguise.' I slick on some pale lipstick and I go to my meeting with DS Mills.

Sitting in the taxi I realize that I don't feel any emotional attachment to my job or to staying in the force. I have no fear of being disciplined, suspended, or even fired. I look at my hands and they are steady and lying relaxed on my handbag. The calmness stays while I go into the building, up the stairs, and down the familiar corridor to the double stable doors. I have a sudden memory of my first trip here. How nervous I'd been. Getting this job had seemed like the most important thing to me. I smiled to think of me then. I have changed.

I push open the stable doors and the usual gaggle of macho men are gathered about regaling each other with tales of their exploits. Robin is not around.

'How's it going, Strom?' one of the men shouts.

'Not bad,' I say, knowing that in less than an hour every one of them will have heard what I have done. The thing is, I don't care. Let them laugh. I glance at my watch. I am perfectly on time. I knock on DS Mills' door and he barks for me to come in.

I close the door behind me.

'Have a seat,' he invites.

'I gather Robin has told you my cover is blown,' I say, sitting down opposite him.

'Yes, you gather right.' He seems unwilling to say anything else. I realize he wants me to 'spill the beans'.

'I didn't tell him I was an undercover officer. He guessed—'

'How?'

'He said I was too clean and too innocent to be a runaway.'

He grunts.

'And Robin also probably told you that we got married.'

He nods. 'He didn't tell me why.'

'He said he married me because that way no one could force me to testify against him.'

'Right. That makes better sense. Are you in love with him?'

'Yes.'

'Is he in love with you?'

'I don't know. He hasn't said.'

'But he has strong feelings.'

I bite my lip. 'Yes. Yes, he has, but the thing is, Sir, I really think we have the wrong guy.'

'Why is that, then?' he drawls.

'Jake Eden is not a drug dealer. I've never once seen anybody take drugs in the club or seen anything that even looks like a drug deal going down. The only thing he seems to be doing is some harmless contraband.'

DS Mills' eyebrows fly upwards and I realize immediately that I shouldn't have used the word harmless. It has clearly revealed my loyalties.

'Smuggling is illegal and carries with it a criminal conviction and a prison sentence for those involved,' he says sarcastically.

'I thought we're going for the big criminals,' I say, hoping to lead him away from my mistake.

'Jake Eden *is* a big criminal.'

'He is not,' I cry passionately.

A look of amusement comes into his cold, ambitious eyes. 'On what are you basing your judgment?'

'He told me.' Oh, that came out wrong.

'And you believed him?' He shakes his head incredulously. 'What did you expect him to do? Tell you the truth when he knows you are an undercover cop?'

I look at him with frustrated eyes.

'I'm afraid, Strom, you have broken the undercover agent's cardinal rule.' His tone is surprisingly calm. 'You've allowed yourself to become emotionally involved with your target. And once your feelings are involved you are easy to manipulate.'

For a moment I don't speak. There is something else going on. I realize that he is toying with me. He is not angry that I fucked up the investigation by sleeping with the target. It occurs to me suddenly

that he wanted me to. I was chosen purely for my looks. He hung me in front of Jake as if I was some kind of bait! Shocked, I watch him lean back into his chair, his face laced with a certain smugness.

'When you say harmless contraband, do you actually know what it is that he is bringing in?'

'I believe it's mainly cigarettes and alcohol,' I say cautiously.

He pins me with his eyes. 'Are you sure contraband is not a euphemism for cocaine, heroin and human trafficking?'

I stare at him filled with dread. He wants me to continue! It is not going to be as simple as I thought. *You are no longer impartial, your cover is blown, and you are taken off the case, Strom.* Why would Mills continue with an operation especially when the agent has fucked up so badly?

His calmness tells me that he must have known from the moment he chose me, an absolute amateur, that Jake would suss me out quickly, and with my cover blown, it would be the perfect opportunity to exploit both Jake and me. My blood runs cold. I study him carefully.

'I've seen the file, and other than the old stuff when he was working for that Schitt guy there is hardly anything there.

What makes you so sure he is what you say he is?'

His eyes glitter dangerously. 'Instinct. When you do this job for long enough you develop strong feelers. Crystal Jake may have the cream of society fooled, but not me. I know his type. I know him.'

'What is it you want me to do?'

He smiles for the first time since I came into the room. 'I want you to go back to Jake Eden and pretend that you have been suspended pending an investigation into your behavior. And since you will be definitely living with him while the investigation is going on you will be thrown off the force. He has to feel so comfortable with...his new wife who is so deeply in love with him that she can never be compelled to testify against him that he loses his inclination to be guarded and starts boasting about what he is really bringing into this country. Rather than it being a setback, what has happened will make Crystal Jake far more accessible to us.'

Mills' smile suddenly breaks into laughter.

'What's so amusing?' I try not to show my irritation.

'The irony of it.'

'Irony?'

'Yes, isn't it ironic that the action he took to protect himself has actually made him more vulnerable?' He laughs

again, but this time, I know, he is laughing at me.

I drop my head and stare at my handbag. It is black and it has a gold button and a gold buckle. I bought it cheap in a sale in John Lewis. I will need a new one soon. The edges are beginning to fray. His words are actually painful, cutting through every layer of my being like a well-sharpened knife. I am an amateur and he has played me easily. When he said, 'I know his type. I know him,' what he was saying was, Didn't I choose you? Didn't I know what would turn him on? Didn't I know you would play the role of slut perfectly?

I feel the blood bubbling in my veins with rage. Rage at being taken for a fool, rage at being used as a pawn for his ambitions, rage at the utter contempt that he has for me. He *knows* I'm in love with Jake and yet he is willing to sacrifice me to get what he wants. I stand suddenly and with such force that the chair skitters on its wheels across the small room and hits the opposite wall.

Mills gets up from his seat and walks without haste toward the chair. I turn and, with my hands gripping my handbag's strap so hard the knuckles show bone white, watch him pull the chair back to where I am standing. He looks me directly in the eyes.

'Sit down, Strom.' For a moment I hesitate. His voice is extraordinarily calm. Then I do as he commands and sit.

'I'm going to ignore what just happened, and put it down to the stress that comes with being undercover, particularly for a new operative.' He moves back around to his side of the desk and rests his palms on the surface of the desk before looming down over me.

'Do you still want to be in the police force, Strom?'

The answer takes me by surprise. It is a clear no. 'Yes, of course,' I say.

'Good. Bringing a criminal like Jake Eden to justice will ensure that you rise quickly up the metaphorical ladder of success and recognition. Do you understand?'

I nod.

'Very good. Now, do you feel you are able to carry out the plan I have laid out for you?'

I feel the beat of my heart high in my throat. 'Yes, Sir.'

'Excellent. From now on you will no longer make any contact with anyone other than me in this office. To all intents and purposes you are suspended. You will also have to vacate your company flat as soon as possible. We'll meet in the Bayswater safe house, and make contact with each other in exactly the same way Robin and you have established.' He opens his drawer and takes out an envelope. He puts it in front of me. 'The key is inside, along with my number and the address. Learn them by heart and destroy the information before you leave this office.' Wow! He had everything ready. How meticulously he has planned Jake's downfall.

'I want names, places, dates. Anything at all.' Mills' eyes are steely.

'Yes, Sir.'

'Any questions?'

'No, Sir,' I say, slitting open the envelope and staring at the phone number and the address on the paper. I commit them to memory and put the paper back on his desk. I take the key out of the envelope and put it into my handbag. Then I stand, even though he has not dismissed me.

A look of fury passes through his eyes. It is gone very quickly. 'I'll be waiting for a call from you.'

'Good day, Sir.' I walk to the door and when my hand is on the handle his words brush my skin like a cold hand.

'Do it for your brother.'

I turn around slowly.

He smiles. 'It wasn't on your file, but it is a matter of public record.'

I nod distantly, my thoughts well hidden.

Outside his door I see Robin leaning against a wall talking to someone, but I can see that he has been waiting for me to come out. I don't want to speak to him. I'm not allowed to, anyway. I wave. He raises his eyebrows as if to ask if I am OK. I show him the thumbs-up sign. He appears surprised, but I quickly walk out of the stable doors. I walk out of the offices and outside the sky is blue and the sun is shining. But I feel cold inside. I have just become a kind of double agent.

I could have walked out of Mills' office and been more than content to leave the force forever, but I know Mills won't stop in his mission to destroy Jake. His determination has become personal and obsessive. It is clear to me that, of the two men, Mills is far more dangerous and unscrupulous in his methods. Me walking away will only mean that I will no longer have any idea of what Mills is planning. I have to find a way to exonerate Jake. Call it sixth sense, or intuition, but something just doesn't make sense. I'll play his game until I get to the bottom of it.

I pass a street painter. He is chalking a large hole in the pavement with people falling in. It looks remarkably real. It seems a shame that talent like that should be so temporary.

I hail a cab to the company apartment in Vauxhall. I pack my things quickly. There is not much. Then I call another taxi, put the keys through the letterbox, and give the driver Jake's address.

As soon as I have put my stuff in the spare room in Jake's house, I text him.

Have been suspended from duty pending investigation.

The phone rings almost instantly. It is Jake. I have already decided that I will not tell him too much. Rule number one—always keep a little back for yourself. For later. For protection.

'What's going on, Lily?' he asks urgently.

His voice makes me feel a little guilty. I should have texted earlier, but I wanted to be clear in my head about what I was going to do.

'I told them that I had slept with you and married you. And that you had figured out that I was an undercover officer anyway. For my trouble I got suspended. Pending a full investigation, I could be dismissed from the police force.'

'Where are you now?'

'At home. I cleared out my stuff from the Vauxhall apartment and brought it here.'

'You should have called me earlier. I could have got someone to do it for you.'

'No, they wouldn't have known my stuff from the other girls'.'

'Are you all right?'

'I guess so.'

'Do you want me to come back?'

'No, absolutely not. There's nothing for you to do, anyway. We'll just end up having sex or something.'

He chuckles. 'I'll be there in five.'

'Honestly, Jake, I'm all right. I need a bit of time alone.'

'All right, we'll talk when I get back.'

'OK.'

'Lily...?'

'Yeah?'

'Never mind. I'll be home early. We'll talk then.'

'Bye.'

'See you soon.'

I put the phone down and think about the words we use with each other and the undercurrents beneath those cautious phrases. I desperately wanted to say I love you, but I bit it back. I wonder what he really wanted to say to me.

NINE

Lily

I go to see my mother.

Her voice bubbles up warmly toward me. 'Have you eaten?' she asks.

'Yes,' I say automatically.

'What time is it?'

'Eleven o'clock.'

'Come into the kitchen. I made a chocolate cake yesterday and iced it this morning. You might as well have some.'

I follow her into the kitchen. My mother has a large kitchen built for her by my dad, who is a bit of a DIY enthusiast. It is airy, clutter free and the exact opposite of Nan's kitchen. There is no kitchen god here. No incense. No sticky cakes, and no firecrackers during the Lunar New Year. She switches on the kettle and reaches for the tin where the tea bags are stored. I don't offer to help because I know she will refuse. She puts two mugs out next to the kettle.

'I've been so worried about you.' She twists the top off the tin and drops a tea bag in each mug. 'I don't think I quite like you being an undercover cop. I've read such horrible things.' She opens a drawer, takes out a knife then walks toward the cake stand where a beautifully iced cake is sitting under glass. 'What if someone offers you drugs? Are you supposed to take them?' She lifts the glass dome.

'Mum, I've left the force.'

Her hands still. She puts the glass dome on the counter, and turns around to stare at me, her face suddenly creased with concern and worry. 'Left the force? What happened?'

I sigh. 'It's a long story, Mum. I'll tell you another day.'

'Does this mean that you are now unemployed?'

I sigh. 'No, I have another job.'

'Doing what?'

'Admin work.'

'Does it pay well?'

'Better than being a police officer, that's for sure. Listen, Mum, forget my job for a minute, I wanted to tell you something more important.'

'What?' she asks almost suspiciously.

'I got married.'

'Oh! When?' she says looking shocked.

I show her the rings. She walks toward me and in a daze takes my hand. I realize then that my mother and I hardly touch. It's been so long since I have felt the texture of her skin.

'How did I not notice it? Did you not want Dad and me to be there then?' She sounds hurt and lost.

I bite my lip with remorse. I realize that I shouldn't have told her. Maybe I should have stayed silent, and if it all works out with Jake we should have just got married again.

'It was a spur of the moment thing. We were in Las Vegas. There was no family from either of us there.'

She lets go of my hand and frowns. 'You were in Las Vegas?'

'Yes, just for the weekend.'

'Dad's been saving up for a wedding for you,' she says softly.

'He can use the money to take you on a nice holiday,' I say, feeling like a total bitch. But what else can I tell her?

'Who is this man?'

'His name is Jake Eden.'

'Jake Eden,' she repeats softly. 'You've never spoken of him before.'

I nearly raise my eyebrows and say, When have I ever spoken to you or Dad about a man? But I catch myself in time and say, 'It was a bit of a whirlwind thing.'

She looks deep into my eyes. 'I'm glad you're happy.'

'I am,' I tell her firmly.

She smiles. 'What does he do?'

I tell her what will satisfy her. 'He's a businessman.'

'Good,' she says approvingly. 'Do you have a photograph?'

'No, I'll bring him over next week.'

'That'll be nice. Dad will want to meet him.' She turns away from me and cuts two slices of cake.

Poor Mum. Her world seems so small, so pointless. For years Dad and I have protected her from all bad news. So now she lives her life baking and cleaning and watching soaps. Sometimes Dad and I intrude into her life and she reacts with surprise. And I realize it from her that I have learned to be so distant with the ones I love.

We eat her cake—it is delicious—and drink tea together.

Once she puts her fork down and asks again, 'Are you happy, Lily?'

I look her in the eye. 'Yes, Mother. I am.'

She smiles and I smile back and for a few seconds it feels as if the sun is shining in my mother's small world.

'That's good,' she says. 'That's very good.'

Jake

We go to Lily's parents' home for dinner. They live in a Victorian three bedroom semi in Hampstead. The décor is pure Scandinavian: white walls, cool blue rugs and brown leather furniture. But an air of immutable sadness permeates it. Here there are unhealed and grievous wounds. Even Lily seems sadder and smaller. She smiles at me uncertainly and it makes me want to hold and reassure her, but I don't. I realize that it is not the done thing in the Strom household. Here everybody is an island unto themselves.

Her father is white-haired, tall, thin, and appears much older than his years, and her mother is small, fragile, and charming. To my surprise she cooks and serves up a superb five-course meal. There is Gravadlax of salmon, pea velouté, an apple and mint sorbet between courses, noisettes of lamb and perfectly cooked vegetables. She finishes with poached oranges and pots of crème brûlée to rival the ones you'd find in the best five star restaurants. Afterwards, we nibble on excellent chocolate truffles.

'Homemade,' Lily's father proudly informs.

I compliment her mother, again.

She smiles modestly.

The family dynamics are interesting. The mother in all her fragility utterly controls her family. Both husband and daughter treat her as if she is fashioned out of eggshell and defer to her in all things.

In the car, Lily doesn't ask me what I think of her parents and I don't offer any opinion. The evening is a success on the surface, but I think I both terrified and fascinated them, in the way a colorful but poisonous reptile might. As for me they are not really my kind of people, they are too straight and proper—not an unpaid parking ticket between them no doubt. Their marriage reminds me of the surface of a pond, stale and passionless. Still, I like them well enough.

In all their careful goodness they made my Lily.

TEN

Lily

After I paint my lips carmine, I step into a long, backless black dress that ties at the nape of my neck. One little tug and I'll be standing in a scrap of lace held together by a bit of string. Carefully I pin a small black brooch on the tie, then step into a pair of black shoes with gold high heels. My toenails, painted gold, poke through. I stand in front of the mirror and look at myself curiously. I have never worn black. Nan's superstitions have colored my thoughts.

'Bad luck color. For funerals only,' she always said.

But Jake bought this dress for me, and now that I see myself in it I realize that I really like black. I think it makes me look long and sophisticated. I touch my meticulously constructed hairdo and wonder what the night will bring. Tonight is the big re-launch party for Eden. Everyone will be there. It is an event.

As I finish fixing a pair of gold hoops in my ears, Jake appears in the doorway. I turn around to look at him and my breath catches. I have never seen him look so dashing. He is wearing a snow white dress shirt, a black silk tie, a beautifully cut black suit and black shoes. There is a red carnation pinned to his lapel. Nothing adds panache to a man's appearance like the confidence embodied in wearing a boutonnière, that symbol of fragile life and beauty caught in a single bloom. I already know that he will be the only man in the entire club wearing a flower on his left breast. The only man swimming against the current. And I love him for it.

He comes forward and stands next to me.

'We match,' I say to our reflections.

'That we do, but you are more beautiful by far,' he compliments suavely.

I smile, wordless, swept up by his beauty, by my good fortune, by the intensity of my feelings.

As he watches I tilt my head back, elongate my neck amorously, and with a single finger, dab perfume behind my ears and at the base of my throat.

In the mirror I see him turn toward me. His hands go toward my earrings. 'Not these for tonight,' Jake whispers, as he gently removes them. From his pocket he brings out two strands of blue gems. Carefully, he hangs them from my ears. My mouth drops open in amazement. They are indescribably gorgeous. I turn my head slightly and the ropes of blue swing into my neck.

'Oh, Jake. They are beautiful,' I gasp.

But he is not finished. From his other pocket he takes another handful of blue gems, and moving to the back of me, places them around my throat. The stones glitter against my skin, like blue stars. Their color is so close to the shade of my eyes that I gaze at them in astonishment. *How did he find these stones?* My eyes meet his, startled, wondering, and awestruck. He smiles and turns me around to face him.

'I was right. They are perfect,' he murmurs, and bending his head kisses the hollow between my breasts where the plunging neckline ends. He watches riveted as through the material my nipples harden. He runs his palms over them and I make a small sound of submission.

His eyes register approval. 'I can't wait to get you home tonight.' There is a softness and depth to his voice.

418

In the darkened confines of the car I feel Jake's hand take mine.

'Your hands are cold,' he says. 'You're not nervous, are you?'

'A bit.'

He squeezes my hand. 'Don't be. I'll be at your side the whole time.'

I smile gratefully at him.

'You do know you will be the most beautiful woman in there.'

'You haven't even seen all the women yet.'

'I don't need to. You are the most beautiful woman to me.'

As we approach the queue of people waiting to get in I feel a little apprehensive, but also a heady sense of excitement. The new Eden's marbled and gilt splendor seems almost garish to my heightened senses. I feel so buoyed up I am almost light-headed. My feet seem to scarcely touch the ground and my stomach feels empty. I suppose it could be because I haven't eaten for hours. I daren't eat, not with this dress. Perhaps I am also anxious that I may not fit in. The shadow of his mother's disapproval looms. I know she will be here. Will she undermine me?

Red ropes are lifted and we are ushered in.

We go past the plum velvet loveseat in the foyer toward the enormous central vase filled with magnolia blossoms.

Struck by two spotlights the blooms seem almost brighter than the lamps.

The music grows louder and my heartbeat quickens.

We enter the club and the whole of fashionable London seems to be there. All the dancers are in their best, and beautiful people are everywhere. It must be true that beautiful models, male and female, have been flown in from all over the world to pretty up the place. Under the chandeliers the supremely rich are casually amused and the air is charged with their intriguingly corrupt whiff. Laughter ebbs and flows like the tide.

The Mayor of London is present; movie star hair, sharp as knives, and as usual pretending to be a good-natured buffoon.

Jake takes me to the table where his mother is sitting. Her eyes meet mine and her back straightens. She drops her eyes to a large bowl of floating orchids set in the middle of the table.

'Ma,' he greets, and bends to kiss her. In the candlelight the pearls around her neck glimmer milkily. She appears softened and yet hostile.

'Hello, Mrs. Eden,' I greet politely.

She nods distantly. I can't blame her. I might be even more ferocious if I thought someone was threatening my son. I remember being in school and aggressively fighting Luke's battles for him.

'Lily, meet my sister, Layla,' Jake says.

I turn to meet a stunning creature in a deep red silk dress standing next to us. She is tall, very tall—she might even be five ten or eleven—and is everything I have always thought of as beautiful. Her hair is the color of bitter chocolate and cascades down her back in rich and lustrous waves. Her eyes are as green as Jake's, but there appears to be either gray or blue in them, too. Her nose is straight and narrow, and her mouth is large and expressive. She grins, vibrantly alive and fiery. She is only nineteen and Jake tells me she has been studying fashion in Paris.

'Layla, Lily.'

Layla claps her hands with delight. 'Oh, Jake. She's a doll.'

I visualize the expression on my mother-in-law's face, extract the disapproval and count the hatred.

Jake looks down at me, indulgent, almost like a proud parent. 'Yes, she is a bit of a doll, isn't she?'

Heat warms up my throat and cheeks.

But in seconds the dynamics of the situation change.

'Who the fuck invited him?' Layla says angrily. The change in her is dramatic to say the least. There are twin spots of color in her cheeks.

'I did,' Jake says smoothly.

I turn my eyes in the direction Layla is looking in and see Billy Joe Pilkington approaching us. He is impossible to miss. He is large and menacing. Everything about him screams *beware of me, I'm lethal*. He is the kind of man I would cross the road to avoid. When he was bloodied and lying beside Jake, the menace had not been so apparent. Now it powers out of him in waves. He is dressed in a navy suit, but he is not wearing a tie, and his shirt is open low enough to see the beginnings of his tattoos. His eyes are dark—either dead fire or black ice. A place to trip up and fall badly.

He stops by Jake's mother first. 'Good health to you, Mrs. Eden,' he says.

Mara smiles. 'God and Mary to you. How is your mother?'

'She's made dying her life's work,' he says with a straight face.

Jake's mother hides a smile. 'May God grant her many years.'

'And me earplugs,' he says with a wink, and turns his attention toward our group of three.

'Hello, Layla,' he greets civilly.

'You have a nerve coming here!' she says rudely. Her whole body has become strangely stiff and hostile. She looks at him with great disdain.

'Layla,' her mother gasps, shocked.

422

'Apologize, Layla,' Jake says with a scowl.

'Why should I?' Layla retorts.

But BJ grins at her. It has an odd effect on his face. It does not soften it, but makes it even more dangerous. 'Layla,' he says softly. 'Look at you, all grown up and still not a shred of manners in sight.'

'See?' Layla turns to her mother. 'He's not being exactly friendly to me, is he?'

They stare at each other for a few seconds. The aggressive sexual tension between them is impossible to miss and makes me wonder which of them is actually resisting it.

'Maybe you'll save a dance for me later?' he says, a dimple forming in his chin. Shit. The guy is actually attractive.

'Hell will freeze over first,' she declares dramatically and flounces off.

BJ laughs, his eyes chasing her into the crowd.

'Sorry about that,' Jake says.

'No, don't apologize for her. She's got spirit. I like that in women and horses.'

Jake laughs. 'Let's call for a drink.'

A waitress materializes and while we are placing our orders another comes around with a tray of little round bruschetta with glistening swordfish carpaccio. The drinks arrive. BJ raises his pint glass of Guinness in a toast.

'Here's to cheating, stealing, fighting, and drinking.'

'May you be in heaven half an hour before the devil knows you're dead,' Jake replies.

We clink glasses. We drink. As ice-cold champagne slides down my throat I see Melanie waving at me. I haven't seen her since Jake came and took me and all my stuff from the flat I shared with her. I know she can't come over to our section so I excuse myself. 'I'm just going to say hello to a friend.' I glance at Jake and mouth, 'Be back soon.'

I weave my way over to her and she grins at me and we exchange kisses that are almost sisterly. She is dressed in a white gown of ravishing simplicity. It flows down her body like liquid. Her lips are ruby and her lashes are as long as an ostrich's.

'Girl, you sure showed us how to do it,' she shouts above the music and the din of the party.

I look back at Jake—he is watching me. I wave and laugh out loud. I know that for most of the dancers the holy grail is finding a fat purse and marrying it as quickly as possible. They know they can't dance after a certain age so the race is on as soon as they start out. Each one will say the same thing: They are here for a short spell.

Melanie is different, though. She is saving up to take the money to Barbados where she plans to buy a beach bar. The last time we talked she figured she would only have to work for another six months.

'Is that adoring admiration I just saw?' she teases.

I flush. 'Maybe.'

'Has he got a big dick?' she asks cheekily.

'Yes,' I admit and we giggle wickedly. I miss her blunt and honest ways.

'Wow, I love these,' she says, touching the blue stones.

'Me too,' I agree happily.

'Listen, I have to go because I'm performing now, but let's catch up soon.'

'All right. How about Friday?'

'Nails and then lunch?'

'OK, I'll call you.'

As I watch her walk away I notice the man who had come to collect BJ after the fight, the man who had shown for a split second that he recognized me.

I start walking toward him.

Our eyes meet, but he lets his slide away, pretending not to see me making my way toward him, tries to disappear through the crowd in the direction of the men's toilet. I let him escape. A few minutes later he comes out of the toilet and looks around him. He does not see me behind the pillar and is startled when I touch his sleeve.

He whirls around.

'Hi, remember me?' I say brightly.

He frowns as if trying to place me. 'Oh yeah, from the fight, right?'

'No, you know me from before, don't you?'

His frown deepens. He is a very good actor.

'No, I had never seen you before that day. You must have me mixed up with someone else.' He smiles, but his eyes are shifty, oh so fucking shifty.

'My mistake,' I say softly, but now I know for certain. He is lying. My eyes glance away from him and fall on BJ across the room. One of the South American dancers has wound herself around him, but he is staring at us. Even from a distance I can see how hard and dangerous his eyes are.

BJ's man opens his mouth to say something else, but is interrupted by Jake's voice. He has come up behind me and curved his hand around my waist. 'Everything OK?' he asks icily. There is tension and warning in the words.

I look up at him. His eyes are dark and watchful.

'Everything's just fine.'

'Hello, Mr. Eden,' the liar says uncomfortably.

'Have a good evening, Tommy,' Jake says curtly, and turning me away leads me back to our table.

'The entertainment is about to start,' he says. Without BJ, Layla looks quiet and subdued. The nightclub becomes dark. Searching spotlights begin to race around the room.

From the darkened ceiling come cages with flaxen-haired nymphs who look like trapped birds inside. The music, a jarring discordant piece of hammering pianos and choppy chords, starts, and the nymphs hang out of their cages, and slowly spiral down on colored lengths of cloth. They land on the stage and form a provocative tableau of glittering costumes and long, stockinged legs. The music changes abruptly.

Something inventive and experimental. My ears start to ring with it.

It is a good evening and I have had more alcohol than I should have. When we step over the threshold of our home, Jake lets go of me and I sway slightly.

'Is it today or tomorrow?' I ask, pretending to consider the matter seriously.

He glances at his watch. 'It's today and tomorrow,' he says very, very gravely. He could be laughing at me, but I don't care. He won't be laughing for very long.

'In that case...' I tug the knot. Just before we left the club I visited the Ladies and took off the little brooch that held the knot. Now it gives way and the entire dress falls around my ankles.

He touches my breasts with the tips of his fingers. As soon as he touches them I feel his excitement like a spark of electricity and rear back.

'What's that?' I ask startled.

'That's amazement,' he tells me solemnly.

'That makes two of us.' I say flirtatiously.

'Guess what?' His eyes are cheeky.

'What?' I'm all wide-eyed and ready.

'I stole some stuff from our room in Vegas.'

'Oh yeah? What?'

'Come with me, Mrs. Eden, and I'll show you.'

Handcuffs. Oh! Handcuffs. They most certainly did not teach me everything there is to know about them at the police academy.

'What do I love more than my wife?
Nothing.'

—Jake Eden

ELEVEN

Lily

I wake in the early hours of the morning with a dream still vividly imprinted on my mind. It is an odd dream. In it I am a child and I have woken up and found Luke gone from his bed. Unafraid, I get out of bed and go down the stairs. The house is quiet so I begin to call out for him. There is no sense of foreboding. As I move to the living room I see there is a plate of cookies and a glass of milk on the floor. And then I wake up.

I lay in the dark thinking about my weird dream; it ushers in a memory of when I was six years old and Luke five. It was Christmas morning and the moment I'd opened my excited eyes the first thought in my head was the presents that Santa brought us during the night. He always left two presents at the bottom of our beds to open first thing in the morning. I turned my head to see if Luke was awake yet, and found that he was not even in bed. Surprised, because we always woke each other up and opened our presents together, I sat up and listened. The house was very quiet.

I knew he couldn't have gone to the bathroom anyway, because he'd rather pee in bed than wait to open his presents. I scrambled out of bed and ran to the bedroom window that faced a field overlooking the woods at the rear of our house.

I opened the curtains and there were almost blizzard conditions outside. Through driving snow I could make out Luke's bright yellow jacket. He was squatting in the middle of the white field building something from the snow, oblivious to the freezing cold. He'd slipped out of our bedroom, down the stairs and gone outside through the back door, without even Mum or Dad hearing him.

Shrugging into my pink jacket I hurried downstairs as quietly as I could. I knew my parents would be mad with Luke and I was so excited about Christmas Day I didn't want anything to spoil it. I opened the back door and felt the sudden bite of cold. I didn't dare shout so I went quite close before I called out to him.

'What are you doing, Luke?'

He stopped building what looked like three steps of a snow staircase and squinted at me through the flurries of

white flakes. His little cheeks were tinged with red and blue.

'If Mum and Dad see you they're going to go mad on Christmas,' I warned.

He reached for a toy tractor half covered with snow.

'I don't want Santa's present.'

'Why?' I asked perplexed. He had specifically asked for this toy. Stood in Toys"R"Us and pointed it out to Dad as the thing that Santa should bring him.

'I've changed my mind,' he said with his bottom lip pushed out stubbornly. 'I want to go to Santa and get an exchange, so I'm making a ladder to climb to the North Pole.'

'What do you want to exchange your present for?' I asked curiously.

'I want Santa to make mummy better.'

How strange that that memory is intact and yet has been hidden from me all these years. Remembering those words from his tiny mouth breaks my heart, and tears rush uncontrollably forward. I begin to cry for my baby brother.

Very quietly, I edge to the side of the bed and slip out. Going into the bathroom I climb into the bath and hug my knees to my body as the tears flow. I remember how my dad found us both building the staircase and managed to convince Luke that we could write to Santa. Santa preferred that, anyway.

That is the thing I'll always remember and miss about Luke, his kind heart and beautiful innocence. He was a gentle dreamer and life should have treated him with care and love, but it didn't.

'Oh, Luke,' I whisper.

I hear a small sound at the door, the whisper of clothes against wood. I look up and Jake is standing there looking at me.

'What are you doing?' he asks me. His eyes are full of concern.

'I want to tell you about my brother,' I tell him.

'OK,' he says and climbs into the bath and sits facing me, his toes nearly touching mine.

'He was a heroin addict and he died from an overdose.' My voice catches at that. I have never admitted that to anyone before. 'I found his body.'

Something flashes in his eyes, but he does not say anything or attempt to hold me.

'It was truly awful. It destroyed me. I became a little mad after that.' I laugh, a rasping, desperate sound. He says nothing. Simply looks at me. I clear my throat and I tell him about the spoon, the rubber tube. The needle still embedded in his bloated arm. Then I tell him about my descent.

'I was barely living. I survived on a mixture of rage and the need for revenge. I was so broken I even tried to kill myself.'

I peer into his eyes, looking for condemnation of my weakness, or pity, but there is nothing, only direct and tenacious focus. At that moment I know I can tell him anything and he will still be there for me. His regard is unshakeable.

I come clean. 'Everything I told you about my parents so far has been lies, part of my cover story. My dad, he's not an alcoholic or a wife beater. He's a good man, a doctor. He put me on anti-psychotic drugs.'

Then I pour out the visit to the pathologist and how it made me so angry with the people who had sold the tainted drugs to Luke that I decided to become a police officer. I tell him about how I joined the secretive undercover outfit called SO10. I tell him about the crack den and how the terrible, terrible smell of it still haunts me. And how I realized very quickly that I didn't want to go after the small dealers, but the huge drug barons, and how the assignment to trap Crystal Jake had dropped into my lap.

'So you went undercover. To catch the big bad guys?' he asks.

I nod.

'If you come upon a case where a wealthy heiress has died under suspicious circumstances and you are the investigating officer, what is the first line of investigation that you would naturally take?'

I frown. 'I'd follow the money.'

'So if you want to catch the big drug barons, why are you not following the money?'

For a second I am confused. 'I'm a foot soldier. It is not my job to do that. My superiors decide the avenues of investigation and I carry out their commands.'

'Has it ever occurred to you to wonder why no one at the highest levels of this "drug war" is doing that?'

I frown again, thrown by the turn the conversation has taken. 'What are you saying?'

'I'm saying that you, your little secretive undercover unit, and all the other departments that are supposed to be fighting the drugs war are all being manipulated. Drug barons are worth billions. They have to wash their money somewhere. That somewhere is some of the biggest banks in the world. Why are they sending you out to trap me when the most obvious thing would be to punish the banks that hide the money, to freeze the billions that the drug cartels own, and to stop the drugs at the source?'

I stare at him. Feeling stupid. It is an issue that I care about very deeply and yet I have accepted the most shallow of explanations about it.

'The most developed form of puppetry in the world is the traditional Japanese puppet theater called Bunraku. The Japanese are very proud of it because it is considered a very highly skilled art form. And it is rather special because unlike other puppet shows the manipulators of the Bunraku puppets appear openly, in full view of the audience. However, the audience pretends not to be able to see them because the puppet masters are cloaked in black robes and sometimes black hoods.

'The war on drugs is the same. The real manipulators of the puppets are not invisible, but we pretend we can't see them. The system has trained us to see only the small-time criminals, the powerless puppets. So they train people like you to go after small fry and to be happy you have shut down a drug den knowing full well that as long as supply is safe another den will pop up even before the arresting officers have written their reports.'

He pauses.

'But as far as I am concerned I'm not even that small-time drug dealer, Lily. You have to believe me.'

'So why do they want you?'

'You tell me.'

I press my fingertips against my temples. 'I have seen the file on you.'

'I haven't touched drugs since I was nineteen years old. Whatever you saw in that file is not me. You see, I've been in a crack den a few times. I've seen clawing addiction first-hand. That intolerable smell you talk about, that's feces, the ammonia of stale urine, sweat, and layers of accumulated dirt. And those blankets that they put up to cover every little gap of light that would otherwise come through? They do that because of their paranoia. They have the unshakable impression that people are watching them.'

'Were you a crack addict?' I whisper in shock.

He smiles. 'No, but I know because I was once that slightly bigger fish drug dealer that all those little drug dealers went to, to get their stock from. I went to a crack house so I could see the bottom of my chain. It made me so sick I started a charity to help them. I don't have a lot of time so I don't do as much as I should, but if you want to help them you can take over. We both know you are bored sick of your job.'

'How did you know I was bored?'

He flattens his mouth. 'Lily, that job was designed to bore the shit out of you.'

'What?'

'Of course. What, did you think I was going to put you into some position where you could get any kind of information that could be twisted and used against me?'

'Right. What does your charity do?'

'We send the addicts to South America to be purged out with ayahuasca assisted treatments. It may seem off the wall but it has been shockingly effective and the reoffend rate is better than anything else I have seen.'

'Doesn't that have a psychedelic chemical, DMT, a Schedule 1 controlled substance?'

'Ayahuasca is a psychoactive brew of vine and plants that has been used in traditional medicine and shaman practices for centuries in the Amazon region. It is perfectly legal in South America.'

'Right,' I say carefully, since I know nothing about this stuff, but my first thought is that if it works that well, why isn't it on mainstream media?

'International research suggests that when administered in therapeutic settings, ayahuasca can reduce problematic substance use by helping promote personal or spiritual insights and self-knowledge. That's the spiel we give our detractors. This is my experience of it. It's fucking brilliant. These kids go there like walking corpses, they projectile vomit, shit like crazy, experience strong audio and visual hallucinations, and come out a few weeks later healed and whole. It is a form of psychic detoxification where they discover the root cause—unpleasant memories, fears, anxieties—of their addictive and harmful behavior. Sometimes that sense of deficient emptiness and inchoate distress that they have felt all their life is gone. It gives them their first taste of victory after being constantly defeated by life. They come to the understanding that they are already the perfect human beings they were born as.'

I experience a stab of pain. Poor Luke. It's too late for him.

'Have you tried it?'

'Of course. I wasn't about to let the kids go through something I wasn't going to try first.'

'What was it like?'

He smiles. 'Ayahuasca shows you the baggage you have carried all your life. You see clearly that all that pain is not part of you. You can put it down. I cried tears of pure joy when I took it. If you want I'll take you one day.'

I look into his eyes and I know instantly that I would like to do that. I'd like to heal, too. I'd like to put my baggage down and live like everybody else.

'Why don't you go around to the center tomorrow and see how you feel about it?'

'I will.' I pause for a second. There is something more important for me to tackle before I get involved in his charity. 'Do you have enemies, Jake?'

'Many.'

'Someone is out for you. Someone is giving untrue information about you.'

'And you think it is Tommy?'

I look up at him, surprised by how quickly he has surmised the situation. 'Yes.'

'Why?'

'Because when I came to pick you up at the barn after the fight he looked at me as if he knew me, but I have never seen him before in my life.'

'And BJ? You think he's involved too?'

'If you were out, he could move in and claim your territory, right?'

He nods slowly. I open my mouth to say something else, but he puts a finger against my lips. 'Don't say anything for a while.'

We sit staring at each other, trying to insert some normality into the scene we find ourselves playing.

 440

Finally, he says, 'Don't tell anyone what you just told me.'

I nod.

'Promise me, Lily. You are making some very dangerous accusations. These people are lethal. You don't know the way they think. The question of honor is not taken lightly in our community. You have to promise to stay out of this. You've told me and you must trust me to sort it out, OK?'

'OK, I promise,' and that should have been the perfect time to tell him that I am still an undercover agent—not trying to trap him, but trying to help him. But I don't because I know he will try to stop me and I don't want to be stopped. I want to get to the bottom of the truth. I have been led by the nose too long.

Later I will regret my silence.

TWELVE

Lily

'**I** am bored with all the restaurants I know. Take me somewhere authentic, but Chinese obviously,' Melanie says after we do our nails.

The only restaurant that immediately comes to mind is the one that Robin once took me to. Even though the service was just shy of surly, the food was surprisingly good. We take a taxi to Soho and go into the restaurant. Like most Chinese restaurants the air conditioning is turned up too high. We are met at the till by an unsmiling waitress and briskly shown to our seats. A laminated, slightly sticky menu is thrust into our hands.

'You want drink?' she asks while noisily clearing away the extra table settings.

We order Chinese tea.

Melanie raises her eyebrows. 'Already I am impressed,' she says sarcastically.

'We Chinese, we tend to be a bit abrupt, but don't worry—the speed and taste of our food will make up for it,' I say in a heavily accented voice.

Melanie laughs but true to form the food arrives with impressive speed. The crispy Peking duck is so delicious Melanie eats more than I have ever seen her eat. Afterwards the egg fried rice, sea bass steamed with ginger and onions, cashew nut prawns, and a mixed vegetable dish arrive piping hot and go down quickly, too. We are nearly finished with our meal when Melanie suddenly chuckles quietly.

'What?' I ask her.

'This is what I love about dancing. You meet all kinds of people without their masks. Don't look now but the guy that has just come in used to come into Miss Moneypenny.'

I know that name. It is another gentlemen's club and if I am not mistaken it belongs to the Pilkingtons.

'Oh yeah?' I say casually. 'What's so special about him?'

'Well. He's arrived here with a policeman and they look really chummy so it's obvious he must be some kind of undercover cop too, but you should have seen him at the club. He has a taste for cruelty. He went for the dancers who were turning tricks on the sly. Once he took a girl home, and she never turned up for work the next day. We never saw her again while I was there. There was

something fishy going on too. All the girls were talking about it. We all knew it was not right.'

My eyes widen with shock. 'What do you mean?'

'She was Romanian. No family. No relatives. Just disappeared. One moment she says, "Bye, see you tomorrow," and next minute she's gone without a trace. Management should have called the police. He was the last one to see her. But nothing happened. And now I know why. He *is* the police. Another time he beat a girl real bad. I heard that *she* was asked to leave! I didn't stay after that. Bad vibes, man.'

I feel a ripple of disgust go through me. There is a dirty cop behind me. 'Who runs that club?'

'You were talking to him yesterday. That slime ball, Tommy.'

I sit frozen. 'Right,' I say slowly. 'Can he see us, Melanie?'

'OK, he's looking at the menu. Quick, turn around and look now. He's the one in trendy yellow designer gear.'

I glance around as casually as I can and my limbs turn to water. I turn back quickly and look at her in shock. 'Are you sure, Melanie?'

'Of course I'm sure. I could never forget that bastard. All the girls were scared of him. It was as if he was the boss.'

'Does he know you?'

'I wouldn't have thought so. I'm not his flavor. He likes Eastern European girls, blondes.'

Her eyes narrow. 'You look like you've seen a ghost. Do you know him?'

I meet her gaze with a frown. 'Yes, I do, but I can't explain just yet.' I take a deep breath.

'Bejesus. You're mixed up with him.'

'Not in the way you think. Look, do you mind if we slip out through the back way? I don't want him to see me.'

She shrugs. 'OK.'

I call for the bill. While my credit card is being processed by the machine I look up at our unsmiling waitress. 'My ex-boyfriend has just turned up and it could be trouble for me, can I please leave by the back way?'

'Cannot. Regulations,' she says shortly.

I take a ten pound note out of my purse and put it into the tray. Her eyes slide down to it.

'I show you the way.'

At a dirty black door she turns to me. 'You come again,' she says with a smile and shuts the door in our faces.

'Come on, Mel,' I say pulling her away. As we hurry away my mind is whirling like crazy. The truth is I am actually frightened. I have the sensation that the ground I thought I was standing so securely upon has turned into quicksand that is sucking me up. Two streets away we hail a cab and I say goodbye to Melanie.

You know what kind of people become undercover officers? People who want to hide under a different skin, unhappy people, people with low self-esteem. On one hand I hate the people that I am supposed to be trapping; in another sense I become them and secretly envy them and their glamorous lifestyles.

I can hardly bring myself to believe that the man Melanie is talking about is Robin. That... That Robin is a bent cop.

Instead of getting another cab for myself I walk aimlessly along the street. I need to think. I know I need to arrange a meeting with Mills in the safe house, but I also know that whistleblowers in the force are not lauded and promoted but disappeared. Anyone who raises issues and problems becomes the problem. And it is doubly dangerous to be the problem of such an ambitious man as Mills. He wants Jake's head on a platter, not Robin's. So I need to protect myself.

I look at my watch. Jake isn't expecting me for a while yet. By leaving the restaurant via the back entrance we would have lost the tail Jake has on me. I disappear into the Tube and get out at Green Park. I exit and hailing a cab ask him to take me to Lea Bridge Road.

Ten minutes after I walk into Lorraine Electronic Surveillance I leave with their smallest audio recorder, a nifty device no bigger than a USB stick, but one that is powerful enough to clearly pick up sound at up to twenty-five feet. It also has a twelve hour record time and is sound activated, so will only begin recording when it hears something.

Then I call the number Mills gave me. To my surprise it is not a telephone operator who will pass on the message but Mills who answers. Our conversation is brief and to the point.

Tomorrow at noon.

Then I catch a cab back to Jake's home. Before Jake comes home that evening I book a rental car and have them park it in a car park that I specify. I pay for a courier to pick up the keys and drop it off to me inside the hour.

Then I sit down and plan my meeting with Mills. When Jake comes home he finds me cooking, a bottle of wine open, me on my second glass, the music so loud I don't hear him come in.

He leans against the doorway watching me.

I grin and point to his glass of whiskey. He picks it up and comes toward me. 'I didn't know we were having a party.'

'I have an Irish joke for you.'

He groans.

'No, no, it's really good.'

'Go on.'

'There's an Englishman, a Scotsman and an Irishman all talking about their teenage daughters. The Englishman says, "I was cleaning my daughter's room the other day and I found a packet of cigarettes. I was really shocked as I didn't even know she smoked."

'The Scotsman says, "That's nothing. I was cleaning my daughter's room the other day when I came across a half full bottle of vodka. I was really shocked as I didn't even know she drank."

'With that the Irishman says, "Both of you have got nothing to worry about. I was cleaning my daughter's room the other day when I found a packet of condoms. I was really shocked. I didn't even know she had a cock."'

Jake laughs and so do I.

That sets the tone for the evening. It is irreverent. We eat with our fingers and laugh a lot. I totally forget about Mills and what I have to do the next day.

Afterwards, Jake makes me wear a pair of my shoes from my dancing days and do a strip tease for him. Tipsy and laughing I start undressing. It is only a game. It is to put the night to bed.

But when I look into his darkened eyes, my mouth makes a purring sound and my sex swells, hot, wet and aching.

Jake

She seems different tonight, her face is flushed, her lips parted. Sweat dampens her naked skin. She is wild for it, in that desperate way that people have on the last day of their holiday. She grinds her bare ass against my erection and I groan and catch her by the waist, holding her tightly. She wriggles away. I let her go. She comes back like a carefree butterfly.

I watch her push the globes of creamy flesh close to my face and shimmy hard

so all her flesh quivers and shakes. That heady, sexy as hell scent of her fills my nostrils and I feel myself losing control. My breathing becomes shallow, my heart races. Your time running around naked and free is nearly over, my love. She turns around to face me, her legs apart. Her folds are swollen and protrude invitingly out of her sex lips.

'Undress,' she orders, in a deep silky voice, utterly unaware of how improbable she sounds giving orders when her bits are protruding or how little time is left for her to play the tease. She's everything I've ever wanted.

My eyes never leaving hers, I tug off my clothes in double quick time. She spins around in a deft lap-dancer move and, pushing me down on the sofa, she moves upwards, and with her thighs wide open she begins to lower her sticky sex into my mouth. I watch it come down, the puffy lips oozing and glistening with raw sexual need, her hole gaping and begging to be filled.

Like a hungry man I swoop upwards to meet it on its way down to me. With her hands flat on either side of my hips she leans forward and slips her warm, open mouth over my engorged dick. The glaze of sweat makes her nipples slide against my body.

I hear the sound of her heart beating faster as her breath rasps with excitement. I lick and suck and fuck her with my tongue until she comes with a force that shakes her to her very core.

I spread her legs wide and look at her. Her gorgeous hair is tangled and spread across the sofa. Slowly I let my eyes travel down to her sex, open and ready for me, and I feel that wild, relentlessly primitive urge to possess and brand her. To mark her as mine. If I was in one of those tribal societies where they ink their women to mark them as their property I'd be right there inking her whole body so there is no mistaking what is mine.

Putting my hands on either side of her I mount her. Her mouth opens into a slack O. It gives me immense pleasure to know that the thick, mushroomed head of my cock is stretching her to unbearableness. She locks her legs desperately around my hips to keep me there. Just the idea of her underneath me, helplessly swallowing my cock into her body, excites me and I pound her hard until I explode inside her, my cock pushing so deep into her that her body buckles and shudders.

For a few seconds I stay inside her while she milks the cream of my body with her own. And during that time I sense her as if she is a part of my body, her heartbeat, the flow of blood inside her veins, the increased heat rising off her skin, and the lift and fall of her chest.

The sensation is unfamiliar, but strangely beautiful. For a long time I watch the moonlight come in through the window and throw its blue light on her cheek. I want to protect her from anything and everything that could possibly hurt her.

How foolish I was to think
That I could catch a butterfly?
—*Butterflies*, Shiv Kumar Batalvi

THIRTEEN

Lily

At twelve I take a cab and direct it to an Indian restaurant in Notting Hill. I go into the restaurant, slip the waiter a twenty pound note, and he gladly escorts me out through the back door. I walk quickly along the back street, take a left and walk up the road to the NCP car park. Inside, I keep pressing the key remote in my hand until a car lights up and clicks open.

I get in and drive to the safe house, where I find a parking space, pay the parking charge and get out, locking the car. It is a small building of six flats in a quiet street. At lunchtime hardly anyone is around. I access the apartment block through the street entrance and climb briskly to the second floor. My heart is thudding hard, but I am not in a panic. I know I haven't done anything wrong. I think I am more bemused than anything else.

I check the concealment of my recording device—all seems well—turn

my key in the door, and push. Inside, I'm met by the strong, disagreeable smell of cigar smoke. As soon as I close the door I can see up the hallway and into the living room. DS Mills is lounging on a sofa with his feet up on the coffee table. He is sucking on a cigar and holding a large goblet of brandy in his hand.

He looks at his cigar. 'You are late,' he says.

I glance at my watch. 'By a minute, Sir.'

'Arrive before I do, in future. I'm a busy man.' He gestures condescendingly with his finger to the sofa opposite him. 'Sit down.' Even beyond the office environment, his arrogance is breathtaking. I've heard that he is married, but I can't imagine the state of the long-suffering wife sitting at home waiting for him. I do as I am told.

'Spit it out then. What've you got for me on Eden?'

On the way here I'd thought of all the different ways I could tackle the subject with Mills, but face to face there is no easy way, so I just blurt it out.

'The information I have is not about Jake, Sir. It's about Robin.'

Mills' eyes narrow dangerously. He carefully places his cigar to rest on the side of his ashtray, and asks coldly, 'Is this some kind of bullshit joke, Strom?'

I stay strong. 'I'm afraid not, Sir. I have information that Robin has been seen in the Pilkingtons' clubs and I believe he might even be working with or for them.'

'You want me to believe this ludicrous accusation verbatim because?' His sarcasm and irritation are obvious. He gets up onto his feet and walks around the sofa.

'I trust the source, Sir.'

'I'll be the judge of that. Who the fuck is your source?'

'A dancer from the club. She's seen Robin and Tommy Saunders, Billy Joe Pilkington's number two man, together at the club a few times. That is highly irregular and should be looked into.'

'A dancer?' he scoffs.

I swallow hard and sit upright. 'My duty is to put out any information I uncover so that any future investigations can be informed by it.'

'Robin can visit any damn club he wants. It's not against the law.'

I flush. 'My instinct tells me something more is going on, Sir. The dancer made some serious accusations. A girl he had gone out with went missing.'

'Do you think I'm going to take the word of some anonymous, two bit stripper over one of my best men? Have you and Eden cooked this cock and bull story up to save his ass?'

'That's not fair, Sir,' I snap back. 'I followed your instructions to the letter. No one, not even Jake Eden, knows about our arrangement.'

'I can't believe you dragged me up here for a bit of stripper gossip.'

'Have you got a magic crystal ball, Sir? Do you know exactly what is happening at all times and you never ever get anything wrong?'

He glares at me warningly. 'Watch yourself, Strom, I'm your commanding officer.'

But at this point I don't give a fuck anymore. He is just a bully. And I don't care if I never work in the force again. 'I'm just curious why you would not be even slightly intrigued as to why Robin might be fraternizing with well-known gangsters.'

'What are you implying, Strom?' Mills stops suddenly in my face. His face looks like it might explode among the bulging veins.

I remain outwardly calm and smile. 'I'm sure you can deduce the implication yourself, Sir.'

My sarcasm causes him to erupt violently. He thrusts a finger in my face. 'I'd be very careful, if I were you. You're walking on extremely thin ice.'

'I'm not afraid of you. I haven't done anything wrong. Yes, it was a lapse of judgment to sleep with my target, but I confessed, and offered to resign.'

Suddenly, like a bolt of lightning, out of nowhere, it comes to me. I see it clearly, the thing that had eluded me all this time, the thing that I had missed. I stare at him with shocked eyes. My eyes are riveted on him, equal parts fear and disbelief. My voice is a whisper. 'You showed no curiosity or surprise about the shipment coming in on the sixteenth. You knew about it before I told you, didn't you?'

He sighs. 'You stupid, stupid bitch. All you had to do was open your fucking legs and distract Eden while we laid our plans. But you couldn't just do that, could you? Oh no, you had to be a little Miss Marple, running around poking your fucking nose into things that have nothing to do with you.'

Suddenly I am afraid. I *have* been running around playing at being detective without any idea of what was really going on in the shadows. Jake is not the gangster. This man is. I see it in his cold, pitiless eyes.

The door. I have to get to the door. 'I'm not listening to this,' I say as calmly as I can manage, and getting up, head for the door. My knees are trembling so hard I am afraid I will not get to it.

Almost there. I'm there... But before I can pull it open, Mills' big palm slams down on it.

I jump like a startled cat, a scream rattling in my throat.

'You're not dismissed yet,' he murmurs so close to my ear that I rear back in terror. He smiles at me and a shiver runs down my spine. There is something truly chilling and frightening about this smiling side of him. He is almost unrecognizable. I can hardly believe it is the same person. 'Back to your seat. I'm not quite finished with you.'

He is six feet plus and sixteen stone so my racing mind decides that it is best to placate him until I can think what to do next. I sit back down and watch him, frightened to my core. He goes to the window, takes his mobile out of his belt holder and dials. While he waits for his call to be answered he keeps his eyes trained on me. I think about running to the door, but I know I won't make it. He is too fast. Too dangerous.

'Things have moved faster than expected,' he says into the phone. 'I'm going to need some help with dispatch.' A pause. 'No, no disposal necessary this time.' He listens again. 'Yes. Right now! Don't forget to knock three times, so I know it's you, and don't shoot you by mistake.' He laughs.

Oh my God! Oh my God. I am a dead woman... I have dug my own grave by doing such a good job of losing my tail. If Mills has his way, I will disappear without a trace. I think of Jake and everything he means to me.... God! He'll never know that I love him with all my heart. Oh God! I've been so, so stupid. What a mess I have made of everything.

Mills ends the call.

I need to think. I'm starting to feel out of control and hysterical. My mind tries to analyze the situation. Who has he called? Robin? Or maybe Tommy Saunders?

'Who have you just called?' I ask.

'That should be the least of your worries, I would have thought, Lily.'

Hearing him call me by my first name makes a wave of nausea roll into my stomach.

'You don't have to get rid of me. I'm off the force, anyway. Just let me go and you'll never hear from me again. I beg of you,' I cry. By his disgusted expression I know I sound whiny and pathetic, but I don't want to die. I want to live, I want to be with the man I love and watch our children playing in the meadows like Jake did on beautiful spring days.

'Don't be pathetic, Lily. We both know that's never going to happen. There's too much at stake for everyone concerned.'

Helpless and frightened tears run down my face. I start wailing.

'All right, I'll let you go.'

I stop and stare at him. He's playing games. 'You're going to let me go?' I know it is nonsense even as I say it.

'Yes, if you call Jake and ask him to come here now. It's not you I want.'

A strange kind of calm washes over me. There is not a single cell in me that can be persuaded to do that. I'll never hurt Jake. Not intentionally.

'I'd rather die than do that.'

Mills breaks into what can only be described as demonic laughter. All the hair on my arms stand. 'That's funny,' he says, getting a hold of himself. 'I'll just have to call him myself.'

'You don't have his number.'

'No, but you do.'

'I'll never give it to you.'

He starts walking toward me. I go rigid with fear. When he is about two feet away he reaches into his jacket, pulls out a gun and, after calmly screwing on the silencer, presses the cold metal to my cheek. I emit an involuntary cry. 'Tell me,' he orders. My eyes swivel sideways and I stare at him in terror.

'Tell me or I'll blow your brains out.'

'No.'

He swings his hand in a wide arc and cracks the barrel of his gun across my temple. The blow sends me flying off my seat onto the floor, pain exploding in my head. I lie sprawled and stunned under the coffee table as he yanks my bag from my clenched fists. Through a haze of pain I see him search for my phone. I try to stand but he presses the heel of his shoe down on my chest and grins down at me.

Warm blood streams down my face. I start mumbling and begging him, 'No, please. Don't bring him here. Leave him alone.'

He walks away from me with the phone to his ear. I feel like I'm losing consciousness, but I know that I must stay awake no matter what. I must warn Jake, if it's the last thing I do. I hear him talking, but I can't make it out through the excruciating pain. Mills is coming back toward me.

He stands over me and calmly presses his heel into my hurt temple.

I scream.

'Is that proof enough for you or do I have to hurt her again?' he asks into the phone. I clench my teeth to stop myself from crying out and try to listen to Mills' side of the conversation. 'That's right. Get the key from under the mat and come in. Don't try anything funny or bring anyone else with you, or you'll be in time to see her skull explode.'

Mills ends the call and tosses my phone away. He then walks to the drinks cabinet and pours himself another brandy. He goes back to his chair and relights his cigar. He puts his gun in his lap and his feet up on the coffee table. He has assumed the same position I found him in. I hold my throbbing temple and remember my surveillance device. If I don't make it I need his confession on tape. Perhaps someone else will find it and put this corrupt bastard away.

'Why?' I ask. 'Why are you after Jake?'

He takes another mouthful of brandy. 'Why? Why anything, Strom? Territory... Money... Power... And a gangster I can control.'

'A gangster you can control?' I repeat.

He watches the smoke rising lazily from his cigar. 'You see, Lily, the real problem here is Eden. He's a fucking dinosaur and there's just no place for people like him in this industry.'

He takes a puff, blows out another plume of smoke and stares at me, his eyes dark and totally devoid of emotion. 'The people I work with can't have large swathes of prime real estate in the hands of someone like him. By running his clubs as if they're part of a legit business operation he's holding back progress.

I make a small sound of disbelief. 'You mean Jake was telling me the truth! He really isn't a gangster?'

'Gangster?' Laughter erupts from his mouth. 'He's fucking soft in the head. With him out of the way the clubs will be run the way they should be. With the right working girls, and our own security people controlling the flow of drugs there's a fortune to be made.' He shrugs. 'I had a different timeline for our takeover, but with all your meddling and interfering you've pushed it forward. After today we'll have it all.'

'Just how do you plan to get away with this? You can't simply make Jake and me disappear. There'll be CCTV images of me and Jake coming here and questions that will eventually lead to you.'

Mills shakes his head. 'My dear naive Lily. It will be my team and me who will be investigating. It's really terribly simple and straightforward. Obviously, you discovered evidence of drug dealing. You came here to pass the information to me. Unknown to you your criminal husband followed you here. A gun battle ensued between him, my associate and me. Eden died. Unfortunately, Strom, you did too. Honorably in the line of duty. A real police hero. So young and good looking too – the papers will love it. We'll award you a medal for outstanding services or something. Your parents will be quite proud of you. The public will mourn the death of a brave officer. Obviously I take the credit for the bust, and Eden, a notorious criminal, is forgotten very quickly.'

I feel my stomach shrivel up inside my body as I hear his voice lay out the future so confidently. But when I speak my voice is full of contempt. At least I will die knowing that Jake is not criminal. He was being set up.

'I had you marked as the type of officer who retires on a nice pension in the countryside somewhere. But after today the only thing you will be looking forward to is a view of the inside of a cell for the remainder of your days.'

He laughs. 'It's kind of you to worry about my well-being when you're about to meet your maker.' He checks his watch.

'Is Robin coming?'

'You're giving me a headache, Strom. I'd appreciate a bit of quiet until your husband and my associate arrive.'

—You know it's true,
baby I'd die for you—

FOURTEEN

Jake

I feel the veins in my neck bulge, my throat narrow. If that fucking piece of dog shit harms one single hair on her head I'll kill him with my bare hands. My right leg starts trembling with nervous energy.

'God in heaven, why? Why, Lily? Why?' I smash my fist into the door. 'Why couldn't you just fucking leave me to deal with it?' Pain flowers into my fist. The pain is good, because it focuses my mind. I need to pull myself together. My secretary comes running into my office. Her eyes are wild. She has never seen me like this.

I hold my palms up.

'Do you want me to do anything?' she asks in a shocked tone.

I don't trust my voice. I shake my head and stride out through the open door. I drive back to the house in a state of such agitation that I speed through every single red light I come across. Horns blare at me from every direction.

They increase my sense of panic. At an intersection I slam the steering wheel.

'Damn you, Lily. Always making promises you don't keep.'

I throw open the front door and race to my safe. There is an icy hand inside my chest: clenched around my heart. I'm so angry I could kill someone. I take out the gun, the one I had hoped I'd never have a need for again. I always knew taking this in my hands again would require a matter of life and death, and this is. I load it up, my movements precise and efficient. It's like riding a bike. You never forget. I slip it into my waistband. Then I slide the backup, a 9mm, into my right ankle holster and sprint to my car.

I input the address into my navigation system. Twenty-three minutes! That's how long it's going to take me to reach her. I tell myself to calm down, but I end up driving like a madman, keeping my foot floored to the pedal even when the near misses become more and more frequent. I sense that Lily's captor means business, but it is me he is after. She's just bait. And you don't hurt the hostage, at least, not until you get what you want.

In this case, me.

I pull up outside the address, adrenaline surging through my body. I switch off the engine and do a quick reconnaissance of the street. All seems quiet. I exit the car and walk quickly up to the discreet entrance. I press the buzzer as per instructions. Someone buzzes me in. Once inside the dimly lit foyer I see the two level staircase that leads up to the flat entrance at the top. I listen. Nothing. I take my gun out and climb the stairs. My heart is thumping so loud I can hear it in the echoing stillness of the stairwell.

I find a key under the mat and use it to push open the door. It swings back to reveal Lily sprawled on the ground and a large man is standing over her. A gun is pointed at her head and her face is chalk white and smeared with blood. I feel myself going into shock.

'Get out. Don't come in. He'll kill us both if you do,' she screams.

I came to get you and I'm not fucking leaving without you.

'Drop the gun, Eden, or I swear I'll splatter her brains right now.'

'Shoot her and you're dead.'

'But she'll be dead, too. You want to take that risk?'

I can see from the man's dead eyes that he is a psychopath. He wouldn't think twice about carrying out his threat. But I'm not giving up my gun, or both Lily and I are dead for sure. Two thoughts occur to me. He is alone. But he won't be so for long. This might be my only chance. My best hope is to distract the ugly cunt, and make him shoot at me, long enough for me to get a clear shot and finish him. I dive to the ground and roll, spin on the carpet, and bump into a lamp stand—it crashes to the ground. I lunge for the protection of a cabinet.

I see him: his eyes on fire, his shiny face contorted. He roars in surprise and rage, as he turns in my direction and starts firing wildly. The shots come rapidly. The shocking kick of the bullet as it smashes into my chest, shattering bone, muscles and sinew, whips me onto my back. The pain is ice-cold, fills my ravaged chest, and then something hits my head, it snaps back. Oh Jesus.... I pull myself upwards and level the arm that's still holding the gun. I pull the trigger.

He doesn't know what hit him as the bullet strikes him in the throat. His throat erupts. A spray of crimson paints the wall behind him as he sinks to the ground, clawing at his open throat, shrieking in agony. His body thrashes and writhes. Then an eerie silence descends. He is dead. I hear a sob, then an elongated wail of horror, the sound of cloth rustling. Lily is crawling toward me.

There is a strange icy throbbing in my chest, but my mind suddenly becomes

calm and serene, almost trance-like. As if I am a calm observer. Outside the mayhem. At peace. Maybe I'm dying. Jesus, that would be a bummer. But at least it's done. The job's done. Lily is kneeling over me and crying, I feel a tear fall on my face. My head is on fire and I can feel my blood pouring out of me quickly. I try not to acknowledge it. I feel faint.

'It's all my fault. I'm sorry. I'm so sorry. I love you,' she sobs. 'I love you so much, Jake.'

Some part of me starts smiling. *Yeah, me too, babe. Like crazy.*

I try to speak, but my lungs are full of fluid, the agony is unspeakable. I try to squeeze her hand, but there appears to be no force in mine.

She starts shaking me. *Oh fuck's sake, Lily. Have a bit of respect. I'm dying here*, I want to joke, but my lips won't move. Oh Jesus, I cannot focus my eyes anymore. The peace envelops me like a fog. But I won't submit to it. I kick furiously against it.

'Don't you dare fucking die on me. Hold on, please, Jake.' She starts rummaging through the pockets of my jacket, finds my mobile, and dials. I don't want to die.

'Hurry, please,' she cries plaintively, urgently.

471

Suddenly I hear Lily drop the mobile phone without giving the address and scramble to her feet.

Oh my God! Something's wrong. She has my gun in her hand and is pointing it at someone standing in the doorway. I can't see who it is, I can't help her. Please... Get away, I want to scream. I try to rise up but I'm nailed to the floor.

I hear voices, Lily's and someone else's, a man's, but I'm drifting away...the blackness is calling.

Lily

I hear him come up the stairs. My hands are shaking so much the gun seems to be rattling in my hands. I hate guns and I have only had two real hours of firearms training during the two week intensive. There is very little emphasis on SO10 operatives to master weapons since there is no need. Someone who can handle a gun will do so in the street compromising their cover. I take a deep breath. I curl my finger on the trigger. I straighten my elbows and point the gun into the open doorway. The sound of steps comes closer. I stare at the empty space.

Suddenly Billy Joe Pilkington fills the doorway. He is big. He is very big. And he has a gun.

'Don't come any further or I will shoot you,' I shout a warning.

FIFTEEN

Billy Joe Pilkington

'Whoa,' I say, dropping my gun and holding my exposed palms up. Hell, what the fuck happened here? I don't know what I expected, but not the one-man-down, Jake covered in blood on the ground, and his missus crazy-eyed and pointing a gun at me carnage I find.

'Hey, I'm here to help you.'

'Liar,' she screams wildly. 'I heard Mills call you and I know exactly what he said so don't try to pretend anything else. I'm not interested in your turf war. Just get out of here so I can call an ambulance and get Jake to hospital. If you don't leave I swear I'll shoot.'

'Listen, I'm not the snitch. Jake told me about it. It's Tommy. We figured it out.'

'So how did you know about this address? It's not listed anywhere,' she asks suspiciously, all the while glancing worriedly at Jake.

'We've been keeping a close eye on him. When he got a mobile call earlier today, he acted so nervous, I knew something was up. So I worked him over and that's when he told me about this place, you, and his bent fucking copper friend. I jumped in my vehicle and came straight here, tooled up and ready for fucking anything, but looks like I got here too late.'

Suddenly, she throws the gun to the floor. 'It's not you. You didn't knock three times.'

She doesn't make any sense but if she's putting down the gun, I'm made.

'I have to call an ambulance,' she blurts out, panicked and trembling.

I crouch over Jake. Fuck! He is in a bad way. He is lying in a pool of blood and more is pouring out of his head and chest. We can't wait for a fucking ambulance. He'll die before one gets here. The closest hospital is only ten minutes away. I might not even make it then.

I grab her wrist. Her eyes swing wildly toward me.

'Listen, we can't wait for an ambulance. We have to take him there ourselves. Do you understand me?'

She nods quickly.

'My car is double parked right outside. A blue—'

'I know it,' she cuts in impatiently.

'Right, I'm going to carry him. I want you to run ahead and open the back doors.'

I go to the curtain and tear a long strip. I tie it around his chest and around his head. Almost instantly the cloth becomes soaked. His breathing is scarily shallow. I don't waste any more time. I heave him off the ground. He's a big man, and unconscious he is a dead weight, but I have lifted men up and thrown them down from a high height during fights. I heave him up with a grunt and make for the stairs. Jake's wife has opened the car doors and has returned.

When she sees me she runs down the stairs ahead of me and holds open the door. I get him into the back of my car and while she cradles his head I run to the driver's seat and get in.

'Ready?'

'Go. Hurry, please,' she begs urgently.

I pull away and slam my foot on the accelerator. Some guy screams at me. 'Fucking maniac.' In ordinary circumstances I would have got out of the car, walked up to him and got him to say it to my face. He's got Jake to thank.

Jake's wife is crooning to him.

'Hang in there, Jake. I never said a bad thing about you. Not to anyone. Not ever. There was never anything bad to say. And I never gave a single important secret away. I'm good for all your secrets. I'll never talk. I'm your wife and I love you to bits. We have our whole lives to live. Don't leave me, my love. We will survive this. You just wait and see.'

The silence that comes from him is deafening.

I glance into the rear-view mirror and tears are pouring down her face. He lies in her lap with his eyes shut, so white, so still. It doesn't look good. This is the man who wouldn't lie down and give up when he was in the ring with *me*. I feel the cold hand of real fear for him.

'Hang in there, Jake. Oh, Jake, Jake, Jake,' she sobs, while the blood seeps through her fingers. She looks up at me. She seems dazed and totally lost. I know her type. She's delicate. She can snap at any moment. I've seen that look before.

'His hair feels so soft and smells so good, but I can feel him slipping away. His pulse is slowing down, too. I think he's dying, BJ,' she tells me calmly.

Fuck me, if that isn't the weirdest thing I've heard today. She must be in shock and rambling. It's not going to be good when she zones back into reality.

I fucking nail my foot to the accelerator.

Lily

BJ gets Jake to the A & E of the closest hospital. I don't even register what it is called. I just sit there covered in his blood as they take him away from me and load him onto a gurney. It seems to me that they are moving too slowly. I feel an irrational fury. I want to scream at them, but I don't. Instead they are surprised to find me perfectly calm. Even I am shocked at how unmoved I am. I don't feel *anything*.

'Hurry, please,' I urge, my voice, as cold as ice.

And they take him away from me.

Someone touches my arm. Slowly I swing my eyes upwards. A long way upwards. Ah, BJ.

'I've got to go. I can't be here when the police arrive.'

'OK. Thank you.'

'I'll be around later.'

 478

He turns to move away. I catch his arm. 'Wait.'

He turns back, surprised.

I reach into my bra and fish out the surveillance stick. 'Can you hold onto this for me? You're the only one I can trust now.'

'What is this?'

'This is Jake's life.'

He takes it, nods, and leaves.

Then I call my old Detective Sergeant and give him the address, briefly warning him what his men are going to find. I take a deep breath and call Shane to ask him to come. As soon as I hear his voice that strange everything-is-under-control, all-is-well cloud that had protected me from fear and panic is suddenly gone.

My heart starts racing. My chest constricts and I can't catch my breath. Sweat starts pouring from my underarms. I feel lightheaded and faint. I am choked by a sensation that I could die right here from pure, unadulterated terror.

The terror of losing Jake.

Someone—a nurse—takes the phone from my rigid hand. Maybe she will tell Shane the name of the hospital. I become aware that other people in uniforms are running toward me. I see visions of me falling to the floor, screaming and kicking, and everyone staring curiously. My brain instructs me to tell the people who are holding me that it is Jake who needs their ministrations.

There seems to be confusion all around me.

Some rational part of my brain concedes that it is possible that I have become hysterical. In fact, I think I have just slapped a nurse. It's not that I want to, but I can't control my arms and legs. They flail out uncontrollably with a life of their own. Someone injects me with something.

I scream for my Jake until I am gone from my body.

SIXTEEN

Lily

I don't know how many hours pass before I wake up. There is no moment of confusion, of where am I? What is going on? Where is Jake? NO! As soon as I open my eyes I know. I am in a hospital and Jake's been taken away from me. He is probably being operated on. I sit up and slide off the bed. My bare feet touch cold ground. There are curtains pulled all around me. I part the curtains and start walking in the direction of voices. I come to the reception desk.

'Ah, you're awake,' someone says.

'Where's Jake?' I ask.

'Calm down.'

'I will calm down when you tell me where my husband is.'

'First we need some shoes,' she says.

'I just want to know—'

But she is already walking back to the curtained section where I had come from and returns with a pair of shoes, mine. I wear them hurriedly. 'Take me to my husband please.'

'He's still in surgery, but I can take you to where the rest of your family are.'

I frown. 'My family?'

'Yes, they are all waiting. Come on.'

I follow her to a sitting room. 'Here they are,' she says cheerfully.

The first person I see is Jake's mother. The nurse makes her exit.

For a few seconds Jake's mother and I stare at each other. Then she stands up and advances toward me. Her small frame is trembling with anger. I look at her and I don't feel afraid. I want her to hurt me. I deserve it. It is all my fault. I was so stupid, so fucking careless. It will be a relief to have her strike me. She stands in front of me and lifts her hand. I think she intended to slap me. I would have done it if I were her. Her hand moves in an arc, but it never connects. Shane catches it.

'Don't, Ma,' he says sadly. 'He's in love with her. When he wakes up, it will break his heart to know you marked her.'

He lets go of her hand and she covers her mouth with it. Her eyes are shocked and huge and her hand is visibly shaking. 'What if he doesn't wake up?'

He turns white. 'Then his soul will grieve.'

She crumples then, sobbing as if her poor heart was breaking. He put his arm around her and gently led her toward the blue chair.

And then Dom is next to me. 'Come on,' he says. 'Let's get you some coffee.'

I let him lead me out of that sad waiting room with its blue seats and Jake's devastated mother.

I lean against the wall. Dom and I have hardly spoken. I've kept away from him.

'Do you want a real drink?' he says.

'Yeah,' I say.

He takes a flask out of his jacket pocket.

I take a long swallow. The alcohol burns my throat. 'How long has he been in the operating theater?'

'Seven hours.'

I become frightened. 'He's not going to make it, is he?'

His jaw goes stiff. 'He's gonna make it,' he says. 'He's gonna fucking make it or I'm gonna kill the fucking bastard myself.'

That's Dom for you: Why open a fucking door when you can fucking kick it down? Tears start flowing down my cheeks.

Jake

I wake up to indescribable pain. 'Lily,' I mutter.

There is no answer. I return to the blessed blackness.

I come back. Lights. Voices. Machines. Searing pain. I go away.

I open my eyes. A woman. 'Lily?'

'Nurse Bourne, I'm afraid.'

'Lily.'

'Your wife?'

'Yeah, my wife. Tell her to get her ass in here now,' I mumble.

And then it is blackness again.

My mother holds my hand. I know that. I feel her. She cries. I want to stop her. I'm all right. She goes. Shane comes. 'Get well soon,' he whispers.

I open my eyes and there she is. She is shaking. She puts her hand in mine. She's not all right. 'I love you,' she says. I'm not there for her.

Then I open my eyes and it is no longer fuzzy. I recognize my mother.

'Where's Lily, Ma?' I ask.

'She's outside,' she says. 'You nearly died because of her.'

'That's right. I nearly died because of her, but I'd be dead without her, Ma. She warned us they had infiltrated BJ's organization.'

That's the thing about Ma, she's not vindictive. She forgives easily. 'In that case I will pray to the Madonna for your wife,' she whispers.

A little while after, Ma leaves and Lily opens the door.

'Oh, you're awake,' she cries with disbelief.

She comes and stands beside me, fragile as a bit of porcelain. There is a bandage on her temple and a long bruise on her left cheek and blue shadows under her eyes, but she is still so beautiful I want to weep.

'I can't wait to get my cock into your pussy,' I tell her and she begins to cry. Huge big tears that roll down her cheeks. I don't stop her. I know they are tears of joy.

SEVENTEEN

Lily

If I had not made the recording I don't know how it would have turned out. For many days the papers ran with the story and it was big news. We killed a DS, a highly respected one at that. I told them everything I knew, but I don't know what happened to Robin. Once I called the office and asked for him. One of the guys picked up the phone and told me he doesn't work there anymore. I never saw anything in the papers so I guess they just did what they always do. Cover their own asses.

It is nearly two weeks before we are allowed to take Jake home. The family rallies round. Shane and Dom set up a bed downstairs in one of the reception rooms so Jake doesn't have to go up the stairs to sleep. Shane and Dom carefully lay him in bed. I hover around helplessly behind them. Jake has become so pale.

'Thanks,' he tells his brothers.

I offer them a drink but they leave pretty quickly once Jake has been installed.

'Back later tonight,' they tell me.

'OK,' I say as I close the front door. I go back to the living room and Jake is grinning at me.

'God, I've missed being home with you,' he says. 'Come and kiss me properly then,' he says.

I go over feeling suddenly shy. I've told him that I love him, but I don't know whether he heard. If he can still remember what happened after his head trauma.

I kiss him gently on the lips and his hand comes around my forearm. 'You call that measly thing a kiss?'

I laugh. 'You're supposed to take it easy.'

'I'm supposed to, but you're not.'

I frown at him. 'What are you talking about?'

'Take off your panties.'

'What?'

'You heard.'

'Why?'

'Don't make me get up and bust all these stitches.'

'This is crazy. I can't believe you're doing this,' I say, taking my panties off. 'Right. They're off. Happy now?'

'Come closer,' he invites, his eyes alive with something I haven't seen for two weeks. Something I was afraid I would never see again.

'Listen, you're not allowed—'

'To strain. I'm not going to strain. You are.'

I bite my lip. I want to go over, but I really don't want to do anything that could harm him.

'If you don't come, I'm coming to get you,' he warns.

I look at him worriedly. 'Jake...'

'I promise I'm not going to move a muscle. You're going to do all the work.'

I take the step closer.

'Spread your legs.' His voice holds an implacable quality.

I inch my legs apart, feeling myself getting wetter.

'Open for me, Lily,' he persuades.

I spread my legs farther apart and he slips his hand between my legs, slipping his fingers into the crack, playing with the wet folds, collecting my arousal on his fingers. Taking it to his mouth. And sucking it off.

'Take your top and your bra off.'

I obey.

'And your skirt.'

He buries his fingers in me. Totally naked with his fingers working on me I moan. 'Lift one leg and put it on the mattress.' With my hands resting on the mattress I lift one leg and rest it on the bed as he commands That opens me up to his gaze. I look down myself at the end of his hand. Dirty. Dirty. Dirty.

My nipples start aching. I am mad for the feel of his mouth on them, sucking, licking, biting. Watching me avidly he glides one finger into me. I shudder, my back arching. He slips his finger out and circles my clit. I push my hips desperately against his hand, wanting the finger back, the blood running hot in my veins. Two fingers enter me. I whimper. His touch slows. The fingers withdraw. A small cry of frustration erupts from my mouth. His fingers hover over the entrance of my sex. I push my hips forward chasing those elusive fingers. He lets me catch his fingers. They slide in.

He stops moving. I look at him, my body twisted, begging for more.

'If you want it, work for it,' he says. 'Fuck my fingers.'

So I do. I ram into his fingers, two then three, stretching me. My hands are numb from gripping the mattress so hard and my body being twisted uncomfortably. Every thrust increases the discomfort but that is part of the pleasure, too. The pleasure of being overwhelmed, commanded and watched while I fuck his fingers with what should have been shame but isn't. He watches me avidly until the climax comes for me.

'Oh God!' I scream, feeling myself fly again with the sensation of being unspeakably filthy, of being wanted so violently by this man. It has been so long.

Naked and strangely exhausted I climb into bed and carefully lie beside him. For a while neither of us speaks.

'Jake.' I lift myself onto my elbow. 'Do you remember what happened in that flat?'

'Some,' he says, turning his head to look at me.

'Do you remember what I told you?'

His eyes gleam. 'Tell me again what you told me and I will see if I remember it,' he says innocently.

I smile. 'I meant every word,' I say.

'Is it beautiful yet?'

I frown. 'Is what beautiful?'

'Remember when you said love should be beautiful. Is it beautiful yet?'

My eyes fill with tears. 'Yes, it's beautiful.'

'I'm glad,' he says softly. 'Because it was always beautiful for me. Our meeting was a "magic" of perfect timing. A few seconds later and you would have gone through that side door and we would never have met. I knew from the moment our eyes met that you were mine. And you were already mine in many other lifetimes.' He reaches his hand out to touch my face, the skin softened by days of lying in bed. 'I've always loved and I'll always love you. No matter what they throw at us they will never separate us. Even our separation will be illusions. After this life is over I will seek you again, and I will find you again.'

It dawns on me as I look into Jake's eyes, that losing Luke tore the life from me, but then the same random hand that took him away intervened again and made the most unlikely suitor become my savior. A tear crawls down my cheek. Maybe I always knew from our first kiss that he was the only one who could have mended my heart.

He smiles gently, my beautiful, beautiful gangster man.

—Baby, it's only for you, it's only for you
Baby, it's only for you, only for you—

EPILOGUE

Lily

I have named them all. That huge one over there is Jakob; his wife is called Elsie. No, I'm not being facetious, she *is* his wife, once mated, male and female crows stay together for life. I have seen their chicks: beautiful, with bits of yellow on their bills and blue-eyed. I call to Elsie and she flies over and lands on my shoulder. I turn my head and she rubs her beak against my nose. I know most people think that crows are a dull black, but in fact, they have a light violet gloss on their bodies and a greenish-blue gloss on their wings. The violet gloss gleams in the sunlight. I know why Jakob chose her. She is beautiful.

When Elsie flies back to her mate I walk away. Soon I will have a chick of my own. Two months ago I stopped taking the pill and this morning I peed on a stick that came up with a thin blue line. For a few seconds I had stared at the stick in shock. Unable to move, something irrepressible opening up like a flower inside me.

I wanted to run into the bedroom and tell Jake straightaway, but I decided to save the news. After dinner tonight. He is taking me away to Paris. I will tell him then. Mine was in a bathroom but let him remember the moment as something truly special.

A gift on the anniversary of our meeting.

A small smile comes to me at the thought of his expression. I know he wants a big family. He has even got names all planned for them. He says he wants at least half a dozen, but obviously he's not getting that. He tried to pin me down to five. I said two. He said four and we finally agreed on three. But in fact, I am open to four. It all depends on how painful childbirth turns out to be.

I hope my baby will be green-eyed like him.

The coming of the child makes my thoughts turn to Luke. I don't dream so much of him anymore. At first I was sad. As horrible as they were, I felt with their passing, I had lost my last connection to him, but then I realised that the nightmares are not my connection to him. The memory of him doing handstands in the rain, building a snow staircase to Santa Claus and the hundreds of other memories of him are what's left of him.

The sky is blue and the sun is warm on my back. I shade my eyes and look to the distance. I can see Jake riding Thor. He is coming in my direction. As ever he is not wearing a shirt. The wind whips at his hair. I feel the vibration of the horse and the man even before I hear them.

My heart swells with love. I smile up at him. The horse snorts and looks at me with big, liquid eyes. From my pocket I take out a lump of sugar and hold it in the palm of my hand. The horse goes for it. His rough lips brush my skin. Jake gets off, picks me up by the waist and whirls me around.

'Hey,' I say, laughing. 'What's this in aid of?'

'Nothing. Every time I see you I feel such a rush of joy it has to be acted on.'

I put my hands on either side of his cheeks, look into those gorgeous, magnificent, grass-green eyes of his, and bending my head, kiss him. 'I love you, Jake Eden. So damn much.'

And it's true. I'm crazy about him. He has totally changed my life. I was covered in cobwebs in a cold, dark place until he laid eyes on me. He never took no for answer. And never gave up on me. Ever. He hung in there no matter how bad it looked. He is truly as he says. As tenacious as a gnarled tree.

'I hope you never tire of telling me that,' he says, gently setting me down on the ground.

'Want some breakfast?' I ask.

'What am I having?'

'What do you want?'

'Well, today is our anniversary so I want something special.'

I look up at him. His skin is tanned and healthy and there is a cheeky smile playing about his mouth. One day his skin will crinkle and hang off his bones, but even then I will never tire of looking at him.

'Well, come into the kitchen then,' I say.

He fakes wretchedness. 'There was a time you would have called me into the bedroom.'

I laugh and open the kitchen door. 'Did you or did you not have an anniversary blowjob *and* an anniversary fuck this morning, Jake Eden?'

'I'll admit, I did.'

I step inside. It is cool in the house. I go to one of the cabinets and open it. 'So...'

He grins. 'I was hoping for something a bit more on our anniversary.'

When he is like this I find him impossible to resist. I take out a wooden box and open it.

Jake comes close. 'Did they bring you something else today?'

 496

I take a bit of a child's broken plastic toy out of my pocket. Red and blue. I hold it out to him.

He takes it out of my palm and examines it. 'Fucking hell, it's hard to keep up with these critters. They keep bringing stuff for my wife.'

I suppress the laughter that is rising in my throat. 'I have an Irish joke for you.'

He groans. 'Not another one?'

God! How much I love, love, love this man. 'Do you want to hear it or not?'

'Does it feature a fork and soup rain?'

'No.'

He leans his hip against the edge of the counter. 'All right then.'

'The thing is, this joke can only be told in the bedroom.'

'Lead the way, madam,' he says, straightening himself eagerly, his eyes shining.

Well, the joke had eight canned pineapple rings and a bit of whipped cream, but my husband is big, so I had to use twelve pineapple rings and half a can of whipped cream.

Did my husband enjoy the joke?

Yeah, any hot-blooded Irishman would. It was good enough to eat.

And guess who ate it?

Yeah, me. I'd eat anything off that Irishman...

In memory of Patrick Eden:

Muldoon lived alone in the Irish countryside with only a pet dog for company. One day the dog died, and Muldoon went to the parish priest and said, 'Father, my dog is dead. Could ya be sayin' a mass for the poor creature?'

Father O'Malley replied, 'I'm afraid not; we cannot have services for an animal in the church. But there are some Baptists down the lane, and there's no tellin' what they believe. Maybe they'll do something for the creature. '

Muldoon said, 'I'll go right away, Father. Do ya think five thousand is enough to donate to them for the service?'

Father O'Malley exclaimed, 'Sweet Mary, Mother of Jesus! Why didn't ya tell me the dog was Catholic?'

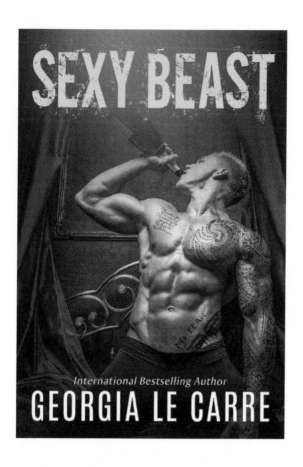

If you have enjoyed EDEN you might like a peek into what happens to BJ and Layla. Their sweltering affair is called **Sexy Beast** and will be available in the summer of 2015.

Want to know what the Billionaire Banker did to his woman?

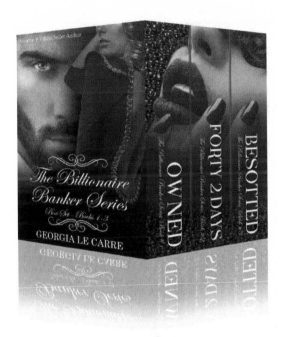

The Billionaire Banker Series

http://www.amazon.com/dp/B00
M08LS6A
http://www.amazon.co.uk/dp/B00M
08LS6A
http://www.amazon.com.au/gp/pr
oduct/B00M08LS6A
http://www.amazon.ca/gp/produc
t/B00M08LS6A

Click on the link below to receive news of my latest releases, great giveaways, and exclusive content.
http://bit.ly/1oe9WdE

or

I just **LOVE** hearing from readers so by all means come and say hello here:
https://www.facebook.com/georgia.leca rre

On another note...

Want To Help An Author?

Then please leave a review. Reviews help other readers find an author's work. No matter how short it may be, it is very *precious*.

United States
http://www.amazon.com/gp/product/ B00X2JUCRC

United Kingdom
http://www.amazon.co.uk/gp/product /B00X2JUCRC

Canada
http://www.amazon.ca/gp/product/B0
0X2JUCRC

Australia
http://www.amazon.com.au/gp/produ
ct/B00X2JUCRC

Coming Next...

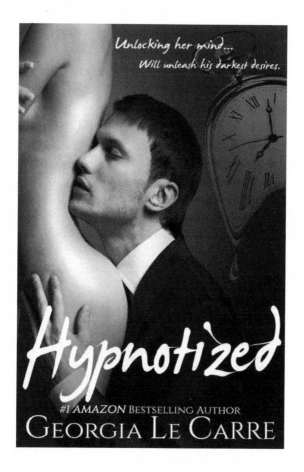

Hypnotized

Georgia Le Carre

The power of a glance has been so much abused in love stories, that it has come to be disbelieved in. Few people dare now to say that two beings have fallen in love because they have looked at each other. Yet it is in this way that love begins, and in this way only.

—Victor Hugo, *Les Misérables*

Prologue

The girl behind the counter smiled at me and licked her lips. Shit. That was an invitation if ever I saw one. Sorry, honey, I'm married. Hey, I'm not just married, I'm in fucking love. I had the perfect life. A beautiful wife, two little terrors, a successful career. In fact, I was poised to dominate my industry.

The results of my research would soon be made public and I was going to be a star! Life was good.

'Keep the change,' I told her.

Her smile broadened and yet there was disappointment in her eyes.

I grinned and shrugged. 'If I wasn't already hooked I'd ask you out. You're gorgeous.'

'I'm not jealous,' she said flirtatiously.

'My wife is,' I told her, and picked up the tray of drinks: cappuccino for me, latte for my wife, and two hot chocolates for my monsters. Suddenly I heard a man shout, 'Fuck me!' And though those two words had nothing to do with me, my body— No, not just my body, *every part* of me *knew*.

They concerned me.

I whirled around, jaw clenched, still clutching the paper tray of drinks—one cappuccino, one latte, and two hot chocolates—as if it was my last link to normality. For precious seconds I was so stunned, I froze. I could not believe what I was seeing. Then instinct older than life kicked in. The tray dropped from my hand—one cappuccino, one latte, and two hot chocolates—my last link with normality falling away from me forever. I began to race toward the burning car. My car. With my family trapped in it. I could see my babies screaming and banging on the car doors.

'Get out, get out of the fucking car,' I screamed as I ran.

I could see them pulling at the handles, their small spread palms banging desperately on the glass. I could even see their little mouths screaming for me.

'Daddy, Daddy.'

It was shocking how frightened and white their little faces were. I could not see my wife. Where was she?

I was running so fast my legs felt as if they might buckle, but it was as if I was in slow motion. Time had slowed down. At that moment thoughts came into my head at sonic speed, but the disaster carried on in real time. Suddenly my wife lifted her head and I saw her. She was looking out through the window

508

directly at me. I was twenty feet away when I saw everything clearly. I kept on running, but it was like being in a dream where your mother suddenly turns into an elephant.

You don't go *What the fuck?*

You just carry on as normal even though your mother has just turned into a green elephant. I just carried on running. I no longer looked at my children. My gaze was riveted by the sight of my wife. I was ten feet away when the car exploded. Boom! The force of it picked me up and threw me backwards. I flew in the air and landed hard on the tarmac. I did not feel the pain of the impact. I got onto my elbows and watched the fire consume my family and the thick, black smoke that poured from the wreckage.

There was no grief then. Not even horror. It was just shock. And the inability to comprehend. The loss, the carnage, the tragedy, the green elephant. People came to help me up. I was shaking uncontrollably. They thought I was cold so they wrapped me in blankets. They sent me in an ambulance to the hospital. I never spoke. The whole time I was trying to figure out the green elephant. Why? How? It confused me. It destroyed my life, past, present and future.

Two years later
London

Marlow Kane

It is the time you have wasted for your rose
that makes your rose so important.
—Antoine de Saint-Exupéry, *The Little Prince*

'**L**ady Swanson is here for her appointment,' Beryl said into the intercom. Even her voice was all at once professional and terribly impressed.

'Send her in,' I said and rose from my desk.

The door opened and a classically beautiful woman entered. Her skin was very pale and as flawless as porcelain. It contrasted greatly with her shoulder-length dark hair and intensely blue eyes. Her dress and long coat were in the same

cream material; her shoes exactly matched the color of her skin. The overriding impression was of an impossibly wealthy and elegant woman. Women like her lived in movies and magazines. They did not walk into the consulting rooms of disgraced hypnotists.

'Lady Swanson,' I said.

'Dr. Kane,' she murmured.

I winced inwardly. 'Just Marlow, please,' I said and gestured toward the chair.

She came forward and sat. She crossed her legs. They were long and encased in the sheerest tights I had seen in my life. Yes, she was an incredibly polished and cultivated woman.

I smiled.

She smiled back nervously.

'So, I believe you refused to tell Beryl your reason for coming to see me?'

'That is correct.'

'What can I do for you, Lady Swanson?'

'It's not for me. It's for my daughter. Well, she's my stepdaughter, but she is just like my own. I've raised her since she was two years old. She's twenty now.'

I nodded and began to raise the estimation of her age upwards. She must have been at least forty, but she didn't look a day over twenty-eight.

'Her name is Olivia and she met with an accident about a year ago.' Lady Swanson paused for breath. 'She nearly died. She had extensive injuries and was in hospital for many months. When she recovered she had lost her memory. She can remember nothing. She can remember how to do *things*—cook, places—but she cannot remember her past.'

I nodded.

'I was hoping hypnotherapy could help her remember her past.' She leaned forward slightly, her lips parted. 'Do you think you could...hypnotize her?'

I watched her and thought of the men in her life. How easy it must have been for such a beautiful woman to get anything she wanted from a man.

'Lady Swanson, I'm not sure I am the right man for the job. Usually I treat people who want to lose weight, kick a bad habit, or who are afraid of spiders.'

'I understand that, but do you think you could help her, though?'

'To be honest, I've never had such a patient.'

'Well, it's worth a try then?' she pressed hopefully.

'But you have to bear in mind that not everybody can be hypnotized.'

She didn't listen to that. Instead she broke into a smile. It was like the sun shining out from between a crack in a

 513

sky full of storm clouds. Yes, she was obviously one of those women who could whistle a chap off a tree, but... I was immune to it. For two years I had wandered around looking for even the smallest spark of the vibrant life that used to course through my veins. All I had ever found was ashes. Even now this beautiful, beautiful woman elicited nothing from me.

'Oh that's wonderful,' she gushed softly. 'You will take her on then?'

I felt almost as if she had subtly manipulated me. 'I'll try. No promises.'

'I did some research on you and your work, and I am certain you are the best person for the job. If anybody can do it, you can.'

I froze at that.

Instantly her face lost some of its glowing enthusiasm. 'I hope you don't think I was snooping into your private affairs? I was only interested in your professional credentials...'

I smiled tightly: the personal stuff came up with the professional stuff. After the accident the two had become inextricably entwined. 'Of course not. It is prudent to check out a practitioner before you go to see him.'

'I just want what is best for my daughter. And you are that. Will you take on her case?'

'Does your stepdaughter know you are here?'

She leaned back and looked out of the window. 'A butterfly wing is a miracle, made up of thousands of tiny, loosely attached pigmented scales that individually catch the light and together create a depth of color and iridescence unmatched elsewhere in nature. Our identities are like the butterfly wing, made up of thousands and thousands of tiny, loosely attached memories. Without them we lose our color and iridescence. Olivia is like a child now. We make all the major decisions for her. The world is a frightening place for her.'

'All right, Beryl will find an appointment for you.'

She smiled. A soft smile. And I had a vision. Her in bed with her shriveled husband. It was not only she who had done a quick Google search. It was not every day that Lady Swanson, of the Swanson dynasty, called my office for an appointment.

For a moment our eyes held and I saw something in hers. Interest. Desire. I let my eyes slide away.

'Thank you... Marlow.'

'Goodbye, Lady Swanson.'

'Ivana, please.'

'Goodbye, Ivana.'

I walked to the door, opened it, and let her out. As she passed me her perfume wafted into my nostrils. Expensive, faint, but still heady. From up close she was even more flawless. I closed the door and walked to my desk. I opened my drawer and taking out a bottle of Jack Daniel's poured myself a huge measure. I knocked it back, swallowed, and closed my eyes. Fuck. Was it ever going to stop hurting? I walked to the window and watched Lady Swanson get into her chauffeur-driven Rolls-Royce Phantom. She stared straight ahead. It was almost as if it was only a dream that she had come into my office and sat in my chair.

The intercom buzzed. 'Can I come in?' Beryl asked.

I sighed. 'Yes.'

The door opened even before I had taken my finger away from the button.

'Well?' she asked, wide-eyed. 'That was a very short first session. What did she want?'

'She wants me to treat her stepdaughter.'

Her eyes became huge. 'What? She wants you to treat Lady Olivia?'

'How did you know that?'

'It was all over the papers. She met with an accident and lost her memory. You have your work cut out for you.'

'Why do you say that?'

'Lady Olivia is known in the tabloids as 'Miss Secretive'. She has never ever

given an interview and furiously guards her privacy. There are no pictures of her behaving badly. Ever.' Beryl came deeper into the room and went to my computer. She typed in a few words and turned towards me, her face filled with gossipy excitement, said, 'Here. This is what she looks like.'

I walked toward the computer screen.

It was not a very good picture. A long lens photo. Grainy. And not even in color. But my cock twitched and woke up from its deep sleep.

Coming Soon...

GOLD DIGGER

Georgia Le Carre

CHAPTER 1

'**W**hatever you do, don't *ever* trust them. Not one of them,' he whispered. His voice was so feeble I had to strain to catch it.

'I won't,' I said, softly.

'They are dangerous in a way you will never understand. Never let your guard down,' he insisted.

'I understand,' I said, but all I wanted was for him to stop talking about them. These last precious minutes I didn't want to waste on them.

He shook his head unhappily. 'No, no, you don't understand. You can never let your guard down for even an instant. Never.'

'All right, I won't.'

'I will be a very sad spirit if you do.'

'I won't,' I promised vehemently, and reached for his hand. The contrast between my hand and his couldn't have been greater. Mine was smooth and soft and his was gnarled and full of green veins, the skin waxy and liver-spotted. The nails were the color of polished ivory. The hand of a seventy-year-old man. His fingers grasped fiercely at my hand. I lifted them to my lips and kissed them one by one, tenderly.

His eyes glowed briefly in his wasted, sunken face. 'How I love you, my darling Tawny,' he murmured.

'I love you. I love you. I love you,' I said.

'Do your part and they cannot touch you.'

He sighed. 'It's nearly time.'

'Don't say that,' I cried, even though I knew in my heart that he was right.

His eyes swung to the window. 'Ah,' he sighed softly. 'You've come.'

My gaze chased his. The window he was looking at was closed, the heavy drapes pulled shut. Goose pimples crawled up my arms. 'Don't go yet. Please,' I begged.

He dragged his gaze reluctantly from the window. His thin, pale lips rose at the edges as he drew in a rattling breath. 'I've got to go, my darling. I've got to pay my dues. I haven't been a good man.'

'Just wait a while.'

'You have your whole life ahead of you.'

He turned his unnaturally bright eyes away from me, looked straight ahead, and with a violent shudder, departed.

For a few seconds I simply stared at him. Appropriately, outside the October wind howled and dashed itself into the shutters. I knew the servants were waiting downstairs. Everyone was waiting for me to go down and tell them the news. Then I leaned forward and put my cheek on his still, bony chest. He smelled strongly of medicine. I closed my eyes tightly. Why did you have to go and die and leave me to the wolves?

In that moment I felt so close to him I wished that this time would not end. I wished I could lie on his chest, safe and closeted away from the cruel world. I heard the clock ticking. The flames in the fireplace crackled and spat. Somewhere a pipe creaked. I placed my chin on his chest and turned to look at him one last time. He appeared to be sleeping. Peaceful at any rate. I stroked the thin strands of white hair lying across his pinkish white scalp, and let my finger run down his prominent nose. It shocked me how quickly the tip of his nose had lost warmth. Soon all of him would be stone cold.

I wondered whom he had seen at the window. Who had come to take him to his reckoning. My sorrow was complete. I could put my fingertips into it and feel the edges. Smooth. Without corners. Without sharpness. It had no tears. I knew he was dying two hours before. Strange because it had seemed as if he had taken a turn for the better. He seemed stronger, his cheeks pink, his eyes brilliantly bright and when he smiled it appeared as if he was lit from within. He even looked so much stronger. I asked him what he wanted to eat.

'Milk. I'll have a glass of milk,' he said decisively.

But after I called for milk and it was brought to him he smiled and refused it. 'Isn't this wonderful?' he asked. 'I feel so good.'

And at that moment I knew. Even so it was incomprehensible to me that he was really gone. I never wanted to believe it.

'In the end you wanted to go, didn't you?'

There was no answer.

'It's OK. I know you were tired. It was only me holding you back. You go on ahead. Find a place for me.'

He lay as still as a corpse. Oh God! I already missed him so much.

'I understand you can't talk. But you can hear me. When it is my turn I want you to come and get me. I'll be expecting you to come in through the window. Go in peace now, my love. All will be well. They will never know the truth. I will never tell them. To the day you come back to collect me.'

And then I began to cry, not loud, ugly sobs, but a quiet weeping. I didn't want the servants to hear. To come rushing in. Call the doctor waiting downstairs to come in and pronounce him dead. I knew what waited for me outside this room. Another hour...or two wouldn't make a difference. This was my time. My final hours with my husband.

The time before I became the hated gold digger.

Made in the USA
Middletown, DE
03 May 2022

65228340R00316